A Thief's Blood

Douglas Skelton has published numerous non-fiction books and crime thrillers. He has been a bank clerk, tax officer, shelf stacker, meat porter, taxi driver (for two days), wine waiter (for two hours), reporter, investigator and local newspaper editor. He has been longlisted for the McIlvanney Prize five times, most recently in 2024. Douglas contributes to true crime shows on TV and radio and is a regular on the crime writing festival circuit.

Also by Douglas Skelton

A Company of Rogues

An Honourable Thief
A Thief's Justice
A Grave for a Thief
A Thief's Blood

Other novels by Douglas Skelton

Blood City
Crow Bait
Devil's Knock
Open Wounds
The Dead Don't Boogie
Tag – You're Dead
The Janus Run
Thunder Bay
The Blood is Still
A Rattle of Bones
Where Demons Hide
Children of the Mist
The Hollow Mountain

DOUGLAS
SKELTON

A Thief's Blood

CANELO

First published in the United Kingdom in 2024 by

Canelo
Unit 9, 5th Floor
Cargo Works, 1-2 Hatfields
London SE1 9PG
United Kingdom

A CIP catalogue record for this book is available from the British Library.

Print ISBN 978 1 80436 883 1
Ebook ISBN 978 1 80436 743 8

Cover design by Henry Steadman

Cover images © Alamy

Look for more great books at www.canelo.co

Printed and bound in Great Britain by Clays Ltd, Elcograf S.p.A.

1

Prologue

London, January 1718

He was not a man to remember his dreams, let alone attach much credence to them if he did, but this one remained in his mind even after he shot up from his pillow, the scream that had begun to form in his nightmare becoming little more than a yelp in the real world. Lying abed, he searched the corners of his room, fearful of seeing a face he had not gazed upon for these long years leering at him from the shadows.

The lady beside him stirred, emitted a slight moan, so he patted her ample hips and soothed her. She muttered something unintelligible before her even breathing told him she had drifted back to sleep.

He would find it difficult to do the same, even if he were of a mind to attempt it, for the mocking laugh from his dream still echoed in his mind, and he again felt agony slicing through an arm that was no longer attached. So fresh was the memory of the pain that, if he were to draw back the covers, he would not be surprised to see the limb returned, the wound at the shoulder gaping and raw, the bedsheets red with his blood. He could still hear the muted sound of battle, as if it were taking place outside his home. He could smell the powder and hear the screams of dying men and horses, the drumbeats carrying orders to the field, the sharp thunder of the ordnance that had marked the commencement of hostilities. He could see the flashes of red around him as the men of the British regiments surged and fought and died, the blur of blue coats as the Royal Horse Guards charged.

And over it all was the whistling, that cursed whistling, tuneful and yet most sinister, crossing the years to haunt him anew.

If sleep did overcome him, he suspected he would be pitched back immediately into that remembrance, and that was not a prospect he welcomed. Not the battle, for he had been a professional soldier and was used to the confusion and the death. No, it was not the conflict that he dreaded to relive but the encounter with the man who bedevilled his dream.

The pain. The laugh. The whistling.

He thought him dead but yet, lying in his bed over 200 miles and eight years away, Nimrod Boone circled his mind as though it had only been yesterday that they had struggled against one another while around them raged the bloody work at Malplaquet.

And for the first time that he could recall, Colonel Nathaniel Charters found himself mortally afraid, for it was his firm belief that the dream coming at this juncture was not a memory at all.

It was a portent.

-

Eliza Berthon was eleven years old and didn't believe in monsters.

Her mother had been born on Dartmoor, a place the girl had never seen and knew only from the legends she had been told at the fireside since she was of sufficient age to understand. Even though their mother had been resident in the city for fifteen years, the wild winds of the moorland still gusted in her tales, despite them being related to Eliza and her younger brother Matthew in hushed tones so that their father, Jacques, could not hear. He had little time for such fripperies, his upbringing rejecting any notion of the existence of pixies and witches and ghosts, but Eliza in particular relished hearing of Cutty Dyer, a most vicious creature who frequented the area of King's Bridge, on the eastern edge of the moor. Her mother had described it as a sprite, an innocuous-sounding term for such a beast.

'We all knows of him, backalong,' Abigail Berthon had said in her Devonshire burr. 'A sprite, they said, and some of them there rogues live by water. Both faerie and goblin they be, evil little things, and Cutty is the worst of 'em. Children, he likes, and men who should know better but whose minds are addled by spirits. He waits for them, he does, waits for them to walk abroad alone, after dark, down by the river, down by the Yeo. And when he comes upon 'em, old Cutty, 'ulking great thing that he be, when he comes upon 'em then the last thing they sees is his eyes, red with bloodlust, and his hair, long and matted, and his talons, crusted with the gore of his victims, as they reach out for them. Aye, that be the last thing they sees, before those talons rip out their throats and old Cutty falls to drinking their blood.' She would pause to let the full horror of that sink in. 'I heard tell of one man, 'ard as a dug's eed he were, and he fell under old Cutty's claws and into the water he went. They found him day after, throat open, eyes staring, mouth stretched in a scream that never reached no human ears. Cutty Dyer. As evil a monster as ever there be. So let that be a lesson to you, Eliza Berthon, Matthew Berthon,' she tapped them each on the forehead as she spoke their names, 'never step out abroad after dark and never partake of excessive spirits, for there be creatures who will take advantage of such lack of care and would look to satisfy their bloodlust upon you...'

Matthew, two years younger than Eliza, had listened with eyes wide and mouth open. Eliza, however, was a most level-headed child and, even though she lapped up the stories, she knew that they were mere fancies. Such creatures didn't exist. Not really, not in the real world.

Yes, there was cruelty, she saw that around her, for London was a cruel city. She was accustomed to it, for this place was all she had ever known, but her gentle soul abhorred the thought of God's creatures, man or beast, being tormented, as they were regularly in the name of amusement. A few months before she had heard of a tavern in Soho, the Boarded House, which had announced an entertainment in which a wild cat from Africa, a tiger they called it, was tied to a stake and then set upon by six fighting dogs. She saw the atrocity only in her mind. The poor beasts would have snarled at each other, the cat sweeping with its claws, the dogs snapping with their teeth, and blood would have flowed and men and women would have stood by and watched and cheered and laid bets as to which of the animals would be left standing. A bear and a bull were also tormented for the pleasure of those people, fireworks attached to their bodies and set alight. In the city streets, Eliza had never seen anything but dogs and cats, as well as horses, cows and sheep, and she wished she could have seen the exotic creature, but not as a figure of cruel entertainment.

Eliza Berthon was eleven years old and she knew how monstrous humanity could be. Yet she still did not believe in monsters.

Now, as she lay in her bed, her brother asleep by her side, she thought of Cutty Dyer and the other creatures of the night of which her mother would speak before being hushed by her husband. The wind howled outside their home in Whitechapel, as it had done the night before and the night before that, for the city was raked by the cold breath of winter. It had not turned as cold as it had two years previously, when Eliza and Matthew had played upon the ice that had transformed the surface of the Thames into a vast area for play. They had slid upon it while their parents had wandered through the frost fair near the bridge, enjoying sweetmeats and warm wine, listening to the singers and musicians filling the crisp air with song. This wind failed to deliver such extremes; it was wet and unpleasant and it pushed at the windows of their house as if desiring entry, its moan one of desperation and disappointment as the casements held firm. Even so, some gusts did find a crack here, a hole there, and Eliza buried herself deep under her quilt to escape them. She could not fully block the wind banging at the closed shutters but knew the house was strong and could withstand its demands.

And then, another noise, another banging, from downstairs. Louder. More violent. Insistent.

She heard her father's voice, angry, surprised, demanding to know who it was that assaulted the door with such aggression, his words ending suddenly with a crash as wood splintered, followed by a gasp and then a gurgle.

Eliza glanced at her brother, who was undisturbed by the disruption below, then peered over the edge of her quilt at the open door. Beyond it lay the narrow hallway leading to their bed chamber, then the stairs leading down, the flickering of the fire and the candles in the room below causing the shadows of the balustrade to dance.

Her mother's voice then, no words, no Devonshire burr, just a scream. Not anger, but terror. And then that, too, was cut off.

Eliza considered calling out to ask what was amiss, but thought better of it. Some instinct told her there would be no response. Her eyes fixed on the shifting shadows on the stairway, her ears perked for further sounds, detecting something being dragged along a floor accompanied by harsh breathing. Then silence.

The wind blew.

The windows rattled.

The shadows flickered.

Her brother slept.

And then…

And then…

Whistling. An old song she had heard her mother sing, said to have been written by a king, accompanied by slow footsteps. Heavy, measured.

And on the stairs, a new shadow appeared, a man's shadow, large at first but diminishing as it left the candlelight behind, something solid, something of steel, hitting each step as he climbed.

Eliza Berthon was eleven years old and didn't believe in monsters.

On that night, as the wind shrieked and howled across the city, she discovered she was wrong…

1

'We should finish him…'

The voice was matter-of-fact, as if the act of murder was akin to ordering a mutton pie. Jonas Flynt knew he should move but the heavy blow that had rendered him near unconscious still reverberated around his skull. He knew his eyes were open but his vision was compromised, the explosion of light that had accompanied the strike continuing to flash and sparkle, the man's voice drifting through the high-pitched whine echoing in his ears.

'We should finish him…'

The man hadn't repeated himself, but those words seemed lodged in Flynt's brain. He tried to move but a heavy boot on his back ensured he remained prone on the rain-soaked pathway. He didn't know whose foot it was, but he suspected that if he didn't do something then he was as good as dead. The only problem was, between the boot holding him down and the effects of the blow rendering his limbs sluggish in the extreme, there was nothing he could do. One pistol was spent, the other lay somewhere in the darkness, and his sword stick was trapped beneath him.

Jonas, he thought, how the holy hell do you get into these situations?

The answer was, as ever, Colonel Nathaniel godrotting Charters…

-

'I wish you to find me a man,' Charters had told him the day before.

'I thought your tastes ran more to the female of the species,' Flynt had said. 'Naturally, I make no judgement…'

Charters pursed his lips. 'Don't attempt humour, Serjeant, it ill becomes you.'

Flynt suppressed a smile. 'Who is this man you wish me to hunt down?'

'His name is Lombre. Not the nomenclature he was born with, of course. You will have caught the meaning behind the name he has adopted, have you not?'

Flynt's grasp of French was tenuous to say the least, but he knew that L'ombre meant the shadow.

'He's French?'

'Nobody knows. What is known is that Monsieur Lombre spies for whoever pays him, whether it be the French, or the Spanish, or the Jacobites, if they can gather the funds sufficient to meet his price, which is generally not inconsiderable, though my understanding is that he will discount his fee if he believes in the cause.'

'A man of principles, then.'

Charters' lips twitched. 'It depends on your definition of principles.'

'But he does no work for us?'

'No, the man has an abiding hatred for our fine nation.'

'I can only wonder why, for we are such an enchanting, peace-loving people.'

Rain drummed on the inn's roof and raked across the streets outside as Charters glared at him across the table, the shadows cast by the candles accentuating the dark circles under his eyes. Flynt would have inquired after his health, but their relationship was not one that lent itself to such solicitude. They had met in the private upstairs room of the Black Lion in Drury Lane, the venue for many of these secret meetings. Flynt suspected the landlord Joseph Hines was also an operative of the Company of Rogues, overseen by Charters on behalf of the Crown. The room was warm, a fire roared in the grate and those candles that cast the shadows were of beeswax, no noxious tallow for Colonel Charters.

'Why would the French wish to spy upon us?' Flynt said. 'They are our allies. Did we not sign the Triple Alliance with them and the Dutch a year since as a buffer against the Spanish Bourbons?'

'I would never have taken you as a naif, Flynt. As a nation we must always be on our guard, especially from allies, for they often seek the soft underbelly in order to drive in the dagger. Hostilities may not rage but we are never at peace, not with the French, and we view the Hollanders with a great deal of suspicion. As for the Bourbons of Spain, they seek to become more powerful and they must be advised, most forcibly if need be, that such an overreach is not acceptable.' He raised the crystal goblet filled with red wine. The tavern's patrons downstairs drank from cups and tankards but only the finest was served to Colonel Charters. 'Peace is as fragile as this glass. As long as you hold it firmly then all is well, but let your attention wander and allow your grip to loosen, and it will shatter. There is forever plot and counterplot and I thank God for it, for otherwise the likes of you and I would have no function in service of this great nation, would we, Serjeant?'

Charters insisted on addressing Flynt with the rank he had held, albeit briefly, when he had served under him. Flynt had come to regret hauling him from the mud and blood of a foreign battlefield all those years before.

'It doesn't prevent you from enjoying French wines,' Flynt said, nodding towards the goblet in Charters' only remaining hand, the other having been left behind, along with the arm, in Flanders.

Charters smiled. 'Nobody is all bad, Serjeant. You above all should know that.' Something clouded his eyes briefly and he added, 'Almost nobody, at least.'

Flynt let that pass. These exchanges often wearied him, for he knew he could never win. Occasionally he would prod at the colonel to generate a response, but Charters was generally too wily to rise to the bait. That he had a temper Flynt had seen in the past but overall he retained his composure, masking any irritation behind a smile that was not quite supercilious, but was certainly on kissing terms with it. Flynt served this great nation, as Charters called it, because he was forced to do so, for the colonel held a charge of highway robbery over his head. Though it was true that Flynt had for a period led the life of highwayman, it was not he who had held up the coach in question on Hampstead Heath and beaten the young lover of a duchess within an inch of death. The true identity of the perpetrator was revealed to Flynt during the summer of 1716, but the knowledge did him no good at all, for Charters would without doubt ensure that the aforementioned duchess and her swain would swear on a mountain of bibles that the highwayman had, in fact, been he.

'Then what business is this fellow Lombre about?' Flynt asked.

'Something nefarious, most certainly.'

'And he is definitely in London?'

'So my intelligence informs me.'

Flynt knew that Charters' network was second to none, and if he had been told that Lombre was in the city, then that would indeed be the case.

'And when – or if – I find him, what then?'

Charters paused for another sip of the wine before setting the half-empty goblet on the table, his fingers resting on the stem. '*When* you find him, I would have you employ those special talents of yours to obtain from him details of his mission and with whom he is in contact.'

'You wish me to torture him?'

'You have done so on occasions previous. I feel sure it will be no hardship to you.'

Flynt couldn't deny he had employed extreme measures to obtain information, even though each time it had caused him anguish, but he didn't argue the point, for he knew it would avail him nought.

Charters raised his eyes to from the goblet to meet Flynt's. 'And once you have obtained the necessary information, I wish you to kill him.'

'I'm not an assassin.'

'You are what I say you are, Serjeant. And do not affect such distaste, for we both know what nature of man you are and of what you are capable. You will do this and you will do it in name of king and country.'

Flynt took issue with Charters' inference that he was a born killer. That he had taken lives was true, but he reasoned only in defence of self or others. Again, though, to challenge the statement would achieve nothing. 'You've never issued such an order so boldly. Is this man such a danger to fat George and his kingdom? More so than, say, Christian de Fontaine?'

Charters frowned at Flynt's disrespect for the king. 'Madame de Fontaine is little more than a whore for hire.'

'So is Lombre, you say, though Madame de Fontaine works for the French predominantly.'

'She works for herself, predominantly, using her undoubted talents for anyone who will pay her. She has worked for me on occasion.'

Flynt had encountered the woman twice before, once when she was employed by a group they now knew was called the Fellowship and once in a personal capacity. She had dropped hints of having performed certain services for Charters in the past, and some of them of an intimate nature. Flynt had little doubt there would have been a coupling, for he was aware of Charters' appetite for the ladies, and Madame de Fontaine had admitted to her own avidity for bed-chamber activities. He had not had first-hand experience of those particular skills as he had managed to rebuff her overtures. Though he had been tempted.

'Christy is devoted to coin,' Charters continued, 'but this Lombre, whatever be his true identity, is a zealot, and such men are dangerous.'

'A zealot in whose cause?'

'A zealot in the Pope's cause.' Flynt had wondered why the Dutch had not been named as potential employers for Lombre, now he knew, for the Low Countries were predominately Protestant. 'The Roman Catholic Church would wish to see England back in the fold under a Catholic king and James Edward Stuart is suitable for that position. Lombre might well see him as the true king, which would explain his apparent willingness to labour for the Jacobites at a cut rate. We know for certain that he was responsible for the deaths of at least two of my Lord Stair's agents on the continent, both found with dagger thrusts to the heart. He shows a preference for the stiletto, it seems, and not only enjoys its utilisation but is most proficient. He truly *is* an assassin, Serjeant, and my fear is that, with His Majesty at present going against his own nature to make himself ever more visible than previous, then I do believe Monsieur Lombre would not baulk at regicide in order to further an enemy's aims.'

'You suspect he may wish to kill old George?'

Charters again winced. 'I merely float this as a possibility. And I do wish you would show just a little respect for your monarch, Flynt. After all, he is your master.'

'I have no master.'

'Not even me?'

'I merely work for you...'

'And are well compensated for your trouble,' Charters interjected.

Flynt could not argue against that. 'I am, it is true, but I risk my life every time I perform these tasks for you. Something I do under duress, remember.'

Charters waved that away. 'You have talents, Serjeant Flynt, and it would be a sin not to employ them in the name of patriotism.'

'I do it in the name of self-preservation, as well you know.'

'Then do so now. Find Lombre, obtain from him what I need to know and then dispose of him...'

'And where do you suggest I begin my search?'

'I know exactly where you will begin, my dear Serjeant, for I know where he will be on tomorrow's eve and at what hour of the clock…'

-

Charters had not volunteered the source of his intelligence and Flynt knew better than to inquire. The colonel had explained that Lombre was to attend a riverside tavern, a ragged, ripe, roustering drinking den where congregated honest seafarers and dock workers as well as the dregs of the riverside underworld, an assortment of rogues who made an illicit living from the commerce based in the Pool of London. Here were the ark ruffians who robbed passengers, the lumpers who not only loaded and unloaded goods to and from vessels but also skimmed a little off the top for themselves, the water pads who preyed on river shipping, the badgers who robbed and murdered the unwary and dumped their corpses in the water.

Flynt had stationed himself a good hour before the appointed time. The weather was filthy but it was no hazard to the tavern patrons, for rundown though this establishment was, it was a palace compared to their living conditions. It was, for the moment anyway, watertight and a fire raged in the grate, causing vapour to rise from the soaked breeches and hose of those seated close to it. A fiddler in the corner stamped his leg in time to the lively jigs in which he specialised. There were also, of course, whores aplenty, for London was awash with opportunities for sexual gratification, limited only to a man's means and not his predilection. The doxies who plied their trade here varied from young women offering their bodies for the first time – the poor, the needy, the desperate who roamed the room eager to engage any interest and in so doing turn a much-needed coin – to older women well-seasoned in the ways of the flesh. Some were so obviously ravaged by disease that there were no takers. Within minutes of his arrival, two enterprising bobtails had separately approached Flynt in the shadowy corner in which he lurked, thinking him ripe for a tupping. He was slumped over an untouched tankard of ale, affecting the demeanour of a man lost to its liquid charms, his hat pulled low, the collar of his thick coat turned up but the folds positioned in such a way that he could, if the need arose, easily reach within to produce his twin pistols, Tact and

Diplomacy. No such action was necessary to divert the attentions of those ladies, for a polite refusal proved sufficient.

After an hour a man entered, his black hat also set low, but as he raised his head slightly Flynt saw a black patch over his left eye. Charters had told him that Lombre lacked his left eye and bore a ragged scar from forehead to chin, and though there were many men in the city with missing eyes, limbs, even noses, ears and tongues, this man had a way about him that suggested he was the one he sought. He recognised something of himself in this man's bearing, his caution upon entering, and the way that single eye had swiftly surveyed the room to satisfy himself that there were no potential dangers. Flynt, in his gloomy corner, ensured he did not overtly study the newcomer. Too close a scrutiny would set warning bells clamouring.

Lombre moved without hesitation towards a door that led to a private room. Flynt had no wish to impede the man's progress because he wished to know who it was he was due to meet. The room was at present empty, he knew that for he had earlier blundered into it, feigning drunkenness, to see only the landlord laying out a bottle and three glasses. Flynt now maintained his relaxed posture and his gaze upon his tankard. It was at that moment an ageing drab presented herself before Flynt's table and leaned low, all the better to let him see the acreage of flesh which seemed desperate to fall from her bodice like a merchant's sign.

'I sees you sitting here all on your lonely this frightful cold night, love,' she said in a voice made loud by an excess of gin. Too loud, Flynt thought. 'Would you not be liking a bit of company?'

Flynt edged to his right in order to discreetly crane around her ample frame. Lombre had not deviated from his path. 'Thank you, but no.'

'The price of a gin, love, is all I ask. I'll show you heaven for a penny or two.'

Flynt shot her a quick gaze, packing into it a warning that should she not remove herself, then physical harm would be imminent. 'I said no thanks.'

Either the liquor clouding her brain, or simple stupidity, meant she did not catch the hint. She straightened, affected a wounded air. 'What be your trouble? You not like a lady with a full body?' Her voice had risen even higher. 'Or is it boys you like, eh? Be that it? You is a goddamned Molly?'

At that point, taking note of the woman's raised voice, Lombre froze, his eye locking on Flynt's, and that instinct of recognition of another professional flooded his expression as he flicked a gaze towards the door to Flynt's right, his hand already easing from his pocket. Flynt swore, began to rise, pushed the woman to one side with his left hand, while with his right he reached under his coat to pull Tact free. Lombre dodged behind a burly dock worker, his stiletto appearing as if by sleight-of-hand. The dock worker bellowed something foul and swung a meaty fist at Lombre, who thrust the blade quickly and easily under the man's arm. The man wheezed and reeled back, assisted by a shove from Lombre which sent him careening into Flynt's table, knocking the doxy off her feet and forcing Flynt to dart away to avoid collision. By the time he had steadied himself, Lombre had reached the main entrance amid a chorus of yells and cursing from the patrons he had thrust from his path. Flynt struggled through the protesting patrons, brushing away any hands that attempted to hold him back, and burst into the cold night air, the wind whipping across the river to hurl rain at him with considerable enthusiasm. The splash of footsteps on the ill-lit pathway towards the Tower of London reached his ears and he ran swiftly in their direction, fearing this would be his only chance to bring Lombre down. To his right the waters of the Thames seethed and foamed in the darkness, the wind churning it into anger. He could still hear his quarry's feet beating upon the sodden ground ahead, but couldn't see him.

When the footfalls came to an abrupt halt, Flynt paused at the steps leading down to the water at St Katharine's by the Tower, listening for further sounds. Lights burned in the buildings to the left, just squares of weak candlelight, but the path here was just as dimly lit as that on which he had just travelled. The wind boomed around him and the rain thundered against the ground but through it he discerned no further sound of running. The timbers of the small vessels moored at the quayside creaked and moaned as they shifted on the choppy water, their ropes slapping wetly against the forest of masts. Beyond them, on the water, a wherry had pulled away from the bank, the waterman's lamp bobbing like a firefly as he transported his passenger across to the southern bank. Flynt thought he spotted a splash of red as the lamp swung, and if so it meant the waterman had won the Doggett's Coat and Badge race, held on the river every summer. For the oarsman to wear it in such inclement weather proved he was most proud of his achievement. It was too dark for Flynt to discern the passenger, but he was confident that the boat was too far out for it to be Lombre. No, he sensed the man remained on dry land. Flynt strained through the ambient sounds for a trace of his quarry, but heard nothing. Had Lombre dodged up a narrow alleyway or continued his onward flight, he believed he would still detect something, so that suggested the man had come to a halt somewhere and was lying in wait. After all, that's what Flynt himself would do. Running was so tedious.

He caught his breath and stared into the dark shadows surrounding him, alert for the slightest movement. He held his breath, feeling the back of his neck tingle, his senses alerting him that the man was nearby and watching him. Crouching to present as small a target as possible, he tentatively closed in on the steps leading to the water, his pistols ranging around him in case an attack came from elsewhere.

Lombre barrelled into him from behind, gripping his wrist with his left hand and bending the pistol away, while with his right lunging with his thin, sharp dagger. Flynt twisted to avoid the blade, feeling its pressure as it slid across the thick material of his greatcoat, then threw a left-handed punch, his knuckles connecting with Lombre's jaw. The man reeled but retained his firm hold, so Flynt jabbed the heel of his hand into his nose. It was a hefty blow and it obviously stung, for Lombre staggered back and cursed in some foreign tongue that Flynt could not identify, allowing him time to bring his pistol level and draw the second one for good measure.

Lombre dabbed a finger at the blood streaming from one nostril, stared at it, then glared at Flynt. 'You were sent by Nathaniel Charters, I presume.'

It wasn't a question, so Flynt saw little reason to confirm or deny. 'Who were you meeting in that tavern?'

Lombre's face creased in a mocking smile. 'You get right to the point, I see.'

'The hour is late and I would take to my bed.'

'Do not let me delay you. A man needs his sleep.'

Flynt couldn't quite place the man's accent, for it bore hints of both England and France, with the lilt of Italy. Flynt was curious as to this fellow's history but this was not the time our place to investigate it.

'I have work to complete first,' Flynt said.

Lombre stared at the unwavering pistol. 'Finish it then.'

'I don't seek your life.'

That was true, for despite Charters' orders he would not kill this man unless he had to.

'What do you seek then?'

'Information.'

'You will not have it, not from me.'

'I will, of that you can be sure.'

Realisation dawned on Lombre's face and the eyebrow of his single eye raised. 'Torture then? You will waste your efforts, my friend, for it will aid you not. Yes, I may tell you something, but you will never know if it be true or it be lie. Torture is seldom the boon to intelligence gathering that our masters believe it to be.'

Flynt knew this to be the case and though he had before inflicted pain on others previously in order to glean information, those men had not been of Lombre's stripe, lacking the wit to put an end to their suffering by lying. Flynt had little doubt that this man would withstand a great deal of agony before he uttered a single word.

Lombre must have sensed something between them, or saw something flit across Flynt's face, for he smiled. 'So we have reached an impasse, have we not, my friend?'

'No. I could kill you here and now.'

'You said you did not seek my life.'

'That doesn't mean I won't take it.'

Lombre shrugged. My God, he was decidedly unflappable. 'I suspect that is exactly the outcome to this little drama that Charters wishes. As such it will be what it will be, my friend.'

'You know Colonel Charters, I take it?'

'We have played games before, he and I. I am correct, am I not? You are ordered to kill me?'

'Yes.'

Lombre affected a little bow in appreciation of Flynt's candour. 'And yet you do not follow your orders.'

'I follow the orders that suit me and ignore the ones that don't.'

Something like realisation crossed Lombre's face. 'Ah – you are Jonas Flynt!'

Flynt was unaccountably discomfited by the news that he was known by one such as Lombre.

'Come, my friend, do not deny this. You are Jonas Flynt, the one they call the Paladin.'

Flynt frowned. 'Who calls me this?'

Lombre waved a hand. 'The people of the streets of this city. Perhaps a few others who have had your acquaintance. You have not heard this before? Do you know of the Paladin from days gone past?'

Flynt knew of the legend. 'A knight of Charlemagne's court.'

'Bravo, friend Flynt. I had been told you have some learning and you do not disappoint.'

'I'm gratified to hear it, but the Paladin was a defender of the faith and I have none.'

'Then you have a void in your soul that will never be filled. I assure you that it is whispered of the one who will defend those who cannot defend themselves.'

'That one is not I.'

Another smile. 'I have it on good authority that it is.'

'Who is this authority?'

'Ah, men such as we live and work in a realm in which secrets are a commodity to be bought and sold, but that is one I cannot trade.'

Flynt had never heard of there being a street name for him. His young friend Jack Sheppard would have caught such whispers and relayed them to him if they were widespread. He suspected that Lombre was spinning a tale, perhaps in a bid to flatter him and garner some sympathy.

'Nonetheless,' Flynt said, raising his pistol slightly, 'we still have our situation to resolve.'

'I believe it is resolved, although you perhaps do not know as yet.'

Flynt was suspicious of the man's calm demeanour. 'In what way is it resolved?'

'I will reply thusly…' Lombre slowly raised his stiletto, his free hand splayed in a display of peace, and then replaced the blade in the pocket of his coat. 'I put away my weapon, as you can see.'

'It brought you no advantage, my friend, for you are too distant for a thrust and my ball can travel faster than you could throw it.'

'This is true, but still, I believe the situation between us to be resolved.'

'And I ask you again, in what way?'

'In this way…'

The blow wasn't debilitating, but it was sufficiently powerful to pitch Flynt forward, his finger triggering Tact, his head filling with sound and fury, his vision exploding in a myriad of colours. He tried to rise, to twist round to catch a glimpse of his attacker, but a foot placed between his shoulders forced him back down and Diplomacy was plucked from his grip. He felt himself slip into a blackness but forced his mind to retain some hold of consciousness. Even so, he was aware that he was sliding back and forth between the two.

A voice drifted through the colours and cacophony. Lombre's voice. A scent also, something familiar.

'We should finish him...'

Silence, before Lombre spoke again as if in reply. 'He is a danger to us... to me...'

Another silence, then an exasperated sigh from Lombre. 'Very well, but it is against my better judgement.'

Flynt tried to roll onto his side but the foot that held him steady was immoveable. He was aware of someone crouching by his side and then Lombre's voice again, closer this time as he leaned into his ear.

'I hold you no particular ill will, Jonas Flynt, but my every instinct tells me that I should remove you permanently from this realm of the living. However, it seems I am to be prevented from taking such action. You have friends, it seems. Cleave to them, for if we meet again, you will need them. Farewell, Monsieur Paladin.'

Footsteps then. Two sets. No... three. Receding. Nothing further said but the scent remained for a moment before it was drenched by the rain and carried away by the wind.

Flynt forced his body to roll over, the rain on his face now proving most refreshing. He risked raising his head, ignoring the pain piercing his temples, to peer into the darkness of the riverside walkway but Lombre, and whoever had struck him, had vanished into the murk. He let his head drop again and stared at the droplets of rain falling towards him; they were blurred but their chill helped him regain his faculties. Moisture seeped through his coat, his waistcoat, his shirt. He was lying in a puddle, but he didn't much care. With a tentative finger he stroked the back of his head, winced at the sudden lance of pain, then checked to see if there was blood. There was a smear on his fingertips, but nothing to worry about. He'd had worse wounds.

He took a deep breath and slowly dragged himself to his feet, stopping while halfway erect as his mind swam once more. Whoever had hit him knew his business, knew exactly how hard to strike without causing permanent damage or even rendering him fully insensible. Also, whoever it was had prevented Lombre from finishing him off.

You have friends, Lombre had said. Cleave to them, he had recommended.

He would do that, if only he knew who they were.

2

Colonel Nathaniel Charters was more than comfortable in his favourite chair in White's Chocolate House on St James's Street reading the most recent edition of *The London Courant*. The buzz of men's voices drifted in and out of his consciousness, for even in such quietude he was ever alert for any casual comment that might reveal something of interest or use. He was studying a report on the Religious Worship Act, still to receive Royal Assent but which would overturn previous acts restricting the rights of those dissenters who had split from the Church of England on grounds of principle. However, Charters was extremely aware that one man's principle could still be anathema to governments for whom the word was something to follow only when expedient. Nevertheless, he was gratified to know that parliament had seen fit to restore at least some of the freedoms to those people who perhaps sought to worship their God without interference from the state or monarch. Charters upheld the laws of his land, although sometimes did stretch them to their limit, but he fervently believed that men and women had the right to worship as they pleased. That said, he was painfully aware of the religious divide that had contributed to the upheaval of the civil war of the previous century and even in these more enlightened times there were men who would use such divisions to grasp as much power as they could. Politicians often thrived on disunity, for in the spaces between opposing views they found the ammunition that would further whatever cause they sought to follow, which was, Charters generally (but not always) found, self-advancement and the lining of their purses.

It was while he considered such matters that he was approached by one such individual.

'Colonel Charters, dear fellow,' said Sir Robert Walpole, 'it be exceedingly pleasurable to see you.'

Charters was skilled at hiding his true feelings and on this occasion he masked his dismay at not only having this rare moment of relaxation disturbed but also that the one disturbing it being Walpole. Nevertheless, he had to present a pleasant face, if only for reasons of sociability.

'Sir Robert,' he said, 'it is good to see you also.' He nodded to Walpole's companion, who stood slightly behind him, still wearing a dark coat beaded with moisture, though he held his hat, similarly damp, in a hand clasped over the other as it held the silver wolf's head of his cane. 'Lord Moncrieff.'

The man acknowledged with a curt nod. Charters had had dealings with the Scottish lord previously and each knew what the other was about. Flynt had killed the man's father back in 1715, then had later encountered Moncrieff the younger while on a mission to the north of England, and why the son still lived was something that Charters would dearly love to know. Flynt remained tight-lipped on the subject and though Charters suspected there was more to that particular adventure than he had reported, he had accepted the incomplete version. At least for the moment.

'You are well, I trust, Sir Robert,' Charters said, most pleasantly, while wishing these men would continue on their way and leave him at peace.

'I am most assuredly so,' said Walpole, his face beaming, his words bearing traces of his Norfolk upbringing. 'I apologise for disturbing you as you take your leisure. You do not game this evening?'

Walpole gestured to the doorway, beyond which could be heard the voices of noblemen and rich merchants as they attempted to best each other at games of chance.

'Not this evening, Sir Robert. I have much need of some quiet reflection.'

He had hoped that would have provided a heavy hint but Walpole paid it no heed. 'I wanted to thank you most personally for the assistance you have provided me regarding my, em, recent fall from grace.'

'Please think nothing of it, Sir Robert,' Charters said.

'Nevertheless, I do think something of it.'

There had been some turmoil in the Whig party, with two factions vying for power. Walpole and his brother-in-law Charles, the 2nd Viscount Townshend, had each formed part of the Cabinet, with Walpole himself holding the position of Chancellor of the Exchequer. However, they had come into conflict over matters of policy with Lord Sunderland and his ally James Stanhope, who were garnering a power base. There had been much intriguing in Whitehall and Hanover during King George's visit to his homeland and, unfortunately for Townshend and Walpole, their rivals had the royal ear. At the end of 1716, Townshend was dismissed from Cabinet and offered the consolation of Lord Lieutenancy of Ireland, an often-poisoned chalice in the eyes of those with political aspirations. Walpole clung on, but when his brother-in-law abandoned the new post, he felt forced to resign. Such loyalty spoke well of him, but Charters was aware that he jumped before he was pushed and that in the man's convoluted political thinking, there was some profit to be made by it. Walpole was not a man to take action without thinking it through and during the intervening months he and Townshend had been politicking against the Sunderland/Stanhope ministry with considerable zeal, causing a schism in the Whig ranks and delighting the Tories, who had languished in opposition for some years. Nonetheless, Walpole now found himself, not completely in the cold but certainly feeling the chill, and so had sought a way back, finally alighting on the means when yet another rift opened, this time between King George and the Prince of Wales. He was active in burrowing his way into the prince's good graces in their new home at Leicester House.

'It is regrettable that our royal family be so riven,' Charters opined.

'Yes, indeed,' said Walpole, affecting pitch-perfect gravity. 'But it be often so between father and son, does it not?'

Charters was forced to agree. Relations with his own father, a distant figure who seemed often cold and callous in relation to the needs of a growing boy, had often been fraught.

'Is it true that the prince challenged my Lord Newcastle to a duel?'

Walpole smirked. There was little love lost between he and the current Lord Chancellor, who the king had wished to be godfather to his son's newborn son, against the prince's wishes, prompting the rift. 'We know not the full truth of it. Newcastle is adamant that it was so but His Royal Highness denies it is the case. Naturally, though, His Majesty has sided with Newcastle.'

Those final words were spoken in a tone that suggested Walpole failed to understand why anyone would believe Lord Newcastle.

Moncrieff stood by, neither commenting nor reacting. He was a man who watched and who listened, something Charters himself understood. And yet, his connection to the group Charters knew only as the Fellowship meant he was also a man to *be* watched.

'But regrettable though it be, if it means you have a way of easing back into government, Sir Robert, then all to the good, eh?' Flattery was always advisable when dealing with Walpole, whose opinion of himself was exceeded only by his ambition. 'The country needs a man of your talents.'

Walpole waved that away, though there was a certain preening quality to the swelling of his chest. 'I am here to serve this great nation of ours, my good colonel, and will do my utmost to ensure that what talents I have to offer will be put to use, despite opposition from men I once called friend.'

Friendship in politics could often be a tenuous thing, Charters thought but didn't voice. It was also true, to an extent anyway, that he thought Walpole to be an able politician. Unlike many others he was most competent, and there were those who thought him destined to hold great office, which was why he garnered support from fellow Whigs but also some Tories. There remained many who opposed him most virulently, for to some in politics there was nothing so dangerous as a capable man, competence being a rare thing in Whitehall. It was for that reason Charters was happy to help him find a way back into those good graces he so craved, for if he were to achieve greatness, a favour owed would be valuable.

'I trust my recommendation has proved useful to you,' he said.

'Yes, indeed. Thanks to your suggestion of intermediary I have the ear of the Princess of Wales, a most fine woman indeed, and am making inroads into building bridges with His Majesty, the prince. She has a fine mind, for a woman. And strikes a most handsome figure.'

George Augustus, the Prince of Wales, shared his father's somewhat dim view of Walpole but he listened to his wife, Caroline, and that should, if all went well, pave the way forward for a more equable relationship, especially when the prince became king.

'Naturally, I would prefer that His Majesty the king and his son were not so alienated,' Walpole added, 'but it be an ill wind that blows no man some good, eh?'

Especially if that man be you, Charters thought, but looked to Moncrieff. 'And you, my lord, how fare you?'

'I am well, Colonel, thank you.'

Moncrieff had made a better job of losing his native accent than Walpole, but the Caledonian flavour roughened the pronunciation of colonel.

'I hear you are to be congratulated. Your wife is with child.'

'She is, praise to God, for we are blessed.'

'That's what we are about this very night, a celebration of my friend James's fecundity,' said Walpole. 'He has managed at last to spread his seed.'

The reaction from Moncrieff was subtle, little more than a flare of the eyes and a thinning of the nostrils as if he breathed in air most sharply, but it was there. Walpole's sense of humour could be too earthy for some.

'A son and heir to the Moncrieff fortune would be most welcome, eh, James?' Walpole slapped Moncrieff on the back.

Charters knew well how that fortune had been increased, if not originally amassed. Moncrieff's late father had left the family most comfortable thanks to investments in plantations in the Indies and the colonies, but the younger Lord James had also worked hard to improve his position, for he was of the Fellowship, an organisation that had fingers in many pies, and not all of them tasty dishes. Charters was building a fuller picture of them, however.

Moncrieff managed to look embarrassed. 'We would be most delighted with a girl, Sir Robert.'

'Yes, but a boy, James. A boy! To carry on the family name, that is the dream, is it not? I have, as you know, recently been blessed with my fifth child, Horace. A fine boy, a fine boy, he will be a credit to me.'

Moncrieff's eyes met Charters', who suppressed a knowing smile. They both knew the gossip. That Walpole and his wife, Catherine, had been estranged for some time and that he may not have sired the boy, so much so that he took little to do with him. Deception and infidelity were the stock in trade of those who laboured in the corridors of power.

Walpole's eye fell on the newspaper. 'Be that the latest edition, eh?'

'It is, Sir Robert, I do like to keep up with current affairs in the public domain.'

'And those in the private domain, too, eh?' Walpole's wink was heavy, suggesting he had already imbibed copiously that evening. Charters smiled politely. 'It won't be in those pages, but have you heard of the horrors out Whitechapel way?'

'I have not, Sir Robert, what has occurred?'

Walpole shook his head solemnly. 'Dreadful business, quite dreadful. A family, I'm told, slaughtered within their own home.'

Charters felt a tingle begin in his fingers and run along his arms.

'Children dead in their beds...'

The tingle conveyed itself to the back of his neck.

'Here we are, James and I, out to celebrate the impending birth of one child while others lie most brutally murdered only miles away. And the perpetrator unknown and at large.' He shook his head. 'I know not what this city, this country, is coming to. I am no innocent, Charters, I know we are surrounded by violence and cruelty, but sometimes I feel this great metropolis is falling into the hands of the denizens of the alleyways and rookeries. We need to take control. Strong government, that's what's needed, strong and robust...'

Charters interrupted him before he could embark on a political speech. 'How have you heard this?'

'In the street just now, the pamphleteers and purveyors of broadsheets are already out with it. The *Courant* and other publications will follow shortly, I would imagine...'

That laugh. The whistling. Charters heard them both again.

Walpole leaned forward to touch him on the shoulder, his face concerned. 'Good God, Charters, are you unwell? You have turned quite pale...'

Charters forced a smile, a glance at Moncrieff revealing that he studied him most carefully. Damn it, this was not the way he wished to present himself to that man. 'I am quite well, Sir Robert. This is a dreadful business as you say and I am shocked at the brutality of what you tell me. I will most certainly look into it.'

'Do that, Charters, use your resources to assist in finding the person responsible...'

3

Though slightly unsteady on his feet, Flynt retrieved Diplomacy from where it had been discarded by his attacker, and made his way from the riverside. He didn't relish the thought of walking all the way back to the city, but for a goodly distance he encountered neither chairmen nor hackney coach to convey him, the weather being so foul that anyone with any sense ensured they were off the streets or at least tucked up in a tavern or bawdy house. However, the walk in the moist air did him some good, for it helped clear his addled brain and return his strength, so he persevered until he found a brace of doughty sedan carriers lingering by St Paul's who had defied the elements to ply their trade. They carried him through the old city wall at Ludgate, to Fleet Street and from thence to the Strand and finally to Covent Garden, where he was deposited at the door of Mother Grady's house on the west corner of the Piazza. The house was still known by the woman's name, despite it being co-owned by Belle St Clair, with Mary Grady now taking less to do with the day-to-day running of the establishment, although still in residence.

It was Jerome, Mrs Grady's nephew and the house watcher, who admitted Flynt, taking instant note of his dishevelled appearance and the mud on his clothes. He knew nothing of the lump the size of a duck egg and blood crusted to his hair on the back of his head.

'You've been int wars, Mr Flynt,' Jerome observed, his solid Yorkshire tones displaying his customary knack of stating the obvious.

'I have, Jerome, and am in sore need of a brandy and some rest.'

'Then you shall have both, Jonas,' Belle said, descending the wide staircase while carrying a two-stick candelabra, a thick night gown wrapped around her slim body, her black hair long and curling about her shoulders.

As usual, his heart quickened when he set eyes upon her, for she was never anything less than beautiful. He no longer thought of another woman who looked like her, one who lived in far-off Edinburgh, for he had at last come to terms with the loss of her affections. Cassie was now a memory he could control. It was thanks to the advice of an old friend that he was able to resume his liaison with Belle, for they'd had a physical relationship previously, albeit one he erroneously thought was purely business, but one from which he had pulled back when the old wound that was Cassie was reopened. That old friend, during an adventure in the north, had made him realise that in mourning the one, he risked losing the other. Flynt had sat at a literal and spiritual crossroads on the road home, agonising over which way he wished to go, whether to Scotland or back to London. Finally, he had turned Horse, his mare, southwards and on his return had rebuilt the bridge he had almost burned. Now he knew that what was between Belle and him was not simply that of courtesan and cull, but something deeper. And he was all the happier for it.

And so she ordered hot water, a clean towel and a bottle of brandy to be brought to her room, where she helped him remove his greatcoat and divested him of his weapons before inspecting the head wound.

'One day you will receive a blow too far, Jonas,' she said, her tapered fingers delicately inspecting the laceration in his scalp.

'This is nothing,' he said, in an attempt to be offhand and manly, but his wince when she touched a tender spot destroyed the illusion.

'Don't be a baby,' she said, with false severity. 'Compared to other wounds of yours I have treated, it truly is nothing, so stop making such a fuss. What did this person strike you with?'

'I know not, for you may notice that I lack eyes in the back of my head.'

'You lack many things in your head, including more often than not good sense. How often do you intend to be beaten, wounded and almost killed?'

'I don't intend any of it. It's all dictated by circumstance.'

'Well, circumstance will one day be the end of you.'

They'd had this conversation before. Belle knew of his past, knew he had left Edinburgh as a youth to go soldiering, but had grown disaffected with the excessive loss of life in order to gain a few miserable yards, even feet, of ground, of watching the deaths of ordinary people – men, women, children – caused by politicians and nobles who supported this king or that king, or disagreed with the way others worshipped their god. She knew he had fled the battlefield. She knew he had found a colonel of infantry lying in a muddy shellhole, one arm all but severed from his body, dead men all around and rats feasting on their flesh. She knew he had carried that army colonel, Nathaniel Charters, to safety and been rewarded with elevation to serjeant, a promotion which he hadn't retained for long thanks to his tendency to insubordination. She knew that he had been thief, highwayman and gambler. What she did not know was that he worked for Charters' Company of Rogues, though she was canny enough to sense that there was something in his life that he didn't share and that it often led him to those circumstances during which he received bruises, cuts and slashes, all of which she had tended to in recent years.

He sighed, deciding that his usual tactic of deflection was not the tack to take this time. 'I have thought the same myself, Belle, but believe me when I say that I have no choice.'

'We always have choices, Jonas.'

'Did you, when you were shipped over the ocean from the Americas after being sold on the block?'

'No, but I had the choice to let it consume me or to turn it to my advantage. I did the latter and here I am, part owner of this house. I have a future here, Jonas, and it is because I was able, and sufficiently lucky, to use my situation for my betterment. Others were not so fortunate.'

Flynt wondered how he could turn his own situation to his own advantage and came up with nothing. Yes, he was innocent of the crime Charters held over him like a headsman's axe, but what did that matter? Guiltless or not, he could still hang for it. And if he did turn his back on the Company of Rogues, what then? The only way he could achieve it was to do as Gabriel Cain, the old friend who had made him see sense regarding Belle, had done, and that was leave London and never return, to disappear into the countryside, or abroad. He could return to Scotland but there was nothing for him there, which was the second thing he had decided upon at that crossroads. He had a father and a stepmother in Edinburgh, and a stepsister – Cassie. There was a boy who he suspected was his son, but who called another man father, and Flynt would never destroy that illusion. But none of these people deserved to be caught up in the whirlwind that was his life. He had allowed such a thing to occur once before, and it had led to tragedy. Flynt had long ago realised that those circumstances of his life that he had so casually dismissed were complex and often steeped in violence, some of which he sought, but which mostly came his way as a matter of course. He didn't think leaving the Company of Rogues would change that, even if Charters would allow it, which was highly doubtful. Belle knew more about him than any other and accepted the nature of man he was, but she still deserved an answer.

'There's nothing I can do, Belle. My life isn't wholly of my choosing, but it's the one I've been dealt and I must play the hand out.'

'And if you lose?'

He forced a smile, found a glibness he really didn't feel. 'I'll endeavour not to lose. The secret is always to have some trick up my sleeve.'

'And if that fails?'

He reached out to touch her cheek. 'Then I'll have lost and that's the game.'

She placed her hand on his. 'Life isn't a game, Jonas.'

'Yes it is. Life is a game of chance between destiny, desire and death, and we are the dice they throw. In the end, win or lose, death always takes the pot.'

–

Colonel Charters studied the pamphlet that he had bought in the street just a half hour before. The vendor had sung out concerning bloody murder in Whitechapel and again that frisson shivered his flesh. It couldn't be, he said to himself, but inside he knew it was possible. He had read it first in the dim light of his carriage, a cold creeping over him that had nothing to do with the wet weather.

Now, at his desk, a glass of brandy at his hand, he read the report again. Detail was scant, so the author had resorted to lurid and dramatic descriptions of the tragedy in order to ostensibly provide readers value for their money. But then what had occurred was lurid and dramatic. To that Charters would add another word – familiar.

In some echoing part of his mind he heard that laugh, that mocking laugh. And the whistling, always that whistling.

He tinkled the small handbell on his desk and sat back in his chair, his head resting on his hand as he considered the account. The dreadful events in Whitechapel might not be connected, of course, to those in

Flanders. After all, he had long thought the man dead. Further detail would have to be gleaned, but discreetly, of course.

The door opened and Jacob, his servant, entered. 'You need something, Colonel?'

Jacob had once been a soldier, like Flynt, like Charters himself. Although a servant, his manner was not in the least subservient. It was that attitude that had landed him in trouble, after engaging in a disagreement with a superior over an order with which he didn't agree. Charters had been impressed with his spirit and had saved him from a flogging, perhaps even execution. He took him on as his servant and he had remained at his side ever since. More than once he had proved useful in his work. He wasn't as ruthless as Jonas Flynt, nor anywhere near as cunning, but he had wit and some knowledge of the city and its streets.

'Nimrod Boone, Jacob,' Charters said.

'Gawd sake, there's a name I never thought I'd hear again. Ain't he dead?'

'So we were led to believe.'

'Then why talk of him now? I know the nights is dark and we likes a good ghost story now and then, but old Nimrod is one to send the shivers down the back of Old Nick himself.'

Charters pushed the pamphlet across his desk with his forefinger. Jacob understood he was expected to read it, which he did, his lips moving as he struggled with the words. He had his letters but he was far from fluent. When he was done he looked up, a frown slashing at his forehead.

'You think this might be his work?'

'There appear to be similarities.'

'There ain't much detail here. It could be coincidence.'

'Or it could not.'

Jacob accepted that, his eyes drawn to the sheet again as he reread it.

'I need you to make inquiry, Jacob. Contact your old comrades. Ask of Boone and if they have seen him.'

'And if they has?'

'I will deal with it. He has other crimes to answer for and justice delayed is justice denied...'

His eyes moved to the window, beyond which he heard – imagined – whistling in the dark.

-

Someone was whistling, happy at his work. There were other sounds, too, as Covent Garden's daytime commerce gathered pace: the clip of hoof on cobble, the shout of wholesaler to porter, the thud of crates and baskets of produce being unloaded, laughter, curses, singing. Around Jonas Flynt the house was silent, however. The bed was soft, the room was warm, but outside the rain rattled at the window as the wind herded it across Covent Garden Piazza. A single candle sat in a silver holder on a tall dresser, but it had long since guttered and died. Daylight now limped through the drapes to cast a grey glow across the room. Beside him, Belle St Clair slept soundly, the warmth of her body against him giving him pleasure. He laid a hand on top of the coverlet, resting it on her hip. It felt good.

Her lovemaking that night had been fierce and desperate and he didn't know why. She had clawed at him, pulled at him, thrust at him with a fervour he'd never before experienced with her. Perhaps she just felt particularly aroused, he didn't know, but when they fell away from each other, their breath harsh and lacerated, he wondered what was behind it. He knew she was adept at such activity, she had been trained by Mother Grady and had honed her skills over many nights, but never before with Flynt, even when he was a paying customer, had she been so heated. Perhaps she was angry with him for resorting to deflection. Perhaps she sensed or feared something in their future that she thought she could burn away with her passion.

As he lay there in the weak light of dawn, his hand on her hip, her breathing now even, he thought of that future. He didn't know what lay ahead but he knew he would do his best to protect her from it.

A gentle knock of the door preceded Jerome's voice, attempting a whisper. 'Mr Flynt, thee awake?'

Flynt eased himself from under the covers to pull on his breeches and shirt before he opened the door.

'Sorry to disturb thee,' Jerome said, keeping his voice low as he glanced towards the sleeping Belle, 'but there be a gentleman downstairs asking for thee.'

Flynt frowned. 'What gentleman? Not like before?'

Once before Belle and Flynt had been disturbed by unexpected callers. A rogue named Blueskin Blake and another man had been sent by Jonathan Wild, the man who called himself Thieftaker General, to convey Flynt to his presence, and when he resisted, Blueskin turned aggressive and insulted Belle. She deployed a small Queen Anne pistol, which she kept hidden, and shamed him. Blueskin had never forgotten that, nor had he forgotten the loss of face when he had to report back to his master without Flynt in tow. As far as Flynt knew, Belle still had that toby pistol under her mattress, so he was careful never to inflame her ire while in her chamber.

'Nay, this gentleman be decided polite,' said Jerome. 'Asked if he could see thee as he had a matter most important to discuss. I've put him int front parlour. We don't have no culls here at moment, so you could have t'room to thyselves if needed.'

'Did he give you a name?'

'He said it be a Mr Pickett.'

Flynt knew of only one named Pickett, first name Daniel, and he was the near constant companion of a man known only as the Admiral, who reigned over the illicit activities of the docklands and riverside. He thanked Jerome and asked him to tell the gentleman that he would attend him momentarily and to perhaps offer him some coffee, or something stronger if he required it. Jerome left to do that, and Flynt dressed, threw some water over his face and rubbed his teeth with a salty cloth. He moved carefully and silently, being anxious over waking Belle, but she slept soundly.

When he reached the parlour, Daniel Pickett stood in front of the fire, catching what heat there was in the faintly glowing coals, a cup in his hand. The housemaid had clearly not been in to resurrect it and either he or Jerome had raked the ashes in an attempt to bring it back to something close to life. It looked as if the effort was doomed.

Pickett turned when Flynt entered. 'I regret the intrusion, Mr Flynt.'

Pickett's accent was surprisingly cultured. Although Flynt had seen the man many times in the past two years, this was the first occasion on which he had spoken. Communication on previous occasions had been with looks and gestures, usually while divesting Flynt of his weaponry before a meeting with his employer, for Daniel Pickett was a very cautious man.

Flynt didn't reveal his surprise but said, 'No apology needed, Mr Pickett. How can I help you? Your employer, he is well, I trust?'

'Quite well, Mr Flynt,' Pickett said, with a dip of his head. 'But he requests your company for a time. There is something he would wish to discuss.'

This was also something of a first. Previously, the Admiral had appeared unheralded, generally in the dark of night and always in his black coach. Flynt was instantly curious as to what lay behind this meeting.

'When and where would he like to meet?'

Pickett placed the cup on the mantle. 'The when is now, if you please, and as to the where, I will convey you. I have a carriage waiting.'

There was no question of Flynt refusing to accompany Pickett. Had this been Blueskin Blake attending him on behalf of his master Jonathan Wild once more, even if he had couched the invitation in similarly pleasant terms to Pickett, he would not have agreed. However, Blueskin was not a man to whom pleasantries came easily, if at all. The Admiral was as dangerous a man as Wild but Flynt enjoyed his company and he had little doubt that whatever he felt the need to discuss would be important. Flynt's mind turned to Belle. He would leave word with Jerome that he had been called away. She would understand, for though she was never certain what business he was about, she was used to him being drawn elsewhere at a moment's notice. At any rate, he could hear further stirrings about the house, and she had a business to run. She did not need him underfoot.

4

The black carriage, pulled by two fine black horses, waited outside. It was the same one in which Flynt had conversed with the Admiral on previous occasions and he knew it to be both sturdy and comfortable. He and Pickett dashed through the rain to reach its shelter and the driver cracked his whip to spur the horses into motion, steering them in the direction of the Strand and thereafter doubling back on the same route east that Flynt had taken the night previous. Pickett was once more silent and Flynt did not trouble himself by asking what matter his employer wished to discuss as he knew it would result in further silence. He was a cautious, silent man, was Daniel Pickett, and Flynt both admired and respected that, for he was prone to periods of quietude himself, although in his case they often led to an excess of introspection,. which was never a pleasurable experience. He had done too many things of which he was not proud, made too many mistakes for which others had paid a price and suffered guilt because of that. In the dark of night, he often saw the faces of men he had killed, some deservedly, others because of those circumstances he had mentioned to Belle. They haunted his sleep and tormented his dreams and when he woke he could still see their features and hear their voices taunting him.

As the coach driver guided them through city streets that, like the Piazza, had already come to life, Flynt made a quiet study of his companion, who sat back in the seat opposite, his face turned to gaze through the carriage window. He knew nothing of him, apart from the fact that he seemed to be devoted to the Admiral. Was that merely because he was paid to do so? Or was there a deeper bond? Familial? Emotional? Perhaps one had saved the other's life, just as Flynt had done with Charters, although in that case he doubted there was any bond beyond the colonel utilising his skills with what seemed like increasing regularity.

Flynt thought perhaps he was being taken to the Admiral's riverside dominion but, at St Paul's, the carriage diverted to turn towards Cheapside, passing the poultry sellers and then the Stocks Market thronged with fishmongers and butchers and the customers who sought their produce, for though the wind still blew, albeit with less vehemence than the night before, and the rain still fell, commerce must continue and Londoners must eat. They continued on to Cornhill and Leadenhall Street to cross the city wall at Aldgate and thence to Whitechapel Road, which took travellers east to Mile End and eventually to Colchester and the port of Harwich. The carriage passed the church of St Mary Matfelon that gave this wide thoroughfare its name, the walls that had once been coated in lime whitewash were now of brick, having been rebuilt some years previously. When they passed a windmill, Flynt guessed they were headed for the huge humpback of earth and dung and detritus that rose from the open land ahead. The carriage came to a halt and Flynt made to disembark but Pickett raised a hand in an unspoken instruction for him to stay, then held that same hand out.

Flynt understood, for he had followed this ritual a number of times previously. He fished both his pistols from their specially sewn compartments within his coat and surrendered them along with his silver cane. Unsmiling, Pickett nodded his gratitude, then opened the door and handed the weapons up to the driver. Motioning to Flynt to remain in the carriage, he fastened his coat tighter around his throat and wedged his hat firmly upon his head before striding towards the tall, powerful shape of the Admiral, who was in conference with two women and a young boy, each carrying with them baskets. They seemed to be at ease with him, the women laughing, the boy though staying slightly distant and merely listening. Pickett said a word and the Admiral turned his head slightly to allow him to see through his one eye, the remainder of his face, as ever, concealed behind a dark leather mask. He nodded, exchanged another word with the women and touched his hat brim before walking towards the coach, Pickett at his back. In all the times they had met, Flynt had never seen the Admiral in daylight, nor less seen him walk, and he now noted that he had a pronounced limp and needed a long cane to support him. Whatever wound or condition had left his face marked had also caused him to be somewhat lame.

Pickett opened the carriage door, waited until his employer had laboriously climbed on board, then closed it again. He remained just outside. He was a cautious man, a silent man and a watchful man.

The Admiral's breathing was even harsher than Flynt had heard before – perhaps the walk and the damp air had irritated his lungs – and he took a moment before he spoke. He removed his tricorn hat and laid it carefully on the seat beside him, but his soft leather gloves remained in place.

'Mr Flynt.' The Admiral's voice was seemingly coated with abrasive material. 'You are well, I trust?'

'Quite well, thank you,' Flynt replied.

'I am right glad to hear that.'

There was a silence then, something Flynt was used to when conversing with this man, for there were times when the act of conversation was difficult for him. He first met him when the city was in the grip of the most ferocious winter Flynt had ever experienced. At the time, he had been recruited to provide some small assistance in removing a Scottish nobleman from the Tower of London so that he might avoid a date with the headsman. Passage from London had been required and the Admiral had been instrumental in arranging it. Since then they had shared one another's company on many occasions, the Admiral eventually explaining that he trusted few men, and respected even fewer, and it was good to find someone in their world of shadow who was capable of sharing a discussion on art, literature and a mutual mistrust of Jonathan Wild, with whom the Admiral enjoyed a long-running struggle for the overlordship of the riverlands. Flynt sensed a loneliness in this man, whose real name he did not know and whose features he had never seen, permanently obscured as they were. Agreeable though the discourse had been, he still retained a suspicion that he was being groomed for some future service and, depending on what that service was, a refusal might prove unpleasant for them both.

The Admiral had turned his face to stare through the window. Eventually a cough grated in his throat. 'Damn this weather,' he said, 'it does me lungs little good.'

He watched the two women and the lad begin to climb one of the pathways on the side of the hill, took a deep, halting breath, and said, 'You are acquainted with Whitechapel Mount, friend Jonas?'

'I have been in the vicinity on occasion, yes.'

The Admiral nodded. 'They say it be many things, a natural feature of the land, or a defensive hill from eons past, a fort from the parliamentary wars, even something as simple as a dunghill. What think you?'

'I'm not native to the city, but I have heard the many theories. A burial mound for plague victims or those who perished in the great fire of '66 are another two.'

'Aye, perhaps there are learned men who know the truth of it, but we will have to be satisfied with conjecture. Whatever its true beginning, it is a laystall now, a resting place for the muck and discards of the city.' His head jutted towards the women and lad, now squatting in the dirt, the wind and rain not concerning them in the slightest. 'They dig through the detritus brought here from the Tower district and others, searching for items that can be repaired, sold again for profit. Those women are but one example of workers who comb the mound for treasures. You would be surprised by what they can find.' He coughed again, the phlegm rattling from his chest. 'I apologise, sir.'

Flynt inclined his head. 'No apology required. The cold and the damp does get into our lungs.'

'Aye,' the Admiral said, the single word a hoarse testament. 'Whatever its original function, a rubbish tip it be today, and a profitable one, for a man of my acquaintance owns the lease and a pretty penny he makes from it. He has other interests, naturally, but there is coin in refuse. Even the dust that is deposited here can be used for brick making, did you know that?'

Flynt suspected that the man in question was the Admiral himself. 'I did not.'

'There are fine views from the summit, not on this day to be sure, but when it is clear you can see south beyond the river and west to the city wall and the Tower and St Paul's.' He paused for a breath. 'On a summer day you see gentlefolk strolling up the various paths, but not after dark, for then there are other habitués, men and women who are less welcome. The footpad, the cutthroat, the rogue. For even in surroundings that are more rural than metropolitan, there are violent men, are there not?'

'It was ever thus, for human nature can be most base and violence is never far away.'

'Aye, that is something of which we both know a great deal, for we are both violent men, are we not?'

'I like to think not without reason.'

A slight grunt then. 'I like to think that too, but sometimes...' A sigh, the mucus that seemed lodged in the man's throat bubbling. 'Sometimes even I am horrified by that of which men are capable. Have you heard of what the pamphleteers have termed the Whitechapel Horror?'

Flynt hadn't. 'I have been somewhat diverted of late and I regret have not kept abreast of affairs.'

'Aye, one diversion being a man called Lombre.'

That the Admiral knew of the man he sought came as no surprise, for the encounter of the previous night had taken place on the waterfront, where little escaped his notice.

'I regret he escaped me.'

'Ah, that was unfortunate.'

'It was more than that, it was incompetence on my part.'

'We all have unguarded moments. Do you wish me to do what I can to trace him for you?'

'That would be most helpful, thank you.'

The Admiral nodded his assent and Flynt was grateful he didn't inquire as to why he sought Lombre. He had no desire to go further into the matter, for his work on Charters' behalf must, by necessity, remain clandestine. 'What was the horror of which you speak?'

The Admiral's head turned again to stare from the window. He seemed to watch the women working but perhaps he was merely gathering his thoughts.

'The family of a man named Jacques Berthon lived not far from here, down by Goodman's Fields.'

'Berthon? He was French?'

'By blood, but Huguenot by faith, and his family took refuge here in the city when the French state waged war against them. They weaved the silk, settling first in Spitalfields. Jacques, though, had little interest in the trade, much to the disappointment of his father. His talents leaned more towards numbers and he forged himself a reputation in bookkeeping, with a particular skill in the exchange of stocks.'

His breath rasped again and he paused to control it. Flynt, used to his speech patterns, waited.

'He was a fine, upstanding man,' the Admiral continued. 'An upright man, but not in the parlance of our people who see such as leaders of rogues, but in the true sense of the word. He was that rarity, Jonas, a true Christian man. He lived modestly, for though he was skilled in the numerical arts he did not seek huge riches. Kind and charitable and educated, he possessed a keen interest in science and the use of mathematics therein. His skills in that regard were of such a degree that, in my opinion, he was eligible for membership of the Royal Society, but that fellowship is closed to men such as he, his birth and even his education not being of a sufficient elevation. Just last year he met with others who shared his interests and formed a society for the furtherance of mathematics in Spitalfields.' Another pause, another ragged breath. 'He further disappointed his father by marrying outwith the Huguenot faith, a lovely girl from Devon by name of Abigail. They had two children, Eliza and Matthew. They were a fine family.'

Flynt had detected the use of the past tense in the Admiral's speech and when the man was forced to stop as his voice had grown rougher, he said, 'What happened to them?'

The Admiral swallowed a few times and cleared his throat before lowering the window beside him to lean out and hawk something nearly solid into the rain. He raised the window again and sat back to catch his breath, his gloved hand fumbling in his coat pocket for a linen wipe, which he dabbed at the mask around his mouth. When he spoke again, his voice was thin and even more husky than before. Flynt suspected it was from rage and horror rather than debilitation caused by his condition.

'They were slaughtered, Jonas. The mother, the father, the children. Someone forced his way into their home and cut Jacques' throat, before doing the same to Abigail. He then attended to the children as they slept above.' He swallowed again. 'I have been told it was as a charnel house. Blood, so much blood. The mutilations were...' He sought for the word. '...inhuman, is all I can say. They were children, Jonas, little children and this butcher cut them up as though they were beasts destined for the hook.'

The mask concealed his expression but the single visible eye revealed much. Flynt had never heard the man's voice so charged with emotion and a single tear burst from its leather prison. The Admiral seemed unaware of it, or felt no shame at being so exposed, for he made no move to wipe it away.

'The family were known to you?' Flynt asked, his voice gentle.

A nod in reply. 'It began as business, just as that between you and I. Jacques handled some of my financial affairs, those that were open and above board, for he was, as I say, a most fastidious man. He maintained my accounts. He suspected I had... other interests, of course, perhaps had heard of my soubriquet.' He raised a hand towards his mask. 'My appearance marks me as unusual, after all.'

'You used your name with him?'

'I used *a* name with him, for I have many and none of them my actual identity. It suits me for my true self not to be known for such could be used against me. I have family beyond London, distant to be sure, but still family, and I would not have them harmed by an enemy in order to wound me.'

That was the first time the Admiral had told him anything of himself. Their previous conversations had been friendly but the man had never revealed his true name, nor anything of his past. Flynt had his theories as to what caused his current condition but the man seldom referenced it or let slip anything of a personal nature, yet here, in the space of a few sentences, he had done both, however vague. The Admiral was, by necessity in what he called the shadow world, a man capable of having great violence committed, but he truly grieved the loss of this Huguenot and his family.

Flynt asked, 'You developed a friendship?'

'Aye, he and his family overlooked my physical appearance, never commented upon it, never asked about it. The children were wary at first, that is understandable. The lad out there, the one with the women workers, he kept his distance, I feel sure you were aware. I scare him, I always do when I make my visits here. On these few occasions when I venture forth in daylight, and to visit here by necessity I must, I usually detect at least a look, of open curiosity, of repugnance, of fear.' He rotated a finger in the air towards his face. 'Often someone inquires as to how came I to be in this condition. I never tell them. Apart from Jacques and his family, there have only ever been two individuals who have been so accepting. Daniel is one. You are the other.'

Flynt grew uncomfortable as the man's single eye shone in gratitude. 'A man's physical appearance does not necessarily reflect his nature,' Flynt said.

'I have done many ugly things in my life.'

'As have I. But I would hazard that your appearance is the result of something other than any evil that you have committed.'

There was a short silence between them, with only the slightly laboured breathing between them, before the Admiral spoke again. 'I have been aware of your scrutiny, aware that you have seen the scarring on these hands, respectful though that scrutiny was, and I do not fault you for it, for I am aware that I present a most curious aspect, but I give you credit for not commenting or inquiring.'

'I surmised that should you ever wish me to know, then you would tell me.'

'Not even Jacques knew, and I trusted him. Only Daniel there knows the truth, for apart from you he is now the only man I in any way trust.'

'I thank you for that.'

'There is no need for thanks, for it is what it is. I know there is talk of me and to an extent I cultivate it. Mystery can be alluring to some but daunting to others. They say that I somehow survived leprosy or the pox but was left hideously disfigured. I heard one that I was birthed during the great fire back in '66 and crisped by the flames. What think you of those theories?'

'I have heard them and rejected them.'

'Then what do you believe caused my condition?'

'I have seen such scarring before. You were in the military, given the soubriquet you have adopted I would hazard at sea, and were caught in cannon fire.'

'Bravo, Jonas, bravo. It was at La Hogue, back in '92, but the irony was that it was not French cannonade but my own that caused my injuries. Whether the gunners used too much powder or whether the barrel was somehow weakened I know not, but it misfired, killing them, and it was my misfortune to have been the midshipman overseeing them.'

He paused, swallowed once more, then began to ease the glove from his left hand. He held it up before his eye, turning it back and forth. Seeing it in daylight for the first time revealed to Flynt the extent of the burns. Even after over twenty years the flesh looked as if it was raw, with what appeared to be blisters still present, black and hard, as if the wounds had been first experienced just a few weeks before.

'The blast seared my face, my body, my hands,' the Admiral said. 'Sections of my uniform were sealed to my flesh and fragments remain still. As you can see, I lost my left eye. The inferno was a powerful one and I breathed in its acrid heat, scorching my throat and lungs, hence my manner of speaking and breathing. I would have surely perished but for the lad at that moment passing between me and the gun.' His voice softened. 'Timothy Roberts, was his name. A bright lad, a good lad, his lack of stature and fleetness of foot made him ideal for the duties of powder monkey. You are not a man of the sea, Jonas, but are you acquainted with matters on a man o' war? You know the duties of a powder monkey?'

'They ferry powder from the ship's magazine to the gundecks.'

'They do. Brave lads all, and I knew young Timothy, for I was not much older than he. He loved the sea, loved the life, even though it be hard.'

'Perhaps no harder than what he had on land,' Flynt said.

'True. He was from a poor family in Plymouth, but a loving one. His mother took his death most grievous, for he was the only one of her children who had survived and her husband, himself a seafarer, had passed. I supported her until she herself was free of this vale of tears, anonymous of course, but it was of little comfort, I fear. Had he not been delivering powder at that moment, had he moved a little slower or a little faster, I would not be here this day. But that is the way of life and death, is it not? A single moment makes all the difference. Even so, I should have died, the surgeon told me, but I did not. I breathe, I think, I talk.' He stopped, caught his breath. 'But something did die. I was once a gregarious individual. I liked to carouse, I liked to wench, for I was a handsome fellow. I am no longer. That fellow died, but his vanity did not, and so I am as you see me now, seldom venturing forth in daylight. But I cannot become fully a creature of the night. A man needs to lay eyes upon sunlight now and then so I visit here and, of course, my docklands.' He paused again, the length of the speech causing his breathing to toil. Once he had it under control, he spoke once more. 'We have much in common, I believe, you and I. You have scars, both physical and, I suspect, spiritual. Perhaps that is why we have bonded so readily.'

'Perhaps.'

The Admiral cocked his head to study him with his good eye. 'You wonder why I tell you this now?'

Flynt had already guessed where it was leading. 'You wish me to know more of you.'

'I do.'

'Because you trust me.'

'Aye.'

'And because you wish something from me.'

The slight laugh that came then was little more than a wheeze. 'By God, Jonas, I am right to have you as friend. I do wish something from you, and if you agree to it then it will be as a friend, and not because you fear me.'

'I don't fear you.'

'Many do.'

'I don't. As you say, you see me as friend and that is how I see you. Friends don't fear one another nor expect it to be so. What do you wish me to do?'

'I would have you probe the murder of Jacques and his family.'

Flynt had suspected as much. 'The authorities will investigate.'

That was dismissed with a click of the tongue. 'What authorities? The Charlies?'

The Charlies were the watchmen, generally elderly men who made a show of maintaining law and order but seldom succeeded.

'The magistrates,' Flynt suggested.

'They will not move their plump backsides from their fireside. They will appoint some constable, a volunteer, who will not be equipped for such work. Or some lawyer more used to poring through documents than walking these streets.'

'What makes you think I am equipped for such an investigation?'

'I know you are, Jonas. You will not be surprised to hear that I have made it my business to learn what I can of you. I am a prudent man, by dint of necessity, by dint of experience, and before I extend the hand of friendship I make it my business to know everything I can about the other party. I expect you did the same.'

'I already knew all I could know of you.'

'And now your knowledge is further extended. But of you, I perhaps know more. Thief you have been. Gambler you are. Those weapons of which Daniel so diligently relieves you have been well used over the years. You have made inquiry into matters that, on the face of it, are not matters in which a thief and gambler would take an interest. I make mention of the death of a judge, the arranging of passage for a certain Scottish nobleman and his wife, and just this past week, the incident with the man Lombre.'

'My interests are varied.'

'Perhaps, and I express no curiosity as to why such things pique those interests. But I also know that you have defended many who cannot defend themselves and though you profess to have no faith you have shown charity and mercy where others have not.'

'I have also shown no mercy all too often.'

'Perhaps, where mercy was not deserved. At heart, I believe you to be a good man.'

'I am not a good man.'

'No man is all good. We all carry elements of both saint and sinner in our hearts and minds, each one struggling with the other for dominance.' The Admiral's voice was little more than a whisper now as he leaned forward to place his scarred hand on Flynt's leg. 'Find the man who did this to my friends, Jonas.'

'And if I do find him?'

'Bring him to me. Dead if you must, but alive would be preferable.'

'You don't trust English justice?'

'Justice takes many forms, I think you know that, my friend, and some are surer than others. You have meted out your own form of it in the past, of this I know for fact. Bring him to me and I will see that justice is done.'

Flynt thought about this. Both he and the Admiral were used to death, had witnessed it and caused it, but from the description given, this crime had been horrendous in the extreme. Whoever did it had no saint remaining in his heart.

'How do men like you and I stop ourselves from becoming like this man?' he asked. 'Which of the two will be victorious in our case? Saint or sinner?'

The Admiral sank back in his seat. 'Which ever one we feed...'

5

Flynt hadn't expected to find a familiar face standing among the spectators who had heard of the horrors perpetrated within the modest brick-built house near to Goodman's Fields. The crowd milling around the street were a mix of gentiles and Sephardic Jews, who had been drawn to the land east of the wall in order to make a home. There were merchants, tradesmen, manual labourers, gentlemen, vagabonds, women with children by the hand, and, without doubt, a few pocket divers on the foist, for where there was a crowd, there was opportunity to lift a purse or a wipe. More legitimate, but equally as enterprising, commercial opportunities were seized by those selling pies, sweetmeats, fruits, ballads and broadsheets. One such purveyor of news held up his product and rasped in a hoarse voice about horrible murder in Whitechapel. He seemed to be conducting a brisk trade, for those who could read had the sheet in hand and consumed details both real and imagined with great interest.

And standing among them was Colonel Charters, his brow furrowed. The rain had dried, at least for the present, but the glowering sky matched his employer's frown.

The Admiral's carriage had come to a halt a goodly number of yards away from the scene, and Flynt spotted the colonel's tall shape easily in his blue woollen coat, his hand fixing his hat to his head against the persistent wind. Flynt didn't see Charters' own coach so presumed it had been left in another street, for he was not a man to walk all this way, nor less take a hackney, chair or boat.

The Admiral wished him God speed but kept himself well back into the interior of his coach, not wishing to be seen. Daniel Pickett gave Flynt a nod as he dropped the window covering. The driver jerked the reins to galvanise the horses and the carriage rolled off south, back to the Admiral's riverside haven.

Flynt eased his way between the men and women gathered, ears open for a choice remark that might lead him towards some sort of trail. Adopting a casual air, he made a point of studying faces, looking for tell-tale signs of guilt and sensing the unease that had draped itself over the crowd with the rain. There was curiosity in those expressions, certainly, but there was also shock. And horror.

'We do not often see you venture beyond the wall, Colonel,' he said quietly as he reached Charters' side.

Flynt was gratified to see that, for once, he had startled his commander, for it was more often he who was caught unawares. As he jerked towards Flynt, Charters' thoughtful, curious look transformed into one of brief surprise, then the forcing of his customary mocking expression. The dark circles under his eyes, clearer even in the dim daylight than in the gloom of the Black Lion's private room, told a different story.

'I be not tied to the city, Serjeant,' he said. 'Sometimes I do like to sally forth and see how fares the rest of the country.'

Flynt had never known Charters to leave London, but he let that pass. 'And you just happened to come by Goodman's Fields?'

Charters didn't reply, but his attention returned to the house.

'What is it about the occurrence here that interests you, Colonel?'

Charters seemed about to admit something, but then thought better of it. He shot a final look towards the front door, which lay broken and open and guarded by a man Flynt took to be either a Charlie of more recent vintage than many of his contemporaries or some form of parish functionary.

'I heard of this dreadful affair from a pamphlet,' he said, keeping his voice low even though nobody was close enough to hear. He jutted his head towards the broadsheet seller walking by them. 'As you can see, it is quite the talk of the town, so I thought I would attend, perhaps offer my assistance, if needed.'

Flynt knew there to be a deeper explanation for his presence, for dreadful though the events had been, Charters was not prone to involving himself in criminal matters unless he had good reason. 'Do you think there is something here that threatens the nation's security?'

For the second time, Charters hesitated. It was a fleeting lapse, however, for the colonel swiftly went on the attack. 'I have my reasons and they need not concern you. But why are you here, Serjeant? Have you not a task to perform? What of our friend Lombre?'

'I lost him,' Flynt said, steeling himself for some blistering comment, Charters not being a man who took well to failure.

'You lost him,' Charters repeated.

'He had assistance.'

'Who?'

'I'm working on it.'

Charters merely nodded. 'You believe him to be in Whitechapel or Spitalfields, perhaps?'

'I spoke to a contact here, who will assist in tracing him.'

'Then go about that business and don't tarry here.'

The colonel's lack of anger, not even a tart comment, aroused Flynt's suspicions, so he probed further. 'What assistance do you think you could offer this investigation?'

Charters shook his head. 'I have already informed you that the matter is not of your concern.'

'But I am concerned, Colonel. I have never before seen you to take an interest in anything that did not directly connect to your work, apart from your affection for the ladies.'

By his expression, Charters was finally prepared to issue a reprimand for being so bold, but he chanced to look back to the house and uttered a soft curse. Flynt followed his gaze and saw two further familiar faces emerging from the house.

'Damn the man, what brings him beyond the wall?'

Jonathan Wild, with Blueskin Blake as ever in his wake, stood in the doorway talking to the guard on duty. The Thieftaker General was most smartly dressed in a brown worsted cape with silver-gilt embroidery protecting a similarly hued and embroidered knee-length coat over brown knee breeches. His hose was a brilliant white but splashed with mud while his black shoes were decorated by a silver buckle Flynt thought to be too dainty for a day like this. His tricorn hat matched his ensemble and he carried his sword in a gilt scabbard, an affectation he thought made him appear to be more of a gentleman. Blueskin, by contrast, was positively dowdy in a black greatcoat that had seen better days, black boots and a hat that looked as if he had used it to beat someone senseless, an unlikely occurrence, but knowing Blake he would give it his best effort should the need ever arise.

Charters turned away. 'I don't want him to see us together, Flynt, for both our sakes. If you insist on taking an interest in this, then here's your chance.' Charters gripped Flynt's arm and pulled him further away from the throng. 'Reacquaint yourself with the not-so-honourable Mr Wild and find out what you can as to his involvement and also further details of the events within that house.'

Flynt was also less than pleased with the appearance of Jonathan Wild, but it at least afforded him the opportunity to keep his contact with the Admiral secret. He had often marvelled at how luck played a part in his life, both good and bad. Here was a stroke of good fortune, for he had been considering telling Charters that he had been asked to probe the murders in return for assistance in finding Lombre. Charters would then have delved deeper into his informant's identity and Flynt would have had to refuse to answer, which would only have intrigued the colonel further. It was often best to keep certain aspects of his life away from his line of sight, for he only used them to his own advantage.

'Are we making this official Company of Rogues business?' Flynt asked.

Charters' lips thinned with irritation. 'No, damn it. This is personal.'

That took Flynt aback. 'In what way personal?'

But Charters was already brushing past him, eager to get away from Wild. 'Meet me in the Castle tavern on Aldgate as soon as you have some information.' He then added over his shoulder, 'Detail, Flynt. Get me details of what occurred within, for pamphlets, broadsheets and rumour can often be wide of the mark.'

He didn't wait for Flynt's reply but walked quickly away from the crowd. Personal, he'd said. What personal connection could Nathaniel Charters, retired army colonel on a pension but independently wealthy and spymaster for the Crown, possibly have with the family of a Huguenot bookkeeper? Let alone a brutal murder? Charters was someone who could order a killing with ease, as he had with Lombre, but Flynt was certain he would not countenance the slaughter of children.

He watched the colonel strut swiftly towards Alie Street, then noted two men detach themselves from the crowd to follow him. One gave Flynt a curt nod as he passed. The colonel's watchers were always present, unseen perhaps, but always there.

Flynt turned his attention to Wild, still at the door with the sentinel, paying no attention to the staring faces, for his stance was all for effect. He was there to be seen. Blake, however, was more circumspect. He lingered in the shadow of the doorway, his sharp eyes scanning the press of onlookers. As Flynt shouldered his way through, it crossed his mind that it was he who would have been more likely to have spotted Charters, Wild being too intent on simply being seen. Blake's eyes settled on him as he stepped through the front rank of the crowd, narrowing in suspicion. The dark-haired rogue, perpetual stubble staining his cheeks and chin no matter how closely he shaved, was forever suspicious of Flynt, and with good reason.

A nudge from his bodyguard and a flick of a finger towards Flynt diverted Wild's attention from the guard. A smile that could very easily have been sincere, if the man was capable of such, spread his face. 'Jonas Flynt, whatever brings you to these streets?'

Flynt touched the brim of his hat towards Wild, then gave Blake a brief nod, which was repaid with a grimace of distaste. Flynt almost smiled. 'I had business in Whitechapel and heard of these dreadful events.'

The thieftaker's smile died and he affected a mournful expression. 'Aye, 'tis most dreadful, most dreadful indeed.'

Like his smile, his words, still echoing of the streets of Wolverhampton, might have been heartfelt, but something in the way he projected them as if he was on a stage in Drury Lane suggested otherwise.

Blake saw no need to feign anything other than his customary wariness. 'What business does you have here, Flynt?'

'A meeting with an old friend,' Flynt said.

'The tall, lank-sleeved cove I sees you having converse with not a moment ago?'

Blake had seen them after all. That would not thrill Charters, so Flynt felt pleasure in the anticipation of informing him.

'No,' Flynt said, feeling the need to at least make the attempt to protect the colonel. 'I chanced upon him when I arrived in the square. He was my old commander in Flanders.'

Blake seemed to accept that. 'Then who was the old friend what you was meeting?'

'Nobody you'd know, Joseph,' Flynt lied, purposely using his given name rather than the nickname. 'He's an honest man.' He returned his attention to Wild. 'What brings you to Whitechapel, Mr Wild? Are there not felonies aplenty within the city to take up your attention?'

'I was informed by messenger of this dreadful business, word being sent by a citizen who remained anonymous but who thought this might be a matter that would benefit from my expertise.' He looked back through the door and shook his head. 'I be not easily shocked, sir, but sometimes the inhumanity of my fellow man leaves me sick to my gut.'

This time Flynt swore there was no pretence in his words. Wild was being as genuine as he possibly could be.

'What knowledge do you have of what truly occurred?' Flynt asked.

Blake displayed no concern over the depravity of what had taken place. 'What business be it of yours?'

Wild raised a hand. 'Come now, Joseph, Mr Flynt here is a gentleman…'

That brought a short but disdainful laugh from Blake. 'He ain't no more gentleman than I is, Mr Wild. He's a rogue and a rum one at that…'

'Joseph, you wound me,' Flynt said, it being his turn to show lack of sincerity.

'Not as much as I would like to one day. And that day will come, you can make book on that.'

'That will do, Joseph,' Wild said, real steel in his voice. 'Return to the coach and await my return.'

Blake was surprised. 'And leave you here with him, on your alone?'

'I'm in no danger from Jonas Flynt.'

'I ain't so sure…'

Wild's temper broke. 'Damn your eyes, Blake, leave us.'

Still showing signs that he wished to continue his protest, Blake glared at Flynt and shouldered past him. Wild watched him go.

'I apologise for Joseph's behaviour, but he really doesn't like you.'

'He has to join a line in that regard,' Flynt said.

Wild laughed. 'Yes, you certainly have a knack of getting under the skin of some people.'

'But not you, eh, Mr Wild?'

'No, not me. I like you, Jonas, for you and I have much in common.'

That thought unsettled Flynt but he forced his face to remain open and friendly. 'In what way?'

'We are both northerners, come down here to make our way, you from Scotland, me from Staffordshire. We are both men of some intelligence and resolve, with our own sense of honour...'

Flynt suppressed a laugh, hoping it didn't show on his face.

'And we are both bad men to cross,' Wild added. 'Joseph there is also a bad man to cross, and I would advise you to be most wary. I can control him only so far, but there is a point when he breaks free and, like a vicious dog, turns savage.'

'I'll keep that in mind, Mr Wild, thank you again for reminding me of his nature.' Flynt gestured to the doorway. 'Now, what of this incident?'

Wild now grew curious. 'What be your interest in this, Jonas?'

'You mentioned my sense of honour and it is outraged at what is rumoured to have occurred within those walls. I would know more.'

'Outrage,' Wild said, thoughtfully, the glimmer of humour that had tickled his lips now gone completely. Again, Flynt sensed this was not artifice. 'Aye, this be an outrage, it is true. All good men should be so repulsed by it. Slaughter, it was, no other word can describe it.'

'What can you tell me?'

'What have you heard?'

Wild was canny, so Flynt being as open as he could was the only way to obtain further information. 'That someone murdered an entire family here.'

'Aye, that's about the sum of it. Man, woman, two children.'

'Will you investigate?'

Wild puffed himself up a little. 'I will do what I can to assist in bringing whatever madman committed these unspeakable acts to feel the full weight of the law around his throat.'

'As any of us should.'

Wild made a study of Flynt. 'You will make inquiry?'

'I am not without connections to the darker side of London, as you know, Mr Wild. Is it not the duty of any man to stand ready when such evil is perpetrated?'

When Wild continued to scrutinise him, Flynt looked beyond him to the guard, still standing at his post, before switching to regard the crowd, the front rank close enough to hear them talk.

'Perhaps it would be best if we stepped inside? There be too many ears to hear and tongues to wag.' Flynt paused as a thought struck him. 'It may also be possible that the man we seek is among this crowd.'

That made Wild study the faces with renewed interest. 'Aye,' he said, 'here to witness the clamour his depravity has created.'

He turned and entered the house, telling the watchman that this was Jonas Flynt, describing him as an associate. Behind his back, Flynt grimaced but followed, not knowing if the sudden tingle at the back of his neck was caused by the thought that they were being watched, or if the thought was the result of the tingle.

-

I sees him.

He dresses puritan, the tall cove in his black clothes and black hat, but he has the looks of a hunter and I knows that look well, for I sees it look back at me every day in the glass. Like knows like, after all.

They don't see me as I sidle closer, close enough for my listeners to catch some of what they say. Flynt, Wild calls him. Jonas Flynt. An associate, he says. They is going into the crib now, the hunter and Wild. I knows him, too, and the cove what was with him, 'cos they has been pointed out previous. Blueskin Blake is what they calls the other cove and he is right tasty, not like the hunter, not as tasty as him, but handy enough. They don't know me, they ain't had the pleasure, nor will they, for they isn't my business. Blake passed right by me, close enough to touch if I'd had a mind. His face was like thunder, so whatever was said to him by yonder fop Wild was not to his pleasure. I seen the look in his peepers, too, when he spoke to the hunter, no love lost there, I'd say.

They is gone indoors now, no doubt studying on my handiwork.

I likes that notion, I do, I likes it a lot. I likes what I see and hear and smell from the folks clustered around me. Fear. Fear mixed with excitement, 'cos there's those what enjoys the idea of what has occurred here. My work brightens up their day, it does. Gent or pauper, they all likes a bit of blood, as long as it ain't theirs. Cockfighting, dogfighting, prizefighting, bear baiting all excites them, sets their own blood a-tingling. But not mine. Watching beasts rip each other to shreds ain't my notion of excitement. No, not the watching. I prefer to be doing the ripping. These people what only watch don't know the full of it. They don't know the thrill of the cut. I wonders how they'd feel if I was to loosen my blade and be in at their beef.

Tempting, it is, but I will stay my hand. Time enough for that. I is still warm from my work in this place, still feel it pulsing in my blood. And I has to report, I has. But no matter, for this here is just the beginning.

There's more to come...

6

The house reeked of blood.

Flynt's nose wrinkled against the stench as soon as he left the small hallway and entered the parlour. It was a comfortable, family home, typical of a man of means, though limited. A fireplace, with the fire screen standing to one side, lay cold and dark. A wooden bench covered in cushions and a thick blanket faced it, alongside a rocking chair of old wood upon which rested a cloth doll, no doubt stuffed with fragments of discarded clothing, as if awaiting its owner to retrieve it. In an alcove to the rear, near the stove and a wooden table where the family would have taken their meals, stood a large Welsh dresser displaying some well-used pewter plates. Congealed blood, hardened to the wooden floor, lay before him, a further spray splashed across the wall leading to the stairway.

'They found the man here,' Wild said, swinging his scabbard at the pool. 'His throat had been sliced open, hence the mark on the wall.'

'You saw the bodies?'

Wild's tone was grim. 'Aye, they were in place when I arrived.'

Flynt glanced at the front door, noted the splintering around the lock. 'The door was forced.'

'Aye. It's likely that Mr Berthon heard the noise and moved to intercept the intruder.'

'Nobody else heard? Came to investigate?'

'The house next door lies empty, the one on t'other side is occupied by a deaf old trot who wouldn't hear Gabriel's horn were it blown directly in her ear.'

'But somebody did come eventually?'

'Aye, friend to the dead 'un, saw the door lying open. Fainted dead away and when he came back to the world alerted the first Charlie he could find.'

'This friend is not one to be leery of?'

Wild shook his head. 'A square cove, he be, on good terms with the family. He didn't do this, I'd stake my reputation upon it.'

It occurred to Flynt that Wild's reputation wasn't much of a stake.

Wild stepped to another bloody stain, larger even than the first. 'The wife was found here, at the foot of the stairs.'

Flynt saw no tell-tale spray on the wall. 'He didn't cut her throat?'

'Gutted her. Ripped from belly to breastbone. Her insides were spilled out where she fell.'

Flynt had seen death in many forms but he felt bitterness in his throat. The Admiral had said that this was more charnel house than dwelling and now he understood why. Until now this had been just another job, even an abstract concept, but being confronted with the evidence of bloody murder, Wild's near matter-of-fact description of what was believed to have happened tinged with the reek of blood, he felt growing horror. He had told Wild he was outraged by what he had heard but at that stage it wasn't true. He didn't know these people, had only heard of them that morning, but now, standing in their home, where they had lived, loved and laughed, and looking down on the stains left by their lifeblood, he felt rage growing.

And there was worse yet to come.

'The little ones were found up here,' Wild said, beginning to ascend the stairs.

Flynt stepped over the woman's blood and followed him, his hand gripping the wooden railing tightly, as if squeezing it was akin to gripping the killer by the throat. He noted bloody footprints on the wooden stairs, the left sole bearing a sharp slice, as if it was cracked. Obviously the killer had stepped in the blood below and tracked it upwards.

There were two rooms aloft, one larger he took to have been formerly occupied by the parents, the smaller one to the right at the head of the stairs. Wild led the way but stepped aside before entering. 'I cannot gaze upon it again. I'm not a weak-willed man, as you know, but the thought of what those poor innocents suffered be too much for me.'

He waved Flynt on and, despite his own feeling of nausea, Flynt stepped into the small room where grey light eased its way through a small curtained window facing down to the street beyond. He could hear the voices of the crowd but it seemed like a world away. A small bed was tucked under the casement, another faced the door. Both were in disarray. Both saturated with blood. He closed his eyes, grateful that he had not been present earlier to see the little bodies, and tried to block the images that flashed before him. He stepped back onto the landing.

'Did you see the bodies?' he asked.

Wild nodded. 'I will spare you the details, apart from telling you that it was a violation.'

Flynt felt his fury kindle further. 'The children were sexually outraged?'

'Not as can be told but, in truth, the condition in which they were found was so extreme there is no way of the telling of it.'

Swallowing his bile, Flynt looked towards the head of the stairs. 'One of them might have seen their murderer approach if this door was open.'

'The girl, Eliza was her name, her bed had full view of the stairhead.'

Flynt thought of the doll down below. Had she forgotten to take it to her bed with her? Would it have provided any comfort at all?

'And now you know all, Jonas. We have four dead and no living person saw or heard anything of the murderer. He came and left in the night like some kind of phantom.'

'He would have had to walk the streets with blood on his clothing.'

'As yet we have found nobody who saw him. It be possible that he arrived and left by carriage.'

'Was there anyone who bore the family animosity?'

'As far as I know, they did not. The father was respected, a Huguenot although not a follower of his faith with any great adherence, I'm told. The mother was from the west country and was liked. They were respectable, they were hard-working. The children were polite and respectful.'

'Then why them?'

'I know not.' Wild turned his head towards the bedroom. 'London is a violent place, Jonas, we both know that. We have even contributed towards it. But this...?' He took a deep breath and swallowed hard, his jaws working as if something had lodged in his throat that required to be expelled. 'I have never seen anything like this. I hope to God I shall never see anything like it again. This is not the work of a man, this is the work of the devil.'

At the entranceway, Wild had been more intent on making his presence known, on being seen, but here he was different. This was the most human Flynt had ever seen him. Wild was a crook and a user of men. He would betray anyone if it suited him or if it helped him turn a coin. He concealed his true nature behind a mask of authority and public service. Of the two, Flynt believed Blueskin Blake was the more honest, for he didn't hide what he was. But in that moment, Flynt saw another side to the self-styled Thieftaker General. He still didn't particularly warm to him, but he saw that within that duplicitous, larcenous heart there still lived some semblance of decency.

-

The Castle tavern on Aldgate was housed in a timber-fronted Tudor building that had been spared the great fire of 1666 by only a few yards. In his highwayman days, while working the empty stretches of the Whitechapel Road, Flynt and his friend Gabriel Cain had often supped here and had come to know the landlord, who had regaled them with this intelligence, as well as boasting that his establishment was the oldest of its kind on either side of the city wall. Flynt was unsure if this were true but he accepted it, for the man seemed greatly proud of the fact.

It was a narrow building, still showing evidence of domestic origins with separate rooms, though Flynt was aware that below street level ran a series of vaulted chambers that pre-dated the present structure. The floor was uneven, the entire house seeming to tilt, as if resting against the adjoining property after a particularly energetic night of carousing and perhaps even coupling. In the entrance passage he was met by Charters' watchers. He didn't know their names, though they had the look and bearing of former soldiers. One acknowledged his greeting but said nothing as he waved towards a doorway to the right. The other, his hand resting on the pistol thrust in his belt, neither greeted nor displayed any form of recognition. He was blank of face and dead of eye, but Flynt felt sure that he was the more watchful of the two and would miss nothing. Charters' wellbeing was in safe hands, he would wager.

He ducked under the low doorway to enter a small, oak-panelled room with four tables each with two chairs, the dark beams crossing the ceiling so perilously close to the top of Flynt's head that he felt them brush the brim of his hat. The room was empty of customers, apart from Charters slumped alone at a corner table, his gaze seemingly fixed on a brandy bottle before him, though Flynt suspected he was not actually seeing it. A glass, near empty, sat by his hand, another unused on the table. Hearing Flynt enter, he looked up and assumed his customary erect demeanour. At his side a fire spat and crackled, and on experiencing the welcome heat, Flynt realised how cold he was. Though his greatcoat was thick and his leather gloves sturdy, the damp air had succeeded in seeping through his layers to settle on his flesh. Even so, he knew that it was the scene within the little house that had truly chilled him.

He dropped his hat and gloves on the table and took a seat in the vacant chair opposite Charters, then poured himself a measure of brandy from the bottle.

'Please, feel free to help yourself,' Charters said, the warmth of the liquor perhaps having revitalised his own spirit, though his eye still held a faintly haunted look.

'Thank you, I have,' Flynt said, then sipped the brandy.

'Is it to your liking?' Charters asked.

'It's not the best of quality but on a day like this quality matters not.'

'It will fire your blood, most certainly, and protect against the elements.'

'It wasn't the elements to which I referred,' Flynt said, draining the glass and pouring another, seeing Charters' eyebrow twitch. He seldom drank more than one measure in his company and never two in swift succession but he felt the need of them this day.

'It was bad then,' Charters said, his voice flat, as if he had been expecting – hoping – for better.

Flynt nodded and wiped his mouth with the back of his hand. 'It was bad.'

Charters breathed deeply. 'Tell me.'

Flynt told him everything he knew. Charters listened, occasionally interjecting with a query, his humour vanishing again, his jaw tightening as Flynt described how the Berthon family had died. When he had been told all, Charters sat back in his chair and refilled his own glass, then Flynt's. His hand shook, Flynt noted. That was another first.

'Then there was little exaggeration in the reports,' Charters said, his tone suggesting that he wished there had been.

'Conjecture perhaps, but it would appear no hyperbole.'

Charters swallowed his drink whole. 'I feared as much.'

Flynt left his glass untouched. 'Will you tell me true why you are so interested in this, Colonel?'

'Can I not be touched by the tragedy of it?'

'Aye, but there's more to it than that, you said so yourself. Had it been mere curiosity then you might have had your man Jacob come to Whitechapel to make inquiry, or me, or any one of the Company. You told me there was something personal in this for you and I would know why.'

The bottle was hefted again and another measure poured and drunk. Charters set the glass down and was immobile for a moment or two. Finally, he spoke.

'Very well, as your current assignment and this seem to have intersected, I will tell you. Does the name Nimrod Boone resonate at all?'

Flynt played the name in his mind but it sparked no memory. 'Should it?'

Another breath from Charters and he reached for the bottle again, but Flynt pulled it away. He had never before seen his former commander in such a low state and he found it concerning. 'Enough, Colonel,' he said, his voice gentle. 'Talk, don't drink.'

Charters, had his mind not been so diverted, would never have allowed Flynt to treat him in such a manner. Instead, he accepted it with a nod and rubbed his hand across his face. He was silent for a moment, then said, 'It was shortly before we first encountered one another at Malplaquet, but I thought perhaps you might have heard the name whispered among your comrades.'

'This fellow Boone was under your command?'

'As much as a man like he was under anyone's command. You have a tendency towards insubordination and lack of respect for your superiors but Boone…? Boone was… unpredictable.'

'Was he an officer?'

'A mere foot soldier,' Charters said. 'I suspect there was a willingness to enlist, probably to escape punishment for some crime.'

'So how did he come to your attention? He didn't save your life, too, did he?'

Charters' smile was as weak as Flynt's attempt at humour. 'No, quite the opposite. You never did inquire as to how I, as a ranking officer, ended up in that crater on the field?'

'I presumed you had defied the traditions of your rank and gone out to get your hands dirty along with the cannon fodder. Or had somehow taken a wrong turn at the officers' mess.'

Charters grimaced and his voice adopted something closer to his usual steel. 'We're not all behind-the-line warriors, Flynt.'

Flynt realised that under the circumstances he had been too flippant and apologised. 'Please, go on, sir.'

Charters' eyes widened slightly at the unaccustomed respect but he didn't comment. He fell silent once again as he gathered his thoughts. 'Do you dream of that day, Flynt?'

'Malplaquet?'

'Yes.'

Flynt shook his head but he was lying. He had dreamed of it, or at least a version of it. The battle itself, the bloodiest of the campaign, was fought in daylight but his dream was much darker. It's not night, but he is surrounded by blackness. And within it he hears the thunder of cannonade and sees the blood and the mangled bodies. And rats, feasting on the flesh of the dead and the living, a multitude of rodents swarming and snarling, their sharp little teeth ripping and tearing. The reality was not quite as dramatic – there had been rats, but not the hordes his sleeping mind conjured.

'I have begun to dream of it,' Charters said, his voice softer than Flynt had ever previously heard. 'Only recently, for in truth I endeavour not to think about that day overmuch. But suddenly I am back on that hellish Flanders field and pursuing Nimrod Boone.'

'Why?'

'Because he was a scoundrel and a murderer and I was determined that he wouldn't escape justice.'

'But he did.'

'It would seem so.'

'Who did he murder?'

Charters sighed, closed his eyes. 'A family, much like those poor souls back in that little house.'

'French?'

'Flemish. It was just a week or two before Malplaquet. He slaughtered them with a bayonet he'd liberated from a French soldier.' He swallowed hard. 'I saw the bodies, Flynt. I see them now, as though they are on this very table before me, laid open as though by a drunken barber-surgeon. I have seen death, we both have. We have seen mutilations on the field, flesh shredded by grapeshot and shrapnel. But this, Flynt, this was butchery.'

Flynt recalled the horror nestling within Wild's words and it was matched in those of the colonel's.

'And it is certain it was Nimrod Boone who was responsible?'

'He was caught quite literally red-handed. He was found by a detachment of soldiers in the little farmhouse, surrounded by the dead, the weapon still warm with their blood.'

Flynt felt a further chill steal over him and, despite himself, sipped at the brandy. 'There were children among the dead?'

'Three,' Charters confirmed. 'Two boys and girl, who was barely out of swaddling. When he was come upon, he fought to escape, slashed at men who were his comrades, cutting two and near killing a third, before he was subdued with a musket butt to the head. Would that blow had been heavier and crushed his skull. They said he was more devil than man.'

Flynt thought of what Wild had described and heard his words about it being the work of the devil. It now seemed to be less of an overstatement.

'And that was when you became acquainted with him?'

'It was. He was brought to me. I tell you this, if I was ever to choose a man capable of such horrors, I would not have chosen him. He was so... ordinary. He was one that should you pass him in the street you would not notice him.'

'Even ordinary men can commit extraordinary acts,' Flynt said.

'I know that is true, for I have seen men – men of poor backgrounds, humble beginnings, tradesmen from the towns and villages – perform feats of bravery. But this was no heroic act, this was barbarism, and to look at Boone you would not think him capable. He stood before me, of slight stature, his features unremarkable, and casually admitted what he had done.'

'Did he say why he killed them?'

'Because they were there.' Charters blinked at the memory. 'His exact words, and I remember them most clearly, as if he said them just this very morning, was that the why of it lay in why a dog licks his balls. Because he could.' Charters paused to let that sink in. 'Naturally, sentence of death was passed.'

'But never carried out.'

'He escaped, killed the chaplain who attended him to bring succour as well as two guards.'

'How?'

'We were in the field, Flynt. We didn't have a permanent guardhouse, so he was housed in a tent. He overcame his guards and fled the encampment.'

'Was he not manacled?'

'He was, hand and foot. That was how he killed the guards and the chaplain. He throttled them with the chains, then hobbled forth. Naturally, I had questions for the sentries on the picket line but it would seem Boone was skilled in silent movement when he had to be.'

Something in Flynt's memory stirred. A whisper from his days encamped ahead of Malplaquet, of a man who had lost his reason, and had managed to abscond while in chains.

He asked, 'His escape was virtually on the eve of commencement of hostilities at Malplaquet, correct?'

'It was two nights before. I didn't have the leisure to track him down, nor less spare men to do so.' Charters paused, eyed the brandy bottle. Flynt pushed it towards him but the colonel shook his head. 'It wasn't the last I saw of him. I thought him long away, or had run as far away as he could in the time he'd been at liberty, but I caught sight of him among the ranks. He had detached himself from his chains somehow, using tools found as he hid, I would conjecture. At first I thought I was mistaken but I pursued him.'

'He came back? Why?'

'Because he could,' Charters repeated. 'My instinct is that he likes the kill. He lives for it. And the confusion of battle is an ideal place for a man with such appetites. And Malplaquet was particularly bloody, as you know, so made an ideal feasting place.'

'So you pursued him. Did you catch him?'

'I did, eventually, and confronted him beside a crater left by the morning's cannon fire. Inside were the bodies of men from both sides. I'm sure you know which crater it was.'

Flynt knew. There was more in that crater.

'He had a sabre, no doubt taken from a dead officer,' Charters continued. 'Or perhaps he killed him and took it, I wouldn't be surprised. I was resolved that he would not leave that field alive and I discharged my pistol.'

'You missed?'

'I did not, but the ball delayed him only a little. A lesser man, one who had a little less devil in him, would have fallen, but he did not. He came at me with the sabre. We fought, two Englishmen crossing swords while around us comrades died and the enemy died, and it was as if there was no other conflict than ours.'

Charters closed his eyes as he remembered. Flynt gave him the space.

'He got the better of me. I was the more accomplished swordsman by far but despite his stature he was most powerful and extreme light of foot. He slashed at my shoulder, cutting me to the bone, near separating my arm from my body, and I fell. He must have thought me dead, for that was where you later found me, surrounded by the dead.'

And more, Flynt thought. The rats. He thrust the memory from his mind. 'And Boone?'

Charters' head shook. 'I know not. I thought perhaps he was felled in battle.'

'And now you think otherwise.'

'I *fear* otherwise, for what you have described to me bears all the hallmarks of his handiwork.'

'It may not be.'

'It may not, that is true, but it is my duty to find out. I have Jacob making inquiry of old comrades in arms to see whether they know of his return, or indeed anything of him since we returned from Flanders.'

Unlike Flynt, Jacob had obviously maintained links with those with whom he served. Flynt had subsequently met with only one man who had been with him during the war, a childhood friend now dead.

'I should have had the creature executed immediately after the hearing but I delayed it for a day, to give him the chance to make his peace with God,' Charters said. 'I should have bested him when we fought on the field. If this is he, back in London, then I must find him and stop him.'

He fell silent again and then leaned forward, his voice little more than a whisper. 'Have you ever known a truly evil man, Flynt?'

The face of a northern lord sprang into Flynt's mind. He was dead now, lying in an unmarked grave somewhere on moorland, a grave that had been meant for Flynt. 'In our world, it is difficult to tell between who is mad, who is bad and who is evil.'

Charters reached for the bottle again. Flynt did nothing to prevent him. 'You know I have committed, or had committed, acts that might be seen as evil. There are those who would look at you, at what you have done both at my behest and on your own accord, and they would say you are evil. I do not hold with that.' Again, the brandy was gone in single swallow. 'But Nimrod Boone is such a man. I wish you to find him, Flynt.'

'I thought you had Jacob on his trail.'

Charters dismissed that with a wave of his hand. 'Jacob is most capable and can handle himself ably, to be sure, but he is a seeker of intelligences only. This needs a man with other skills. Your skills. Find Nimrod Boone, Flynt, find him and end him.'

That was the second time in a matter of days that Charters had ordered him to kill a man, but this time Flynt suspected he would obey and do it right gladly.

7

Jack Sheppard supped a tankard of ale as he fixed an appreciative stare at the ample behind of a serving girl while she bent to retrieve empty cups and bottles from the table in front of him. Around him, the Black Lion tavern enjoyed its customary brisk trade, the air as ever thick with smoke from the blazing fire, the burning candles on the walls and the tobacco puffed from a myriad of pipes. The assault on the nose and eyes was matched by the din: raised voices, raucous laughter, the cries of the landlord Joseph Hines as he bellowed at the pot boys and wenches, and the blind man in the corner tooting away at a bone flageolet in return for the price of a drink or two or, if he was lucky, perhaps even some of the meat Flynt could smell roasting in the inn's kitchen.

'I thought you were faithful to Bess, Jack,' he said as he dropped his hat on the table and, without even thinking about it, took a chair that afforded him clear views of the room and the doorways.

Jack took his eyes away from the girl's charms. 'A fellow can look, Mr Flynt, ain't no harm in that.'

'Bess might see it differently.'

Jack scowled. 'Bess can see it as she pleases, for she ain't no angel. I ain't seen her these two weeks past because she's working up Holborn way.'

Jack was only around sixteen years of age, Flynt was never sure, and Jack himself was somewhat hazy, while Edgeworth Bess was a few years older and a working girl. She had not yet been aged unduly by her life but she was getting there. Jack was infatuated by her, even though their liaison was, at least ostensibly on her part, an occasional business arrangement. Flynt suspected though that, despite her tendency to deny it, Bess held tender feelings for the lad.

'You knew how she made her living from the off,' Flynt reminded him.

'I knows it but...' The lad's words halted as he attempted to find the correct way to phrase his feeling. 'Look, I understand it, you knows I do. It's the way of our streets, ain't it? We all grift and grab and Bess, she's a looker and no mistake, and the culls they like that. But I don't like her working on her lonely. She don't have no bully watching over her like some of the girls out there.'

'Do you see yourself as taking on that mantle, lad?'

Jack grinned. 'Me? No, you know me, Mr Flynt. I'm a grabber, not a grappler. You want a crib cracked or a purse foisted, then I'm your man...' His voice cut off sharply when he realised what he'd said. To cover himself he added with some haste, 'At least I was, but the hard stuff I leaves to others. Like you, Mr Flynt, begging your pardon for being so bold.'

Flynt inclined his head to grant the requested pardon. 'I tried to have her placed in a decent house, as you know, Jack.'

Fearful for Bess's safety after she had shot a man, Flynt had taken her to Mother Grady's in the hope that she would be safe from any revenge the deceased's brother might seek. She had remained there little more than a single night before she fled.

'That ain't her desire, but I thanks you again for trying. She be an independent sort, is Bess, but I do wish she were less so.' The serving girl passed by again and Jack's eyes wandered in her direction. 'So we has this arrangement, her and me. She tups her culls and I gets to look at whatever rich apple dumplings or fine full nancies what comes me by.' As if in example of his words, Jack's gaze took in the girl's breasts and buttocks in one easy sweep. She saw his appreciative look and ducked her head in a shy smile. The girl was of Jack's own age and Flynt noted that she had no good reason to pass by their table other than to let him see her. He smiled at the lusts of youth, recalling his own wandering eye as a lad.

'I have work for you, Jack,' he said.

The girl had weaved between the tables and exited towards the kitchen, but not before she shot a quick glance back at Jack. He was a handsome fellow and had a ready wit. Flynt thought she could do a lot worse than to take up with him, while he would do better for himself than to continue with Bess, whether she had tender feelings for him or no. That way only lay heartache, Flynt believed.

When she was gone, Jack gave Flynt his full attention. 'I is at leisure presently, so what does you need?'

'I would know of a cull by the name of Nimrod Boone.'

Jack's brow furrowed. 'That ain't a common chanter, Nimrod. What manner of name is that? Scotch? Welsh? Foreign maybe?'

'Biblical,' Flynt explained. 'Do you know your scripture?'

Jack shrugged. 'Passably. Don't set much store by it. After all, the Bible tells us that thou shalt not steal but if me and my brother Tom went in for what's written we'd've starved long ago, and so would my old mum.'

'I thought you had given up the flash life now that you are apprenticed to Mr Wood?'

Jack was learning the carpentry trade under Owen Wood, who had a workshop in Wych Street, off Drury Lane, a position that Flynt himself had arranged in a bid to keep the lad away from the road to Tyburn on which he seemed bound. Jack had also expressed a desire to keep his head down after he came to the notice of Jonathan Wild.

'I has, Mr Flynt. Straight as an arrow me now, but you will recollect I did say we'd've starved long ago, like in the past like, not now.'

His face was open and genuine but Flynt knew him to be a flash lad, capable of lying with such fluency it would shame a politician. 'Then why are you here and not at your labours?'

He could see Jack's sharp mind working. 'Things is quiet at present and Mr Wood, he's a decent cove as you know, he's let me come here for an hour to eat and take my leisure. So, who was this Nimrod cove then?'

Flynt sighed, sensing deflection in the lad's manner, but it wasn't something for him to investigate at that moment, especially as he had a task for him. 'Nimrod was the king of the land of Shinar and a great-grandson of Noah...'

'I knows of him, built hisself an ark and survived a flood.'

'That's right. They say Nimrod was a mighty hunter but also, some say, a despot who wanted to turn his people away from God and instead worship him. Some scholars believe it was he who built the Tower of Babel...'

'I knows that story too. God smited them somehow.'

'Well, he found they were all speaking the same language, so he changed that until none of the workers could understand each other by making them speak in many tongues.'

'So this cove you seek is named after him?'

'I'd say so, as you say it's not a common name. His parents clearly knew their Bible, for Nimrod is mentioned practically in passing. I take it then he means nothing to you?'

'Don't know no Nimrod Boone but I believes there is a Boone what I has heard of, Caleb be his Christian chant. If I'm right, he's an upright man what runs a crew of wild rogues.'

Caleb was another name drawn from the Bible, a spy sent by Moses to reconnoitre the lands of Canaan. The use of names from scripture was not uncommon, but it was a connection that Flynt couldn't overlook.

'Can you find me a way to reach this Caleb Boone?'

Jack's expression told him that was not in any way a challenge. 'Easily, Mr Flynt. I takes it there ain't no point in me asking why you want these coves?'

Flynt smiled but said nothing and Jack nodded. 'That's what I thought. Give me an hour or two, I'll have the best way to get to this cove for you sharpish.'

An hour or two. Owen Wood was being most generous with his time. Flynt picked up his hat. 'Good lad.' He dropped some coins on the table. 'One thing more, have you heard the nickname the Paladin being used in the streets?'

Jack slid the coins with one hand into the other and dropped them into the pocket of his breeches. 'Street legend, is all.'

'Then you have heard of it?'

'Some mutterings in the past year or so but not too wide. Some cove what supposedly does good deeds, like a bleedin' crusader or something. Defends those in need. Wishful thinking, is my take from it. Poor people need some sort of saviour rather than fend for themselves.'

'And nobody knows who he is?'

'No, nobody does, and there's an explanation that is dead simple for that – because he don't exist. The streets is full of people what has nicknames and some of those people don't actually draw breath other than in the minds of the weak.'

'If you hear anything further about this individual, tell me, will you?'

'Why you so interested, Mr Flynt? You ain't never asked me about no bloody street tale before.'

'It intrigues me, Jack. Keep your ears open.'

'Always does, you know me…'

A voice boomed across the tavern. 'You there, boy!'

Both Flynt and Jack followed the voice to the entrance from Drury Lane where stood a man whose prosperity showed in his fine topcoat, full dress wig, powdered to perfection, an Italian tricorne hat made of fine beaver felt complete with gilt edgings and carrying a gold-tipped stick. His wealth was also revealed by a belly running to corpulence. He pointed his stick towards them and said again, 'You, boy!'

Jack swore softly and Flynt knew for certain that his claim to have forsaken his former light-fingered ways had been somewhat overstated.

'Go now,' Flynt said softly, 'out the back, and be swift about it. Seek me at Belle's later.'

Jack had no need to be told twice. He bolted across the tavern to the kitchen door while Flynt moved to intercept the rotund gentleman who was demanding that someone stop the boy. Nobody moved, however. In fact, many adjusted their position to give Jack free access.

'Damn you all to hell,' the man cried, 'I will have that little thief arrested!'

Flynt had positioned himself in the man's path, his hands held up to placate him. 'Easy, sir, what harm did the lad do you?'

'He is a thief, sir, a damned, nimble-fingered little picker of pockets who just this very day relieved me of my silk kerchief while I had discourse with a young lady outside the Theatre Royal.'

Jack had lifted the wipe while the man was negotiating a price for a tupping, Flynt assumed.

'I was told that the rascal was often to be found in the taverns on the lane and here he was,' the man said. 'Now, sir, step aside for I will have him, by God I will, and see him in the Newgate before this very night is over.' Flynt didn't move and the man raised his walking stick. 'I said stand aside, sir, or I will strike you.'

'Then you will be charged with assault and it will be you in Newgate and not the boy.'

This gave the man pause. 'You are obviously in concert with the little thief, sir, and no magistrate would countenance a charge against me. I will prosecute him, by God I will, and have my satisfaction through the assize. And then the boy will hang, or be branded and whipped, though I would prefer his life to be forfeit to prevent him from a-going thieving once more.'

Flynt stood his ground and held the man's gaze. 'Why not wield that walker, friend, and let us see what charge would be countenanced. If it ever connected, that is.'

Something in Flynt's tone made the man take a step back. 'You threaten me, sir?' He looked around him. 'I have witnesses to your threat. I will see *you* in the assize dock and in Newgate, by God I will, sir. For I am a most formidable man, a most deliberate man.'

He cast his eyes around again but all around seemed to find something incredibly fascinating in any direction but his. Gradually, the conversation that had died after the man's entrance began to resume. The blind whistler, taking his cue from that, picked up a sprightly tune.

Flynt smiled and held his hands out in an unthreatening manner. 'I make no threats, friend. I merely discern that you are a gentleman, and such violence is not in your bones. You are a kind man, a good man, yes, formidable as you say, but your anger and your outrage has gained the better of your reason. The boy is gone from this place and you will never see him again, of that you can be certain. Lads like him are like the mist from the river. They come, they go and sometimes you fail to notice their passing.'

The man grew quite red in the face. 'Well, sir, I noticed his passing, for I was light of a silken kerchief. Property, sir, property. It be the cornerstone of this nation, from the great estates to the lowly kerchief, and it will be protected, sir, by God it will, by law and, yes sir, by me.'

Judging that Jack would be well away by that time, Flynt shrugged and stepped aside to allow the splenetic gentleman to pass.

'I wouldn't go through that door,' he said, his words causing the man to stop and turn.

'You threaten again, sir?'

'Not threaten, a caution against exiting that way. A man of your station in life would be easy meat to the rogues and vagabonds who lurk in that alleyway. You might lose more than a silk wipe.'

The man sneered a little and peeled back his coat to reveal a brace of fine pistols, the butts bearing what looked like a golden monogram. 'I am no neophyte to this city, sir. If any rogue wishes to tangle with me I will accommodate them most severely.'

Flynt was tempted to let the man take his chances beyond the door but his conscience wouldn't allow it. 'Come, friend, the boy is long away and placing yourself in jeopardy is foolhardy. Let me buy you a drink and reimburse you for the price of your stolen property.'

The man's eyes narrowed in suspicion and he took a step back towards Flynt. 'You are something to this young rapscallion. I saw you in congress with him as I entered. You and he are somehow in league, I'll be bound.'

'I had merely exchanged a word with him, looking for some accommodating female company free of disease and thought perhaps he could direct me accordingly. These street boys are most educated in the ways of men of the world such as you and I. I feel sure you understand.'

'I do, sir, but that explains not why you would be willing to part with your own coin to make up my losses at his larcenous little fingers.'

'Let me say that, having inadvertently delayed you, I feel some responsibility. In addition, I am most fervent in my desire that you do not lay yourself open to harm by pursuing him.' Flynt gestured to the table on which lay his hat. 'So, I beseech you, sit with me for a while, we shall share a bottle and you shall be recompensed for your loss.'

The man hesitated, glanced at the door through which Jack had vanished, then reached a decision. 'Very well, sir, I shall accede to your request. But I will make this clear at the outset, I cannot accept anything less than a crown in compensation, for I have been put to considerable inconvenience this night, by God I have...'

As he led the man to the table, Flynt resisted a sigh. Being a Paladin was an expensive business.

8

The rain had resumed and soaked near through his thick coat by the time he returned to Covent Garden. He had spent what seemed like an eternity pacifying the gentleman, who owned a small estate in Surrey and whose conversation consisted of little other than money. He was in town to discuss his investments in various enterprises such as the East India Company, the Hudson Bay Company and the South Sea Company. Flynt concealed his distaste, for he knew that part of that last company's interests in the region was the provision of slaves from Africa to the Spanish and Portuguese holdings. While most men accepted the trade as legitimate, Flynt had a unique perspective because his father had brought home a wife from the Indies who had once been a slave. And, for course, there was Belle. He took some comfort in the knowledge that the expected riches had never materialised, for the Spanish cared not a fart for the enterprise being granted a monopoly by parliament and had restricted trade in the area to little more than a trickle, leaving investors bemoaning the lack of return. The gentleman, however, was confident that situation would soon change. Flynt hoped he was wrong.

Jerome met him in the vestibule and took his wet apparel with a promise to dry the coat and hat before the stove in the kitchen and informed him that Miss Belle was in the private parlour, along with Mother Grady. Flynt thanked the young man and made his way to the rear of the house where he found the women alone, seated on either side of the fireplace, Belle reading a book of poetry and Mary Grady picking at some embroidery, which she had taken up on her retirement. She said it helped soothe her but her face, when she was bent to the task, was often contorted with frustration and he had been present on one occasion when she had thrown it across the room accompanied by language strong enough to have blistered the paint from the walls.

'A quiet night, I take it,' Flynt observed, for he had expected there to be gentlemen in attendance in the vestibule.

Belle looked up from her book and cast her eyes over him as if ensuring he had no new injuries. 'It has been most active, in fact. The gentlemen remaining are currently engaged above and this is merely a lull in proceedings.'

Belle herself, since being emancipated by Mother Grady and assuming the role of partner, had given up engaging with gentlemen above, apart from a few choice customers. Flynt was not a customer, however. He was special, she had explained.

Mother Grady set her embroidery aside and watched as Flynt poured himself a brandy from a decanter on a table beside the door. 'You are here most regular, Jonas Flynt. We should perhaps be charging you rent.'

Flynt turned and smiled. 'I like the company.'

She grunted. 'You like something for which you no longer need to pay. Have you given up your rooms at the Golden Cross?'

Flynt had lodgings in the coaching inn on Charing Cross. He was comfortable but he had to confess he had not spent much time there of late.

'Mother,' Belle said. She never called her Mrs Grady and never Mary, always Mother. In a way, the woman had been like a mother to her, despite having had her transported to London while but a girl. 'You know Jonas is with me.'

'Is that so now?' Mother Grady's native Irish accent giving that question an edge. 'And for how long this time, I wonder.'

Flynt had seated himself on the sofa facing the women and the fire. 'For as long as Belle will have me,' he said, taking a drink. This brandy was of a far finer vintage than that which he supped in the Castle on Aldgate.

'So you love her, do you?'

'Mother!' Belle was shocked by the question.

'Hush, Belle, we shall have this out, for I won't be seeing you hurt again by this man.' She made the word man seem like an insult, even though she had made a living out of servicing the needs and desires of the gender. 'He has drifted off before, he is capable of doing so again and this time he may never return.'

'It isn't my intention to drift anywhere,' Flynt assured her, feeling some irritation at the woman's accusation but at the same time understanding that she had come to care for Belle very deeply.

'Is that so?'

At that moment, Flynt grew aware that there was something he didn't know. 'Mrs Grady, what lies behind this questioning? It can't be because I no longer pay for Belle's company, for you must know I have offered.'

Mother Grady made a sibilant noise with her lips. 'You think we need your coin to turn a profit here? And Belle has given up lying with men, you must know that. Only you now because you are *special.*'

Flynt shot a surprised glance at Belle. He had believed she was still seeing certain customers. She looked down at her book.

'So, Jonas Flynt, I will ask you again,' Mother Grady said, her eyes piercing. She had grown noticeably frail in the past few months but had lost none of her ability to recognise lies when she heard it. 'Do you love this woman?'

Flynt found himself unable to express his feelings because he was unsure of what they were. He was never one to discuss emotions, and being confronted in this way made him uncomfortable. Men could come at him with knives, pistols, swords, clubs and he would deal with it, but such talk left him near defenceless.

Mother Grady waited for him to respond but when he didn't, she made that disparaging sound again. 'Tell him, Belle.'

'Mother, it wasn't anything...'

'Tell him, Belle,' she insisted.

Belle sighed before slowly closing her book and tucking it between her leg and the arm of the chair, then folded her hands on her lap. Flynt watched her, both interested and fearful of what was coming. She took her time in speaking, as if gathering her thoughts, or perhaps courage.

'Last evening, while you were... doing whatever it is you do,' she said, 'we had a little gathering here. It was a quiet night, the weather was most foul indeed, tonight is bad but not near as inclement as it was...'

'Damn it, Belle, get on with it before I die of old age or apoplexy,' Mother Grady said.

Belle shot her a sharp look but said nothing. She looked down at her hand, paused, but when she raised her eyes to meet Flynt's he saw within them a determination that he had seen many times before.

'We invited a certain Mrs Fairfax to see us, do you know of her?'

Flynt shook his head, that mix of curiosity and dread remaining prevalent.

'She is a most interesting woman, extremely talented, and her skills have made her quite the talk of society.'

'And what are those skills?'

Belle hesitated and it was left to Mother Grady to reply. 'She reads the cards.'

Flynt felt relief spill out from him in the form of a laugh. 'Cartomancy? In the name of God, you had me worried...'

'Don't you be mocking, Jonas Flynt.'

'Mrs Grady, you can't believe in this sort of thing?'

'There are more things on this earth than that which you can see, smell, taste and touch, that I do know.'

Flynt looked to Belle. 'Please don't tell me you believe this?'

'I neither believe nor disbelieve. My mind remains open to all possibilities.'

A mocking retort died on his tongue as he saw a warning in her eyes that he knew well and he had no desire to risk her ire. Instead, he tried to keep the scepticism from his voice as he asked, 'So, tell me, what did this spey-wife have to tell you?'

Belle's eyebrow twitched a little at his use of the Scottish term for fortune teller but she didn't remark upon it. 'She said that I had a man in my life, that he wasn't English.'

Flynt's rational mind told him that perhaps that was a guess, given Belle was black and lived in a brothel, but again he said nothing.

'She said that the relationship began as a professional one but that there was something deeper.'

Another guess, based on Belle's reaction to the woman's first statement.

'But she said that I was to be on my guard, for there was darkness ahead.'

'What sort of darkness?'

'Someone would come between us. Someone would rip us apart.'

'She used that term? Rip us apart?'

'She did.'

'And did she say when this would occur?'

'Soon, was all she saw.'

That was why Belle had been so ardent the night before and her discourse with him carrying an edge. Mother Grady continued to glare at him as he leaned towards Belle. 'Look, Belle, we are both adults.

We are both rational people. We read, we discuss. Of course something could happen that might end what we have, but it's not because this cartomancer, whatever her name was…'

'Mrs Fairfax,' Mother Grady said.

Flynt acknowledged the prompt with a jerk of the head. 'It's not because this Mrs Fairfax says it is so. The cards are mere pieces of board with printed designs upon them. They mean nothing but win or lose. They do not hold the secrets of the future.'

'The cards are but conduits to the other world,' Mother Grady said. 'It is the reader who has the gift, not the cards.'

Flynt pressed his lips together, wishing to say there was no other world, just this one, filthy, stinking and dangerous as it was, and that we should live in it, find what light and life there was without the fear or the influence of a mythical other place. But he didn't. He kept his counsel because it wasn't his way to challenge other people's beliefs. However, he could not let this pass without another appeal to Belle's reason.

'There is nothing I can say that will put this from your mind, Belle, because these people, these spey-wives, are most accomplished at planting the thoughts there in the first place. Perhaps she can see a future, but it is only that – *a* future. There are many paths down which we can walk and we don't know which one we will take until we come to it. As to someone ripping us apart, let us look on it as being forewarned and we can take steps to prevent it, should that moment arise.'

'Life is a game of chance between destiny and ambition, is that the way of it, Jonas?'

'Yes,' he said, grateful that his glib response earlier carried some meaning now, 'all is chance, not preordained.'

The reasoning part of Belle saw some truth in this, for she nodded. Mother Grady, though, was not to be dissuaded. 'You have not yet answered my question, Jonas Flynt. Do you love this girl or not?'

Flynt didn't look at the older woman. He couldn't. He stared at Belle, as if willing her to understand. She returned his gaze, her expression difficult to read. 'Belle…' he began, then halted again, the words not coming.

Mother Grady snorted. 'There you have it. He can't say it because he doesn't feel it.'

Belle's gaze dropped away from him. 'Let it lie, Mother, for in truth in this situation I couldn't say it to him, either. It's a word that trips most easily from the tongue when it is not meant, but more difficult when there is true feeling.' She was defending him, but he could hear the disappointment under her words. 'Jonas is right when he says we are adults. Words such as love are not for such as he and I.'

Flynt wanted to say something, anything, but still found he was unable, so when Jerome knocked politely at the door, opened it and stuck his head around the jamb, he was never so grateful to see him.

'Sorry to interrupt thee all,' Jerome said, spotting the glare from his aunt and clearly wishing he hadn't, 'but there's a lad here asking for Mr Flynt. Says it's urgent.'

Jack, Flynt realised, showing some unintended but impeccable timing. He rose quickly, apologised to the ladies and with a final look at Belle, who had picked up her book of poetry once more, and left the room.

Jerome led him towards the kitchen. 'Poor beggar was soaked through, so I took him in here to dry a little and gave him some broth, too. He looks like he needs a good feed.'

It was Jerome's job to deal with rowdy customers to the house, even though Mary Grady when she was in her prime had been more than capable of manhandling them herself, but he had a soft side too. Jack sat at a wooden table, his hair plastered to his head by the rain, his clothes obviously soaked, energetically spooning broth from a bowl. Given what had occurred at their last meeting, the boy had the decency to look ashamed when he saw Flynt appear.

'Would you be so good as to leave us alone for a moment, Jerome?' Flynt asked. 'I need a word with Mr Sheppard here.'

Jerome nodded and left without a further word. He was a man who had come to learn the meaning of discretion while in his aunt's employ as the house was frequented by men of property and influence.

Once alone, Flynt took a chair opposite Jack, who couldn't meet his eye. He said nothing for a good minute, allowing a look to do all his talking, at least for now. Eventually, Jack could take the tension no longer but still didn't raise his head.

'Mr Flynt, it's right sorry I am about what happened in the Black Lion,' he said. He stared down at the spoon in his hand, which remained dipped in what remained of the broth.

'You told me you had given up thieving,' Flynt said, his voice even.

'I knows it.'

'You told me that you wished to remain out of Jonathan Wild's orbit.'

A slight catch of Jack's breath before he said, quietly, 'I knows I said that.'

'You told me you wanted to make an honest living.'

'I knows that too.'

'You are unhappy working for Mr Wood?'

Jack still averted his gaze. 'No, I likes it well and I is learning so much from him.'

Flynt had a nose for lies and it twitched now. 'And yet, you dipped that man's pocket and took his silk wipe.'

Jack said nothing as he stirred the broth with the wooden spoon.

'If the gentleman had laid hands upon you it would have meant Newgate and possibly even Tyburn, you do know that?'

The boy continued to swirl the spoon slowly in the broth.

'Which was why I arranged the apprenticeship. I don't want to see you hang, Jack.'

'I knows all that, Mr Flynt.' His voice was soft, a hoarse whisper.

'And yet, you dipped that man's pocket and took his silk wipe,' Flynt repeated, the words intoned slowly for emphasis. 'Why risk everything, your future, your life, for a wipe?'

Jack finally returned his gaze, this time his voice more animated as he tried to explain, or excuse, his actions. 'It were right there, Mr Flynt, hanging from his gropus while he had his words with that Drury Lane vestal, trying to bring down her price, and next thing I knows it was in my paw and I was away with it. He was asking for it, if you ask me.'

Flynt maintained his composure, but really wanted to reach out and clip the boy across the ear. 'Whether the wipe was hanging from the man's pocket or not is immaterial, Jack. A dive is a dive, it matters not if the wipe is hidden or showing.'

Head drooping again, Jack mumbled, 'I'm sorry, Mr Flynt. I think once a diver, always a diver. It's in my blood, I thinks. I've tried the life of the square cove, you knows I has, but I reckons the call of the foist will always be upon me.'

Flynt sighed, but he was no longer angry. Part of him had always known that Jack Sheppard would forever be a thief. Another part of him recognised that he had himself made use of the lad's larcenous tendencies in the past, and was currently utilising his vast array of contacts in the flash world to his advantage. Flynt's own record of thievery did not give him any right to judge another. The stab of guilt caused by his own hypocrisy was sharp and intense.

'Then God help you, son. But all I ask is that you try to make a success of your work with Owen Wood.'

Jack mumbled something that might have been assent, accompanied by a brief bob of the head as he returned his attention to the broth. Flynt sensed a truth struggling to break free of the boy's natural tendency to duplicity but he knew he would get no further with him, so he turned to the matter at hand. 'What of this Boone fellow?'

Jack, sensing the lecture was over, brightened considerably and began spooning the broth again. 'I was right, he's an upright man, leading a crew of swaddlers. He's a right bastard, he is, I'd be most careful of him if you is going up against him.'

Swaddlers were the most vicious of criminal street gangs, not only robbing their victims but beating them and even on occasion committing murder.

'I only want to talk to him, Jack, not interfere with his business,' Flynt said.

A noise escaped Jack's throat that was half grunt and half laugh. 'Anyways,' he said, after a final mouthful of broth, 'he has a crib up Rookery way.'

St Giles, to the north and west of Covent Garden, named for a saint but far from saintly. When would Flynt ever not have to visit that godforsaken hellhole?

'Do you know where exactly it is within the Rookery that he bases himself?'

'No, but if you gives me more time I can nose around up there, see what I can finds for you.'

Flynt considered this but then decided against it. 'No, I'll go there myself. You get off to your bed. Mr Wood will be concerned for you.'

As apprentice, Jack had a little room in the workshop's basement. It wasn't much but, as a child of poverty and the workhouse, it was better than that to which the lad was accustomed.

'Ain't no need for worries there, Mr Flynt,' Jack said, with some eagerness. 'I popped in and told him I was about your business and old

Wood was right accommodating. He holds what you did for Katherine with that mace cove in high regard.'

Flynt had performed a service for the carpenter regarding a flash lad who led his daughter astray. She had become infatuated with the former soldier who lived his life on the mace, swindling all and sundry. He used her to entice men into a sexual adventure, before arriving at a propitious moment, when the man was naked and vulnerable, claiming to be her husband and demanding money as a means of assuaging his outrage. Katherine loved the ex-soldier with such a passion that it blinded her to his true nature, though to his ever-so-slight credit, in the game he played, the interruptus always came before the coitus began. Such care obviously did not extend to his personal interaction with her, for she found herself carrying his child and he dropped her like a hot stone. Owen Wood offered Flynt money to track the mace cove down. Flynt refused payment but traced him and duly obtained funds as compensation for the heartache caused to Wood's daughter and to help with maintenance of the child. Some physical damage had to be meted out because the soldier thought it an affront to be approached over what he saw as a trifling matter. Flynt pointed out to him most forcibly that it was indeed far from a trifling matter. The real tragedy was that the baby never drew breath, for she was delivered stillborn. Unknown to both the girl and her father, Flynt exacted a further penalty of a more painful nature, ensuring that the former soldier's face would never again prove appealing to a young woman.

Flynt thrust the image of his ability to deliver his own brand of justice from his mind. 'No, Jack, you've done enough. I'll assume the search for Boone for now.'

'I would give you caution again about poking your sneezer in this cove's affairs, Mr Flynt,' Jack said, 'but I knows it wouldn't do me no good. You is one what seems to enjoy sniffing out trouble and though I doesn't know this Boone cove personal like I hears he is a sly boot of a Turk.'

A Turk was street slang for a cruel man, with Boone also being cunning, but Jack was correct in that such a warning wouldn't deter Flynt from seeking him out.

'There's one other thing,' Jack said.

'About Caleb Boone?'

'No, that other cove you was asking about, the Paladin, was it?'

'Yes, did you hear something?'

'I did. There is some what talks of him like he is Jesus down from the cross.' There was a curious gleam in Jack's eye, his earlier shame now banished by his customary cockiness. 'As I said, he does good deeds, but he don't walk on water, do he?' He paused. 'Although you did, didn't you, Mr Flynt, when the Thames was solid.'

Flynt had ended up under that water, but that was not a memory he wished to relive. 'And is there word as to who this Paladin is?'

'We both knows who it is, Mr Flynt. I didn't know until I started to nose around, but then it began to become clear as day when I hears some of the tales. Some was most familiar, like the one about Katherine Wood, though there was some pulling of the long bow in the telling. The tale now goes that you crucified that mace cove on a floor in Southwark.'

Flynt dreaded how exaggerated the stories had become. Rumours such as this could impede his work. 'I hurt him a little, is all, but not like that. How widespread are these tales, Jack?'

'As I says, they doesn't range terrible wide, but there is whispers.'

'Any indication as to from whom or whence it began?'

Jack sucked in a breath. 'That's the thing with these whispers, Mr Flynt, nobody knows where or when they begin. Someone says it, another repeats it, then another and with each telling it grows so quick that before it gets back to the whisperer it's like a tale to be told over the fire.' He smiled. 'You knows what they says, Mr Flynt? About this here cove?'

Flynt waited.

Jack's grin grew. He was enjoying this. 'Between heaven and hell there is the Paladin.'

Flynt almost groaned.

9

Lord James Moncrieff had not expected to see Bailie Andrew Wilson that evening. As far as he knew, the man was not in London, and to find him awaiting him in his own parlour, enjoying his best port while conversing most courteously with his wife, was a far from pleasant surprise. He had known the man all his life and had found him distasteful but in recent years he had come to despise him.

The bailie stood as he entered, his head slightly stooped, his eyes averted towards the floor as befitted a petty official from Edinburgh. When he spoke, his voice was coated with servility. 'My lord, I do apologise most fervently for arriving at your lovely home unannounced. I found myself in the city on business and thought it would be remiss of me if I didn't call upon you and Lady Moncrieff was most gracious in her welcome.'

Moncrieff hid his irritation as he waved away the apology. He poured himself a port. 'And what business brings you to London, Bailie Wilson?'

'Town matters, my lord, for the work of an official in the service of Edinburgh can be far-ranging.'

'I have invited Mr Wilson to room here for the night, James,' said Lady Moncrieff, forcing her husband to conceal a sudden flare of displeasure.

'Your ladyship is most generous,' Wilson fawned.

'It's the least we can do for such an old friend of the family, is that not so, James?'

Moncrieff barely paused before speaking, hoping that the tightening of his throat was not apparent. Dear God, it's bad enough the man sits by his fireside without having to endure him all night and at breakfast. 'Of course, it will be our pleasure.'

Wilson bowed his head again, then said, 'I understand congratulations are in order, my lord. Lady Moncrieff informs me that she carries a bairn.'

Moncrieff shot a quick look at his wife. 'Yes, we have been blessed.'

Wilson raised his glass, which was nearly empty. 'Then may I propose a toast?'

'James, perhaps refilling Mr Wilson's glass would be welcome.'

Moncrieff forced a smile as he carried the bottle to where Wilson sat in the warmth of the fire to top up the crystal, all the time avoiding catching his eye. The bailie raised his glass. 'To you, dear lady, and to you, my lord. And also to the bairn that grows within you. He will be a strapping lad, of that I feel sure, a credit to the proud house of Moncrieff.'

Moncrieff raised his own glass in return and the two men drank.

'I thank you most kindly,' said Lady Moncrieff, then rose from her chair. 'But I'll leave you two men to your business talk.'

Wilson also rose. 'Please, don't leave on my account, I feel most guilty at my presumption...'

She waved him to be seated again. 'The lady of the house has many duties, Mr Wilson, and like town officials those duties never seem to end. I'll have an extra place set for dinner and your room prepared. Your lodging will be humble, for we've never managed to have that bedroom decorated to our complete taste.'

'It'll be as a palace to me, my lady. I'm an ordinary man myself, as you ken. I live humbly, without ostentation, for I work only for the betterment of my city, which though not as great as London, is deserving of all my efforts. Since my dear wife's death, I've found that work even more rewarding, for it has filled a gap in my heart.'

'I was most distressed to hear of Mrs Wilson's passing, Andrew,' Lady Moncrieff said. 'She was a fine woman and to die of a sudden in such a manner was a tragedy.'

Muriel Wilson had died in their home the year before. She had been hanging drapes when she tumbled from the ladders and struck her head on the sharp corner of a table.

'She was a grand lass, a grand lass,' Wilson agreed, his tone wistful, and Moncrieff swore he saw a tear form in his eye. 'And she was the love of my life, you ken. There'll be no other lass like her.'

Lady Moncrieff crossed the gap between them and laid a hand on the bailie's arm. 'You cannot know what lies ahead, Andrew,' she said, softly.

'I thank you, my lady, for your kindness.'

Lady Moncrieff smiled at him, then, with a brief look towards her husband, left the room.

Almost immediately after the door closed behind her, Wilson changed. His posture straightened, his face lost its obsequious aspect, and even the tearful eye Moncrieff had seen had dried. This was the real Andrew Wilson before him. Stern, arrogant, dangerous.

'I was unaware you were in town, Grand Master,' Moncrieff said.

'I didna ken I was required to inform you of my movements, boy.'

'The Fellowship High Council should be aware that…'

'The Fellowship High Council will be made aware of my movements when I wish them to be made aware. You forget yourself, lad, remember to whom it is you speak.'

Moncrieff swallowed back the rebuke. This was the Fellowship's Grand Master before him, and he held the power of life and death over the membership. Being of the Fellowship brought great rewards, but with it came the knowledge that whoever held the premier position always had the final say. It had become part of the rules ever since the Knight Templar Jerusalem Mordicant formed the brotherhood after he fled the purge of his order in France over three hundred years before. Mordicant had the foresight to see the bloodletting coming from a king and pope both hungry for the power the Templars held and their riches. He had escaped to Scotland along with others, but unlike his fellows his own fortune was intact and he used it to build a financial empire, a secret one to be sure, gathering like-minded men around him, avaricious men whose greed was not only for coin but for power. Wherever there was a profit to be made there was at least one member of the Fellowship guiding – manipulating – events to their benefit. They controlled politicians and nobles, businessmen, generals, admirals and potentates across the world. One of Mordicant's rules was that the Grand Master must be a Scot because, at least according to legend, he had risen from lowly beginnings in the borderlands. Andrew Wilson was the latest incumbent of the role, a dour, parsimonious and quite ruthless individual who hid his true personality behind that of the fawning bailie of Edinburgh. Even Moncrieff's own father had been taken in by him. Wilson had always blocked the elder Lord Moncrieff from joining the ranks of the Fellowship, deeming him too undependable thanks to lusts that he seldom controlled. Moncrieff the younger now recognised his late father's failings and had come to terms with them, but was himself of a different stamp. He loved his wife and was faithful to her. It was that and his business acumen which had smoothed his passage to the inner circle of the Fellowship and there were those who whispered that he was destined to be the next Grand Master. Whispered only, for if Wilson were to hear of them then he might take steps to neutralise any threat to his own position.

Moncrieff tightened his jaw. Lately it took all his self-control to deal with this man. 'May I ask how I can assist you, Grand Master?'

'I merely needed a bed for the night.'

'As my wife said, you are most welcome.'

Humour glinted in Wilson's eye. 'Aye, and right sincere you sound, boy.'

Moncrieff should have apologised but he would be damned if he would. He held Wilson's gaze, refusing to be bullied by this guttersnipe of a petty politician who only held the chair of the Fellowship through long-extinct family connections.

'There is always a bed in my home for you, not just as Grand Master but also as one of father's oldest friends.'

Wilson grunted and drained his glass again, refusing with a wave of the hand Moncrieff's inquiry as to whether he wished another.

'Whether that be true or no, I won't trouble you long, for I am for Edinburgh on the morn. So, boy, tell me what news of London. You retain Walpole's confidence?'

'I do.'

'And you still believe he will worm his way back into the government?'

'He will, without a doubt. I shall ensure it so, with the aid of the Fellowship of course.'

'And he is a worthy investment?'

'I believe so.'

Wilson nodded. 'Then I'll leave it with you, for I have other fish to gut...'

During the conversation that followed and the more innocent one that accompanied dinner, Moncrieff's mind raked over what those other fish were and why Wilson's visit to London was so furtive that the High Council knew nothing of it.

-

Jack finished another bowl of the broth before he left. At the rear door, he promised Flynt he would no more go a-thieving and Flynt replied that he believed him. Each one knew the other was lying.

Flynt could not leave without speaking again to Belle. He couldn't let what the cartomancer had told her lie between them like an unexploded cannon ball, so he returned to the parlour where to his immense relief he found her alone. Mother Grady's contempt for him, her suspicion, had been displayed many times but not perhaps as openly as it had that night. She was growing ever meaner as she aged, a feat which Flynt would previously have thought an impossibility.

'The lad calling upon you was young Master Sheppard, I presume?' Belle asked, her voice so level he couldn't discern whether there was a coldness there, while her head didn't rise from her book.

'Aye, it was,' Flynt said, suddenly anxious as to whether he should sit or remain standing.

'You are on another of your mysterious activities, then?'

'I have work, it's true.' He spoke carefully, still unsure of her mood. Belle had learned in difficult circumstances how to hide her feelings, both as a child enslaved and then as a courtesan. Mother Grady had affection for her now but it had not always been the case.

She turned a page. 'Then you had best be about it, Jonas.'

Now he knew her temper. He moved a little further towards her. 'Belle...'

Once again he couldn't find the words. Her glance towards him was sharp, as was her voice.

'At a loss for words, Jonas? Is your tendency to the taciturn still upon you? Perhaps we should bring in a rogue or two to bring out the facile part of your nature. God knows you talk more to the scum of the streets than you do to me.'

'You're angry with me.'

Back to the pages again. 'I'm not angry.'

'Hurt then.'

'I am beyond being hurt by men, Jonas.'

A silence fell between them. A log shifted in the fire. The clock on the high mantle ticked. Somewhere upstairs a man laughed. Belle raised her eyes to the ceiling. 'His lordship is in a fine mood this night,' she said.

Flynt didn't inquire as to which particular lordship was dancing the bedroom jig with one of the girls. He didn't care.

'Is this coolness because of what the spey-wife said?'

'Please stop calling her that.'

'Is it?'

She laid the book face down on her lap. 'No.'

'You know that these people read your expression.'

'I said it wasn't about Mrs Fairfax.'

'Then what is it, Belle?'

'It's about you, Jonas, you and I and what we have together, whatever this is we have together. Am I nothing more to you than a tumble? A place to go when the night is cold and damp or when you have been beaten, stabbed, kicked or shot?'

'No.'

'Then what is it, Jonas?'

'This is all because of Mother Grady's question, then? Whether I love you?'

'No, it's because you failed to reply and then scuttled from the room at the first opportunity. If I hadn't known better I would have thought you and Jack had planned it thus.'

He realised he had to sit down after all, so he perched on the edge of the couch. She watched him carefully as he sought the words, her eyes then softening.

'I know you better than you think, so I'm aware such matters do not come easily to you. We both have pasts that are best ignored, if not forgotten, and perhaps for that reason we are drawn to one another. But if my past, my life here with Mrs Grady, is what casts a cloud over us then you must leave now and never return.'

That stung. 'Do you think so little of me that I would hold such against you?'

'I believe I have made it most crystal that I think far more than a little of you, but I know not what you think of me. Oh, you are most tender, the most tender man I have known, and you are aware I have known many. But you hold so much of yourself back. I have tried to break through that crust but it has proved exceeding difficult. So many times I have tried. So many times I have spoken to you in this manner. And when you returned from the north and took to my bed once more I thought perhaps we had broken through but still you hold back. And then you disappear on this work of yours and I know not whether you will ever return again.'

When she saw he was about to speak, she held up her hand.

'No, I know you cannot tell me what this work is, although what a man cannot tell a whore about his life is most puzzling. We are, after all, not easily outraged. I didn't expect a declaration of love this night, to be true. Truthfully, I didn't expect Mrs Grady to challenge you in such a way, so I was also taken aback. But she did and you failed to respond. You sat there like a landed fish gasping for life.'

She paused, noticed the book still lying open but spine up on her lap so she closed it slowly, then carefully set it upon a little table between her and the fireplace. Then she smoothed down her dress and regarded Flynt once more.

'We have never danced.'

The statement took him by surprise. 'What?'

'You and I, we have never danced. Not once. We have laughed, we have tupped and supped and conversed on matters of the day, if not of the heart, but we have never danced.'

Flynt didn't know quite how to respond. 'I am not much fleet of foot in that regard.'

'I like to dance, did you know that, Jonas? Mother Grady has ensured that I am well tutored in the social graces, as well as the private arts. There have been men who have taken me to entertainments in great houses where we have danced.'

Flynt felt a stab of jealousy. Or was it regret that he had been so careless in not expressing his affections?

'Of course, that was business only,' she continued. 'Sometimes the girls and I dance together here, when such business is slow. I like to dance, Jonas. And yet we never have.'

She let that lie between them for a moment. He didn't know how to respond.

'So here is the way of it,' she said, traces of sadness now in her tone. 'I will leave it with you to decide the nature of our connection, whether I am but a tup and tumble or if there is something deeper, more meaningful. It's up to you, Jonas.'

Again she saw him move to speak and again she held up her hand to silence him.

'No, say nothing now, for whatever you say will not be as considered as I wish it and you may be tempted to be glib or deliver platitudes. Go, do whatever you have to do and when – *if* – you come back to me, then you will have an answer. Do your work and think on my words.'

He knew better than to try to protest so he stood and walked to the door. He turned back with his hand on the handle.

'This Mrs Fairfax said that someone would come between us, correct?'

'She did.'

'What if that person is she? What if she planted that thought in your mind knowing it would fester and perhaps prove to be correct.'

Belle's shake of the head was mournful. 'This was a conversation we should have had some time ago, Jonas. It has nothing to do with her, as I said. But I leave you with this thought. What if that person who comes between us, is you…?'

10

There were a number of rookeries in London, but St Giles was the only one known as *the* Rookery because it was by far the worst, or at least the worst Flynt had encountered for, well travelled through he was, he had not visited every corner of the city. They were dubbed rookeries because the tangle of streets and alleyways was like a nest in which all manner of peoples found some sort of home. St Giles-in-the-Fields, as the parish was called, could be babel-like in the varied accents and languages spoken by those who came here looking for cheap accommodation. The dark, narrow streets stank with the effluence of daily living that clogged the central gutters, if gutters there were. The maze of alleys and lanes were treacherous tunnels in the nighttime and not much better during the day, for little direct sunlight reached them. Ropes and strings connected the decaying buildings on opposite sides, rags hanging from them like banners. Many windows were blocked to avoid payment of the government's window tax. Backyards were muddied with the waste that flowed into them, criss-crossed with walkways of rotting wood and dotted with pens for pigs and other livestock, although some roamed free, even unto the streets, adding to the overall miasma and ensuring that stepping out could be most perilous. The old city of London was no nosegay but at least some residents and merchants made efforts to clear the way. Here there was no such attempt made. The Rookery was where anything close to civic pride came to die.

Flynt eased off Drury Lane and then along Castle Street to cross beneath the tall sundial with its six faces, the original plan for this junction being to have six streets diverging from it but in the end there was one extra, hence the area being termed Seven Dials. He pondered how often he had to come here in the course of his work, both legal and otherwise. He had been told the Great Plague had stemmed from St Giles and then spread outward across the city, but there was another plague here, that of men like Caleb Boone. Flynt had robbed people but he had never resorted to brutality to relieve people of their purses. He had threatened people at gunpoint as a highwayman on the high toby, he had crept into their homes in the dead of night during his period on the crack lay, but he had never used violence in order to take what wasn't his, which made the bogus charge that Colonel Charters used against him even more galling. He was no stranger to violence, the cold rage with which he had dealt with the mace cove who had both shamed and sullied Katherine Wood being a more extreme example, but he utilised such excesses only when he felt it necessary, and was prone to regret afterwards. The violent part of his nature was useful and had more than once saved his life, but it troubled him, for he feared that one day he might lose himself within it. But the men Jack had called swaddlers were a breed apart. They brutalised their victims for the sake of it and then vanished into the labyrinth of the Rookery, where no watchman, constable, justice or sheriff dared venture.

There was one place that he might find a clue that could lead to tracking Boone down. The Rat's Castle sat in the centre of the district like a spider plucking at the web of streets and alleyways that waved around it. It shared part of its name with the inn in which he had supped brandy with Colonel Charters, but that was as far as any comparison went, for while the tavern on Aldgate boasted the charms of the Elizabethan age, this Castle had all the allure of a rotting corpse.

It was situated on the ground and first two floors of a tenement that had been constructed, or rather thrown up, only a few decades before but was already ramshackle. The original intention of the area around Seven Dials was to create a fashionable residential area for gentlefolk. That dream was soon dashed and now the wider St Giles was filled with the transient and the lost, the worker and the grifter, the honest and the flash, and all came together in this one establishment.

The large room that Flynt entered was like any other inn or tavern in the city, filled with people, with noise, with smoke. But the patrons here, men, women, children, were more often than not ragged and some were so drunk they could barely raise their heads thanks to having temporarily released themselves from the daily struggle of living through the imbibing of gin and rum and cheap wine. They lay on the earthen floor, or propped against walls that were discoloured by damp, the wattle and daub plasterwork bulging like a festering boil, the cups and bottles from which they had swilled their gin dangling loosely in their hand. There were bunters, of course, working the room, offering their charms and services at cut-price rates to those still *compos mentis*, for even the poor and the desperate needed some physical contact, however unwashed and perhaps even diseased it may be. A staircase at the far end of this bar room led upwards to a large room where the atmosphere was relatively more convivial. There food could be purchased and revellers could sing and dance if their blood, or the gin, demanded it of them. The thud of boot on bare floorboards thundered overhead, some very nearly in time to a sprightly tune played on a fiddle and a flute. There was another level above that, one that Flynt had only once visited, as ever in search of a man, so he was aware it was left to the more carnal pursuits, with straw beds rented by the hour laid out in a vast open space that left every intimate moment open to those rutting and panting on either side. Heavy beams ran from floor to ceiling, against which others could enjoy a tuppenny upright when there was no room on the floor. This, then, was the Rat's Castle, a place of refuge, a place of business, a place where the poor, the lonely, the desperate and the dangerous rubbed shoulders and bodies and, in the main, lived in harmony, for there was an unwritten law, rigorously enforced by the landlord and his team of Abram coves, tough men, violent men who roamed the floors with clubs, that there be no violence beyond its threshold. The Rat's Castle was in this manner a liberty zone, where men and women may seek their pleasures or their escapes from life without fear of molestation. Nonetheless, Flynt made sure that both Tact and Diplomacy were within easy reach under his coat, while he twisted the handle of his cane for ease of drawing the sword concealed within.

On entering, he took a moment to scan the faces around him, seeking the one he knew would be here, finally settling on the wrinkled visage of a man seated alone against the far wall, he having the luxury of a chair, his right leg stretched before him, the wooden peg that formed it from the knee down tapping in tune to the music drifting from above. Nobody was sure exactly how Jury Leg Thompson came to lose the lower half of that leg, for his story had changed over the years, depending on what he thought might bring him some coin or a drink or two. According to his telling he had been both soldier and sailor and the limb lost in battle. On other occasions he was the victim of a childhood ulcer that had putrefied. Then there was the carriage that had run him over in the street, owned by either a gentleman, a peer of the realm, a Jacobite lord fleeing the authorities, and, once in Flynt's own hearing, even a member of the royal family.

Flynt first purchased a bottle of gin, ignoring the curious look from the brawny man standing with arms folded behind the bar, then found a vacant chair which he picked up and set down beside Jury Leg, who nodded to him most amiably. 'Now that's a face I ain't seen in an age. Captain Flynt, down here among the ordinary rogues and vagabonds.'

'Captain Flynt no longer, Jury. It was honorary from when I made my living on the high toby.'

Everyone referred to him as Jury, his Christian name having been lost in the mists of time and gin.

'As is the custom in the nighttime trade on the heaths, but still, honorary or not, it is a title of which the captain should be proud, and no mistake, and the one with which I shall continue to address him, by his leave. But I does wonders what brings the captain here to this here den of iniquity? He is not normally an inhabiter of the Rat's Castle, him much preferring the hospitality of the houses down the Drury and the Garden.'

'I come seeking information, Jury,' said Flynt.

'Information, be it? That I has, as you well knows.' Jury's eyes alighted on the bottle in Flynt's hand. 'And is that there a tall boy of this here establishment's finest Old Tom that I spies there in the good captain's bunch of fives?'

Flynt held the bottle up, knowing that the gin within it was harsh enough to wash down a gun deck but was still the best the establishment could offer. 'It's yours in return for the intelligence I seek, Jury.'

The man looked at the cup in his hand and then at the bottle resting beside his good leg. 'As it seems both old Jury's own tall boy and drinking bubber be as empty as a hangman's conscience he will gladly assist the good captain with what information he requires, if it be within his own limited knowledge.'

Flynt's smile was slight but genuine over the man's modesty, feigned though it may be. 'It's known across London that a man can't spit in the Rookery without old Jury knowing of it.'

He smiled, revealing teeth broken and blackened like an old saw blade. 'Aye, I prides myself on keeping my listeners and my peepers open, I does, that be the solemn of it.' His eyes had not wavered from the bottle Flynt held. Realising he would receive nothing of its contents until he had fulfilled his function, he licked his lips. 'So in what way can I assist the famous Captain Flynt?'

'I seek a cove by the name of Caleb Boone.'

Hearing the name dragged Jury's eyes away from the bottle and his smile died. 'It is not a name which is at all familiar, I has to admit.'

'Don't lie to me, Jury.'

'There be no lies, and that's the solemn of it, captain. Ain't never heard of the cove.'

Flynt moved the bottle away. 'In that case, I will take this Old Tom and pour it out in the street.'

Jury's hand reached out. 'Now, let us not be so hasty, for that would be criminal waste, that would.'

'Then tell me of Caleb Boone.'

Jury's eyes flitted around him and he leaned towards Flynt. 'Wouldn't be saying that name too loud in here, if the captain don't mind some advice, for it ain't only old Jury what keeps his listeners flapping. Saying that chant too loud, and too often, can get a cove hushed right proper, even in this here place.'

'I'll take my chances. Where can I find him?'

'What business does the captain have with this man whose name will not be given breath by these lips, I wonders?'

'That is my affair. Now, where can I find him?'

Jury made a show of considering this, as if doing his best to drag the location from the darkest recesses of memory. 'The finding of him don't quite occur to me, Captain. As already intimated in our converse, there is some coves what it is best for other coves not to keep track of.'

'That be a pity, for then this Old Tom will have to go to waste.'

Flynt popped the cork of the bottle and began to tip some of the contents out. Jury emitted a soft groan as the gin spilled onto the floor, staining the earth ever darker than it already was. Flynt could have sworn he saw smoke rise but the light was bad and there was smoke aplenty curling around them.

'Oh, that be a regular shame to see, is that,' Jury said mournfully, his hand stretching again to grab the bottle. Flynt again snatched it further away but did replace the cork. Jury looked from the bottle to the dark stain on the dirt floor. 'It pains these poor old peepers to see it.'

'Then tell me what I need to know.'

'The captain drives a terrible hard bargain, and that's the solemn of it.'

'I mean the man Boone no harm, I merely have questions for him, so you have no need to be afraid, Jury.'

'There be every need to be afeared of this man. I reckon that you be a man of your word and harbour no ill intent towards him, but if it be in passing that you did, for I does know of the captain and his ways, then that would a occurrence that I would caution against most fervent. The rules of the house, as you knows well, do prohibit such matters most fervent. In weeks past there was a young bobtail what got herself grievous cut, lost a listener, she did, the poor soul. The landlord and his crew did the cove up something proper and then carted him away to Gawd knows where. My point being that they don't take much to claret being spilled, unless they is doing the spilling.'

'Let me worry about that, Jury. Where can I find Caleb Boone?'

Jury considered further denial of knowledge but the lure of the gin was too strong. Again, he ensured nobody was listening before lowering his voice. 'He has established hisself down Satan's Gullet.'

Flynt hid his apprehension. The Rookery was bad enough but Satan's Gullet was worse. It was one of the narrowest lanes in the district, the ground strewn with waste both human and animal, jetties jutting from the tenements on either side. In that way it differed little from the rest of the area, but the Gullet was a dangerous place. The last time he had entered he had been forced to kill five men and it was not a locality to which he yearned to return.

Jury held out a trembling hand in expectation of payment and, a bargain being a bargain, Flynt handed the bottle to him. The old man instantly plucked the cork then saved some time by ignoring his cup and raising the neck to his lips to absorb a prodigious amount of the gin. He lowered the bottle with a satisfied sigh and wiped his mouth with the back of one filthy hand. 'That be a good drop of the creature, that be.'

That testimonial to the quality of the liquor was something Flynt doubted very much.

Jury nodded his gratitude. 'Thank you, Captain, you is a man of his word, always said that, and you hasn't proved me a liar.'

'I have a further task for you, Jury.'

The bottle faltered on the return passage to Jury's lips, but only momentarily. He took another long drink then gave Flynt a suspicious look, as if he sensed that whatever was coming would not be to his liking.

'Take a message to Mr Boone,' said Flynt. 'Ask him to meet me here.'

The suggestion seemed outlandish. 'You wants me to go talk to Caleb Boone?'

'Or get a message to him. I know you have the means to do that without making actual contact.'

'And exact why would I wish to do this, I wonders of the captain?'

Flynt fished a purse from his coat pocket and tipped some coins into the palm of his hand. 'Because as much as you like Old Tom, you also like the jingle. So, this will be yours once you have done what I ask. Send word to Mr Caleb Boone that I will meet him here at his earliest convenience. It's possible that he has heard of me so the fact that it is in this place will afford at least some element of protection, for us both.'

As before Jury reached out for the money but Flynt clasped his fingers over it. 'Ah-ah, not until you tell me that you have fulfilled your part of the bargain.'

A sly gleam crept into the old man's eye. 'So, lets me see this straight and true, I needs only get word to this gent's listeners that you is here and a-waiting his pleasure, is that the solemn of it?'

'That is indeed the solemn of it.'

'And once that is done the bunce will be transferred direct to these here fives?'

'Directly into your hand, yes.'

Jury's smile suggested that somehow Flynt had been gulled but couldn't see how, so he watched with some interest as the man rose with extreme sprightliness before, in a mix of hop and limp while still clutching his bottle, he made his way around the lounging patrons to the bar opposite. Once there he leaned closer to a slender man whose features would have proved attractive if viewed by a ferret. A few whispered words, a jerk of the head over Jury's shoulder, followed by a long look from the sharp-faced little creature in Flynt's direction before he then turned instantly and left the establishment. Jury returned to Flynt's side and gave him a slight bow. 'Word has been sent, Captain.'

He held out his hand and Flynt, smiling, duly deposited the coins. The sly Jury had clearly identified the man who would get word to

Boone while appearing to demur. He inspected the denominations, his eyebrows working in approval. 'You is most generous, Captain, as I would expect from a gentleman such as yourself. It's a pleasure doing business with you. But if you will excuse me, I would prefer to vacate these premises most sharpish, for I knows of your reputation and I knows of the other cove's reputation and it is to be presumed that this here place is not a healthy place to be at present, landlord's rules or no landlord's rule. So farewell to thee, good captain, and God be with you, for I suspects you will need His help.'

With that, Jury stomped quickly away, the bottle of Old Tom clutched tightly to his breast as if he feared someone would attempt to wrest it from him. He left the tavern without a backward glance.

Flynt settled back in his chair to wait, his eyes ever watchful, for within this single room he would wager there were rogues who should not be at liberty, but should instead be locked in the St Giles Roundhouse before being taken to Newgate. The landlord's rules were nigh on sacrosanct but not everyone was a believer. He recognised that he was also a rogue, but one who did his best to atone for his thieving ways. Damn it, now that he considered it, perhaps he was some sort of Paladin after all, though he did ponder on how such a rumour began. It took someone with education to come up with that cognomen. The question was who?

His thoughts turned to Jack. The lad was on an irrevocable course towards Tyburn, or a swift and bloody death in some back alley, he could feel it. He had done his best to divert him but larceny ran through to the lad's soul. He was a bright boy, he was likeable, but he was a born thief and he was not to be deflected from that path. All Flynt could do was watch over him when he could and do his best to keep him out of Wild's clutches, for he knew the thieftaker already had eyes on him and would have work for a bright and nimble lad.

And then there was Belle. He played over their earlier conversation in his mind. No, conversation wasn't the correct word, for in truth he had conversed very little, except to become a little defensive, and only that because he was ill-equipped regarding such matters. He thought he had loved Cassie, but he had deserted her all those years before. At that crossroads in the north he had to decide whether to continue longing for Cassie in Edinburgh or enjoy the reality that was Belle. He had chosen the latter. Did that mean that he loved her? That their connection was more than the mere physical he had known already. That he held her most fondly in his mind was also something of which he was profoundly aware, but his dilemma was that he didn't know if he was actually capable of love. Tender feelings, yes, loyalty, yes, but the fact was he didn't spend much time considering matters romantic, the day-to-day pressures of his life precluding such thoughts. His difficulty with the concept was deeply rooted, for though he had convinced himself that he had loved Cassie, he had never professed it. And when challenged by Mother Grady earlier he had been unable to do the same to Belle. The why of that he could not identify. All he knew was that while other men could say those words, even Gabriel, who claimed not to believe in the emotion, Flynt found it could not pass his lips. Did he love her? Did he want to lose her? What in God's name was wrong with him? If he didn't bring his faculties into some order then he would most assuredly lose her, for Belle St Clair was not a woman who made idle threats.

The appearance of two men in the doorway brought his focus from the inward to the outward, for they carried an air with them that was most singular. Their coats were streaked with rain, their hats drooped, but that was not what made them unique. It was the way they held themselves ready and their eyes roaming the room that told him they were not in the Castle for entertainment. Flynt himself had seen it in Lombre, and the landlord of the Rat's Castle had recognised it in him when he purchased the gin for Jury. At their back was the rat-faced little man who Jury had spoken to. He nodded in Flynt's direction and the men's gazes finally settled upon him. He didn't know them but knew their type all too well. Their eyes were watchful, their faces etched not just with the harshness of life but also of the hardness they carried about them. Flynt knew that look well, for he saw it every morning in the looking glass while scraping his beard. These men were dangerous.

They split up and crossed the room in his direction, each taking a separate route through the drinkers. Their coats were open and both men rested one hand on the butt of a pistol. Flynt adjusted his coat to afford him ease of access to Tact and Diplomacy if the need arose. The rat-faced individual didn't accompany them but instead took a direct route towards the stairway from which vantage point he observed the proceedings. The two men halted close enough for Flynt to hear them speak over the din, but far enough away to draw weapons and fire if such was required.

Flynt didn't move, but affected a casual demeanour, even though every nerve was tense. 'Gentlemen, may I make an assumption that you are associates of Mr Caleb Boon?'

The one on the left said, 'You'll be Jonas Flynt then?'

'I am indeed.' He looked beyond them to the doorway. 'Did not Mr Boone accompany you, or am I be conveyed hence? For if that's the case I must make myself plain at the outset, I don't intend to leave this delightful establishment.'

'You will go where we bid or you will not speak with Caleb, on that you can make a firm wager,' said the second man standing to Flynt's right. There was no heavy emphasis to the words, they were most conversational. 'But you ain't leaving the Castle, if that sets your mind at ease.'

'It certainly does, for thus far things have been most companionable and I would be most displeased should they turn in any way unpleasant.'

The first man raised his left hand to point briefly in the direction of a door set beside the stairway. 'If you would be so good as to step through that there door, you will find Mr Boone waiting.'

The men were very polite but their tone suggested that they would not brook any resistance. Flynt pursed his lips. It was clear that Caleb Boone had entered the premises through the rear and so was a cautious man. Flynt was also a cautious man. He had gone through many doors without knowing clearly what lay beyond but on those occasions he ensured he at least had the element of surprise on his side, not to mention Tact and Diplomacy in his fists. He didn't relish the idea of stepping through that one with these two at his back.

The one on the right either sensed or guessed his thoughts. 'We won't be coming with you, ain't no need for no worry in that regard.'

'All you needs do is step through that there door where you will find Mr Boone awaiting,' said the one on the left.

'But don't be keeping him awaiting too long.'

'He ain't a cove what likes to be kept awaiting, is he, John?'

'No, Harry, he ain't got no patience.'

'Not like us. We can await till the horn blows for Judgement Day.'

'So, we would advise most strong that you go through that there door right smartly, otherwise you will not speak with the cove what you comes here to speak with, for he will not linger beyond it long.'

Flynt assessed the situation and came to the conclusion that he would have to risk it. He needed to speak to this man Boone and this seemed to be only opportunity to do so. He rose and turned towards the door but John, the one on his right, stepped in his path.

'You is carrying, I'll wager,' he said. 'What you think, Harry?'

'I would say he is a cove what is prepared for any eventuality, John.'

'I'd say you is correct. So, Mr Flynt, we would be obliged if you would part with your barkers.'

'Just deposit them there on that chair you has just left,' said Harry. 'We shall watch over them, don't you worry.'

Flynt switched his gaze from one to the other. 'You expect me to enter that room unarmed?'

'That is correct.'

'If you wants to see Mr Boone, that is,' John said.

'Remember, it was you what asks to see him,' Harry reminded him. 'He don't know you from Adam and bears you no ill will but you might have grievous intent upon his person and we could not have that.'

'So if you would be so good as to place your barkers where Harry said and then you can take yourself in there with no fear of molestation.'

'You has our word upon that.'

Flynt's smile was ironic. 'And you are men of your word, I'm sure.'

Harry laughed. 'When you was born on the streets and brought up on the streets and you has nothing, the only thing you has of any value is your word.'

Flynt knew this to be true. Rogues could be underhand, they could be devious, but for some, once their word was given, it was held as true as if it were a written covenant. Some, not all. Others from the streets were slaves to the underhand and devious part of their nature. He now had to decide if these men were of that sort or had some measure of honour. They seemed professional, there was no direct threat, no posturing, no bluster. They stood easily, their manner relaxed, despite the hands on the weapons wedged in their belts. It was true that it was he who had requested this meeting and they had made it clear that if he chose not to do as they ordered then it would not take place and that would mean nothing to them. He took a deep breath of the smoky air through his nose then reached under his coat to produce his brace of pistols. Both men instinctively tensed, their fingers tightened on their weapons. Flynt slowly eased Tact and Diplomacy free and carefully set them down on the chair.

John craned forward a little to see the weapons more clearly. 'Them barkers be right pretty.'

'Most elegant,' Harry agreed.

'I will expect them to be as I leave them when I return,' Flynt said.

'Don't you be worrying yourself over them, my friend.'

'We shall not take our peepers off them,' John assured him. 'We has become known well in this here place and none of this here populace will as much as look in their direction.'

'They is as safe there as they would be in the London Tower,' Harry assured him.

Flynt knew that to be not as safe as they thought but nonetheless was of no doubt that these men would be as good as their word. As he moved to the door, he noted that rat-face scurried ahead of him, knocked and entered, leaving it open. Flynt felt somewhat underdressed without his pistols but he still had his silver cane, and the blade concealed within it, which was something. His step faltered just a touch as he tightened his grip on the cane, took a deep breath and stepped across the threshold.

11

Caleb Boone was not a large man but he had the face and build of one who had fought for a living. His nose was broad and flat and the flesh above and around his eyes bore the permanent swelling and scarring associated with too many blows. His ears, too, were ragged and thickened, for street fights were vicious and any grip presented was one of which advantage must be taken. His hair was dark and short, his clothes were of quality but bore signs of frequent mending. He sat in a chair in the centre of the room with one leg casually draped over the other, a boarded window behind him, while at his side stood the rat-faced man. There were no other men present, which surprised Flynt greatly. He had expected, perhaps dreaded, to find the room bristling with weaponry.

'That's the cove,' Ratty said, stooping closer to the man's ear, his voice as reedy as his features suggested. 'He is the one what sent Jury with the word.'

'He is the one *who* sent Jury,' Boone corrected as he studied Flynt before him. 'Who, not what.'

Ratty actually gave him a little bow. 'Begging your pardon, I did knows that, I meres slips on my tongue, is all.'

Boone's eyes closed briefly and Flynt noticed a barely perceptible shake of the head as he listened to the mangled speech. When he opened them again, he waved Flynt towards an empty chair sitting opposite him. 'I will admit, sir, that I was most intrigued by your invitation to parlay.'

Flynt was surprised by Boone's voice and diction. It was deep and the flavour of the streets lurked among the vowels and the occasional dropped consonants but there was a quality to it that suggested some education. Jack's information was incorrect, for this was no mere upright man heading up a crew of swaddlers. Perhaps at one time, but not now.

'Allow me to introduce myself, Mr Boone,' Flynt said as he took a seat. 'My name is Jonas Flynt.'

'Yes, we had that from Jury Leg Thompson. He also intimated that you are an upright man. Which crew do you run, pray tell?'

'I have no crew, Mr Boone. I operate alone.'

'I has heard of Jonas Flynt,' Ratty interjected. 'Captain Flynt, they calls him. He was on the high toby up the heaths.'

'You have heard, not has. Please, try to mind your manner of speech.'

Irritation flashed across Ratty's expression but was soon replaced by fawning respect. 'Right sorry I is, I shall be more carefuller in my expressiveness.'

A smile flattened Boone's lips as he again addressed Flynt. 'A highwayman, sir? Was that your game?'

'In the past I have been highwayman and also cracksman. Currently I gamble.'

'Tats, flats, or do you favour the cockpit?'

'Both dice and cards, but the cockpit was never to my taste.'

'You do not favour the sight of blood, perhaps?'

'I've seen more than my fair share and will no doubt see further, but I have no desire to see man or beast tear at each other for sport.'

Boone accepted that. 'So then, what does a highwayman, cracksman and gambler wish to discuss with me?'

Flynt decided to get straight to the point. 'I seek a man who carries your surname. It is possible he is related to you.'

'Who is this man?'

'Nimrod Boone.'

Boone sat back, his head tilted a little as if he was playing the name in his mind. 'Tell me, did Jury know of your purpose in summoning me?'

'No, he needed only know that I wished it and not why I wished it. I'm sure I don't need to point out that with men such as he, you tell them only what they need to know in order to perform the task you set.'

'Very wise, for Nimrod was my cousin and I wouldn't want his name sullied on the lips of one such as Jury Leg Thompson.'

Flynt noted the use of the past tense. 'Your cousin is dead?'

'As dead as a man can get.'

'And you know this for a fact?'

'He went off to war and never returned, I would take that as close to fact as can be gleaned in wartime. I expect his body rots with thousands of other men under the sod of some foreign field. But what interest does my poor dead kinsman hold for you?'

Again, Flynt opted for at least a partial truth. 'I've been asked to find him. An old comrade of his was certain he saw him in the street.'

'Nimrod was hardly an eye-catching fellow and there will be hundreds of men walking these streets who resemble him, I'll wager. I believe if he still breathed and was in the city he would have sought me out.'

'You were close?'

'As close as two young men could be. We were raised together, Nimrod and I. Our fathers were brothers and we became as such ourselves.'

'You were raised in these streets? Here in St Giles?'

'No, we both hailed from Sanctuary, as did our fathers and our father's fathers. They say the Boones originally stemmed from beggars and debtors who took refuge there in times past, but I have no way of knowing if that be true or just family legend.'

Sanctuary was an old name for an area near Westminster Abbey. Under a right granted by Edward the Confessor, the abbey once offered refuge to nobles who had transgressed, but those whose birth was not so elevated had to make do with hiding in the filthy tenements and cottages nearby. The right of sanctuary was abolished in the previous century but pockets of rancid housing remained.

'But we managed to get out, he and I,' Boone continued. 'He to a life and death in the military, serving as it was then his queen and his country, me to the splendours of the Rookery, such as they are.' He smiled as he waved his hand around him. 'So, as we were like brothers, I am certain that, had he returned from Flanders, I would be aware of it. I do believe this old comrade who has retained your services was mistaken.'

'He was most convinced.'

Boone accepted that with a jerk of the head. 'Nevertheless, as I have stated, he was mistaken. Nimrod is dead, may the good Lord have mercy on his soul.'

'Did he need such mercy, Mr Boone?'

'We all have need of mercy, Mr Flynt, for we are all sinners, are we not? We will all one day be called to account for our transgressions. The trick to life is putting off that day for as long as possible while bettering our lot and taking our pleasures when we can, is that not correct?'

'Moving from Sanctuary to the Rookery was bettering your lot?'

'No, but in Sanctuary I was but a lad. Here I can be king. In case you didn't know it, Mr Flynt, the Rookery is now my domain, and you are welcome to enter it when you please. But, given your proclivities, you should know this – if a person has a job in mind, whether it be high or low toby, then I demand a taste of all such activities. If he has intentions to set up a game or two then I also get a piece of that.'

'With respect, the pickings within the Rookery are slim indeed.'

'That they are, but should a person wish to base himself within its confines in order, say, to avoid the attentions of the magistrates, but continue to work within the world of the straight arrow, then I also expect my due of the proceeds and winnings.'

'Out of interest, what happens if that person declines to pay such fealty?'

A sharp, unpleasant little laugh spat from Ratty's mouth. 'You has met Harry and John outside. They is the coves what would be ensuring that you pays your bunce to Mr Boone here, and you would do that right sharpish, otherwise you'd be feeling something right sharpish between your ribs.'

He smiled at his own jest, revealing sharp little teeth, but Boone winced. 'What my friend is saying in his customary crude manner is that a person would be ill-advised to ignore the rules of these streets. My streets.'

Another look of irritation from Ratty. He didn't like the way Boone spoke to him but he accepted it, at least for the moment. Flynt resolved to ensure that his back was never turned on this little man. He had a vicious streak but only through stealth and betrayal.

Boone continued, 'They've been in my employ for a mere month, but John and Harry have proved themselves extremely efficient. Even if they fail, then the law can be brought to bear. A word to a thieftaker here, an arrest there, a trip to Tyburn at the end of it and the message is sent that I have sovereignty.'

This man had apparently carved himself quite an empire from these teeming, filthy streets and Flynt was surprised he hadn't heard of him before. But then, men like him were like head lice in this city. You can catch and kill them but there are always more hidden away.

'I regret, though, that your quest has come to such an end,' Boone said, raising himself from the chair and indicating the door. The interview, it seemed, was over.

'Perhaps not,' Flynt said. 'I believe I will continue to search, for my principal was most convinced it was your cousin he saw.'

Boone shrugged. 'That is your choice, but I would urge you to have a care. These streets can be most treacherous for the unwary.'

'Mr Boone, I assure you that I am never unwary.'

Boone stopped in the doorway and gestured into the tavern, then smiled at Flynt, but there was little humour. 'Even the most careful, not to mention capable, of men can come to grief.'

John and Harry appeared in the doorway, the latter carrying Flynt's pistols but making no move to part with them yet.

'See Mr Flynt to the street and safely from the Rookery, boys,' Boone said.

'I need no such assistance, Mr Boone.'

'Nevertheless, accept this small token of my goodwill. I would be most conscience-stricken should any harm befall you. I wish you continued safety, Mr Flynt, but beyond this small measure I cannot guarantee it.'

Flynt thanked him, for their meeting had been most polite, and followed the two men from the tavern, knowing well that he had been warned off from inquiring further. But if Nimrod Boone was dead as his cousin stated, what need was there of such counsel?

12

Tact and Diplomacy once again snug under his coat, Harry and John having relinquished possession once they reached the outskirts of the Rookery, Flynt decided that it would not be politic to return to Covent Garden and take to Belle's bed. Instead, he took St Martin's Lane to Charing Cross, the rain having died to a wet mist that draped itself over him and hung around the lamps burning outside buildings. He would be glad to get to his own room in the Golden Cross, for it had been a long day. Even so, he remained on the alert, Caleb Boone's veiled threat still fresh. The lane was not deserted but was far from busy so there were no crowds into which any followers could merge. His ears strained for footfalls that echoed his own, but none reached them.

His landlady, Mrs Wilkes, met him as he entered the inn and informed him that a gentleman had been awaiting his return for some time and seemed most eager to have converse with him in private, if possible. As he was obviously a gentleman of some quality, she said, she granted him use of her special sitting room, which boasted a fireplace of its own, decent candles of beeswax and a serving hatch that opened up to the bar from whence he had ordered claret and oysters.

Flynt at first suspected the visitor to be Colonel Charters, come to demand a report on what progress he had made even though he had instructed him to attend him on the morrow, but the man who sat at the table in the centre of the small room, scribbling in a calfskin pocket notebook with a graphite stick, was unknown to him. He was, as Mrs Wilkes had intimated, extremely well dressed, though Flynt saw some patchwork on the fine wool coat that dropped to the knee while the silver-gilt embroidery on the front was threadbare in places. The cuffs of a white silk shirt puffed from the sleeves but on examination the edges were a little frayed. His silk stockings were of a white that had faded and his shoes were scuffed. His dark periwig was long and full, cascading to the shoulders of his brown coat. In short, this was a man who had known prosperity at one time but Flynt surmised was now not so fortunate.

He rose to reveal that he was not overly tall, but was of medium size and stature. His grey eyes were sharp, as was his hooked nose, and he had a large mole near his mouth. There was a familiarity in his features that Flynt could not quite place.

'Do I have the honour of addressing Mr Jonas Flynt, sir?' The man's accent was of London but cultured, not the feigned polish of Caleb Boone but genuine. This was truly an educated man.

'You do, sir, and you are?'

The man held out his hand in greeting. 'My name is Defoe, Daniel Defoe, and it is a genuine pleasure to make your acquaintance.'

Flynt shook the offered hand. He was aware of the man's reputation as a journalist and chronicler, of course, and had even read some of his writing, but could not help but keep suspicion from his voice when he asked, 'How can I help you, Mr Defoe?'

Defoe was astute and so caught the note of caution and in return gave him a reassuring smile as he waved towards the table. 'Please, Mr Flynt, let us make ourselves more comfortable, for I have me a matter of business that I am most desirous to discuss with you.'

Curious as to what business a man such as Daniel Defoe would have with him, Flynt took off his hat, peeled off his damp greatcoat and took a seat, grateful to be off his feet. The writer picked up the bottle of claret, which Flynt saw had been well dented already, and raised it in the manner of a question. To be sociable, Flynt nodded in assent and watched as he poured a fresh glass before topping up his own. Defoe passed the glass to him and resumed his seat, gulping back some of the claret. Flynt didn't touch his, for something told him he would need a clear head for this conversation, and he was already weary from the day's travels.

'What manner of business do you have in mind, Mr Defoe? I cannot see what interest a man such as I would have for a man of letters.'

Defoe gave him a sideways look with those penetrating grey eyes of his. 'Come, Mr Flynt, we are alone here and are men of some experience. Let us not be bashful.'

Flynt's first thought was that Defoe had somehow become aware of his involvement with the Company of Rogues. It was well known that the writer had a deep connection with the Tories, a connection which had cost him dear in the past when the Whigs took revenge for some of his writings, and it was possible that some senior Tory had knowledge of the colonel's work and had passed the same to Defoe, politicians being most garrulous when under the influence of drink or the scent of a woman. Or a young man, come to that. There was also some talk of one senior member having had relations with a pig, but that was not something even Flynt, who was accepting of most sexual proclivities, could countenance.

'Truly, sir, I am most confounded as to why you would seek me out,' Flynt insisted.

Defoe exhaled and took another mouthful of claret. 'Very well, we shall play the game this way. You called me a man of letters, so you know of my work...'

'I do. I particularly enjoyed your report on the great storm of 1703. I was not in England at the time so reading it brought to life what must have been a most distressing time for all concerned. It was a magnificent example of reportage.'

Defoe accepted the praise with some humility. 'I thank you, sir, I did my best.'

'And your Hymn to the Pillory is most moving. Is it true that it was thanks to that poem that when you yourself was thus punished that the populace threw flowers rather than rotten fruit and dead cats?'

Defoe's smile was secretive. 'That is what they say and who am I to countermand it?'

'Yes, apocrypha has a way of becoming fact, has it not?'

'It most certainly does, Mr Flynt, and it is on that very subject that I have sought you out.'

Flynt took the brief pause to sip his claret. 'How can I help with such matters?'

Defoe was silent for a moment as his clever eyes studied Flynt. 'Tell me, sir, have you heard of the Paladin?'

Flynt didn't know whether to be relieved or concerned. That it was not about the Company of Rogues was welcome, but this man's knowledge of that damnable cognomen was vexatious. Nevertheless, Flynt was an astute gambler and had no difficulty in maintaining an even demeanour. 'The twelve Paladins were knights at the court of Charlemagne who defended the faith, if memory serves.'

'I do not refer to literature or legend, but to a living, breathing Paladin here in this city. A man who defends those who cannot defend themselves, who stands for virtue where there is none. A rough justice is what he dispenses, to be sure, for he is a man who himself walks a fine line between light and dark, good and evil.'

Flynt's smile was not forced, for he found Defoe's rather grand description of the few favours he had performed very amusing. 'It sounds very much to me like the ravings of someone who had supped too long and too well on claret such as this.'

'Perhaps, but would it interest you to know that it is your name that has been attached to this particular raving?'

Something stabbed between Flynt's ribs but he maintained the smile. His name being bruited was not a fortuitous turn of events. 'Pure fantasy,' he said, his gambler's skill making his short laugh sound unforced.

'Is it, sir? Is it really? On balance, I do believe I would beg to differ.'

'I'm a gambler, Mr Defoe, nothing more, nothing less. I'm no crusader. Where would you hear such a thing?'

'I am a listener, Mr Flynt, and I hear things. And I have heard of this and of your name. But if it be untrue, how came you to be associated with this individual?'

'If such an individual exists.'

'I believe he does.'

'And that is your right, for a man must believe what he wishes to believe. But if I were you, before I put quill to parchment and ink to press, which I presume is the intention, I would have to be certain that what is printed has some veracity.'

Defoe laughed. 'Ah, Mr Flynt, you have a fine, if naive, view of the newspaper world and I applaud it. However, that is why I am here this night, filthy though it be, for I wished to present you with the claim and give you the opportunity to refute it.'

'Which I do, wholeheartedly. The existence of this nameless protector of virtue is pure invention.'

'Then tell me this, why would my informant link your name to this invention and also direct me to this very coaching inn?'

The issue of who would attach his name to the rumour, someone who knew where he lived, was perplexing in the extreme and its solution was something Flynt himself would dearly enjoy discovering, but he suspected Defoe would not reveal his informant. He had not only been in the pillory, but had played some part in the Monmouth Rebellion. Flynt was unsure if he was involved in any of the skirmishes or the climactic battle at Sedgemoor but he had heard he was in the west country at the time James Scott, Duke of Monmouth, landed to take up the Protestant cause against a Roman Catholic king. Defoe had also spent some time in Newgate on matters unrelated to the rebellion. Certainly it was likely he was not in the lowest ward of that hellhole but he had still survived. There was a steel to the man's gaze that told Flynt he was not easily intimidated. This Paladin matter was rapidly becoming one that might be best referred to Colonel Charters, lest it open up the Company of Rogues to inspection.

'There is nothing I can say that will prove that I am not this person, if he even exists, for it is most difficult to prove a negative,' Flynt said, carefully. 'All I can do is but deny it and trust your basic decency that to somehow align me with this man might prove most perilous to my wellbeing.'

'Perilous to your wellbeing in what way?'

'The city is a dangerous place and there are those who would not take kindly to even the suggestion that there was a man such as the one which you describe. I am, as I said, a mere gambler but that is one wager I would not relish.'

Defoe drained his glass but continued to examine Flynt's face for any sign of perfidy. Seeing nothing, he exhaled again. 'I see you are either a speaker of truth or a man very greatly used to concealing his true self, Mr Flynt.'

'I am as you see me, Mr Defoe, as imperfect as a man could be, but no sainted battler for justice.'

The writer made a decision, or at least seemed to. 'Very well, sir, I will take you at your word for the moment, for I remain suspicious that you are more than you seem.' He stood and plucked his hat from the table. 'I shall take my leave, but let me assure you that I have no intention of letting this matter rest. I will have this tale and I will write of it, you may take that as gospel.'

There was nothing Flynt could say that would prevent that so he let it go. He also rose and donned his hat. 'Let me walk you to the street from whence you will find carriage or sedan to carry you to your home.'

Defoe gave him a smile that was not unfriendly. 'And there we have it, Mr Flynt, the very instinct of a Paladin.'

Flynt matched the good humour, even though he didn't feel it. 'Courtesy merely, Mr Defoe.'

The writer accepted the offer with good grace and Flynt led him through the somewhat labyrinthian corridors of the Golden Cross to the entrance on Charing Cross. The misty rain and the strains of a plaintive ballad being played on a fiddle from a tavern somewhere in the vicinity hung in the air. Defoe looked towards Pall Mall and then the Strand before searching the road to Whitehall, but saw no coach nor chair to convey him. He pulled the collar of his coat up and tutted.

'It be ever thus, is it not? There is never transport to be had when you are in most dire need of it. It be exceeding vexatious that...'

Flynt heard the scrape of a boot and sensed rather than saw a furtive movement in the shadow cast by the archway leading to the inn's stables. By instinct he pushed Defoe back into the doorway, twisted his blade free and whirled to face the two men who lunged towards them, each holding a weapon – one a pistol, the other a knife. He dealt with the pistol holder first, thrusting the tip of his sword into his shoulder, causing him to drop the weapon with a curse. The wound was not overly deep but it was of sufficient force to make the man step away. As Flynt prepared to face the attacker with the knife he found he had come to a sudden halt, the knife held at chest height as if ready to lunge, and for a brief moment Flynt thought he had been discouraged by the wounding of his companion. But he was wrong.

'I would not pursue this matter further, my friend.'

It was Defoe who spoke, and when Flynt looked to him he saw a small pistol held in a hand that barely wavered. The rogue considered the wisdom of ignoring the advice, decided that to continue with what appeared to be a low toby would profit him little, and without a word turned to help his wounded friend, gripping him by the uninjured arm and all but dragging him away. Flynt watched them scuttle down the Strand then turn up St Martin's Lane towards, Flynt noted, St Giles and the Rookery. That, however, was a subject for further deliberation.

He turned to Defoe. 'I see you are more than a man of letters.'

'I am not unaccustomed to the low taverns and inns of this fair city and often walk the streets after nightfall in pursuit of my trade, Mr Flynt, and a man who chooses to do so without some form of defence is a man who asks for trouble.' Defoe indicated the sword Flynt was in the process of returning to its silver scabbard. 'I note you are of such a philosophy also.' One eyebrow raised as he regarded Flynt with a faintly sardonic expression. 'A mere gambler, you say. I think not, I say. Your reaction to this attempted footpaddery was most expert.' He dropped his pistol in his coat pocket. 'I bid you a good night, Mr Flynt. We shall meet again.'

He touched the brim of his hat before passing beyond Flynt to walk to the Strand.

Damn it, he had almost convinced the man that he was not what he believed. The attack marked yet another attempt on his life, such a common occurrence to be sure that it was almost monotonous, but the fact that it had occurred at the Golden Cross caused him sadness for it brought home once again that too many people knew where he lived. There had been a surfeit of instances in which people had found him there and he had known for some time that he was long overdue decanting to fresh lodgings, a prospect he mourned. He was comfortable in the Cross and he both liked and trusted his landlords, Mr and Mrs Wilkes. He would be sorry to leave.

-

He is tasty.

I hadn't expected those coves to serve him out, they was mere tools to test him, but as soon as I sees him tap that one's claret with that sneaky Toledo, I knows this man truly was a tasty cove. I senses it outside the house in Whitechapel, senses it in his eye and in his manner, and I sees it now with my very own peepers.

It weren't nothing to track him here. Hunter he may be but he ain't learned the lesson that the best hunter keeps a-moving. Flynt, Wild had calls him in my hearing, and it wasn't no great trouble to find out who he was and where he lodged. A fingersmith, a cracksman, a proper don with the flats and the tats, but also a husher of men known to stand buff, not run away. He didn't disappoint.

Yes, Jonas Flynt, I sees you well and I knows you well. I ain't no thief, I ain't no gambler but I is a husher of some skill. And I also stand buff against all comers.

It will be a pleasure to spill your claret…

13

It was ironic that Charters had chosen to meet Flynt the following day in the Chapter Coffee House, located close to St Paul's Cathedral on Paternoster Row. It was here that the newsmen and scriveners of the city often met, for the row was at the centre of the city's printing trade and boasted many book shops with presses in the rear or in rooms above producing pamphlets, broadsheets and newspapers. Flynt hoped that he would not find Mr Defoe here, for being seen with Charters might stimulate further interest, even though the colonel took great pains to ensure that his name was not associated in any way with the work the Company of Rogues undertook. As Flynt had already considered, that didn't mean that Defoe had not been told by his mysterious informant of that connection.

Charters had arrived on time, as was his wont, but Flynt lingered for at least half an hour, hidden from view inside a dark doorway, observing the comings and goings around the coffee house, but of the writer there was no sign. It was already 10.30 a.m. and it was possible that the man was not an early riser, but it was also possible that he had ensconced himself within prior to Flynt's arrival. That was something he would have to risk. He crossed the narrow street, nodding to the colonel's two watchers as they lounged far enough away so as not to attract attention but close enough to intercede should anything untoward occur. Flynt paused in the doorway to peer into the coffee house and was relieved to perceive no sign of Defoe.

Charters was at a table at the rear of the premises, near to a back door, with no other customers close to him, apart from the faintly familiar gentleman with whom he was in companionable conversation. The man was around Flynt's own age and was resplendent in full periwig, and dressed most neatly, his features what some women might view as comely but tending towards the fleshy, while his body would have charitably been described as well built but was, in fact, showing signs of corpulence. The stranger leaned closer to mutter something softly which caused Charters to erupt in a hearty laugh. Flynt waited until the man delivered a short bow and then moved on.

'Serjeant Flynt,' Charters said, loudly enough for all to hear, 'why, man, it is good to see you again. Please, sit with me, if you have the leisure.'

It was all play-acting, for the benefit of those who might take note of the colonel having the society of a man who dressed in the manner of a puritan. That they had known each other while in service was no secret, thanks to Charters circulating the intelligence in order to give their appearances in public together some provenance. Charters had also adopted an air of good humour, but the drawn cheeks and shadowed eyes proved it to be false. The affair of Nimrod Boone weighed heavily upon him.

As Flynt settled in the chair, Charters caught him watching the man with whom he had recently been talking to in further conversation with two men near to the door. 'Do you know Mr Handel?'

So that was who he was. Flynt had never met George Frideric Handel but he had seen him occasionally. 'I know *of* Mr Handel.'

'Fine man, fine musician,' said Charters, waving to a serving boy and indicating the need for two coffees. 'I had the pleasure of being present to hear his Water Music last summer.'

In July, a barge carrying King George and his courtiers headed up the Thames to Chelsea, accompanied by a host of smaller craft and yet another barge carrying an orchestra of around fifty musicians, playing the newly composed suite to which Charters had referred.

'It's as well that the hearing of it was a pleasure, Colonel,' Flynt said, 'for I understand that old George ordered it to be played three times.'

Charters gave Flynt a brief but pointed look. '*His Majesty* did indeed request the suite to be played numerous times, for he is most appreciative of music, Mr Handel's in particular.'

'It certainly brought Mr Handel back into royal favour.'

'He was never out of it. Although he holds the title of the Kapellmeister to Hanover, Mr Handel has been here in London these many years under His Majesty's grace, despite what the rumour mongers may say.'

Handel turned back to Charters, as if sensing they were discussing him, and gave him another short bow, before sweeping his hat to his head with a flourish and leaving the coffee house. One of Charters' watchers was in the process of entering and stepped aside to allow him to pass, the two men each inclining their heads in respect.

'I have the honour of being numbered among the maestro's circle of friends, Flynt,' Charters said, 'so do have a care with what you say of him.'

The watcher took a seat at the table beside theirs, positioning himself as a buffer between them and the rest of the room while his colleague remained outside. Charters' acquaintance with the composer explained the nod of recognition in the doorway. Flynt wondered if Handel questioned why a retired army colonel on a pension would require bodyguards. Charters would have conceived some explanation that passed muster, he was sure.

'I have nothing to say of him,' Flynt said, 'for, as I said, he and I have never met.'

'Then you are much the poorer of it, for he is a most charming man. Granted, a fellow must have a working knowledge of not only English but German, French and Italian in order to have discourse but even then he is a most accomplished storyteller. In truth, had his command of our language been greater then there are those who say he would rival even Dean Swift for his wit.'

Flynt knew this was all preamble, for while talking Charters had been surveying the room in order to see who might be listening. Satisfied that the few patrons present seemed more intent on their own interaction with their friends, he nevertheless waited until the serving lad had brought them the coffees he had ordered before he spoke again, this time the darkness of his underlying mood colouring his words.

'What news of our friend Boone?'

Flynt quickly and quietly told him of his conversation with Caleb Boone and his belief that his cousin was dead.

Charters nodded, his lips pressed tightly. 'Yes, it seems to concur with what my man Jacob has learned from his inquiries with old comrades. Nobody saw him after Malplaquet and it is presumed he be dead.'

Flynt sensed something behind the words. 'And yet, you don't accept it.'

'I don't.' Charters paused and Flynt was convinced he detected a slight shiver run through him. 'He walks among us, I can feel it.'

Nathaniel Charters was not a man to surrender to such feelings easily, so Flynt was inclined to accept his instincts. 'I'll continue my inquiries. If he is, in fact, in London then I will find him.'

Charters gave him a brief nod. 'What will be your next step?'

'Caleb Boone said they were raised in the Sanctuary. It is possible they will have family remaining there so it is not unreasonable to assume that if Nimrod did indeed return from the continent then he would make those familiar streets his first port of call.'

The colonel's eyes narrowed. 'You seem most invested in this mission, Flynt. I confess you are in general extremely professional but your attitude in this matter seems somehow different.'

'Two children were murdered, Colonel, most brutally from what I gather. My attitude is honed by that knowledge.'

Charters considered this as he sipped his coffee. 'You affect an air of a man who is distanced from the world, Flynt, but I have always known that you are not untouched by it. It is both your strength and your weakness.'

Charters' words gave Flynt the opportunity to broach his other concern. 'On that, Colonel, we may have an issue.'

'Oh?'

'I may have unwittingly been dubbed with a street name.'

'That is most careless of you, Flynt. What would this street name be?'

'The Paladin.'

This seemed to lighten Charter's mood. He savoured it for a moment then smiled. 'Good God, the individual who attached this appellation to your name both knew you well and also not at all. How did this begin?'

'I know not.'

'And it is generally known that this defender of the faith is in fact you?'

'No, I don't think that is the case. Yet.'

Charters' smile thinned. 'Yet? I don't like the implication of that, Flynt.'

'I was visited last night by Mr Daniel Defoe.'

Charters' eyebrow raised. 'You know Mr Defoe?'

'I believe I have seen him in a tavern or two, but we didn't meet until last night.'

'And I assume he has heard of this soubriquet?'

'Yes, and also been informed that this Paladin was, in fact, I.'

Flynt told him of the meeting and the subsequent attack in the street which seemed to confirm in the writer's mind that Flynt was more than he claimed.

Charters contemplated this intelligence for a moment. 'I am aware of the activities you have pursued beyond the scope of your work for me and I have tolerated them. This desire of yours to right wrongs is, as I say, both your strength and weakness. However, they were not widespread enough for me to expect them to gain currency in the streets.' He stopped again to consider the issue. 'Really, Flynt, this could prove most inconvenient should Mr Defoe choose to publish.'

'I have performed favours for people I know and trust. Also, some of these actions have been taken in furtherance of your various agendas. I am no Paladin.'

'That matters not a jot, for the truth of the matter is that Mr Defoe's writing need bear no relation to fact. He is a most brilliant man and can be decidedly tenacious in his inquiry but less scrupulous in his conclusions.' He halted again, still mulling it over. 'And you have no inkling as to who started this rumour?'

'None, but it is someone who knows me, for they told Defoe where I lodge.'

'Someone then who wishes you revealed and, in so doing, rendering you wounded most grievous in terms of the work you do for me?'

'That is possible.'

'Or someone who wishes you harm and would have the combined might of the London substrata looking in your direction. Although sometimes, Flynt, you do manage that without external influence.'

'That is also possible.'

'The attack on your person last night,' Charters said, 'is not unusual, let's be forthright about it. I have commented before on your ability to enrage people.'

'And I have said before, often while doing my work for you.'

'Often, Flynt, but not always. What is your feeling of it?'

'It was a most clumsy attack, the men employed in its execution were not skilled but they did retreat along St Martin's Lane, which suggests they were headed back to the Rookery.'

'So it may be that this Caleb Boone fellow sent them after you?'

'That would mean they followed me when I left, and I take the utmost care in that regard.'

'Unless he was already aware of where you lodged.'

Flynt had to concede that possibility. 'True, but he has a brace of men at his back who I would hazard are most skilled, so why wait until I was at my lodging when he could very easily have had me vanish from the streets of St Giles?'

It was Charters' turn to accept that. 'So, it is then a choice of solutions. That these ruffians were sent by someone else who bears you ill will, as we have established that be hardly an unlikely eventuality, or it was just as it appeared, a mere street robbery, a low toby as you might call it. But I posit a third option, that Defoe himself arranged the attack to test you.'

Flynt had considered that. 'If that's the case then he will be in considerable danger, for I wounded one of them and they will take most unkindly to that.'

'Defoe can look to himself, if he was the true mover behind it. He is most accomplished at self-preservation and no stranger to perilous situations.'

'I understand he was with Monmouth.'

Charters dismissed that. 'I am informed that he was merely swept up in that doomed enterprise. But he performed functions for our country at the time of the Act of Union that, had they become known to certain parties, might have seen him on the wrong end of a Scottish dirk.'

'He was a spy?'

'He gathered intelligence, shall we say. Leave him to me, for I have some influence with him.'

In that moment, Flynt wondered exactly what influence Charters had over the writer. That Defoe had been in Scotland ten years before was a surprise, especially given his activities, and it occurred to him that when Charters returned from Flanders and assumed the mantle of commander of the Company of Rogues, that he might have inherited the writer as an agent.

Charters continued, 'In the meantime, curtail your more altruistic tendencies and concentrate on the work you have for me. Speaking of which, what of Monsieur Lombre?'

'I have heard nothing from my contact but I am due to speak with him today.'

A messenger had arrived at Flynt's lodgings earlier that morning with a request that he meet the Admiral in Wapping.

'Is it possible that Lombre was behind last night's assault upon your person?'

Flynt thought of the Frenchman's comment regarding 'friends' who didn't wish him harmed. 'It is always possible, but given what you have told me of his skill in the art of killing I would expect any such attack would come from him and not be left to the vagaries of street bullies.'

Charters nodded his agreement. 'Continue your quests, Serjeant. Find him. Find Nimrod Boone. Save the country the trouble of trial and execution...'

-

Moncrieff felt duty-bound to convey Bailie Wilson to the coach stop in Holborn, where he would find the stage to convey him first to York, then on to Edinburgh. It would be a long journey but Wilson had stated he was in no hurry and would welcome the leisure time following a harried few days in London.

Once again, Moncrieff was curious as to what contributed to that flux but he knew better than to inquire again. Wilson wasn't the man to be interrogated.

As Moncrieff's coach busied itself through the clamour of the streets, the Grand Master fixed him with his astute eye. 'What news of Jonas Flynt?'

The now customary flutter of nerves agitated Moncrieff's gut. 'I have had no contact with him.'

'Since your adventure in the north? The disaster that was Gallowmire?'

Moncrieff endeavoured not to rise to the man's mocking tone. 'None at all.'

'You've accepted that you share your father's blood with him then?'

A deep breath. 'I've accepted that it is stated as fact by a few but with no firm evidence to support the claim.'

'And you do not feel the fellow will seek an inheritance?'

'He has shown no interest.'

Wilson's smile remained mocking. 'Yet. He has shown no interest yet. A man's mind can change when it comes to silver.'

Moncrieff had no desire to discuss this subject so remained silent. Wilson snorted a little laugh then transferred his gaze to the streets beyond the carriage window. 'It's of no consequence. I have set in motion a scheme that will remove him from our path, perhaps for a year or two, perhaps permanently if all goes well.'

'What is this scheme, may I ask?'

Wilson's smile was secretive and guarded. 'That's for me to know, boy, and you to be grateful…'

14

Daniel waited beneath the sign of the Ship and Anchor, a Wapping tavern near to Execution Dock. He relieved Flynt of his weapons with his customary silent efficiency before leading him to a door down an alley running beside the tavern and thence to a set of uneven steps that carried them upwards to a small room where a fireplace roared. The low roof was seemingly set at a most curious angle, so much that though the floor itself was level, Flynt had the impression that he was walking uphill. The Admiral was at a table in conversation with a man whose burnished skin and beefy forearms testified to a life at sea. Flynt's own father bore such a complexion, having spent years on a merchant vessel plying its trade across the Atlantic and beyond, though a few years of Edinburgh winds and rain had washed away some of its sheen. At least, he had told Flynt that he was a merchant sailor, but he suspected there was more to his father's travels than hauling ropes on an honest ship.

The sailor touched his hand to his forehead in an informal salute and left, his walk the rolling gait of a man more recently used to the pitch and yaw of a deck than dry land.

'An old friend, just docked from the Indies,' the Admiral said. 'He brings me news of my business interests abroad.'

'Thriving, I trust.'

A growl from under the mask that might have been a laugh. 'There is always coin in illicit pursuits, Jonas. Even in the hardest of times, a man can show profit if he is both astute and resourceful.'

'And ruthless,' Flynt added.

Another laugh, but this transformed into a cough and the Admiral reached out to a linen kerchief on the desk to press it to the mouth of his mask. 'I apologise, my friend, the dampness of this season continues to irritate my lungs most fearful. Yes indeed, this business in which we engage does require a degree of ruthlessness, although perhaps not of the sort you were confronted with in Whitechapel, eh?'

'No,' Flynt agreed, 'that was most extreme. It shocked even Jonathan Wild.'

The Admiral wiped his lips. 'He was present?'

'He was.'

'For what reason?'

'He said he had received notice of the severity of the crimes and wished to offer the authorities his assistance.'

'The devil he did.' The Admiral's tone was thoughtful. 'That lying son-of-a-bitch only looks to assist in matters that make his purse heavier.'

He rose to face the window behind him, where the Thames and the sky were a grey canvas awaiting an artist to daub further detail. Even the Southwark shoreline opposite was little more than a shadow in the misty rain. The Admiral was silent for a moment, no doubt pondering Wild's appearance beyond the wall.

'If you crane your neck just a little,' he said, 'you can see where they executed Captain Kidd.' He turned back to face Flynt. 'Do you know the name, Jonas?'

'Pirate, was he not?'

'He was no pirate. Privateer he was only. A respectable trade, if there be such a thing, and one backed by many men of the city. He was a countryman of yours, did you know that?'

'Of that I was not aware.'

'Aye, from Dundee, in your county of Fife, though he had uprooted to the colonies, New York to be precise. He was a seaman and a merchant and it was the governor of that colony himself who commissioned him in the name of King William to seize enemy ships and those of any pirates for profit. But the enterprise fared badly. He killed a seaman in a fit of anger and captured the wrong ship, a rich prize belonging not to a buccaneer or enemy, and was declared pirate. He was betrayed by that same governor of New York who had first commissioned him, and arrested. On return to England, he was tried and executed. Below us lies a stretch of rocky foreshore revealed at low tide and that be where they build the gallows for pirates.'

He was silent for a moment. 'I was here, at this window, but Daniel was present on the shore, were you not, my friend?'

Daniel, standing by the doorway, nodded briefly.

'It were a carnival, as these things are. Hundreds, perhaps even thousands, it be difficult to tell, followed the procession from Newgate. Hours it took, as these occurrences do, but they got here late afternoon. The month of May, it was, sixteen summers ago. Ten men there were original set to die, but six received their pardon in the shadow of the boom. Four met their maker, Kidd, the Scot, as well as an Irishman and two Frenchies. All the English were spared.' His liquid laugh was sharp. 'I know not for certain what that signifies. But Kidd died that day, proclaiming his innocence, though that gallows crow Paul Lorrain claimed otherwise.'

Flynt knew of Lorrain. He was the chaplain of Newgate, what they called the Ordinary, and among his duties was the expectation that he would exhort the condemned to confess their crimes and make their peace with their God. These confessions he noted down and later sold in printed form, the penal system being a lucrative money-making enterprise.

Without turning, the Admiral said, 'But Daniel was close enough to hear, were you not?'

Another nod from the silent man.

'Kidd was twice hanged, did you know that, Flynt?' The Admiral continued. 'The other three went to eternity right off, though it was a horrendous sight, but Kidd's rope snapped. They should have deemed it an act of God and pardoned him there and then, but not Kidd. He was a pirate most notorious and he would be damned, act of God or no. He was hauled back up on the boom and this time they did the job correctly.'

Flynt asked, 'And what was it he said if he didn't confess nor ask for divine forgiveness?'

The Admiral's gaze remained fixed on a point just to the left of his window. 'Daniel?'

'He asked that his love be sent to his wife and daughter in New York,' said Daniel, quietly. 'And that she forgive him for the shame of his death.'

'No request for absolution from God, no admission that he was pirate, despite what Lorrain peddled to the masses, damn his pious, larcenous little heart. And after his body, and those of the other three, had been tied to a post and thrice washed over by the tides, as the Admiralty demanded, his remains were taken down river to Tilbury, where the Thames meets the sea, and there put on display on the gibbet. It hung there in chains for three years, as a salutary lesson to any man of the salt who might wish to follow the life of the buccaneer.'

'But if the expedition was sanctioned by king and men of note, then were there not documentary proofs?'

'There were such proofs, but they miraculously disappeared. Politics, Flynt. The men who backed Kidd were Whigs and the Tories were in the ascendant and saw an opportunity to disgrace them. Had he named these men of wealth in his defence then perhaps he would have been treated with some leniency, but he refused. A man of honour, Flynt, perhaps even a fool, but no pirate, of that I am gut certain.'

Of a sudden, he turned to regard Daniel, who stood by the doorway. 'Daniel, if you would be so good as to ask Bartholomew in the Ship to provide some coffee. It is a most disagreeable day and I would have something warm inside me. Have you eaten, Flynt?'

'Not yet.'

'Then have Bartholomew prepare those sausages of pork I gave him. You may leave Jonas's weapons behind. I feel sure that he means me no harm, for we are firm friends now, are we not, Jonas?'

'I like to think so.'

Daniel accepted that with his usual display of emotion, to wit, none. He placed the pistols on a chair behind the door and left.

'Always such a talkative fellow,' Flynt observed.

'He does lean towards the silent, but he is loyal and he is trustworthy, and as I believe we have both agreed previous, those are rare virtues in this world of ours, as the case of poor William Kidd tells us. Which returns my thoughts to the snake-like charms of Mr Wild. What be your opinion on his interest in this matter?'

Flynt shrugged. 'He is a difficult man to comprehend.'

'Indeed, he has many layers and all of them rotten.'

'But in this case my sense was that he was sincere. He was horrified by what had occurred.'

The Admiral grunted, as if he found the notion of the thieftaker being horrified by anything difficult to believe. 'Perhaps, perhaps not. You are aware that we have had our differences, he and I?'

'I am, but I understood they have been settled.'

'They have settled, but not *been* settled, if you understand my meaning. We have reached an understanding, is all. If he could strike at me in a fashion that would not have suspicion fall upon him, then he would do so.'

'Even an act such as this?'

'Yes, even an act such as this.'

Flynt considered Wild's reaction to the scene inside the house. 'He was genuinely repelled by what occurred.'

'That may be, but consider this possibility, that he had some intelligence of Jacques' connection to me and had one of his creatures, perhaps that swine Blueskin Blake, go after him. The attack might have been in the hope that there was some accounting on paper within the Whitechapel house relating to my interests of which he could make use.'

'But the family?'

It was the Admiral's turn to shrug. 'His blood was up, he desired to leave no witnesses to the crime.'

Flynt could not bring himself to believe that Wild, or even Blueskin, would have anything to do with the murder of children. 'With respect, I believe you to be wrong.'

'Perhaps, Jonas, but I will say this – if there be any hint that Jonathan Wild has directed this crime then I will strike back with equal ferocity. You said that men like me must be ruthless and should I deem it necessary you shall see how ruthless I can be.'

This was no idle boast, for Flynt was aware of how single-minded the Admiral could be in pursuit of his business. He had never experienced that ruthlessness first hand, so the tales may have been exaggerated, much like the exploits of the Paladin, but at their core there would be some truth. The Admiral did not become the ruler of London's waterways without spilling blood, but the prospect of some form of war between he and Wild was not an eventuality to be desired. He decided to throw the man another possibility.

'Do you know of Caleb Boone?'

A phlegmy rasp at the back of his throat revealed what the Admiral thought of him. 'A glorified pounder born of the Sanctuary with ambitions beyond his ability. He believes himself equipped to move upwards from being street brawler and dock badger.'

A badger was a robber who threw his victims' bodies into the water after he had plucked them clean. 'He worked the riverlands?'

'Aye, until I chased him out and he scuttled to the Rookery, which is just the place for such an ignorant lout.'

'He seems educated.'

'As I said, ambitions beyond his abilities. Like Wild he adopts some airs and graces, and like Wild it is but fineer only, something more palatable covering rough wood. He has his letters and he has read books, yes he has, and he speaks most prettily for a Sanctuary scallywag, but that changes nothing. Caleb Boone is all artifice on the surface but underneath there remains nothing but old, gnarled timber. So what does he have to do with this?

'He has a cousin by the name of Nimrod.'

The Admiral let out an explosive laugh at the name. 'Caleb and Nimrod, names ripped from the pages of scripture and applied to rookery scum. So what of this Nimrod?'

'He has committed acts similar to that in Whitechapel. Not in England as far as is known, but in Flanders.'

The Admiral grew more interested. 'Has he, by God. And where is he?'

'That is what I am trying to find out. His cousin says he is dead and lost across the Channel.'

'Then that would be the end of it, if Caleb Boone was a trustworthy man, but speaking personal I would put no credence to his words if he told me I wore a mask.'

'A gentleman of my acquaintance also remains unconvinced. He believes the deaths of the Berthon family bear all the marks of Nimrod's handiwork.'

The Admiral digested this. 'And this gentleman of your acquaintance is who, may I ask?'

Flynt gave him a slight smile, as if he were embarrassed to deny the Admiral the knowledge. 'I am not at liberty to reveal his identity, but he was an infantry officer who had dealings with Nimrod Boone in Flanders, to his great cost.'

Even at that Flynt felt he had said too much but he felt honour bound to reveal something.

'And you are on the trail of this Nimrod Boone?'

'As much as I am able, yes. I would appreciate any indication that you or your people might learn.'

'Of course.'

The Admiral sat behind the table again, his finger sadly picking at the linen kerchief, even though he had not coughed.

Flynt asked, 'And on that matter, have you news of the man Lombre?'

'Ah yes, our mysterious foreigner,' the Admiral's voice seemed distant, his mind perhaps on Caleb Boone and his cousin. 'His name be French but my people tell me there may be more in his blood than garlic. His speaks with a tongue that suggests other lands.'

Flynt had noted the man's curious amalgam of accents. 'He has travelled widely, I understand, and speaks many languages. That may account for his curious manner of speech.'

'Aye, I have heard many tongues on the riverlands, it be a veritable Babel.' Flynt caught the reference and knew for certain the man's thoughts remained around Nimrod. 'The man you seek has been seen on two occasions at least in the company of a gentleman. They met secretly, but not secretly enough, for I have eyes and ears in walls the length of the river.'

'And who is this gentleman?'

The Admiral sighed. 'I regret his identity remains unknown. He is not known in the docklands, that be for sure. However, one of my men tells me he heard him speak but once, and his voice was as yours.'

'A Scot?'

'So my man informs me, and his ears are especial acute.'

Lombre meeting a Scot. That suggested a Jacobite connection.

'Tell me, Jonas, what is your interest in this man Lombre and this mysterious individual?'

Flynt smiled. 'Admiral, we are friends, but we are also men of secrets, you and I, and this is another that I must keep. Rest assured that my interest does not impinge on any of your business interests.'

The Admiral's breathy laugh was genuine. 'We are indeed friends, Jonas, and so I will trust you and, as I've intimated previous, that is not something I do readily. But have a care. My intelligencers have been unable to glean the nature of his business here, but they recognise that he be a most dangerous individual. My little wharf rats have a special sense when it comes to such things.'

'Admiral, the city is replete with dangerous individuals, including you and I.'

Another laugh. 'That be true. But let me add a further word of caution. In addition to this man Lombre, be also most wary of both Wild and Boone. Wild makes it his business to curry favour with those in authority. My sources tell me that Boone has also found himself some men of influence.'

'For what reason?'

'Illicit enterprise is still enterprise and be most profitable. William Kidd was lured by the promises of such men and to his cost, for when it came time for them to stand by him, they were nowhere to be seen. On the day of his death they were supped and caroused as if in celebration. He learned in a manner most egregious to put not his trust in princes. Wild and Boone will no doubt learn such lessons, too, and when the time comes may God help them as no assistance will be forthcoming from those men in rooms and offices in the west end or in Whitehall. And, my friend, I make you this vow. If it be either of them behind this horror, then the blood of that poor family will not be the last drop to flow and it will take aeons of rain to wash the streets clean.'

15

At some point, Daniel Defoe was bound to patronise the Chapter Coffee House and all Colonel Charters had to do was wait. He could have sent one of his men to fetch him but given that he was going to prevail upon the man to ignore what he had heard about Flynt, such a heavy-handed approach might not be advisable. Luckily he had the leisure that day to linger, for which he was grateful as his sleep continued to be disturbed and he knew he would not find rest until Boone was discovered and despatched. In truth, he enjoyed the time to chat with friends, like Mr Handel, and others among those who frequented the coffee house with whom he was familiar, for not only did the encounters serve as welcome diversions from his troubled thoughts, but such establishments were a hotbed of discourse. The Chapter was particularly useful, it being patronised by many of those who worked in the field of printing and publishing, for such people were prone to gossip and within gossip there was often the kernel of what could become useful intelligence. Nathaniel Charters was a man who prized useful intelligence.

On this occasion, however, much of the gossip concerned the events in Whitechapel and the ramifications of such horrors on the community. The ferocity of the acts had caused great distress and trepidation among the populace. There was, as yet, no sign of panic, Charters gleaned, but there was a growing agitation that a slayer of children was abroad, an agitation he understood well.

Defoe arrived before lunchtime, hailing men he knew, his eyes beginning to scan the room for those whom he might wish to avoid, whether out of dislike or because they held an outstanding debt, and falling almost immediately upon the colonel. A slight frown puckered but was dispelled as he edged between the tables to greet him.

'Nat,' he said, affecting a slight bow, 'I haven't seen you in this establishment for some considerable time.'

'Pressure of business, Dan,' said Charters, for he had known the writer for many years and he was one of the few people who he permitted to address him with the hypocorism of his Christian name. 'Please, sit, my friend, let us talk.'

Defoe hid the recurring frown well, but not well enough that Charters didn't notice it.

'I will,' he said as he dropped himself into the chair, 'and right gladly, for I have been at my own business all morning and I do believe I have worn out the sole of my shoes walking these streets.' He sat back in his chair, all the better to study Charters' face. 'You look fatigued yourself, Nat.'

Charters attracted the attention of the serving boy and signalled that a coffee should be served to his guest. 'A minor disturbance of my sleep, nothing more. A good draught from a physic, perhaps a little bleeding, and I will be all the better for it. But what business do you have that calls for such wearisome activity in this unwelcome weather?'

Defoe glanced around him in a most furtive manner before lowering his voice. 'I will tell you, Nat, for you and I have known each other for many years and I am confident that you will not break my trust, but there are those within these walls who would seize any chance to undermine me by stealing what I have in mind.'

Charters decided to get straight to the point. 'And that would be the Paladin?'

Defoe sat back, surprised. 'By God, how did you...?' He left the remainder of the sentence unsaid, his mind already piecing together Charters and Flynt. 'You know Mr Flynt?'

'I was his commander in Flanders. It was he who saved my life, if not my arm.'

'And he asked you to speak with me?'

'He mentioned to me that you and he had a conversation and that you believed him to be this Paladin. It troubles him.'

'But this merely confirms it. He wishes to muzzle me and he uses an old friend to do so. I will not have it, Nat. I will not...'

Charters raised his hand to hush him, for the writer was becoming most excitable. Defoe realised the serving lad was heading their way with his coffee. He fell silent but it was evident his anger was only further enhanced by being unable to say anything. When the boy left them again, Defoe leaned forward, his agitation evident in the set of his jaw, but he remained astute as to his surroundings so ensured his voice remained low.

'Damn the man's spleen, I cannot stand for this.'

'Calm yourself, my friend, Flynt did not ask me to speak with you,' Charters said, truthfully. 'He was concerned over what effect your writing would have on his work.'

'His work? The man is a thief and a gambler and worse. And yet, he performs acts of humanity, though often accompanied by great violence. What work could he...?'

Again, Defoe halted mid sentence, his sharp mind adding another piece to the mosaic that was Charters' relationship with Flynt. His voice dropped. 'He is in your employ?' He lowered his voice to a whisper. 'He is of the Company?'

Charters had used Defoe in the past to gather intelligence, for the man was most accomplished at gleaning information from others. Defoe had done so willingly, for his business affairs could be chequered and he found himself often in need of funds. That, and the antipathy with which the Tories held him, meant he needed the protection of a man like Charters from time to time.

'I break this solemn vow to reveal the identity of one member to another because it is of vital import that you do not cause any form of attention to be brought upon Jonas Flynt.'

Defoe gritted his teeth. 'But in the name of God, Nat, this is a wonderful story. The sinner who punishes others for their sins.'

'Wonderful story it may be but it is one that I exhort you to forget. I have need of Flynt's skills and if you reveal him to the populace then he will be of limited use to me. Can you understand that?'

Defoe drew himself more erect. 'You cannot silence the presses, Nat. Kings have tried, ministers of the Crown have moved to stifle the truth but...'

'Please, Dan, let's not allow our pomposity to overcome our common sense. You have written and printed scurrilous rumour and pernicious lies that could it be proved were penned by you then you would have been in the stocks more times than you have already. Or perhaps worse. The fact that you didn't append your name to these documents proves that you are not some seeker of truth but just another ink-stained hack wallowing around Grub Street for coin.'

Defoe stared at Charters for a moment, his mouth slightly open, clearly taken aback by the insult from his old friend. Then a smile began to spread. 'By God, you most certainly have given me my character, have you not?'

Charters returned the smile, knowing that Defoe was self-aware enough not to take offence at his words. 'It had to be said.'

'Aye, but damn it, this Paladin was a tasty tale for me to tell.'

'You cannot tell it. Find something else.'

'Such tales come not in huge numbers, Nat,' Defoe said, his tone mournful. 'But in name of friendship, and in gratitude for the coin you have put in my pocket in past years when I was most in need, even though it were not charity for I did provide great service, I will agree to stay my quill.'

'I am grateful.'

Defoe drained his dish. 'I suppose it will give me leisure to return to something I have been working on of late.'

'Is it another of your histories? I did so very much enjoy your history of the union of Great Britain.'

'It be more than mere journalism or pamphleteering, it will be a tale told in longer form. Mr Cervantes, I believe, showed us the way with his tales of "Don Quixote", and then Mr Bunyan with his "Pilgrim's Progress" and Mrs Aphra Behn's "Love-Letters between a Nobleman and His Sister" and her "Oroonoko".'

'This will be what then?'

'I have been inspired by the story of Alexander Selkirk – another Scotsman, much like your Jonas Flynt.'

'The castaway on the southern seas?'

'Aye.'

'You will tell his story?'

'No, not his, I said I have been inspired by his adventures, I will not recreate them. I shall construct a fable around the notion of a man set alone on a desert island, a man of my own creation who will engender the sympathy of the reader by being virtuous and intrepid. I do believe such works of imagination are the future for men such as I.'

Charters finished his own coffee and stood up. Defoe noted the two men at a nearby table also began to rise and smiled. 'You are never alone, are you, Nat?'

Dropping some coins on the table, Charters said, 'I cannot afford to be.'

'Being never alone must be lonely at times, my friend.'

Charters didn't reply. Instead he produced a leather purse from his pocket and set it before the writer. 'For your trouble.'

Defoe seemed offended. 'You would buy my silence?'

'Not your silence, for the service you have done by agreeing to forego this tale and also as a donation to aid you in creating your proposed volume.' Charters plucked his hat from the chair beside him. 'I wish you luck with your endeavour, and I will look forward to reading it when published. What will you call it, by the way?'

'The Life and Strange Surprising Adventures of Robinson Crusoe of York.'

Charters nodded his approval of the title. 'It will be a success, Dan, of that I am sure.'

'From your lips to God's ear. Or rather the ears, and purses, of booksellers and readers.'

Charters smiled and stepped away, then turned back. 'One thing more, from whom did you hear of this Paladin rumour?'

Defoe had picked up the purse and weighed it in his hand, his lips puckering appreciatively. 'You have been most generous, but you know I have a long-standing rule never to reveal a source unless I have good reason…'

'I think you can break it on this occasion, between friends.' Charters indicated the purse still in the writer's hand. 'I believe I have given you an abundance of reasons.'

'Between friends, or even if you were enemy, I cannot and as for your reasons then you may have them back if you wish. A man may be as rich as Croesus but if he does not have his word, then he is little more than a pauper. I will not tell you, my good friend, and for that I heartily apologise, but that must be the way of it.'

Charters noted that there was a hesitancy in the way the purse was held out to him, but he waved it away. 'That's yours. Keep it, along with your word.'

God help me from honourable men, he thought as he turned away.

-

The waterman was squat but broad, his shoulders and biceps straining at his tunic as if desperate to break free. He had to be powerful in order to handle the strong currents that flowed up and down the Thames, currents of which he took advantage to complement the powerful strokes on the long oars to speed them westward. He was an elderly man, his face weatherbeaten as Flynt would expect of one who lived life in the open, and his tunic bore the badge of the Company of Watermen and Lightermen. He seemed not to have a care for the dampness of the air nor the bite of the breeze, well used to such unpleasant climes was he.

Flynt had picked up the boat at King Edward Stairs to carry him up river, it being the fastest way to traverse the city from Wapping. A handful of such watermen gathered with their cries of *oars, oars, sculls, oars, oars,* and exhorted him to choose their vessel above the others but he climbed into the nearest and instructed the rower to take him to Westminster. It was bitterly cold and the rain draped itself over him so he slumped in the wherry with his greatcoat collar up and the brim of his hat down. He crossed his arms, tucked his gloved hands under his armpits and closed his eyes. On the river, he could relax, for nobody would attack him here.

The waterman, as many of his trade were prone to do, maintained a continual barrage of verbosity. The murders, of course, was top of his agenda. A terrible thing it was, he opined, a family sacrificed in such a foul manner. Too many foreigners, was his judgement, too many non-Christian folk with strange means of devotion.

Flynt decided not to be drawn into that conversation, nor did he voice any views of the subject of the king, or the government. Finally, the waterman spoke of an apprentice who until recently had shown great promise at the pull of the oars and had taken well to learning the vagaries of the currents.

'I has him no longer, sir,' he said, as he heaved and stretched, back and forward, back and forward, head always at the swivel should an errant boatman veer into his path, for the river was dotted with craft, small and large. When a vessel did stray too close to him, the waterman fired off a verbal broadside of such coarseness that it would scrape the barnacles off a ship's hull.

'He gave up the work?' Flynt only asked the question out of politeness, for he would much rather have sat in silence and allowed the rhythms of the trip calm his mind.

'No, begging your pardon, sir, but he fell victim to a press gang, the pox-ridden curs,' the waterman said, lobbing something from his mouth into the water as if the thought of the Royal Navy's process or recruiting volunteers by force and sometimes at the point of sword had left a bad taste. 'Men such as we are long desired by them scabiferous wretches, God rot them. He was a stout lad, good and strong, and he was an ideal prize for them.' He expelled another blob over the side, his gaze drifting towards a navy vessel docked nearby. 'He be somewhere aboard ship, I'll be bound, though we know not where. Get out of the way, you pucker-arsed piece of shite!'

This last was directed at another waterman who had skimmed alongside as it proceeded east, but the verbal attack was accompanied by a smile to dilute the vehemence. This fellow Thames voyager was obviously a friend, for he retorted with similar roughness also delivered with a grin.

'They does like a fellow what has knowledge of the waters,' the oarsman continued as if he had never been distracted, 'and young Samuel, he was near at the end of his 'prenticeship. Best 'prentice I'd ever had, he was, lived with his sister over there in Southwark, I'm Wapping myself, but he was a good lad no matter to that. But they took him, may God smite them with the flap dragon, and left me without a 'prentice and his sister relying solely on the sewing what she takes in. He was set to turn good coin on these waters, he could pull an oar, could Samuel, he would've taken the Doggett, he would, and there ain't no doubts about that, but now he's off somewhere being whipped by some bosun. Sons of whores, they is, who be better at buggering each other below decks, if they can get them lobcocks of theirs to perform that is, than they be at honest work, begging your pardon, sir, for the language, but that's how I feels about it.'

Flynt smiled, knowing that the man was suddenly fearful that he would be reported to the Company of Watermen for his water language, and subsequently fined. He assured him that all was well, that he had heard worse than that, which he had. The man, his broad shoulder tugging at his oars, grinned in appreciation, then resumed his tirade against the Royal Navy, the practice of impressment and expanded his views on the working nature of their genitalia, all interspersed with further comments yelled at his fellow rowers.

Flynt let the verbiage wash over him like the gentle rain and allowed the rhythms of the journey to still him. He seldom had leisure to allow his mind to rest, for the life he led was one of constant tumult. Even now, as he tried to relax while keeping track of the old waterman's constant prattle, his thoughts ranged widely from the job in hand to other matters. He knew not where Nimrod Boone's mother lived, or even if in fact she remained within the area still known as Sanctuary, for Caleb Boone may not have been completely truthful. That thought led to another thought and yet another; the murders, the involvement of Jonathan Wild, the Admiral's threat of dire repercussions, the dark future facing young Jack, the whereabouts of Lombre. The Paladin…

There were people who believed they understood him and claimed to know what stripe of man he was. Charters saw him as a weapon to point and let loose, a thief, a killer who was interested only in protecting his own neck and garnering coin. In a way, Flynt fared no better than this waterman's apprentice, for he too had been pressed into the country's service. Jack saw him as a mentor, a protector, an employer. Belle perhaps saw him as a man who was in need of loving, who was better than he actually was. The truth was that he was all of these things. The further truth was that, even though he was a man prone to introspection, too much and too often, he still didn't understand himself.

'I'll tell you this, sir,' the waterman said, bringing Flynt out of his brooding, 'I ain't thinking that we shall ever see young Samuel nevermore, not in this here life, and that be the bounden truth.' He glanced at yet another ship at anchor, a merchant barquentine. 'It's my nose what tells me these things. It tells me the way the wind blows on this here water and it tells me if a cove what wants me to convey him is a wrong 'un. And my nose tells me that Samuel won't be heading back to these waters any time soon. My nose ain't never wrong…'

16

Noses.

Flynt had lost count of the number of noses with which he had been presented over the years, poking round the edge of partially opened doors, usually accompanied by suspicious eyes. And there he was, in another dark hallway in a rundown building in a dangerous part of London, being confronted by another nose, another pair of eyes. Often that introduction was followed by violence, or threat, or merely unbridled antagonism. What this nose and eyes would reveal to him was unknown, for the lady may be elderly but she was a Boone, so he knew well to be on his mettle.

What sunlight there had been on that grey day was waning by the time he disembarked from the wherry at Parliament Stairs, making sure he left a decent gratuity because the trip had been most smooth and swift, the entertaining narration diverting him from his thoughts for a time. He walked beyond Parliament House towards Old Palace Yard, heading for Westminster Abbey, and then to the warren of streets that made up the area to the west of the ancient building. Although some streets were better than others, by and large the swampy land and ramshackle buildings that had grown up in the intervening years attracted many of the lost and the lawless. There had been attempts to revitalise the district but pockets of destitution remained and the fact that some portions of the land itself were constantly in danger of flooding from the River Tyburn suggested that many of these good intentions would lead to a fresh hell.

There were two taverns in the vicinity of which Flynt was aware, the Quaker and the Three Tuns, the latter being housed in a bell tower of indeterminate age. These were his first ports of call in his search for the mother of Nimrod Boone, for the chances were that he would encounter someone who might be able to direct him. He was met with suspicion for he was not a well-known face in this vicinity, but the liberal application of coin did loosen a lip or two and he was able to glean from a woman nursing a gin in a dark corner of the Three Tuns that a Patience Boone lived in what they called Little Sanctuary, a dank, narrow set of ancient streets and alleys close to the abbey.

The address he'd been given was situated in a street that had changed little since it was constructed back when the Tudors ruled the land. The building was of wooden construct with an overhanging jetty that left not much more than a sliver of air between it and the one opposite. To Flynt's eyes, both structures seemed in danger of crumbling at any time. Certainly, in the wake of the Great Fire many buildings had been erected with such speed that they were known to collapse even after only fifty years of standing, but that cataclysm had not reached these environs, so this tenement's decline was purely a matter of age, for it had once been a fine structure indeed.

A stairway formed in the gloom of the interior – another old building, another old stairway – and he ensured Tact and Diplomacy were near to hand before he began his ascent, for though the concept of king's sanctuary had been abolished for many a year, there yet remained desperate men who might make the mistake of seeing him as an easy victim. Despite the vintage of the boards, the floor felt sturdy underfoot and he had no need to step as gingerly as he might do in some of the Rookery tenements. He proceeded from the head of the stairs on the second storey to the front of the building and knocked upon a doorway set beside a window blacked out by the landlord to avoid payment of the window tax. The tenements as a whole would have had over twenty windows and therefore the owner would be liable for payment of around fourteen shillings a year. The blacking out and bricking up of windows that the owner no doubt thought superfluous would reduce his liability by a few shillings but did nothing to illuminate the hallway.

He gave the peeling wood a gentle knock with his gloved knuckle and almost immediately a woman's voice asked who it was.

'I wonder if I may have a moment of your time, if I have the honour of addressing Patience Boone,' he said.

Shuffling feet approached and the door opened a crack. A flickering light from the nub of a candle held in a hand that trembled slightly revealed the nose, the pair of eyes that were wary but were also bright and missed nothing as they regarded him from foot to face.

'And what would a man such as you be wishing with someone such as I, eh?'

Her voice shook along with her hold of the candle but her diction was near perfect. This was not a woman born to Little Sanctuary, on that he would stake his fortune.

'A word or two, madam,' he said, removing his hat to appear less threatening, but crossing his arms in front of him to ensure his pistols were within easy and swift reach. 'About your son.'

She showed no surprise at this, merely nodded once and stepped back to allow him to enter. She shuffled across the small, sparsely furnished room to a wooden chair set before a window with no glass in the frame, but enclosed by wooden shutters which, even if open, would reveal only the building opposite. Flynt hesitated but a moment, first peering into the dingy room, for he had no way of knowing if she was alone, then pushing the door open fully in case someone hid behind it. Patience Boone had turned and by the dim light of the candle watched him with an amused tilt of the head.

'You need have no fear, sir, I am quite alone and an old lady such as I is no threat to a man such as you.'

Flynt had known old ladies such as she who could be as vicious as any street rogue, but he stepped into the room nonetheless and closed the door. The candle cast faint shadows dancing across peeling walls and he managed to make out a low bed to his left, its straw mattress bare of any coverings, a wooden crate beside it with an unlit half-spent candle stuck on an old roof slate. Against another wall was a fireplace with a cooking pot hanging upon a hook, but the hearth was dead and there was no wood set at its side. The floor's naked boards hadn't tasted water for a considerable time and so needed a vigorous scrubbing. A nail hammered into the door behind him was draped with a threadbare shawl and an equally as worn dress.

She placed the candle on the windowsill then pulled a thin blanket from the back of the chair and wrapped it around her shoulders before she took her seat. 'I cannot offer you somewhere to rest for I have only but this single chair, as you can see. What others I've had have long since been used for fuel. I have been in straightened times for some period of time.'

'I am happy to stand, madam.'

She reached down to the floor to pick up a long clay pipe that had been propped against the chair leg. A thin trail of smoke rose from the bowl. 'Then stand and state your business.' The pipe was thrust into her mouth and her lips worked to transform the trickle of smoke into a plume. 'But first I would know your name.'

'Jonas Flynt.'

She displayed no sign of recognising his name, which didn't surprise him for he was seldom in this part in London. 'So, Mr Flynt, you speak of my son, what of him?'

'I seek him and I wondered if you would have any knowledge of his current location?'

She puffed at the pipe, the aroma of the tobacco filling the air between them. 'I hope this smoke causes you no irritation, sir. The baccy is not the best quality but it burns well and heats me from within.' Her lips worked at the stem for a moment. 'So tell me, what has Nimrod Boone done?'

Interesting. She didn't say he was dead. And she seemed to know that he was guilty of something.

'I am an old comrade from Flanders, seeking him out to pay a debt owed these long years.'

He had decided that he would shield her from the true nature of his inquiry, for no mother needs to hear such tidings about her son. Her eyes narrowed again, perhaps against the smoke that drifted from the pipe bowl or perhaps because she sensed his prevarication. His vision was now fully accustomed to the brown glow of the candle so he could see that, like the building around them, she had once been handsome but the years had not been kind. Her face was leathered, her upper lip criss-crossed with wrinkles, as was the flesh around her eyes. Her jowls had sagged but her cheeks had narrowed. Only the alert gaze retained that hint of the woman she may have once been.

'You must ask his cousin, Caleb,' she said finally. 'He is someone of influence now, up there in the city. He will help you.'

'I have,' Flynt said, 'but he seemed to think he was dead.'

She displayed no emotion at that thought. 'But you don't believe him, elsewise you wouldn't be standing before me now.'

'Let me say that I am thorough.'

Amusement danced in her eyes. 'Aye, I wouldn't believe Caleb Boone either, for the truth would be stranger to his lips,' she said, and the bitter tang coating her words amplified her obvious lack of affection for her nephew. 'Caleb and Nimrod, fine names for men such as they, but then their fathers were also blessed with names from holy writ. Abaddon, Nimrod's father, and Elijah, he who sired Caleb, were by their own proclamation deeply Christian men, as was their father and his father.' She snorted. 'Deeply Christian but not a drop of Christian charity did they possess. Abaddon, God damn his eternal soul, would spout catechism even as he tupped me or when he beat me, and you can take my word as gospel that there was little to choose between the two activities.' She puffed at her pipe, once again fixing those keen eyes on him. 'And you owe Nimrod a debt, you say?'

'Aye. He saved my life in battle but we lost touch when the war ended, I was wounded most severe. I feel it my duty to at least thank him for his service.'

'Saved your life, he did? That would be a most unusual experience for Nimrod, to be sure.'

Flynt felt a thrill of anticipation. He had expected this woman to be circumspect but she seemed most open about her son and his cousin.

Her gaze reverted towards the window. 'Cruelty ran through that boy like a deep well. He got such from his father, who was an evil man. My father didn't want us sisters to marry the Boones, but we did. Prudence, Caleb's mother, was my sister, did you know that?'

'I didn't.'

'She's gone to her reward, God rest her and keep her in His embrace. We were from a good family, a decent family, our father was a cooper by trade and a true God-fearing man was he, and the Boone boys came by full of charm and trumpeting their faith like they were apostles of the Lord. Good-looking they were, handsome boys both of them, Abaddon fair and Elijah dark, just as Nimrod and Caleb took after them. But fair of face can mask darkness of soul and my sister and I soon learned the truth of that.'

Flynt let her speak, for he felt that she didn't have much in the way of conversation with anyone other than her own thoughts. She kept her eyes on the window but he knew she didn't see through the shutters to the building opposite or the fluttering candle flame on the sill but into a past of pain and disappointment.

'Nimrod began life as a sweet child, a beautiful child, a lovely fair-haired angel. Do you know he cried but once in my sight, 'cept when he first drew breath in this world? It was over a stray kitten that he'd taken to feeding. He loved that creature. But he found it dead one morning, just beyond our door. That broke him, it did, and he wailed and wailed. Abaddon watched and I saw in his eyes that he was the one who had killed the poor little thing, just before he took a strap to the boy's back for showing weakness. It was after that I began to see a change in him. His father, it is, that I blame. The cruelty he issued, the rage, the beatings, for when he wasn't laying on at me he was at Nimrod, right from when he was a little one. Aye, and more than violence, of that I am sure, for Abaddon was a man of secret passions and vices, which he slaked with his own son. My lovely angel died to be replaced with something that was other. There are young 'uns who have to have the devil beaten out of them, but Nimrod?' She sucked on her pipe, shook her head, stared at the dark window. 'It was as if his father had beaten the devil into him until the dark one had hold of the boy. When I looked in his eyes it wasn't anything of me no more that I saw looking back. It wasn't even his father, may he rot. What looked out of those eyes was not human, I swear to you on the soul of my dead sister, God rest her and keep her in His loving embrace. It was pure evil. And sometimes it convulsed him, made him shiver and shake most uncontrollably. I would see him on the floor of our lodgings – not here, we didn't live in this hellish place, not then, for Abaddon could steal sufficiently to afford better surroundings – and he'd be rolling around, shivering and shaking, with the most filthy phrases issuing from his mouth and other times speaking in languages that I couldn't identify. It was the devil within him that caused that. It was the devil that made him commit murder.'

'Who did he murder?'

'I only know of one for certain. He had taken to carrying with him a knife and sometimes I would see him washing it in the gutter. But the one I know as fact was his own father, not that he didn't deserve it, as it be true that the devil takes his own. Nimrod cut his throat while he slept off a bottle of rum, cut it clean through, as like he intended to take it right off. Nimrod fled that night, wasn't seen here for many a long year.'

That was when he was able to evade the law by joining the army, Flynt surmised. Charters had been correct.

'But you have seen him, am I right?' he asked.

Patience sucked at her pipe for a moment. 'I've seen him, but once. The years had changed him. He was still slight, but there was another look in his eye, one that told me he had grown comfortable with what he had become.'

'When was this?'

'It were two months since, at least. He came by, not as the dutiful son to pay his respects for his mother, but in search of Caleb. I thought when he stood upon that threshold that he had come to do for me as he did for his father, and to tell you true that might be a blessing.'

'Where had he been?'

'On foreign shores, was all he said and I asked no further. I knew he had done terrible things while away, I could sense it hanging in the air between us. When I told him that Caleb was up Rookery way he left and I haven't seen him since. I don't want to, either, for though he be born of my loins there is nothing left to love.'

There was sadness coated on this final words and Flynt felt sorrow for a woman whose life had turned out in a way the girl within had never planned.

'I regret to hear that, madam.'

She studied him through the smoke again. 'I sense sincerity there, Jonas Flynt, and I thank you for it, but my life is my own doing. I defied my father and took Abaddon Boone to husband. I could have fled when the life he promised me turned out to be nothing more than the smoke from this here pipe, vanishing into the dark like it wasn't ever there, but I didn't, so don't pity me, Jonas Flynt, for I am a wicked, wilful old woman who has been too long upon this earth. But I pray you do me one favour.'

'Name it, madam.'

She favoured him with another long appraising look, taking in the greatcoat, the boots, the silver cane he held along with his hat. He fancied she could see through that coat to the pistols concealed within. She took a deep breath and removed the pipe from her lips. 'I know you lie when you say you seek Nimrod Boone to repay a debt.' She held her free hand up when he made to speak. 'No, sir, I do not condemn you for it. I know not the true why of your need to find him and I do not wish to know, for there has been an abundance of pain in my life. So my favour is this: when you do find Nimrod Boone, I would appreciate it if you would give him the rest he needs. God forgive me for the thought, but the sweetest child that ever sucked a tit is no more. Give him rest, I implore you, and I pray he will be folded into the Lord's embrace.'

First Charters, then the Admiral and now Patience Boone had urged him to kill the same man. If Nimrod Boone was truly guilty of the murders of the Berthon family, then he would happily oblige. As for the Lord's embrace, if Flynt believed in such things he would have doubted that likely. But he saw the hope shining in her eyes and he nodded his assent.

He replaced his hat. 'I thank you for your assistance, madam.' He produced a handful of coins from his pocket. 'For your inconvenience...'

She waved his largesse away. 'I will not take your money, Jonas Flynt, for there was no inconvenience and I have not provided any service. In truth, I was grateful for the company, even though it be for a short time only. I see few now. Some old friends but they dwindle in number most rapidly, the landlord of this palace but he's scum.' She cast her eyes to the ceiling and Flynt presumed the owner of the building occupied the upper floor. 'Time was he pestered me for my favours and I granted them, God help me, for in return he would give me some makings for the fire and a few paltry victuals for the pot, but not now. I'm too old now, and he would not touch me with some other man's roger, says he.' She made a tutting noise. 'It wasn't much a thing, to tell you true, but I do miss that firewood and victuals.'

He made his goodbye and left her seated in her chair, once again staring towards the window, and reliving a past that perhaps she wished had been different. But the past cannot be changed, it can only be endured.

In the hallway he hesitated for a moment, his gaze taking in the flight of stairs to the upper floor. He wished to get back to the city. He should not interfere. Nevertheless, he climbed those stairs to the top floor where there was but one door, which he banged with the flat edge of his clenched fist, then drew the blade from his cane. Footfalls approached and the door opened to reveal the corpulent figure of a man, his bald pate dotted with brown flecks, his clothes of decent quality but careworn, a lantern held in his free hand to illuminate the hallway.

'Who bangs my door as if...'

The man's eyes widened as the tip of Flynt's blade tickled his throat. 'You are the owner of this hovel?'

The man nodded, the movement delicate lest the steel slice his flesh. 'I am, sir, but there is no need to...'

Flynt prodded him slightly with the sword point to propel him back into the apartment, which was considerably larger than that occupied by Patience Boone and in daylight would be exceedingly better lit thanks to a large skylight. The candles that were dotted around joined the lamp in the man's hand to illuminate the entire room. It was well furnished, if somewhat cheaply, with painted floorcloths relieving the tedium of bare wood and on a table beside a comfortable winged armchair a book lay face down with a half-empty glass of wine beside it. The woman below could not read in the light of her single candle nub and she could not afford to burn two. Flynt's jaw tightened as he scanned his surroundings but there was no other person present, though another door undoubtedly led to at least one further room.

'Your name,' Flynt demanded.

'Shuttleworth, Howard Shuttleworth,' the man replied, swallowing hard, his meaty fingers trembling as they reached towards the blade but then came to a halt at chest level. 'If you come to rob me I should tell you that I have nothing of value, for I am a poor man and...'

'Be silent and listen to me most intently, Howard Shuttleworth,' Flynt said, stepping towards the table, the tip of the sword still at his throat meaning the man had no choice but to back away to match his movement. Flynt dropped the coins he had been about to offer Patience beside the book. 'You are to look after the lady below...'

'The lady below? You mean the Boone woman?'

'I mean the Boone woman. You will supply her with wood for the fire and with food for the pot.' He looked at the abundance of candles around him. 'And you will give her a goodly number of candles, good ones, ones that burn bright and burn long. And you will continue to do so until you have exhausted these funds, do you understand?'

The man's eyes had fixed on the money and he nodded.

'And don't even consider taking this coin and not doing as I say, for I will return, and if I find you have reneged on our compact then it will go badly for you, do you understand?'

Another nod, most fervent this time.

'And one more thing, you will treat her with respect, for she has earned it.'

Something like courage rose in Shuttleworth's eyes and lifted his top lip in a sneer. 'Earned respect? She's been nothing but a cheap bunter these many years...'

He might have said more but he recoiled when Flynt whipped the blade away, stepped closer and delivered a back-handed slap to his face. Even though the hand was gloved, the blow was firm, its report like a gunshot. 'Better than you have had to live that life, you had best mind that, Howard Shuttleworth, for if you don't we shall have a conversation in future that requires no words.'

Shuttleworth stammered an apology while rubbing his cheek where it bloomed red. Flynt stared at him for a moment then sheathed the sword and turned away.

'Begging your pardon, sir,' Shuttleworth said, 'but what are you to that bun... that lady? And what is your name?'

Flynt didn't turn as he stepped through the open door. 'I'm friend to her, is all you need to know.' And in the darkness of the hallway he smiled, for he knew Shuttleworth could no longer see him, but could hear his voice. 'And you can call me Paladin.'

He knew he should not have added that, but even so, a laugh built as he descended the stairs.

17

He couldn't say what it was that made his scalp prickle as he neared the bottom of the stairs. Whatever it was, instinct, some supernatural premonition perhaps that required none of Mrs Fairfax's painted boards, he made sure that he was prepared before stepping from the entranceway of the tenement building into the night-shrouded street.

They awaited him under the shelter of the jetty opposite, the Ratty and two others flanking him, rough looking individuals with faces that were no stranger to blow or blade. Flynt paused in the doorway, his cane in his right hand but held upwards to tap on his shoulder as he appraised Ratty's companions with a practised eye. Neither of them were likely to turn the head of a lady, unless it was in the other direction. One had a scar of a vintage no more than a few months running from forehead to chin, making his left eyelid droop a little, the flesh still a little raw. The other had a nose that was squashed and the hollowness of his cheeks in an otherwise broad face suggested he had lost most of his teeth. Flynt recognised them as adequate thumpers, perhaps even capable of murder.

'We knowed you would come see the old girl,' said Ratty, baring his little teeth in what might have been a smile if it wasn't so unpleasant. 'And we kept watch for your arrival. Caleb Boone wishes to be seeing you, Flynt.'

'I'm flattered,' said Flynt.

'We is here to fetch you to him.'

'And if I don't appreciate being fetched?'

Ratty revealed his pointed teeth again. Had Flynt been faced with an actual rodent, he would have been disturbed, but that wasn't the case. He had taken an instant dislike to the man, and all he wanted to do was pound that sharp little face for a time.

'Then we would have to be forcing you, wouldn't we?' Ratty said, his tone suggesting a desire that they be afforded such an opportunity.

'That is something I wouldn't advise,' Flynt warned.

Ratty looked to his friends. Scarface's hand under his coat was neither scratching flea bites nor warming his fingers. Toothless allowed a hefty club to slide into his palm from his sleeve.

'We is three to your one,' Ratty pointed out, and Flynt was impressed by the fact that he hadn't required the use of his fingers to reach the tally. 'The odds is in our favour.'

'Others have thought similar and have lost the wager.'

Flynt had the measure of this man. He would not come at him; he would allow the other two to do that. He had seen such as he before. They talked and they talked but when words led to action, they hung back to observe from a safe distance and only moved in for the kill when the victim was incapacitated. Sure enough, Ratty made a signal with his finger and Scarface began to draw a pistol from his coat while Toothless crouched in preparation of an attack.

They both froze when Flynt raised his left hand to reveal Diplomacy, which he had drawn before he stepped into the street and hidden in the folds of his own coat, while, with a jerk of his right wrist, he sent the silver case of his cane flying to reveal the blade, having already twisted it free. Scarface hadn't even cleared his pistol from his belt but it would take only a moment to jerk it free, so Flynt ensured he kept a close eye on him, ready for any sign that he might intend to do so, at which point he wouldn't hesitate to put a ball in him. Toothless would be slower in crossing the distance between them and so he was confident he could take him down with his sword. Neither man displayed appetite for any such action, however.

'Well, gentlemen, here we are,' said Flynt. 'What say we cool our passions, eh? Before I am forced to cool at least one of you permanent. You, friend, take your hand off that barker and with the other ease it out with finger and thumb only.'

Scarface was astute enough to do as he was bid. Flynt flicked his pistol from side to side.

'Now, set it down and kick it into yonder puddle.'

The man protested. 'It's my barker, I needs it.'

'Then you should be more careful upon whom you threaten to draw it. Drop it or I'll drop you.'

The man reluctantly placed the pistol on the ground and nudged it with his foot.

A slight change in stance from Toothless brought a warning look from Flynt. 'You, let the cudgel fall and kick it away also.'

Toothless did as he was told with considerable enthusiasm. Meanwhile, Ratty had backed away as far as he could and was looking for an avenue of escape when he became aware of Flynt's glare upon him.

'And as for you, Ratty, you will remain as immobile as a statue for now.'

The man froze, his palms flat upon the wall of the building behind him, his eyes blinking at speed.

Flynt flicked Diplomacy at the pistol on the ground and again addressed Scarface. 'A little more energy, if you please. Into the water with it.'

Scarface gave the weapon a harder push to slide it across the dirt into the puddle, which was of sufficient depth to cover it almost completely. The powder within would soon be rendered useless.

'Do you have further weaponry?' The man shook his head. Flynt didn't believe him but he wasn't about to narrow the distance between them to check. 'Button your coat,' Flynt instructed, and the man did as he was told, ensuring that the need to unfasten would impede him sufficiently to give Flynt an extra few moments of warning.

'Both of you raise your hands and keep them raised.'

The men did so.

'Now, I want you to walk fifteen paces that way and then stop,' Flynt twitched his pistol to the left, 'but remain where I can see you, your backs towards me. If you speak to each other, if you even look at each other, if you glance over your shoulder, then I will kill you.'

The men shuffled away and Flynt monitored their every move, prepared to act if they made any move to turn back. Ratty stepped after them but Flynt brought his pistol to bear on him. 'No, Ratty, you remain where you are.'

The man bristled at the name, showing some defiance, perhaps because Flynt had touched a nerve concerning his physical appearance. 'My name ain't Ratty.'

'My apologies,' said Flynt, 'it was an easy mistake to make. Do me the service of retrieving my sheath, there's a good fellow.'

The man's sharp eyes cast around in the gloom and finally alighted on the silver cane. He eagerly stooped to pick it up.

'Slowly, now,' said Flynt, extending his sword and turning the pistol on him, 'slide it over the blade. I urge you not to try anything underhand and force me to do something that you might regret.'

Ratty gingerly eased the scabbard into place then returned to his refuge against the wall.

Flynt thrust the cane into his belt, produced Tact and trained it on Ratty's head, while swivelling Diplomacy back in the direction of the two men who had so far followed his instructions. 'Now, Ratty, why don't you take me to see Mr Boone.'

The man's expression changed from resentment to surprise, then confusion. 'Eh? I don't get you, I don't. You said you wasn't going to come see him.'

'No, I said I didn't wish to be fetched,' Flynt said, for he did desire further conversation with Caleb Boone. 'I like it to be my idea.'

–

The one face Flynt didn't expect to see on his return to the Rookery was that of Lombre. The one-eyed man didn't see him, for Flynt was ensconced within a coach that had waited for them on King Street beyond the abbey. It had kindly been provided by Caleb Boone, a touch perhaps learned from the Admiral. Lombre emerged from the narrow street that led to the Rat's Castle just as the coach slowed to a halt. Flynt placed his hand on the door to pursue but then realised Ratty's beady little eyes were upon him so forced himself to relax and look elsewhere. He was frustrated, however, for he was aware he might not have such an opportunity again, but he could not let this man know of his interest. As they alighted from the vehicle, the lane being too narrow to carry the coach, Flynt allowed himself what he hoped was a nonchalant gaze in the direction Lombre had travelled but he had vanished from sight.

The fact that he was walking away from the Rat's Castle troubled him. Was it possible he was meeting Boone? He could simply be taking refuge within the Rookery, for it was easy for a man to vanish if he so chose within its tangle of streets and alleys. But if he truly was rendezvousing with Boone, what would be the purpose? What business would he have with a street rogue from the Rookery?

He made Ratty walk ahead of him. He didn't think the man was dangerous unless he gave him his back, but he kept his pistol to hand though again hidden within the folds of his coat. The Rookery was lawless but it didn't do to walk its streets with naked weaponry. As they entered the Castle, which was as lively as a fair, Flynt surreptitiously replaced his pistol in his belt, for it being visible would not be countenanced by the landlord and his watchers. Ratty shot an inquiring look to the bully behind the bar, who jerked his head to the room in which Flynt had first met Boone.

Ratty opened the door and stepped within. 'I has him, Caleb,' he announced, as if he were Columbus making landfall.

Boone was in the same chair as before, Harry stooped over him as though they had been in conversation. He straightened, his hand already resting on his pistol, but Boone smiled. 'I grew to half believe that you would not have encountered Mr Flynt, or that you, Mr Flynt, would refuse to come.'

'What can I say, Mr Boone?' Flynt said. 'Ratty here was most gracious in his invitation, so how could I refuse?'

Ratty shot him a look that was at first grateful but then became a glare over the continued use of the disparaging title.

Boone looked past them to the open door then at his man. 'Where are Thomas and Robert? They haven't tarried at the bar, have they? You know I don't like my people drinking when there is work to be done.'

Flynt replied on Ratty's behalf. 'They decided they would rather walk back.'

Boone let that sink in for but a brief moment. 'And that would have been your idea, would it not, Mr Flynt?'

'I thought perhaps they could use the exercise. They had to return to Sanctuary to retrieve their weapons in any case.'

Amusement glinted in John's eyes as he shot a glance at Harry.

Boone was not so amused. 'You disarmed them?'

'It seemed like the wisest course of action under the circumstances, as they had indicated their desire to do me harm.'

This information seemed to please both John and Harry, leading Flynt to suspect that there was no love lost between them and Scarface and Toothless. Professional rivalry, perhaps, or even disdain for the men's crude methods. At any rate, Flynt was certain he would not have vanquished them as easily.

John stepped forward, his hand outstretched. 'While we is on the subject, I'll have them fine barkers, if you please, Mr Flynt.'

'Not this day, John,' said Flynt with a shake of the head.

All amusement vanished and the man's hand edged towards the weapon in his belt. Harry followed suit. Surrendering his weapons as a matter of course for the Admiral was one thing, as they enjoyed mutual respect and even some form of friendship, but to do the same for Boone was not a hand Flynt would play. 'You requested my presence, Mr Boone. You will forgive me if I remained prepared for any eventuality.'

'You are safe within the Castle,' Boone said, 'for as you know the landlord and his men take a poor view of any unpleasantness on the premises and that is a propriety that even I respect. Was it not Cicero who said that even thieves have laws which they obey?'

Despite his suspicion as to his motives for lying about his cousin, and now the possibility that he had some association with Lombre, Flynt was impressed by Boone's erudition. 'He did indeed, and as I also respect it, does that not mean that you are, in turn and by house rule, safe from me?'

Boone smiled and jerked his head to order John to step back. Harry also relaxed, but the hands of both men never strayed far from their own weapons.

Boone sat back in his chair. He was most at home here and gave the impression that he was master of all he surveyed. 'The fact you are here tells me you saw the old woman.'

'I saw Patience Boone, your aunt, yes.'

'She is well then?'

'As well as she can be without the sustenance of her family.'

Boone's eyes flashed, just briefly, but then he smiled. 'You rebuke me?'

'I state a fact.'

'She is not likely to accept any assistance from me.'

'Was it ever offered?'

Boone's sigh told him that no such offer had been made. 'What did she tell you?'

'That her son lives.'

This was not unexpected to Boone. 'I thought she might. Perhaps I should have sent my friend here to explain to her the meaning of family loyalty.'

Flynt glanced at Ratty, who sniggered as if imagining how he would tutor the woman. 'Then he would have had to hush her, for my take of her character is that she would not oblige. She is a strong woman.'

'She is a headstrong woman.'

'She would have to be in order to survive the tender ministrations of her husband and the travails visited upon her by her son's violent nature.'

That flash of anger once again, then quashed. 'She told you much when you were with her.'

'That she did.'

'I would not set too much store upon all that she says. Patience Boone likes to present the appearance of martyr, but she was no innocent. Abaddon Boone was not a saint, it is true, but she was guilty of crimes as much as he. Did she tell you how she and he met?'

'She merely said that he came by with your father and swept she and her sister off their feet.'

Boone laughed. 'They were good, decent women, corrupted by my father and his brother, correct? Their father a God-fearing man?'

'A cooper, she said.'

'Aye, that much be true, as was the God-fearing part, but Patience and Prudence were far from decent women. They were both wild girls with a liking for the tupping. Their father banished them from his house and that was when they met Abaddon and my father.'

The woman had perhaps thought it necessary to make her past more palatable to avoid judgement, but it made no difference to Flynt.

'My point is that you should not believe everything she told you,' Boone said.

'I believe her when she said your cousin still lives. And I will admit to curiosity as to why you wished me to believe he was dead.'

Boone chose not to reply. 'Perhaps it be best that you tell me exactly why you seek him. And please, Mr Flynt, no tales of an old army comrade seeing him in the street, for that will not wash with me.'

'Nevertheless, it is partly true. I was retained by someone with whom he served, but who admittedly did not see him in the street. He does, however, have reason to believe your cousin is in London.'

'And what is that reason?'

Flynt quickly assessed how much of the truth he should tell, deciding in the end to be frank. 'You will be aware, no doubt, of the murders in Whitechapel?'

'It is the talk of the streets, even here in the Rookery.'

'Nimrod may have been responsible.'

Flynt had been purposely blunt, for he wished to see what reaction it brought. Boone, though, kept his true feelings guarded. 'He is capable of such, most certainly.'

'He is. He committed similar slaughter before, in Flanders.'

Again, no show of surprise. 'As I said, he is decidedly capable.'

Flynt waited for him to speak further but Boone remained silent. 'Two children were murdered most brutally in Whitechapel.'

'I know.'

'And this does not disturb you? We are rogues, you and I, but I refer you to Cicero. We have rules and the murder of innocents is proscribed.'

'I know this too.'

'Then if you know where Nimrod is you must tell me before there is further atrocity.'

Boone said nothing for a second or two before he rose and walked to a table beside a stairway to the left. A wooden box sat on its side and upon it was a decanter of fine crystal filled with red wine and two matching goblets. Both retained traces of having been used previously. Had one of them recently been touched to Lombre's lips? Flynt longed to question Boone on that matter but instinct held him back. It was doubtful that Boone would confirm any meeting and it was best Flynt did not show his hand yet. He needed to know more.

'Would you care for a glass?' Boone asked, most politely. 'It is an exceedingly fine claret, straight off the boat from France.'

And delivered here by Lombre, perhaps.

'I will not, but I will have an answer to my query,' Flynt said. 'Come, Boone, surely you have not lost your humanity? Tell me where your cousin is and let me stop him before more innocent blood is shed.'

Boone poured himself a goblet of wine. 'You are executioner now, Jonas Flynt?'

'When I have to be. Now, where is he?'

Boone carried the goblet to the chair and took his seat once more. He sipped it and held it up to the lamplight. 'It is a fine drop of

Bordeaux, this. Over the years I have developed a taste for the finer things and I will have them.'

Flynt fought his exasperation to hold his silence.

'You have no doubt made inquiry of me, as I have of you,' Boone said. 'I'm a rogue, as you say, as are you, but you settle unwillingly into the life, though you are most accomplished at both the thieving and the hushing of men from what I am told. I, on the other hand, am unapologetic in my roguery. It is what I am and it is what I do and I am also skilled at the game. I take it none of this is news to you.'

'No. I have also heard you have ambitions to break out of the Rookery.'

Boone shrugged. 'That may or may not be true. We shall see. Patience, my dear aunt, may have been most promiscuous in her desires but she never fully accepted that the family into which she married was on the flash side, though she was happy enough when it put bread on the table, and, as I said, she was on occasion art and part in the execution of the crime, though she deluded herself that she wasn't. It is that flash side of the family which still does support her, for who do you think pays the rent for her room? Certainly not her.'

'I take it that you pay it?'

'I did not offer assistance but I provided it, and more, for her comforts.'

'She has precious little of that. She has no fuel and no food and the room is only slightly better than the street.'

Boone took this in with a slight puckering of his lips and then gave John a glance. 'I have little affection for her, but she is family. My mother loved her and I loved my mother so in her memory I have sent funds most regular to her landlord. It would seem he merely pockets my coin and does not use it for its true purpose. I think a visit to Shuttleworth is necessary, John.'

John nodded his assent and Flynt took some satisfaction in the knowledge that the proposed visit would be far from pleasurable for the landlord.

'And what of Nimrod?'

Boone's mouth downturned and his tone grew mournful. 'I regret that poor Nimrod was always… different, shall we say? Perhaps even difficult.'

'Where is he, Boone?'

A sigh as he drained the glass and handed it to Ratty. 'He didn't die across the Channel, you are correct. He did return to London. He lives yet. I said he was dead and he might as well be.' His raised his eyes to fix them firmly upon Flynt's own. 'This is not easy for me to say as I loved that man like a brother. It pains me, Mr Flynt, pains me most grievous. Nimrod's *difficulties* finally got the better of him, I am sorry to say.' He took a deep breath. 'He is quite mad, irredeemably so, but he didn't kill that family, for he couldn't. My cousin Nimrod is at this moment within Bedlam, where I had him committed for his own good and that of the rest of us, for his confusions and difficulties have made him most unbalanced. If you seek him, you will find him in the Palace Beautiful in Moorfields. He is in Bedlam, Flynt, where he is kept under lock and key and constant supervision…'

18

Flynt was especially vigilant while making his way back through Seven Dials and onto St Martin's Lane. He reached the Golden Cross, confident that nobody had shadowed him, and entered through the rear door, nodding to Mrs Wilkes as she carried a tray of oysters and ale from the kitchen.

'Your friend has returned,' she said as she passed. 'I placed him in the parlour once again. Very nice gentleman, he is, most mannerly. Not like some of the coves what come see you here, Jonas.'

The last line was delivered with a smile. Flynt had been visited by some colourful characters indeed, one of the reasons he would have to give serious consideration to moving on. However, that did not concern him at that moment, for his mind was set upon the return of Daniel Defoe. He steeled himself for the encounter as he made his way through the web of corridors to the small room at the front, where the gentleman was seated in the same chair, another bottle of wine at his elbow, as before scribbling with his carpenter's graphite pencil in the calfskin pocket notebook.

He stood as Flynt entered, his smile genuine. 'Ah, good to see you again, my friend, especially as I now know a little more about you.'

Flynt didn't find that particularly reassuring and said so.

Defoe held out his hand. 'Fear not, I today had a most enlightening discourse with our mutual friend, formerly of the military but still in service, if you understand my meaning.'

Flynt became even more guarded but nevertheless clasped Defoe's hand. He detected a difference in the writer's manner but he remained reserved concerning the colonel. Defoe was a journalist and as such would be skilled in artifice in order to garner information.

'Please, seat yourself,' said Defoe, waving to the chair opposite, 'take a glass with me.'

Flynt remained standing. 'I regret it has been a long day, sir, and I am for my bed.'

'Come, my friend, have no fear. I have given my friend Charters an undertaking not to pursue the matter of the Paladin and my word, especially to that man, is as safe as Mr Paterson's Bank of England.' When Flynt still hesitated, Defoe lowered his voice. 'I pledge upon my honour that the matter you and I discussed last evening, and whatever we discuss this night, will remain between us. After all, we are both keeping *company*, shall we say?'

The secretive little smile told Flynt that Defoe also knew of the Company of Rogues. He sat down and waited while Defoe poured a glass of wine and handed it to him.

'How can I help you, Mr Defoe,' Flynt said, his tone still cautious.

'Dan, please, call me Dan. And I will call you Jonas.'

Flynt tilted his head in acknowledgement and sipped at the wine. It was one of Mrs Wilkes' better vintages.

'We shall be stout friends, you and I, that is my belief and it be most firm,' Defoe said, his voice animated. 'For, by my truth, I have never before had acquaintance of a fellow toiler on behalf of this great nation, the good colonel being most opaque as to those others who do his bidding.'

Flynt kept his counsel and that provoked a laugh. 'By God, Jonas, you are a canny one, and that is no jest. A typical Scot, I would say. Laconic to the point of taciturnity. You must take your ease, for I am here to offer my assistance in whatever way you feel necessary.'

'I thank you, Mr Defoe...'

'Dan.'

'I thank you, Dan, but I have no need of assistance.'

'Perhaps not now, of course, but at some time in the future. If it is Colonel Charters who concerns you then let me put your mind at rest. He and I are old friends and, as I have intimated, I have performed tasks for him and his...' His eyes darted to the door, as if ensuring it was closed. '...Company many times in the past and I shall do so again, mark me. I know not on what business he has you currently employed but I am sure it is of the utmost importance and I would pledge my faith and my honour to your assistance.'

'Thank you, Mr... Dan,' said Jonas, still unsure of the ground on which he currently stood, and wishing to steer it to a firmer footing. It was clear that Charters had discussed the Paladin with Defoe, so there was something regarding that Flynt would wish to know. 'In relation to our subject of last evening...'

'The Paladin, yes,' Defoe said, taking a drink. 'You wish to know from whom I heard the name, am I correct?'

Defoe was no fool. 'I do.'

'Understandable, my dear Jonas, and as we are brothers in arms, so to speak, I have no hesitation in revealing my source, although I denied same to the good colonel earlier today. We are friends, he and I, but I find it most advisable to keep some information from him. What do you say to that?'

Flynt nodded his agreement. He had also failed to be fully open and frank with Charters in the past. 'So who was it that told you, Dan?'

'It were a lady, a most comely one at that. If I were not devoted to my Mary then I would have most enjoyed a tumble with her, if she were willing.'

'And did this lady have a name?'

'Aye, French it were in sound, though she herself be not of Gallic birth, for there is a cast to her voice that you might recognise if you were to hear it...' He stopped suddenly and tilted his head to study Flynt carefully. As a writer he would be alert to any slight change in expression or demeanour. 'I see something in your eye, Jonas. You know this woman?'

'I think I may. Did she have a companion?'

'She most certainly did, a large fellow, who was as silent as the grave and my feeling was he had been responsible for consigning many a poor soul into theirs.'

'Was he wanting of a hand, but now had one of wood?'

'He was indeed, but though the flesh, bone and blood had been replaced by an artificial limb, it was most certainly not of wood. It is of iron, covered in a glove to be sure, but most cunning in design, for it makes use of levers and springs in order to fashion a grip. The lady had him display its function for me and it be most ingenious, though by my faith certainly most unnerving to gaze upon. So you do know this most unlikely pair?'

'The lady is Madame Christian de Fontaine, correct?'

'God's truth, Jonas, you do know her!'

Flynt couldn't help a smile from teasing his lips. 'Our paths have crossed. The silent man is Gregor, who was once part of the Russian royal guard, and he once near throttled me in a room in Southwark with that hand, though I was certain that it had then been fashioned of wood.'

'That be the beauty, I hazard, of such artifice, for it can be changed if desired.' He held up his own hand. 'We must by God's grace live with the hand we are dealt.'

Flynt saw the logic in that but on balance he preferred to retain all his limbs. 'I would be most grateful if you would tell me where I can find her.'

'I will do that right gladly, from one defender of the nation to another. She is in Leicester House, as guest of the Prince and Princess of Wales…'

-

Walter Newell didn't know, on that damp winter night, it would be the last time he entered his home. He didn't know it would be the last time he would kiss his wife and talk to his children and sit down at the table and eat pork and sup wine and smile and laugh with his family. He didn't know all this for it is not the way of existence that a person has precognition of his own mortality. He was only thirty-three, after all, his wife five years his junior, his two boys ten and eight years. But on that damp winter night they all faced death's cold stare.

It was a house full of life and love and when he closed that front door he left the work he did for Jonathan Wild behind. He wasn't happy with what he did, but he reasoned that he was a mere keeper of records and not involved in the actual acts that necessitated those records being kept. A bookkeeper's world was one of figures, not deeds, and though he knew that Mr Wild was responsible for many things that did not bear scrutiny, he could keep them at least the length of a quill from him by concentrating on the numbers.

But numbers didn't save him. Numbers couldn't protect his family from what was to befall them that night.

He didn't know how the man got in, for he hadn't heard any noise. He first realised that something was amiss was while he was preparing to retire in the cramped bedroom he shared with his wife. The children had been abed for some time and his wife Judith below was clearing away dishes. He heard her footfall on the stairs, a strange dragging sort of noise, and he pulled his nightshirt on hurriedly to step to the door just as it swung open and she staggered in, her eyes wide, one hand outstretched to him, the other clutching her breast where streamed dark blood. He cried out in horror and caught her as she stumbled into his arms, her body bucking as she issued a disturbing choking noise.

And then he saw the man, just briefly as he looked to the door, but not enough to register anything but a smile and swinging movement of his hand followed by a sharp searing pain at his own throat. He dropped his wife, he didn't mean to, he didn't want to, but he dropped her and fell backwards himself, one hand reflexively darting to his own throat as if it could stem the blood, but he knew even in his terror that he would die soon and his thoughts were of his children. He must have spoken of them for the man's face swam before him, the smile intact, and now he saw his scalp was bare, his face scarred.

'Worry not, friend Newell,' the man said, 'for I will attend to your little ones right sharpish. You and your wife will see them again soon...'

Walter Newell felt fingers pat his cheek as if in affection before the man turned towards the door, the long blade dangling in one hand. The last thing Walter Newell saw was his wife's glazed eyes as he reached to clasp her hand but not quite making it. The last thing he heard was the man whistling...

19

Flynt spent a disturbed night, his mind roiling with thoughts of Lombre and Boone, Madame de Fontaine and Gregor. He had no firm evidence of the agent's connection to the Rookery upright man but he felt in his gut that there was one. The reason behind it remained clouded, though the suggestion that Boone had influential backers in his bid to amend to the criminal hierarchy of the city did cause something vague and shadowy to grow. Influential backers could suggest the hand of the Fellowship at work.

As for Christy, what business she might have with the son and daughter-in-law of King George could only be guessed at, though he would wager his last crown that whatever reason she had to be near to them it was nefarious. Her presence in London at the same time as Lombre might be coincidence but he thought not. Flynt's mind leaped back to that night near the Tower, when Lombre had him at his mercy. He had been struck from behind by someone powerful, someone who could have been Gregor. While hovering between consciousness and otherwise, he had detected a scent and heard three sets of footsteps moving away. And then there was Lombre's statement that he had friends who didn't wish to see him harmed. Christy de Fontaine was extremely mercurial in her allegiances but she had only once tried to have him killed and that was when they first met. Since then she had proclaimed affection for him, in her innately flirtatious way, but he had no doubt that if it suited her purposes she would not hesitate to have him assassinated. She would regret it, he was certain, but she would do it. As he would her.

And then his mind flitted back to Nimrod Boone, committed to Bethlem Hospital by his own cousin, after he had taken a frenzy and almost killed not only Caleb Boone himself but also the man Flynt had dubbed Scarface. They had moved to prevent him from doing murder to a bobtail by the name of Kate Miller, who had importuned him while Nimrod had been supping ale in the Rat's Castle. Old Jury had made reference to the incident but had not mentioned the Boones' involvement.

'He had been most morose that evening,' Caleb had said, 'and who can say what dark thoughts stalked what remained of his reason, for the poor girl had no sooner invited him upstairs for a tupping than he launched himself at her, drawing a blade that even I didn't know he had upon his person. He had already severed an ear and would have opened her throat if Thomas had not pulled him free, receiving the mark upon his face that you will no doubt have observed earlier. It took the combined strength of myself, John and Harry to subdue my poor cousin. As we have already discussed, the landlord of this establishment will not tolerate violence upon the premises and he was all for summary execution in the alley beyond this room. Believe me, such action has been taken before. But blood is blood, Mr Flynt, and I interceded on poor Nimrod's behalf, pleading for his life. It was not something I enjoyed, for I am not a man to beg as you might gather, but I did on this occasion. The Castle is close to sacred ground and we need such a safe space in our world, but I was successful in my entreaty, though only on the condition that Nimrod would not be allowed to roam the streets. And so it was with deep regret that I entrusted his poor, deranged mind to the learned physics of Bedlam. And there he rests, Mr Flynt, in the incurable ward, his true mind detached from his soul, lost in whatever hell he finds himself in.'

When Flynt awoke, far from refreshed, he considered what step to take first, whether to pursue Lombre further, to confront Christy or to visit Bethlem. He had never previously had occasion to visit the hospital and it was not something he relished.

In the end, while he breakfasted on eggs and coffee in Mrs Wilkes' special parlour, a messenger arrived bearing instruction from Colonel Charters to attend an address in a lane near to Lincoln's Inn Fields immediately. There was no explanation, no amplification, but Flynt knew in his bones that for whatever reason his presence was required it was not a good one.

As soon as he turned from the relatively open ground of the Fields into the narrow lane, he knew his bones had told him true. A crowd milled in the narrow thoroughfare, the feeling restive, even ugly.

Blueskin Blake stood by the door to a tenement, his hand resting upon his pistol, and his eyes rolled as soon as he spied Flynt pushing his way through.

'I should have knowed you would show here, Flynt,' he said. 'You has a nose for trouble and you is most skilled at sticking it where it don't belong, too.'

'And lovely to see you too, Joseph. What's occurred here?'

'You mean you ain't heard? There's been another family hushed above.'

Although he had been expecting something, Flynt's stomach churned. 'Who this time?'

'What interest do it hold for a rogue and gambler like you? This is Mr Wild's business.'

'Joseph, I don't intend to explain my motives to you. Now, who is it?'

Blueskin either smiled or displayed his teeth, which showed the want of a good scraping with an abrasive stick. 'Well, whether you explain your motives or you explain them not, I ain't telling you nothing.'

'It's a slaughter, is what it is.'

The voice came from immediately behind Flynt, a round-faced individual who, by the evidence of his garb, was a reasonably well off man of business, perhaps from the grander houses on Lincoln's Inn Fields and in this lane to see what was happening.

'Shut your blabber,' Blueskin said. 'It ain't no business of yours neither.'

'This is all our business, sir. A family has been slaughtered under our very noses...'

'You've been in there?' Flynt asked the man.

'No, but there is talk.'

'What sort of talk?'

'That this is the work of some ritualist, that symbols most esoteric were daubed upon the walls.'

Blueskin dismissed that with a snort. 'That is just street flam, pure gammon from them what don't know better so they just makes it up.'

The man seemed puzzled by what Blueskin was saying so Flynt translated. 'My friend here suggests that what you say are mere street tales and have no basis in fact.'

'I had it from one who was in the vicinity and who saw a man who looked most foreign leaving this very portal with blood upon his clothing. He was wild of eye and a-muttering in a strange tongue.'

Those within earshot began to murmur assent and as Flynt studied the faces he knew now that what he had sensed in the heightened air was a mixture of fear and hatred. Fear because of the brutal nature of the crimes, and hatred because sometimes fear needs a focus. The boatman had already given voice to it the day before. Now two families had been murdered and a foreigner would make an ideal scapegoat. A little way back in the crowd, he was unsurprised to see, stood Daniel Defoe, as usual jotting thoughts and observations in his notebook. The writer looked up from his scribblings and gave him a nod of recognition.

Flynt pulled Blueskin away and muttered, 'Where is Mr Wild?'

Blueskin jerked his arm free. 'He is above. And I will not have your fives on my person, Jonas Flynt.'

Flynt let the aggression pass. 'Do you have other men here?'

'Two, they is within.'

'I'll send them out. And despatch a boy to the garrison at the Tower. We might need the military here before long.'

Blueskin grinned. 'You has concern with this?' He waved a hand to the crowd. 'That is nothing but blabber.'

'Blabber can soon turn to action, Blueskin, believe me.'

He had seen looks in men's eyes similar to those he now witnessed in this little lane. Previously events had ended with a man dead at the hands of a mob and he was in no hurry to see it repeated. Ignoring Blueskin's protests, he turned towards the stairs to go in search of Jonathan Wild.

As he entered the door of the building someone behind him began whistling 'Greensleeves'.

-

I knowed he would show his face here and it pleases me that I am right about him for I sees his face and I sees that he senses what I has hung upon the air. He smells it, he does, the violence what bubbles just below the surface. It was an easy thing to do, setting that a-simmering. A word in this ear, a comment in that one, as I moves through the crowd, putting the broth to the fire. So easy, so very easy, for people is always ready to believe what they hears, if it suits their presuppositions. So I moves through them, just another cove in a multitude of coves, a multitude what grows ever greater as the words what I dropped is passed from one to the other like a plague, though it be a plague of my making. It will blow soon, I feels it in my guts, like a tingle. Not nowhere close to the tingle what I feels when I rips but close enough to pleasure me, to warm my blood on this cold morning.

He's gone inside now, has Jonas Flynt, off to see Wild, I has no doubts. Blake stands there on his lonesome but I seen him arrive with two other coves, tasty looking like him, but they won't be tasty enough, I'll wager, not to hold back what I feels is coming.

There will be further blood spilled on this street this day and I is looking forward to it most fervent.

-

The stairway took Flynt to a single door, which lay open, so he stepped through and was faced with a further set of stairs ahead and a door to his right that opened up into a parlour, where Jonathan Wild was at a table, his head in his hands. Flynt heard footsteps above and subdued voices. He also thought he heard the sound of someone retching.

Wild removed his hands when he entered and Flynt was surprised to see tears welling in his eyes and the tracks earlier ones had made on his cheek. 'The children, Flynt,' he said, his voice choked. 'My God, the children.'

Flynt didn't know what to say. He had never seen the man like this before. He was usually so assured, so in control. But here he was crying over the death of innocence. It occurred to Flynt that Wild had been shocked by the severity of the murders in Whitechapel but had not wept over them and he guessed the reason.

'You knew these children?' Flynt asked.

A nod. 'I played with them, Flynt. I bounced them upon my knee when they were small. I even on occasion helped Mistress Newell put them abed.'

An ugly thought began to form in Flynt's mind. 'What were these people to you?'

'Walter Newell was the keeper of my books, he and his wife Judith I numbered among friends, of which we have damnable few in this life of ours. And now they lie above, their throats cut and the children…' His words became strangled as the emotion took command of his throat. 'My God, the children...'

He buried his face in his hands again and began to sob. Flynt, uncomfortable with witnessing a man such as Wild displaying emotion so nakedly, eased himself from the room to climb the stairs. He perceived muddy footprints upon the steps bearing the same evidence of a slit sole as he had found in Whitechapel. Alongside was the residue of blood, droplets that had fallen from a wound or dripped from a weapon, while the wall to the left was smeared, as if bloody fingers had reached out to trail along the plaster.

A man carrying a leather bag, his flesh as ashen as his hair, rounded the bannister at the top and halted to let Flynt progress. They caught each other's eye as they passed and the man shook his head in a sorrowful manner.

'I would advise not viewing what lies beyond, sir,' he said. 'I have been a physician for thirty years and I have never seen the like. No, sir, not in thirty years.'

He didn't wait for Flynt to respond before he moved down the stairs swiftly, as if wishing to put some space between him and what lay beyond the two doors on this landing. Flynt had no desire to proceed further but knew he must. On the panel of the nearest door he saw another bloody handprint, that of a woman or a child he judged. Beyond it he found another man whom he took to be one of Wild's men. Flynt's nose twitched at the coppery tang of the near black blood pooling around the corpses of a man and a woman. The dead man's throat lay open and one hand was stretched out to the woman's as if in his final moment he had strained to grasp it.

'The physic ventures that one was done on the stairway, the woman likely, then carried in here where the other was then done,' said Wild's man, his tone and evenness of stare showing he was not discomfited at all by the sight of the dead. 'He then moved next door and did his bloody work there.'

Flynt inspected the small bedroom, but saw no sign of any ritualistic signs painted in blood, then became aware of the man studying him.

'I'm sorry, I don't know your name,' Flynt said.

'Godfrey, and you be Jonas Flynt.'

Many men who Flynt didn't know were aware of him, so this was no surprise. 'You had best take to the street, Godfrey,' Flynt said. 'Blueskin may have need of you.'

'And what of these? Mr Wild instructed me to watch over them till they is carted away.'

'They don't need company,' Flynt said. 'They're beyond being lonely now.'

The harsh sound of puking came from the other room, but it was a dry sound, for whatever had lain in the man's stomach had long since been dispelled and only the need of the body to continue purging remained. Godfrey smiled a little. 'That be Hal. His stomach ain't as hardy as mine, but then he has little 'uns of his own and what's next door is a hard sight to take, even for me.'

Flynt was resolved not to look at it. He didn't need to see it. He wouldn't see it. 'Fetch him and take him with you.'

'But Mr Wild said...'

'I'll explain to Mr Wild presently. All will be well with him, of that I promise.'

The man accepted that and as he moved to the door Flynt asked, 'Are there any symbols scrawled upon the walls in the other room?'

'You mean pictures or such like?'

'Yes, or words.'

The man was puzzled. 'Words?'

'Yes.'

'No, nothing of such in any way. There's blood, all over the place it be, even the ceiling, but nothing what you might call as being distinctive.'

Flynt hadn't expected there to be but he thanked him anyway. When Godfrey left, he knelt beside the bodies, staring into the open eyes as if they might have captured a final image but the flat gazes were locked together, as though they had sought each other's faces one last time as their life ebbed.

He straightened, took another long look around the room to see if there were any secrets it could reveal, but it was a perfectly normal bed chamber, a bed, a dresser, a window looking onto the street. He stepped over the man's body and edged the drapes back to stare down at the street. He couldn't see Blueskin or his men but he could see the thickening crowd, the heads waving to and fro like a tide. He studied some of the faces, saw the fear and the anger still building. It wouldn't be long until that tide turned. Defoe moved among them, asking a question here, taking a note there.

He returned downstairs, pausing to examine the main door. The lock and wood remained intact, so whoever did this hadn't forced his way in. The killer may have pushed through when it had been opened by Judith Newell, if the doctor was correct in his assumption. It was also possible that the killer used a dub to spring the lock and then surprised her. The area between the door and the stairs was free of blood so she had not been murdered immediately upon the killer's entry. Flynt climbed halfway up again to make a closer study of the bloodstains which began in a marked manner and continued upwards, as if the killer had propelled her upwards and stabbed her as they moved, the blood dripping from both wound and weapon, her own hand reaching out to steady herself or possibly prevent their ascent leaving the smears on the wall. Then to the landing and the bed chamber, where Walter Newell waited. And thence to the children asleep in their bed.

He returned to the parlour where Wild remained at the table. Everything in the room was in order, just as it had been in Whitechapel, so robbery was not the motive. The floor and walls revealed no traces of exsanguination, so his theory regarding the sequence of events may be close to the truth, not that it mattered. Not now.

'You have to compose yourself, Jonathan,' Flynt said, his voice gentle but firm.

Wild's hands dropped away again, revealing those red-rimmed eyes and tear-streaked cheeks. 'I am composed.'

Noting Wild's voice was stronger than before, Flynt accepted his word. 'Then I must ask you a question and you will reply in truth, for you know me, and you know I will see the lie take shape in your eye before it reaches your lips.'

A frown from Wild and a hardening of his jaw. 'I don't appreciate being spoken to in such a manner, Flynt. You forget your place...'

'To hell with such nonsense. Children are dead, Wild, two in Whitechapel and two above. I have no time for place.'

Wild seemed ready to argue but then he changed his mind. 'Ask your question.'

Flynt stared down at him for a moment. 'Did you have anything to do with the murders in Whitechapel?'

Wild's shock was genuine. 'What? Good God, man, how can you ask that? You said yourself there were children...'

'Jacques Berthon was bookkeeper to the Admiral. Do you deny that you knew that?'

A denial flashed in Wild's face but again he thought better of it. 'No, I do not deny that. And before you ask whether I attended as a means of goading him a little, I do freely admit that, for at the time I knew not that infants had been slaughtered. The Admiral and I have our differences but I do not attempt to settle them with the blood of innocents.' He returned Flynt's stare, a thought occurring to him. 'You think that damned masked creature has struck back at me, believing me guilty?'

That was indeed the ugly thought that had troubled Flynt. The streets would be awash with blood, the Admiral had promised. Had he cause to believe that Wild was behind the Whitechapel outrage and had struck back? Flynt struggled to keep his face impassive. 'I don't believe he would have children killed either.'

'Yet you thought that of I?'

'No, I asked you because it is something I must ask.'

'And will you ask your friend the Admiral?' A smile appeared, Wild becoming his true self once more. 'Oh yes, I know you and he have been in congress most regular.'

'As have you and I.'

'True, true. I like you, Jonas Flynt, and you have done me service in the past, that business with yon viper in my nest two years ago, for instance. But I don't trust you. Blueskin tells me constant that you are a rum cove and I agree with him. I have come to believe that when you speak, as Mr Milton wrote, there is more meant in your words than meets the ear. So, you tell me, Jonas Flynt, what is your true interest in these murders?'

Flynt considered obfuscation but settled, not for the first time, on a version of the truth. 'One reason I have already told you. I feel a sense of outrage over the death of the children. The other is that I have been asked to investigate by a gentleman with more than a passing interest.'

'And this other gentleman, would he be our masked friend on the waterfront?'

'No.' Here Flynt was only telling a half-lie, for though the Admiral had pointed him at the murders in the first place, his promise in return to seek news of Lombre forged a link to his mission for Colonel Charters. They were silent for a moment while Wild weighed the truth of his words before shouting drew Flynt to the window. He still couldn't see Blueskin or the other men but the crowd grew ever more restive and beginning to push forward. 'There's trouble brewing in the street.'

'What sort of trouble?'

'Someone's spreading lies about what has occurred here.'

Wild's face crinkled. 'What lies could be told about this horror?'

'That the killings were ritualistic and perhaps committed by a foreigner. The mood is incendiary and all it'll take is a single spark to set it aflame.'

Wild took this in. 'And what is it I can do?'

'You're known in the streets. You are even respected.' Flynt was stretching the truth in that regard but he needed the man to rise to this challenge and the best way to achieve that was to flatter his vanity. 'They will not listen to me but they will listen to you.'

Wild was still for a moment, his only movement the slow blink of his eyes as he regarded Flynt with a suspicious expression. The Thieftaker General was devious, greedy, deceitful but he was far from stupid and his previously avowed mistrust of him caused Flynt to fear that he had gone too far when paying tribute to his reputation.

And then a roar rose up from the street, followed by the report of a pistol.

20

Wild lagged a little behind as Flynt took the steps two at a time to hit the corridor at street level, drawing both Tact and Diplomacy as he rushed towards Godfrey and Hal at the entrance. Godfrey slashed with a sabre at a man edging closer and Hal raised a pistol in a wavering hand. A man sat on his haunches before them nursing a shoulder wound. The front ranks of the crowd backed away but weapons had appeared and there was a determined set to faces. Over the prevailing din, voices called for an attack.

'They tried a-rushing us,' Godfrey explained without taking his eyes from the mob, his teeth gritted, 'they wished to see for themselves what lay above but old Blueskin, he stopped them by putting a ball in that one's wing.'

'Where is Blueskin?' Flynt asked.

'They dragged him away,' Hal said, his voice pitched high, as if stretched, and trembling in concert with his hand.

Flynt craned his head to see over the crowd and found a group of men struggling with Blueskin, his face contorted with fury.

Flynt was aware of Wild at his side.

'This is your chance,' Flynt said softly. 'Show them what you're made of. I told Blueskin to send for help but I doubt he did so. If you quell this disturbance before anyone else is hurt then word will spread, even unto the ears of men in offices in Whitehall.' He saw that thought land. Wild was always keen to increase his influence with those of influence. 'A man of deliberation, of courage, is a rare thing, and they will recognise that,' Flynt pressed. 'A mob is a beast and it has to be cowed and the best way to achieve that is to dominate. You are a figure of some considerable authority. Use it now.'

Wild paused as he calculated what benefit there was to him interceding.

'Damn it, Wild, that's your man they have,' Flynt snapped. 'I've seen this before and I know what will occur if something is not done. Do you wish to see Joseph Blake dead? He has been a most loyal servant to you, now it's your turn to show him the same loyalty.'

Wild blinked, swallowed, then his expression tightened as he drew the sword he had adopted as a symbol of the authority he was about to exercise.

He stepped forward. 'Listen to me!'

His tone was too soft, too uncertain, so the yelling continued.

'I will have silence!' Wild's voice was firmer, his northern tones amplified, but still the clamour continued. Wild turned to Godfrey. 'Fire your pistol into the ground, Godfrey. Let us attract their attention...'

'No,' said Flynt, loudly, his glance at Godfrey warning him against it. 'That will only cause further anger, perhaps panic, believe me. You must calm this with your voice alone, Wild. Use your position, man!'

Wild swallowed but he nodded his acceptance of Flynt's judgement and took a deep breath. 'My name is Jonathan Wild. I am the Thieftaker General and by God, I will have silence!'

His voice was much stronger now and the crowd began to still, beginning with those closest to them and then filtering backwards as his name was passed from one mouth to another. Wild straightened a little and in an almost nonchalant motion waved his sword.

'I would be obliged if you would clear a path, gentlemen.' The bodies parted but only slightly to afford a clearer glimpse of the men holding Blueskin. Wild levelled the point of his sword in their direction. 'You there, let that man free.'

No move was made to obey. Wild hesitated, the knuckles of the hand gripping the sword whitening. Flynt swore softly and pushed between the bodies closest to him. Most moved immediately, some tried to stand their ground but the hard look in his eye convinced them that such defiance was folly. Finally, the crowd parted like the Red Sea before Moses, except Flynt was no biblical prophet and instead of a staff he had two pistols. He risked a glance back to Wild, who remained immobile at first, but then he straightened his shoulder again and strode after him.

A knife was held at Blueskin's throat, a scratch already oozing blood, while four men subdued him by gripping his outstretched arms. It looked as if he was being crucified by hands.

'Remove that blade,' Wild instructed.

'Ain't going to happen,' said the man with the knife, his eyes hard little dots.

Flynt aimed one pistol directly at him. 'I would do as he asks.'

Though the man seemed unafraid, he still ducked his head behind Blueskin's, his knife again nicking flesh, causing his prisoner to curse most vociferously. Another of his captors swung a fist into his mouth to bring the flood of invective to a halt.

'Shut your hole, you dark-skinned bastard,' said this second man. 'That little nick ain't nothing to what you deserve.'

Flynt aimed his second pistol in the speaker's direction but Wild had summoned something within himself to lay a hand on his arm and step forward. 'Let us all take a moment to breathe,' he said, his voice most pleasant. 'Most of you know me, I assume…'

Wild's name flowed around them again. 'Aye, and some of us to our cost,' cried a voice from somewhere within the crowd.

Wild ignored that. 'That man you hold hostage is one of my constables.'

Another voice, like the last the source unseen. 'How do we know he ain't the one what hushed those poor people?'

'I can assure you…'

'You can assure us of exactly nothing, Jonathan Wild, Thieftaker General,' said the man who had punched Blueskin. He stepped forward, regarding Flynt's raised pistols with a sneer. This was the one to watch. This was the leader. 'And you has but two pistols, and as you can see there is far more of us than that. What good will they do you in the face of these vast odds, eh?'

There were murmurs of agreement from the crowd, and among them Flynt caught a name. Such an argument had been used with him before and though he hoped this time the outcome would be greatly different, Flynt had a ready response. 'Yes, I have two pistols and that means at least two of you will go down. The question being, which two? And you, Edmund, was it?' The man appeared surprised that Flynt knew his name, as though he had not heard it being uttered a moment before. 'You have nominated yourself for one of the positions.'

'Gentlemen, has there not been enough bloodshed this day?' Wild said. 'Show some respect for the poor family back there…'

Edmund jerked a thumb at Blueskin. 'They was hushed by a foreigner and this here cove looks foreign to me, don't he?'

'I'm as English as you, you bastard,' Blueskin snarled.

'Then why did you spill the claret of my friend over there? He's an Englishman too.'

'He came at me with a knife and I wasn't about to let him stick me with it.'

'If you didn't have nothing to hide in them rooms then why did you wish to stop us?'

'Because it was my job and it was my orders.'

'Joseph speaks true,' Wild said, his demeanour still cool, which impressed Flynt no end. 'He acted under my instruction.'

Edmund returned his belligerent stare to Wild. 'Then what is it you has to hide in there, Wild?'

'Dear God, friend, there has been murder committed in those rooms, foul murder, brutal murder. Children...' His voice broke a little but he swallowed it back. Had Flynt not seen him genuinely moved both in Whitechapel and in that little house behind them, he might have thought it feigned. Perhaps that was where he had found the courage to take this stand, within his grief and anger at what had occurred. 'You think it should be open to public scrutiny like some attraction at the fair?'

'There was foul things a-painted upon the walls...'

'There was nothing painted upon the walls, on that you have my oath.'

Some laughter greeted that but again Wild ignored it. 'I want you all to disperse and let the authorities get on with the work in hand.'

Edmund was not about to let this go, for he was clearly a man who had seized hold of a belief he was unwilling to relinquish. 'And what is that work? Covering up the real nature of them killings?'

'Why would we do such a thing?'

'I couldn't say, because the workings of the likes of you is beyond an honest man such as me. But we had it from someone who knows that a foreigner was seen leaving the house and that there be something unholy writ upon those walls.'

'And what was the nature of these imaginary daubs?'

This perplexed Edmund. 'We doesn't know for certain...'

Voices in the crowd seemed to know exactly what, for they volunteered a mixture of Papist catechisms, to Hebrew symbols, Jacobite slogans and signs of the devil.

'I heard it be Arab writing,' Edmund said, not wishing to be left out. 'I hears the fellow what was seen was black as hell and big, like them two what attend the king.'

King George had brought with him to England two Turkish servants, Mustapha and Mahomet, whom he had found while on a campaign.

'In the name of God, man, now you suggest His Majesty is in some manner responsible?' Wild, despite his grief, couldn't help the laugh from rippling his throat. 'That is treason.'

'Not the king, just them servants of his,' Edmund said, realising he had taken a step too far.

'You talk utter nonsense,' Wild said, waving his hand in a dismissive manner. 'Now, set my man at his liberty and let's be done with this before it grows too late. Soldiers are on their way and I would fain see anyone arrested for high passions.'

Edmund laughed. 'There ain't no soldiers on their way...'

'Ah but there are, for I sent word as soon as I arrived and saw the crowd had gathered. I could tell that passions ran high and rightly so, but high passions can lead to extreme folly, as we are now witnessing. The presence of a justice of the peace is also imminent and the reading of the Riot Act will indemnify the soldiers over whatever action is seen fit.'

The act had been passed in 1715 and allowed for the prevention of tumults and riotous assemblies with swift punishments for such allowed by law. The expressions of some in the multitude displayed alarm at the thought of the military on their way to enforce such punishments. Wild was hoodwinking them, of course, and it was a ruse that could have gone either way, but it seemed to have a calming effect. Flynt continued to be impressed by Wild's demeanour, for he showed a steel he would never have believed existed within him. The men subduing Blueskin did not relinquish their hold, but they did look to Edmund for guidance, their expressions lacking certainty. Even the blade had dropped from the throat closer to Blueskin's chest. But their leader's stern countenance told Flynt that he was not about to give way.

'I would hearken to Mr Wild's advice, Edmund,' Flynt said, deciding it was time he added weight to Wild's bluff, 'for my patience wears thin.'

Edmund sneered again, believing he still held the advantage. 'You ain't going to discharge them barkers. You knows what will happen if you does.'

Flynt did know all too well but he refused to back down, deploying a pretence of his own. 'What will happen, will happen, but you may rest assured you will know nothing of it, and neither will your friend with the blade.' Edmund shot a glance at the man in question, who ducked further down, his eyes only in view over Blueskin's shoulder. Flynt's lips thinned. 'Are you a gambling man, Edmund?'

'No, it be for fools and wastrels…'

'Perhaps, but you're gambling that I won't drop you first. Your knife-holding friend is gambling that I cannot take out his eye with a ball.'

Blueskin's own eyes widened as his head jerked a little to see what kind of target the man presented. When he looked back in Flynt's direction, there was genuine alarm in his face. Flynt enjoyed that look but maintained his severe demeanour.

It seemed as if everyone within earshot held their collective breath as Flynt, Edmund and the man with the knife stared at each other. The silence was broken by Wild.

'Come, this has gone on long enough. Unhand my man and disperse, with no further questions being asked. The rumours of ritual or some religious connection to the horrors behind those doors are false. The murders are the work of a madman who will be found and he will suffer the full weight of the law upon him, on that you can be certain. Leave now, all of you, before it is too late.'

Further murmurs circulated but Flynt sensed a change in the nature of the gathering. The heat of such passions rise swiftly and just as easily evaporate. Many of the men and women now had no wish to be part of this and some had begun to drift away. The crowd clustered around them thinned, leaving only Edmund and his friends, though most of those still clinging to Blueskin continued to exchange uncertain looks. Flynt knew the danger had not yet fully passed and though he maintained his focus on them, he became aware of a solitary figure watching from a corner. A tingle of excitement coursed through Flynt's veins as he recognised Lombre, giving way to annoyance that he could not pursue. Lombre knew this, for he grinned and raised a hand to his hat in salute, before he stepped back into a side street.

Flynt glared at Edmund, blaming him for preventing him from running the agent down.

Wild addressed Edmund directly. 'Well, sir? Much of your force has the good sense to disperse, why do you not do so?'

'Because you're lying, Wild. There ain't no Justice coming here, there ain't no soldiers.'

'Damn it, Wild,' Flynt snapped, his frustration at being denied pursuit of Lombre boiling over, 'let me put a ball in him. I've had enough of his nonsense.'

'Calm yourself, Jonas.' Godfrey and Hal had now joined them and Wild indicated them. 'You have no evidence that I am lying, my friend, but even if I were I would say that those odds to which you referred earlier have now evened somewhat.'

Edmund's gaze slid from Wild, to Flynt and then the two men behind them. He weighed up the odds and found them wanting on his side so he sighed but said nothing as he backed up slowly, then turned and walked quickly away, veering abruptly into a narrow passageway and out of sight. His friends followed suit, the one with the knife practically running in Edmund's wake. Wild watched them go, his features stiff but relief shining in his eyes. He turned and walked back to the entrance to the Newell's house, his back straight, his pretence of solid authority remaining intact. Godfrey and Hal trailed behind him, never turning their backs on the remaining stragglers.

Flynt considered following Lombre down the side street but there would be no point. He had lost too much time and missed him for the third time, first on the waterfront, then when he glimpsed him in the Rookery and now here. He stared at where the man had stood, now certain that the agent was involved in these atrocities, but puzzled as to what he had to gain from the slaughter of innocent families.

From somewhere far away he again heard the strains of 'Greensleeves', the whistles echoing from walls in the strange silence that followed the excitement.

Blueskin dabbed two fingers at the cut on his neck and stared at the blood. 'If I ever sees that chuckle-headed cur again I'll stop his claret good and proper, on that you has my solemn vow and oath.'

The words snatched Flynt from his thoughts. He made no reply as he thrust his pistols back under his coat.

Blueskin's gaze was curious. 'Would you have taken that shot if matters came to it?'

Flynt paused before replying. 'We'll never know, will we?'

That wasn't enough for Blueskin. 'What if you had and you missed him and hit me?'

Flynt saw Defoe approaching and he turned away from Blueskin. 'Then we wouldn't be having this conversation.'

He left him to consider the vagaries of chance and fate as Defoe tipped his hat in his direction. 'Nicely done, Jonas.'

Flynt indicated the notebook that Defoe was in the process of stowing in his pocket. 'You will publish an account of these proceedings?'

'I will, for they were most notable and the city at large must learn of them. As we have witnessed, there is great unease concerning these atrocities. I will, naturally, keep your name out of print, although it does mean credit will be given to that abominable rogue Wild.'

Flynt was relieved. 'He deserves it, for he acquitted himself well this day.'

'Perhaps, but I would suggest that had it not been for your words he might not. I saw you speak to him most urgently before he found the courage to step forward.'

Defoe missed little, it seemed, but his reporting could be of some use. 'You might wish to mention, and soundly dismiss, the fantasy of a foreigner being responsible.'

'You know that for fact?'

Flynt was careful. 'I find it unlikely.'

'And the suggestion of expressions of an esoteric nature daubed upon the walls is also doubtful?'

'More than doubtful, they are bogus. There is unrest enough over these tragedies, Dan, let's not add to the instability with fantasies. You saw what occurred here. Unless the rumour is scotched then it's only a matter of time before someone loses their life because their skin is dark or they speak with an accent.'

His thoughts flicked to Lombre and his curious manner of speech, not quite continental, not quite English, and his facility with a stiletto. The wounds he had observed in that house had not been caused by such a blade, of that he would take his oath. From what he understood the children had been hacked at with fervour. A stiletto was surgical, selective. Lombre had been present perhaps, but he didn't commit the murders.

A glint of disappointment shone in Defoe's eyes. Suggestions of ritual would have made it a better story.

'I did not know you were such a close acquaintance of Mr Wild,' Defoe said, his gaze directed towards Blueskin, who watched them from the entranceway to the building.

'We have acquaintance, but not close,' Flynt said.

'And that other gentleman? He of the swarthy complexion and belligerent demeanour?'

'Joseph Blake,' Flynt said, wishing he could be present when Blueskin saw his name in print. 'But permit me, Dan, for I must away to Wapping.'

'Business for the colonel?'

'Yes,' Flynt replied, aware that the business in question was also for his own benefit. He needed reassurance that the Admiral was not behind this latest tragedy.

Defoe laid a hand on his arm. 'One further question, Jonas. Mr Blake there, he is friend to you?'

Flynt laughed. It felt good after the tension of the previous few minutes. 'Not hardly.'

'And yet you rushed to his rescue. Why?'

Flynt saw in his mind a friend being dragged away by a mob and then murdered before his eyes. 'It seemed like the thing to do.'

Defoe smiled. 'Most certainly, for a Paladin.'

21

The rain remained absent but the window behind the Admiral's desk was speckled with moisture, perhaps lifted from the grey waters of the river and thrown at it by the wind. Flynt had asked him the same question he had posed to Wild and the Admiral had fallen unusually silent. Even his harsh breathing had eased.

'You think me capable of ordering the death of children, Jonas?'

His voice was soft and Flynt was unable to glean anything from it, whether anger or pain at being questioned about the murders in the city.

'I must put it to you,' Flynt replied, just as he said to Wild. 'You threatened repercussions if you had any evidence that Wild was behind the murders of Berthon and his family.'

'I have no such evidence. I remind you that it was I who asked you to investigate and assured you that I would leave it to you before I took any such action.'

The presence of Lombre at the scene meant Flynt had been more or less certain the Admiral was not behind this most recent atrocity but, as he said, he had to ask the question. 'I regret any offence, but I must be free to make inquiries without fear or favour.'

'Which is why I asked you to do it. And you have not offended me, for I do understand why you felt forced to make such an inquiry.'

'Then why do you seem so pensive regarding it?'

'As to that, I proffer another suggestion, that Wild could have had these poor souls murdered also.'

Flynt's head shake was emphatic. 'No, Wild is ruthless certainly, but his shock and grief is very real. There is no profit for him in such a thing.'

'Perhaps to take my suspicions from him?'

'Wild's mind is a labyrinth of chicanery, it is true, but I don't believe he is responsible.'

'Then who?'

'That remains unclear, but it has all the hallmarks of the work of a madman.'

'A madman with the reasoning powers to strike at both Wild and I. What kind of madman does that?'

There was method to this madness, he was certain of it, but he couldn't yet make sense of it.

'I don't know. But I'm actively engaged upon the answer.'

The Admiral leaned forward. 'Then work swiftly, my friend, for I grow restive. There are many in this city who cast voracious eyes upon my little empire and wish to take it from me, either in whole or in part. Wild and Boone are only two. There will come a day when I must make an example of someone, to encourage the others that I remain the true power on the waterfront. I would prefer that example to be the guilty party, but as time progresses that becomes less of a priority, do you understand?'

Flynt understood all too well, casting his eyes to the clock upon the mantle. He had sent a message to Charters to meet him at five of the clock in the Black Lion, and what light there had been in the sky was already on the wane. The image of Lombre and his salute flashed across his vision.

'Do we have further news of that man I sought?'

'The foreigner?' The Admiral settled back again. 'He has gone to ground, it seems.'

'Is it possible he has repaired to another part of the city, away from the river?'

'Anything is possible with men such as he, and given he was discovered here just recently by you and bearing in mind that he may have heard of my inquiries, I would think it likely that he would take himself elsewhere.'

'There remains no suggestion that he has fled the country?'

The Admiral's tone was emphatic. 'That I would have heard. Unless he has engineered a most radical change of appearance, he would have been seen by someone. He hides in London, of that I am sure, but what is occupying his time is still unknown.'

That was something that had exercised Flynt's mind since seeing him in the Rookery and his suspicion that he had met with Boone. Sighting him near Lincoln's Inn Fields only strengthened a slim notion he had, but to fatten it up he would require the aid of Nathaniel Charters. It was time to lay everything before the colonel.

-

'Bedlam, you say?' Charters said, as they walked the perimeter of the Covent Garden Piazza. The rain continued to hold off but as Flynt had come up river from Wapping the darkening sky was filled with full-bellied clouds desperate to unload. Nevertheless, after the rain of recent days, whether passionate in its intensity or a mere wet kiss, it was a relief to walk in the air, chill though it was and pregnant with the expectation of a further downpour. Charters had suggested they get out, rather than be trapped in the dim and frankly noxious atmosphere of the upstairs room of the Black Lion, where the piss pots behind a screen in the corner were again unemptied – a not uncommon occurrence – and the air carried the fumes of cheap tallow. The London streets were no nosegay but there was the benefit of a brisk wind that sometimes whipped the aroma away.

'That is what his cousin said,' Flynt replied.

'And do you believe this Caleb Boone?'

'I neither believe nor disbelieve. A visit to the hospital will confirm it either way.'

Charters thought about this as they walked, his watchers maintaining a respectful but vigilant distance behind them. Around them milled the merchants and porters of the fruit and vegetable market, the working day nearing its end, the domestic staff who had attended to make purchase for their households giving way to the pleasure seekers who made the Piazza theirs after dark. Carters clattered back and forth, bodies milled to and fro, and mixed with the whirl of movement there was the noise, hawkers crying out for late sales, men cursing, laughing, calling to one another, singing, Covent Garden nuns offering the delights of an early evening tumble to any cove who looked as if he yearned to open his purse and unbutton his breeches before dinner. The foists, of course, were present during all hours, for where there was honourable profit to be made, then so was the opportunity to make a dishonest one. As Jack had reasoned when he robbed that gentleman outside the Theatre Royal, when a man's guard was blunted by pre- or post-prandial glow he may be less likely to feel the loss of a wipe or purse.

'And the fresh murders by Lincoln Fields?' Charters asked, his voice trembling. 'They bear similarities to those in Whitechapel?'

'They are near identical.'

Charters cast his eyes down in a mixture of sadness and shame. He considered for a moment before he reached a decision. 'I will accompany you to Bethlem, Flynt. I will see this man with my own eyes.'

Flynt had expected that.

'But if this Bedlamite be Nimrod Boone, and speaking frankly it is the best place for him apart from the grave, that means we have another madman on the loose in London,' Charters said, and Flynt couldn't be certain that there wasn't some hope clinging to his words. If Nimrod Boone was indeed tucked away in Bedlam, then that would alleviate his guilt.

'I think there be reason working here, repulsive though it may be,' Flynt said, before outlining the connections Wild and the Admiral had to the victims and of his conversations with them regarding the murders.

Charters asked, 'And you are acquainted with this Admiral of the underworld?'

'I am.'

'You are friendly with him?'

'I would say, yes, although near accusing him of the murder of children may have planted the beginnings of a wedge between us.'

'He knows nothing of your work for me, I trust.'

'Of course not.'

Flynt's word satisfied the colonel. 'You do associate with some choice individuals, Serjeant.'

'I often find criminals such as he are more honest than supposedly decent men. He at least has no illusions as to what he is about, unlike the likes of Wild and many of those who walk the palaces and corridors of Whitehall. The Admiral knows he is corrupt and offers no excuse or artifice, but they mask their larceny with patriotism and the good of the people. Give me an honest criminal any day before an honest politician, for the latter is often these days a contradiction in terms.'

It was a sign of Charters' preoccupation that he made no form of defence regarding men in power. Even though he knew that among those in parliament there were too many men who used their position to better themselves and not the country, they'd had similar conversations before and generally he had engaged in them with his good humour but today he remained fatigued. The circles under his eyes had deepened and his skin was waxy. He had admitted to Flynt that bad dreams had, to use the words of Shakespeare, murdered sleep.

'That does bring me to another facet of this matter,' Flynt continued. 'Caleb Boone has been seeking the support of powerful men, it seems, in a bid to improve his situation.'

'What sort of powerful men?'

Flynt shrugged. 'I know not whether merchants, nobility, government...'

Something of Charters' spirit rose. 'Really, Flynt, do you seriously suggest that men such as they would work in concert with a cheap rogue from the Rookery?'

'Colonel, we have had experience of such men who have worked in concert with rogues before.'

Charters was quiet for a few paces. 'You sense the hand of the Fellowship in this?'

'It seems possible. I would take it further; I saw Lombre at Lincoln's Inn Fields.'

That made Charters frown. 'You think he is responsible for these killings?'

'All I can say for certain is that he was present. But I also saw him near the Rookery the other day.'

'And you think he was meeting Boone?'

'A suspicion merely,' Flynt said, then told him of the two glasses he had seen in Boone's lair.

'I congratulate you on your perspicacity,' Charters said.

'Sometimes attention to such details can mean the difference between life and death.'

'Quite so, quite so, but it is a slim observation on which to hang a connection between them.'

'I admit that Lombre may simply be hiding in the Rookery...'

'Yes, if a man must lose himself, then that is the place to do it.'

'...and it be possible that his presence at Lincoln's Inn today was mere chance.'

They both fell silent at this, neither much taking the idea of the agent's presence anywhere being a coincidence.

Flynt then added, 'But I am also informed that he has been seen in the company of a Scotsman in a waterfront tavern.'

'Has he, by God? This last intelligence gleaned from your friend the Admiral, I suppose?'

'Yes.'

'And you think, what, Flynt? That Lombre has met with Lord Moncrieff, who uses him as intermediary with Boone?'

'It has crossed my mind. You told me yourself that Lombre's services are not cheaply bought. Boone is the upright man of a band of Rookery rogues but I would hazard he has not the funds to meet the agent's price. Coupled with the knowledge that he has the backing of some rich men...'

Flynt let that dangle.

Charters took up the thought. 'It is possible, I suppose, that the Fellowship has some design in mind and would indeed utilise Lombre's services. We know they use chaos and confusion as a means of filling their pockets. However, his lordship has all but eliminated his Scottish accent and it would take a trained ear to detect any trace, a talent I doubt the scum and villainy of the waterfront would possess. That said, it is a line of inquiry. You will beard Lord Moncrieff concerning this?'

That was not what Flynt intended. 'I believe it would be better coming from you, Colonel. He and I have history, as you know, and it is unlikely he would respond well.'

'Ah yes, there is little love lost between you, is there? I wonder why?'

Flynt avoided the query, but did consider whether Charters knew more than he revealed about his relationship with Lord James Moncrieff. Charters had a knack of knowing everything and disclosing little, a tendency Flynt often found disconcerting and maddening. There might come a time when he would have to reveal that he and the Scottish noble were half-brothers, but that time had not yet come.

'His Lordship and I also have a history,' Charters pointed out.

'And yet you are more likely to gain access to him than I. I understand you both frequent Mrs White's Chocolate House.'

Charters breathed in. 'Very well. I shall do so this evening if his lordship is present. And you, Flynt, what will you be about?'

'I have business regarding the Paladin. I know the source.'

'Do you, by heavens? How came you by this intelligence?'

Flynt was determined to honour the compact made with Defoe not to reveal him as the source. 'I made inquiries.'

'Where and of whom?'

'Here and there,' Flynt said. 'This person and that.'

'You have been busy,' Charters said. 'So who began this rumour?'

Flynt took a beat before replying, savouring the moment, for he knew how Charters would react. 'Madame Christian de Fontaine.'

'Ah, that damn woman.'

The colonel's words were expected but not the manner in which they were spoken. It could have been because Charters' mind dwelt more upon the murders, the involvement of Lombre and the search for Nimrod Boone than the return of Christy de Fontaine, but it could also have been because the revelation was not completely unexpected.

'It would seem she is back in London,' Flynt said, making a careful study of Charters' face.

Charters became aware of the scrutiny and adopted a frown that Flynt found most unconvincing. 'How does she flit back and forth from the continent without my Lord Stair's agents knowing of it?'

Lord Stair was the ambassador at the court of Louis of France and headed an intelligence network that almost rivalled that of Charters in England. Almost being the operative word, for Flynt doubted if anyone would have a network that could rival the colonel's, the foundations of which went back to Elizabeth's spymaster, Walsingham, the man who first realised that the diligent utilisation of rogues and vagabonds working for money, some for patriotism and others simply to keep their heads from a noose, brought results.

'Madame de Fontaine is most adroit at coming and going without hindrance,' Flynt said.

'That woman is something of a menace.'

Again the words were what he would have expected Charters to utter but there was a flatness in the tone that Flynt found extremely dubious.

'Would you have me kill her too?'

Charters gave him a sideways glance. 'No, Serjeant, that is not necessary. Not as yet, at any rate. And did this or that person to whom you conversed here or there provide the reason as to why she promulgated this Paladin fantasy?'

'No, simply that it was she who began it. It's my intention to interview her and learn from her the reason why.'

Charters continued a few paces before he said, 'No, leave her be.'

'Leave her be?' Flynt repeated. 'I have to say, Colonel, that I find your reaction to this news most perplexing. We have a woman known to have worked against your interests once again nestling within London and you say leave her be?'

Charters' tone sharpened. 'Leave her be, Serjeant, that is an order.'

Flynt didn't like rats but he knew one when he detected its scent and there was one walking at his side at that moment. Charters knew more than he was saying regarding Madame de Fontaine.

Something like Charters' old humour sparkled as he attempted to lighten the moment. 'You seem to have a special connection with this damnable woman, Serjeant. Tell me, in your encounters, did you and she ever make connection beyond the verbal?'

Christy de Fontaine was, as Defoe had noted, most comely and she used her beauty, wit and – yes – undoubted charm to snare and captivate men. 'No,' he said, truthfully.

'Good thing too, for she is not above using her body as a weapon to prise an advantage from man or woman.'

'I'm sure you would know, Colonel.'

Christy herself had hinted that she and Charters had been intimate, and the colonel had never denied it. Nathaniel Charters was a man who enjoyed his pleasures and, though the model of tact, was not one to allow himself to be deterred by the existence of a husband or even if the woman was an enemy of the state.

The sound of whistling somewhere in the Piazza brought Charters to a halt again, the relaxation that had begun to steal over his features vanishing to be replaced by a wary, haunted look. His eyes darted around him until he found the whistler, a rotund porter carting a pile of empty baskets to a waiting cart. The relief was evident, but for a moment only, for he saw Flynt regarding him and he forced a smile.

'I cannot abide a man who whistles, Flynt, remember that.'

Flynt was not one to put his lips together and blow but he knew that Charters was lying. He had never before shown any sort of disdain for those who whistled. Charters' eyes dropped away as if he had read Flynt's thoughts. Then he tutted and adopted an irritated tone that Flynt was convinced masked his true feelings.

'Damn this Madame de Fontaine. Another blasted Scot, of course. Between Lombre's mystery man and now this woman de Fontaine, not to mention that you can also be nothing but trouble, Flynt, I find you a most vexatious race. I do sometimes wonder why we went to such lengths to form the union, for you and your kind are too proud, too inflexible and too rebellious for your own good.'

He was making an attempt to goad him and though Flynt was glad to see it, he didn't rise to the bait. His suspicions as to the colonel's attitude towards his news were too strong to ignore. 'I believe I should interview Madame de Fontaine, for it's possible that she's part of whatever this conspiracy is. Remember, she's been known to employ her considerable skills in service to the Fellowship.'

'I think not,' Charters said. 'I say this for a final time, Flynt, leave the woman be. The curtain has fallen on this Paladin farce so let us be done with it. Do not attempt to see her in Leicester House.'

Defoe had told him that during a musical evening he had attended that Madame de Fontaine had entertained the gathering upon the spinet in a most accomplished manner and that she had a most melodious singing voice. Christy was accomplished in many things, including deception and betrayal when either or both suited her purposes, which made Charters' lack of concern regarding her proximity to the royal family most suspicious indeed.

That, and the fact that Flynt had not mentioned she was in Leicester House.

22

Before he devised a way to reach Christy de Fontaine, Flynt resolved to speak again with Belle. After all, she was only a few paces across the Piazza from where he'd left Charters. He hadn't seen her since she delivered her ultimatum and that didn't sit well with him. She deserved at least an attempt at building a bridge, to assure her that he did care about her, even though he was extremely lax in making it clear. He had to remedy that.

The rain recommenced as expected. It was soft but was merely building to a full deluge. He had been soaked enough the past few days and an hour or two in the warmth of the parlour, if Belle was inclined to allow him that comfort, would fuel him to venture forth again.

He climbed the three steps and rattled the iron ring. Normally, Jerome would have opened the door almost instantly, for by custom he stationed himself in the foyer, but on this occasion it was not he who greeted him, though such an eventuality was not uncommon. After all, Jerome could not be at his station permanently. A successful house of pleasure such as Mother Grady's required more than the girls who toiled upstairs, so a cook and two maids also found employment. It was one of the latter who opened the door.

'Good evening, Dorothy,' he said, taking off his hat and shaking it before entering. 'Jerome is otherwise engaged, I take it?'

'Yes, Mr Flynt,' Dorothy said, giving him a slight curtsey, which she was wont to do whenever she met him. It made him feel slightly uncomfortable, for not only did he scorn bowing or taking the knee to any man or woman, he also didn't welcome it being done for him. 'Business be quiet this night, the murders you know. They keeps many of the gentlemen close to their own hearth. Jerome attends Mother Grady and Mother St Clair in their private parlour. We have instruction to see they are not be disturbed, except by you.'

The addendum to the directive that the owners were to be disturbed only by him was perplexing, for they could not have known he would call that evening. As he crossed the foyer towards the rear of the house, Flynt felt something tingle at the back of his neck. Something here was amiss. He heard the laughter of men from the main parlour and the rattle of dice, so not all gentlemen tended to their families. From upstairs came the sound of footfalls and the occasional giggle of a young woman. No priapic emanations reached his ears for the house was most sturdily built and each room was sufficiently secure to stifle sound, for Mother Grady and Belle valued their patrons' privacy above all else.

As he reached the door of the small parlour, tucked away down a narrow corridor, that tingle had grown to a full-strength itch, as if an army of fleas bit at his flesh. He drew Tact from its pocket and pressed his ear against the wood. Like those of the chambers on the upper floor, the door was most solid but he could discern voices. Belle's, Mother Grady's, her words indistinct but by the angry timbre she was fit to blister paint. He took a step backwards, studying the door. Normally, his first instinct in such a situation would have been to kick it open and use the resulting surprise as a means of overwhelming whoever lay beyond. However, such action inevitably led to damaging the frame and he believed Mother Grady would not take kindly to that, and, in any case, he was unsure if he could budge such a masterfully built door. He decided that simply throwing it open would have to suffice.

In the end, he didn't have the chance.

Hands gripped him by the coat collar and held his right wrist immobile while propelling him with considerable force forwards. He managed at the last moment to turn his head sideways before his nose met with the door's stout wood and though the impact on his cheek was painful and an explosion of fireworks filled his vision, it was better than his nose breaking. It was a small mercy but he was thankful for it. His collar was relinquished but a strong blow to his lower back forced him to his knees with a sharp gasp. The pain of it, coupled with the deep throbbing across his face, was temporarily debilitating. Tact was snatched away and he heard it clatter on the wooden floor. He tried to turn but his attacker rammed him once more against the door, sending more fireworks bursting. His right wrist was again caught in an unyielding grip, his hand forcibly splayed upon the surface of the wood, followed swiftly by his left, while at the same time his legs were kicked open and back, causing him to lean forward at something of an angle. The flashing lights and shrieking in his head having subsided, Flynt decided that this encounter was proving to be somewhat one-sided, so even though he was in a difficult off-kilter position, he snatched his left hand free and jerked his elbow back, hoping to strike flesh. His attacker was prepared for such an offensive, for the arm was blocked and forced back to its previous position, then a kick delivered behind his knee caused his leg to buckle and his forehead was bounced against the door with such force that his faculties spun. His attacker then reached under his coat and rooted around. Diplomacy was found first, then his cane, both weapons being plucked away to join Tact somewhere down the hallway. The hand continued to roam over his body searching for further weapons with no sign of coyness as to where it probed.

'I normally have to negotiate a fee before this is done to me, friend,' Flynt said, forcing the words through the pain and overall disconcertion of his senses, 'and generally the touch is of a more feminine nature, not to mention considerably gentler.'

A low guttural sound was the only reply and, despite the agony, Flynt grinned.

'I recognise that grunt. You move quietly for a such a big brute, Gregor.'

He was jerked back from the door slightly and the man's hand pointed at the handle.

'I'm sorry I don't speak finger,' Flynt said, trying his best to mask the discomfort spreading across his back, only to find his face pressed against the wood once more for his trouble, which did nothing to alleviate the throbbing of his cheek and forehead. Gregor's finger stabbed at the handle again. 'Ah, you wish me to open the door? Why didn't you say so?'

He turned the handle and was immediately thrown bodily through the open door. He was grateful that the parlour boasted floorcloths, for they softened his landing, although not by much.

'Jonas, nice of you to join us.'

Christy de Fontaine sat in one of the winged armchairs by the fire, two small pistols in her hands, one trained on Belle in the other armchair, the second on Mother Grady on the sofa. Jerome was propped up in the corner of the room, conscious but only barely, blood streaming from a wound on his temple. Gregor's booted foot on his chest held him in place when he showed signs of rising. Flynt saw him now, big and broad and bearded, slotting a flintlock pistol into the artificial hand Defoe had described, which he displayed openly with no glove to disguise it, and using his other to manipulate the system of levers running along the wrist to the forearm to cause the metal fingers to clench. 'I see Gregor's grip has improved.'

'Yes, a craftsman in Germany who is most skilled in the art was kind enough to replace his former appendage with this most versatile new one,' Christy said.

'That's handy,' said Flynt, then lost his lightness of tone to address Belle and Mother Grady. 'Are you ladies well?'

'They are quite well,' said Christy. 'I mean them no harm.'

'The pistols say otherwise,' Mother Grady said, her words like a whip crack.

'A precaution only, for I didn't wish you to alert Jonas to our presence.'

Flynt asked. 'May I ask how you knew I would call upon these ladies?'

A tiny little frown puckered her brow. 'You did not receive the message?'

'What message?'

'I sent a boy with an invitation to attend here, in Miss St Clair's name, of course, to your lodgings. You still reside at the Golden Cross, do you not? You didn't displace yourself after our last little encounter in your rooms.'

That brought a pointed look from Belle, which Flynt did his best to ignore. 'I thought perhaps you'd had me followed.'

'It would have had to be a shadow most expert in that field, as you are not an easy man with whom to keep abreast.' A familiar smile taunted her lips. 'Although I wish you would keep mine.'

Flynt risked a glance towards Belle whose gaze was like an accusing finger. He wished he could explain that this was Christy de Fontaine's way. She was flirtatious, enigmatic, mischievous, and mercurial and she obviously knew of Flynt's connection to the house so would be doing her best to provoke some form of reaction.

Deciding it best to move away from that line of conversation, Flynt nodded towards the recumbent Jerome. 'If you mean no harm, what happened to Jerome?'

'I'm afraid he became a little boisterous and Gregor had to pacify him,' Christy explained. 'Worry not, Jonas darling, he knows exactly how to measure his blow to merely incapacitate, as you know.'

The memory of the blow to the back of his head on the waterfront, and more recently in the hallway, caused twinges. 'It was he who struck me the other night?'

'It was indeed. We had arrived at that rather dingy tavern in time to see you in hot pursuit. If we hadn't interceded then we would most certainly not be enjoying your company this very evening. Our friend with the eye patch and scarred visage would not have allowed you to walk away.'

Flynt didn't wish to go into that with Belle and Mother Grady present so he gave the big Russian a sour look. 'If Jerome is permanently damaged I will seek reparations.'

Christy's laugh was most melodious. 'Oh, Jonas, I do like it when you comport yourself in a manly fashion, even though you know that Gregor is more than capable of besting you.'

Gregor returned Flynt's stare impassively. 'I seem to remember besting him once or twice,' Flynt said.

'You had the upper hand, certainly, but when Gregor truly bests someone, that someone is generally dead.'

Flynt knew that to be true. On the two occasions he had found himself in direct opposition with the Russian he had only just escaped with his life, or at least without permanent injury. He looked to Belle again, trying to read something in her eyes, but they now bore a hooded quality that masked her true feelings, whether they be rage or fear or jealousy, or all three at once, he could not say. 'What of the patrons and staff?'

'All are hale and hearty, of that I can assure you,' Christy said. 'As we awaited our moment in the Piazza we witnessed men of some importance entering and leaving and it would not do to discommode them in their leisure pursuits.' She inclined her head towards both Belle and Mother Grady. 'You ladies are to be commended on the success of your venture. It's not easy for women to progress in this world but we do find ways, do we not? And men's weaknesses are often our strengths.'

'If you damage our enterprise in any way, lass,' Mother Grady said, 'It'll be my pleasure to claw your eyes out.'

Christy regarded the older woman for a moment and then laughed again. 'I do believe you would. She's a feisty one, Jonas. I like her.' She turned her attention to Belle. 'And Mistress Belle St Clair. Don't look so surprised, Jonas. I make it my business to learn everything I can about my friends and enemies.'

Belle was extremely calm when she spoke. 'So which is he to you, madame, friend or enemy?'

'That, my dear, is a conundrum I believe both Jonas and I often ponder, for we have a most complex relationship, do we not?'

That was putting it mildly, Jonas thought, as Christy made a study of Belle, who didn't flinch under her gaze. She had been scrutinised many times before so she examined Christy in return.

Christy smiled. 'I congratulate you on your good taste, for she is most certainly a beauty. I can see why you would forsake the pleasures of my bed to enjoy the pleasures of hers.'

Jonas felt Belle's eyes sharpen as they turned back to him. Despite knowing what Madame de Fontaine was doing, he felt himself flush. 'Christy, you and I have never been intimate, and you know it.'

Christy appeared for a moment to be tempted to continue her assertion but then reconsidered. ' 'Tis true, Belle, Jonas and I have never been tupping partners, though it was not for the want of trying on my part. He has nobly resisted all my advances. I can assure you that he has been most faithful to your trust.'

Flynt felt a need to get to the nub of the matter and steer her away from this avenue of conversation. 'Why are you here, Christy?'

'I grew impatient for you to come to me, so I thought I would come to you.'

Flynt rubbed his forehead. 'And your visits are always such a pleasure. To what do I owe the pleasure this time?'

'I come with a prophecy.'

'And that is?'

'That if you continue on your present path, you will most surely die. Despite the intercession of Gregor and I, that gentleman I mentioned earlier would see you perish in a most painful fashion.'

Flynt couldn't probe further before Belle and Mother Grady. 'This is not a subject for the ears of these ladies.'

'Please, Jonas, these ladies are not fluttery wives or daughters of noblemen. These ladies are most redoubtable.'

'Nevertheless, these are matters best discussed in private.'

This amused her even further. 'My goodness, you are so noble, so gallant, but so be it. Gregor, please take the ladies to another room while Jonas and I talk further.' Gregor shot her a glance. 'Worry not, my dear, he is a man of honour and will not attempt to molest me, is that not so?'

'You have my word,' he said. 'You also have the pistols.'

She laughed again. Despite his situation, he always found the sound of it pleasurable. Gregor kept his eye on him as he jerked his pistol towards Belle and Mother Grady to order them to move.

'And if we refuse to leave?' Belle asked, her head high.

'Gregor would then be obligated to use force and that, Mistress St Clair, is something I would not recommend. He is not as honourable as Jonas here and has no compunction concerning gender.'

Mother Grady was the first to rise, treating Flynt to one of her special glares as she moved to assist the still-groggy Jerome to his feet. 'What have you brought to this house, Jonas Flynt?'

Flynt couldn't answer. An apology would be feeble and, in any case, not accepted. He maintained his focus on Belle, trying to convey in a wordless fashion that he had never wanted this part of his life to intrude on theirs. Her expression was tightly set and he couldn't glean from it whether she understood as she helped Mother Grady with her nephew. However, she stopped at the door and gave Gregor a disdainful glance before addressing Christy.

'I will go but I will say this, madame. I know not who you are. I know not what connection you have had with Jonas in the past and what business you have with him now, but let me tell you this. If you harm a single hair of his head I will come looking for you, and when I find you please believe me when I say that no bulging ape will stop me from doing you harm in turn.'

Then, with a final look at Flynt, she left the room. Gregor seemed to show no offence at being called a bulging ape. Flynt was certain he had been called worse.

'I repeat, I can see why you would remain so faithful to her,' Christy said, and her tone was sincere. 'The old jade is most hardened by life and her tongue is sharper than a dagger but Mistress St Clair is truly the one to watch. Beauty, brains and deliberation is a most formidable combination. I should know, for I possess the same attributes.'

'Even if you say so yourself.'

'Come, Jonas darling, we know one another well enough to preclude the need for false modesty. And I would appreciate it if you would be so good as to arise from that floor, reclining as you are makes this nicely appointed room so untidy.'

Flynt rose to his feet and waved his hand towards the sherry, port and wine on the table beside the door. 'I need a drink to dull the pain of Gregor's kind invitation to join this reunion. May I get you something?'

'If that is a fine sherry, then I will have a glass, thank you for being so considerate.'

'It's my pleasure.' He began to pour. 'Do we need the weapons now? I have given you my parole not to make any attempt to assault you in any way.'

She placed the pistols on her lips and tutted. 'You have indeed made a promise not to molest me, more's the pity. But as ever, I live in hope.'

As he conveyed the sherry to her, he wondered at how easily they had slipped into their usual mild flirtation, and in her case sometimes more brazen challenges. He took a seat in the armchair Belle had vacated and sipped his wine. Christy tasted hers and nodded in satisfaction.

'A fine drop of sherry,' she said.

'Nothing but the best here.'

'Mistress St Clair included, I'll wager. If I hadn't made such a poor impression this evening, I might have been tempted to come back and test her skills in the boudoir. She accepts patronage from those of her own gender, I expect?'

Flynt hid his discomfort at this line of questioning. 'I never ask her about her profession.'

'Ah, not so open-minded as you might appear, eh Jonas?'

Flynt had no desire to discuss his emotional shortcomings with Christy de Fontaine. She already knew too much about him. 'Before you tell me more about your prognostication regarding my mortality, tell me why you had me dubbed the Paladin.'

A slight widening of the eye told him he had caught her out but she covered it with her secret little smile. 'You have been conversing with Mr Defoe, I take it?'

Flynt didn't reply.

'Never mind,' she said, airily. 'One should never trust a scribbler.'

'Christy, you knew he would come to me and you knew he would reveal his source, so I suspect that you were making mischief, correct?'

'It was a dull evening. I grew bored with entertaining others and sought a means to entertain myself.'

'And you did so by perhaps placing me in jeopardy? You had to know that if Defoe had named me in print as this fictional Paladin of yours then my life on these streets would have been most difficult, if not forfeit.'

'Oh, Jonas, let's not be so dramatic…'

'This is no drama. You know what I do, Christy, and you know I must by necessity remain in shadow.'

'Then perhaps you should not indulge yourself in these philanthropic activities, Jonas. However, I remain confident that you would have handled whatever might have occurred with your usual aplomb. I was also aware that Defoe would never make it into print with the story, for he, like you, is one of Colonel Charters' rogues. Mr Defoe has had a career most colourful. He was a spy for England…'

'I know…'

'But were you aware his name is not even Defoe?' She smiled when he shook his head. 'He was born Daniel Foe, he added the prefix De because it gave him an aristocratic flavour. Like all scriveners, the man is a rogue at heart.'

Flynt glared at her.

'Don't be so stern with me, Jonas.' She pouted. 'I had my little jest, it went no further, so let that be an end to it. We have something far more serious to discuss. You mentioned your life being forfeit and that is exactly why I am here.'

Flynt knew he would get no further with the Paladin matter so was forced to let it drop. 'Then let us talk about my impending demise. Can I assume that the engineer of it will be the enigmatic Monsieur Lombre?'

'Your assumption would be correct.'

'And you are currently working in concert with him?'

'I am not.'

'And I should believe you for what reason?'

Her eyes widened as if in innocence. 'Jonas, darling, you wound me. Would I lie to you?'

Flynt made a show of considering this and then said, 'Yes.'

She laughed. 'Regrettably that is also correct, but in this case I do not.'

'Then why are you in England and why were you meeting him that night?'

'Believe it or not, my sweet, I am in England on legitimate grounds.'

'You'll forgive me when I say... ha!'

'It be true, of that I can assure you. I was asked here by none other than Sir Robert Walpole.'

Flynt hid his surprise. 'Then if that individual is concerned, I have strong doubt as to the legitimacy of your function.'

'Come now, Jonas, your cynicism is most unbecoming. He is a fine man.' She sipped her sherry, then added. 'For a politician.'

Flynt decided to set aside any debate on the virtues of the former minister of government. 'And what *legitimate* function does he have you do?'

She said nothing for a long moment. 'If I tell you, do I have your word that you will not inform our good friend Colonel Charters that I have done so?'

'I give you my word.'

His word meant nothing when it came to Christy de Fontaine. What's more, she knew it.

'Then I know you will not betray my trust,' she said, brightly. 'You see, Jonas, I have faith in you, even though you have none in me.'

'With good reason, Christy.'

'We are friends, Jonas.'

'A friend does not have their pet behemoth pummel another friend into submission.'

She dismissed that with a wave of one hand. 'That was business, Jonas. It was nothing personal.'

'That is business I can do well without,' Flynt said, as well as the more recent bruises also recalling Gregor's hand at his throat some years previous. 'So what is your mission for Walpole?'

She set her glass down on a small round table beside her armchair. 'As you know, he is out of favour with government.'

'I'm sure he will connive somehow to find his way back in favour. Especially if he has employed your talents.'

'I find him most charming, in a robust, country squire way,' said Christy.

'But you find his money even more charming, correct?'

She smiled, taking no offence. 'You know me so well, dear Jonas. The result is that Stanhope and Sunderland now have the power and, importantly, the confidence of the king.'

'Old George never had much time for Walpole and his brother-in-law Townshend anyway.'

'Well, that in part was thanks to his mistress Mademoiselle Schulenburg. She never forgave them for refusing to sanction her raising to duchess. Have you ever set eyes upon the mademoiselle?'

Flynt shook his head. 'I do not travel in those circles.'

'You would have to travel in very large circles, for she is a big woman and far from fair.'

'Old George himself is no Adonis.'

'Yes, but he is a king and that makes all the difference. However, I feel sure you know there has been a breach of the familial bond between His Majesty King George and his son, the Prince of Wales.'

It was Flynt's turn to smile. 'His Majesty? When did you become so respectful of royalty?'

'When Sir Robert paid me, of course.'

Despite their differences, he couldn't help but like this woman. 'From what I hear, there wasn't much of a bond between father and son.'

'Well, given George has had the boy's mother imprisoned in a castle for the past thirty years, can you expect there to be? And then there was the recent unpleasantness over the king's refusal to appoint his son regent while he was back in Hanover. Guardian of the Realm, I believe, was the compromise.'

'All nonsense, as most things are with royalty.'

'Nevertheless these things do sting and all came to a head last year, as you will know, when the king banished young George from St James's Palace following a row over his insistence that the Duke of Newcastle be godfather to his grandson.'

Flynt suddenly became aware of the ridiculous situation. Here they were, discussing current events as if they were old friends in a coffee house while Belle was being held hostage by Gregor somewhere within the house. 'Will you get to the point, Christy?'

'I'm getting there, Jonas darling, please keep your breeches on.' She glanced at the door. 'Unless you fancy a quick tupping here. How delicious would that be, with your inamorata not a few feet away from us?' She saw Flynt's dry look and affected a pout. 'Honestly, there is no fun in you at all, I fail to see what Mistress Belle sees in you.'

Flynt sighed theatrically. 'Fat George the younger and his wife have taken up residence in Leicester House, where you have also been residing. Now, will you please tell me what the hell you're doing for Walpole?'

'My goodness, you are most eager. Are you like this while making love with Mistress Belle? Is it a case of,' she lowered and roughened her voice, 'get on with it, lassie, for I have business elsewhere?' Her natural tone returned. 'We women like to take our time, you know.'

'Christy, for God's sake!'

'Very well. Walpole recognises that his path back to power lies with the future king and so has employed me to smooth his way.'

'And how can you do that?'

'Through Caroline, of course. She and I met in Anspach some years ago and we struck up a firm friendship.'

'You cultivated a firm friendship, you mean, in case it would aid you in the future.'

'Let's not quibble over motivations. The point is that she trusts my counsel and Walpole learned this and has retained me to speak for him, for with Caroline on his side, he will ultimately be granted the good graces of the prince. Caroline is young, George's greatest asset, and he is devoted to her. Well, as devoted as these Hanoverians are to their spouses. Look at his father, one wife imprisoned and two mistresses that we know of. Princess Caroline will be a force to reckon with at court, I can assure you. Have you ever seen her?'

'I told you, I don't travel in such circles.'

'You would be quite taken by her. She is an intelligent and handsome woman, and she was the most agreeable princess in Germany. Her father-in-law might accommodate the latter but the former is something with which he cannot cope, for he does not know how to handle intelligent women. Retaining their children in his care has not endeared the king to his daughter-in-law, I can tell you.'

'And you work only for Walpole in this matter? You have accepted no commission from, say, the French court?'

'Why, Jonas, whatever do you suggest? That I would play some sort of double game?'

'A rift within English royalty would be most certainly in the interests of foreign powers.'

'Even those who are allied?'

Flynt recalled Charters' words. 'Allies are only allies when it is expedient.'

Christy had to concede that point. 'I assure you I am not in the pay of either France or, before you suggest it, the exiled Jacobite court.'

Flynt almost smiled, for he was to make that very suggestion. 'So you work only for Sir Robert in this regard?'

The very slight hitch before she replied told him she was about to offer a prevarication and that she wished him to know it. 'I will say that I work on this occasion on behalf of your realm.' She smiled. 'Do you remember once I told you about wheels within wheels?'

Flynt put together Charters' orders to leave Christy alone in Leicester House and what she had just admitted. She did not work solely for Walpole in this matter, she was also funnelling information to the colonel, for he stored secrets like a squirrel does nuts for winter. Madame de Fontaine was ever on the lookout for a way to maximise her income and it mattered not if it meant labouring under two masters, in this case Walpole and Charters. Flynt would lay decent odds that it was she who informed the colonel of her assignation with Lombre.

'But there is one who would have wished me to be more indiscreet,' she said.

'Monsieur Lombre?'

'Yes.'

'That was why you met with him?'

'Yes, he wished to recruit me to use my position in the heart of the Prince and Princess of Wales' court for the good of the Jacobite cause. They would wish to see this rift widen.'

'To what end?'

'As you say, any weakness among the heads of state is something on which to capitalise.'

'And you refused, of course.'

'I told you, on this occasion I work on behalf of the English realm.'

'And yet, Lombre agreed to spare my life at your insistence.'

'He and I share... memories... and for the sake of that he agreed to stay his hand. But rest assured, Jonas, it was on that single occasion only. Next time you and he meet he will not be so merciful.'

'The next time we meet, neither will I. And is that why he is in London? To recruit you to spy on royalty and do what you can to extend this father and son feud?'

'Word that I was here had reached Rome and the ears of James Francis Stuart, the king across the water or the Pretender, depending on which flag you wave. Royal courts do have a tendency to leak intelligence like a holed bucket. Too many people seeking advancement, too many wagging tongues, too many eager ears. Lombre was prevailed upon to make contact, but that was not his only reason for being on these shores.'

Flynt prevented himself from leaning forward, for he didn't want to appear too keen. 'What other reason?'

'I remain unsure of this other mission but he was in the vicinity of the waterfront for some function other than meeting me. He had met another individual on a previous occasion...'

'Lombre freely told you this?'

She smiled that sweet smile. 'Unlike you, he trusts me and, as I said, we have a certain bond.'

'Did you know this other man?'

'Oh yes, I've worked with him in the past, specifically when you and I were in Edinburgh back in '15 during the affair of the late queen's will. He also was most interested in the split, although why I could not tell, and whether Walpole would work his way back into the royal graces.'

This was the Scot that the Admiral had heard about. 'Who was he?'

'You will know him as the lickspittle that followed the late Lord James Moncrieff around like a little dog, but he is more than that, far more. Andrew Wilson was his name, and he is just as dangerous, even more so, than Monsieur Lombre.'

23

Charters found Moncrieff in conversation with three other gentlemen of means. He had no desire to intrude on their obvious conviviality, further congratulations on his future fatherhood perhaps, although Moncrieff himself seemed to be enduring rather than enjoying it, just as he had when he was with Walpole. They were gathered around a gaming table in White's, though Moncrieff himself didn't gamble. Charters recalled him stating once that he did not game.

As he made his way to his own favourite chair, Moncrieff glanced in his direction and Charters held his gaze momentarily in order to convey his wish to converse. Moncrieff frowned, as he would expect, but gave him a small nod of understanding. Charters took his seat beside the fire and when the servant approached, ordered a dish of coffee. The flames in the grate were insufficient to ward off the cold, or perhaps it was this business that had chilled his blood. In both war and peace he was renowned for his cool head and clear eye when handling matters both sensitive and perilous but the suggestion – no, the fear – that Nimrod Boone walked among them had made him most anxious. His sleep was disturbed, his decision making was cloudy and he had to force himself to focus. Nathaniel Charters had never before felt such preoccupation and he did not appreciate it. This matter had to be concluded and perhaps on the morrow, when he and Flynt visited Bethlem Hospital, it would be, at least in part, for if Boone was safely restrained in that place then it was to be hoped the nightmares would cease. The murders remained an issue, and though such matters were not usually within his purview, the suggestion of Lombre's involvement, and that of the Fellowship, did mean they were wrapped around a potential threat to the security of the nation.

The chocolate house was unusually lacking in clientele this night, Charters noted. The streets were abuzz with the tales of the fresh horrors, and the broadsheet sellers were enjoying a most profitable period spreading lies and rumour as fact. The damp air was alive with tension, as families kept their doors locked and husbands remained at home, pistols cocked no doubt. London was a trigger's breadth from tragedy. It was a matter of time before some innocent individual called at the wrong door and received a pistol ball for payment.

By the time he stood before him, Moncrieff had donned his black coat, suspicion and curiosity mixed in his gaze. 'You wished a word, Colonel?'

'I did, my lord,' Charters said, indicating the armchair opposite. 'Please, won't you take your comfort.'

Moncrieff hesitated for a moment, then seated himself, both hands resting on the silver wolf's head that adorned his cane, his hat gripped between two fingers. 'I have but a moment, as I must be to home with my wife.'

'I understand, and I will detain you only briefly. How is Lady Catherine?'

'It is early in the pregnancy and she is quite well.'

'I am gratified to hear it so, and wish that her good health continues.' The servant returned with Charters' beverage. 'You would take a cup?'

Moncrieff shook his head and Charters nodded his thanks to the servant, who left them alone.

'How can I assist you, Colonel?'

The conversation thus far had been polite, even respectful, but it would not, could not, continue in that manner. Charters was a man who walked in a maze of lies, half-truths and threats hidden behind a veil of courtesy but he had little time for such intricacies. This night was a time for blunt speech. Before he spoke again, he ensured none of the other gentlemen were close enough to overhear.

'Are you familiar with a man named Lombre?'

A mere flicker in the eye told Charters that Moncrieff was but nevertheless he shook his head. 'I confess I am not.'

Charters leaned forward, lowering his tone even further. 'Come, my lord, your time is short and the matter I wish to discuss is too grave for such prevarication. You have my word that I lay no traps for you, I do not seek to inveigle any confession of wrongdoing…'

'I am guilty of no wrongdoing…'

Charters nearly laughed. 'Really? And what of your involvement in a certain affair in a village in the north? There was wrongdoing most grievous there.'

Moncrieff was not moved. 'If that were so, you would have moved for a prosecution.'

'I had no interest in prosecuting you, and my man reported that you were instrumental in bringing a villain to heel.'

Moncrieff's smile was thin, his eyes narrowed. 'As you are being frank, sir, I shall do you the courtesy of the same. The reason you do not prosecute is because you cannot bring *your man* before the courts, for to do so would reveal his true function and also imperil the secretive nature of your company. That means you do not have proof sufficient to make a case.'

'I am glad, my lord, that we are being frank, for I have no wish to dance around the nature of our relationship as though we were children about a maypole. We know each other, you and I. You know of my work and I know of your associations, but I tell you true that they concern me at this moment only insofar as they might assist me to unmask a murderer.'

That seemed to hit home. 'You took Sir Robert's urging to heart? You seek the perpetrator of the horrors in Whitechapel and Lincoln's Fields? The murders of children?'

'I did, but I have other reasons to investigate. Now, I ask you again, do you know of a man named Lombre?'

Moncrieff's lips twitched slightly as he considered his reply, finally settling on something that Charters sensed was close to the truth. 'I have heard the name, yes.'

'But you have had no dealings with him personally of late?'

'I have not.'

'I have your word on that?'

'You do.'

A man's word was only as true as his character but Charters had to accept it. He knew Flynt had spared this man's life for some reason. Perhaps because he had seen the error of his ways in the Gallowmire affair, but Charters suspected there was something deeper. Flynt had shown at least a sliver of trust in this Scottish lord and Charters trusted Flynt, though he would never reveal that to him.

'Are you aware of any other member of your…' he paused, seeking for the correct word to use, then thought damn it, they both knew what it was. 'Any other member of your Fellowship having recent connection with him?'

Moncrieff hesitated a fraction, but Charters suspected not over the naming of the Fellowship. 'I do not. But what does this man have to do with the murders? Do you think him responsible?'

'I know not for certain but there is reason to believe he may have some involvement. Let me put to you further names – Nimrod Boone. Caleb Boone.'

Moncrieff's head shook. 'They mean nothing to me. Who are they?'

'Caleb Boone is a rogue with ambitions of betterment and Nimrod his cousin. It be possible that Monsieur Lombre has had contact with one, or both. He has also been seen in the company of a Scotsman under covert circumstances.'

Something flashed in Moncrieff's eye but he covered it by thinning his lips and going on the attack. 'And you think that Scotsman was I?'

'I do not,' Charters said truthfully. 'But Caleb Boone, as I intimated, has a desire to improve his position, at least within his criminal world, and my information is that he has the backing of powerful and influential men.'

'And on that flimsy premise you accuse me?'

'On my honour I accuse you of nothing, my lord. We are having an open discussion here and you have assured me that you have nothing to do with Lombre or these other men.'

'I could be lying.'

'You could be, but I think not in this case. I saw your expression when you mentioned the murder of children. It is my belief you would have nothing to do with such depredations.' He paused. 'It is also my belief that when I mentioned a Scotsman that you had some notion of who it was.'

Moncrieff fell silent.

'Your silence tells me that you do. I thank you for not lying, my lord.'

A laugh as dice were rolled drew Moncrieff's gaze away but he was not interested in the game. Charters knew he was turning something over in his mind. 'If there is something you would wish to tell me, Lord Moncrieff…'

Moncrieff's attention slowly shifted back to him. 'There is nothing I can tell you, Colonel. I know nothing of this man Lombre, I have never met him, though his name has been uttered in my presence in the past.'

'Not recently?'

'No, not recently. I do not know these other names either.'

Charters pressed, 'But you do have some suspicion regarding the Scotsman?'

Moncrieff didn't reply.

'On this occasion, and perhaps this occasion only, I believe we are on the same side,' Charters said. 'You are set to be a father. Can you really sit there and allow someone who has perhaps ordered the slaughter of innocents to go free? You were moved to do the honourable thing in the north when a boy was so threatened.'

'You have no evidence that Lombre has had any firm connection with the crimes, much less that his meeting with this Scotsman related to them. What you have presented to me is conjecture only, an amalgam of somewhat spurious evidence presented as an incomplete whole.'

The words were strong but the delivery wasn't. Something preyed on the man's mind, something in what Charters had told him had sparked a suspicion.

'My lord,' he said, as Moncrieff rose to his feet, 'what you say is true. The evidence is far from compelling but people have gone to the gallows on less. I assure you I will pursue this matter with the utmost fervour and I will get to the nub of it, and when I do judgement will be swift and it will be severe. I urge you not to be on the wrong end of that judgement. If you know anything, if you even have suspicion, then share it with me now.'

The man seemed tempted to speak, his manner uncertain of the way forward, but then pulled back as he resumed his normal bearing. 'I wish you luck in your investigation, Colonel Charters, but I cannot enlighten you in any way. There is nothing I can say.' He paused, just for a moment, then said with considerable emphasis, 'On my oath, I cannot.'

And in those few words, Charters understood why the man could say nothing.

-

Flynt saw Christy to the main door, where Gregor waited along with Mother Grady and Jerome, now fully *compos mentis,* though his head was bandaged. Christy raised herself on her toes and kissed Flynt on the lips. It was a fleeting kiss but to his shame he enjoyed it. She then rubbed the back of her fingers down his cheek.

'Be most wary of Lombre, Jonas darling,' she said. 'He is not a man to be trifled with.'

'Neither am I, Christy,' he said, shooting a glance at Mother Grady, whose lips pressed tightly together, as if she was holding back her rage, which was probably accurate.

'If you continue to interfere in whatever his true mission is, then he will come after you.' Christy jerked her eyes towards the older woman and her nephew. 'And those you care for.'

'And if he learns that you have given me warning, what of you?'

That coquettish smile returned. 'Why, Jonas, do you mean to say that you care for me?'

Flynt was acutely aware of Mother Grady's glare. 'Concerned, Christy, let us say that.'

She laughed. 'Fear not, I am too valuable a commodity to the people who employ us both. And, of course, I have dear Gregor to watch over me. Monsieur Lombre is most formidable, to be sure, but even he is no match for Gregor.'

She craned upwards and kissed him again, again on the lips. This time it was more lingering, soft and inviting and, despite his manful vow to resist, Flynt felt himself respond. Damnation, he thought, we men are such weak creatures.

Christy broke away and her eyes revealed that she knew full well the effect she had on his flesh if not his heart, then looked to Mother Grady. 'We are close friends, madame, and often share a kiss and embrace most chaste.'

'There's nothing chaste about you, girl,' said Mother Grady. 'Your innocence, if you ever had such, was tarnished many years hence, I would say.'

Christy smiled her sweetest smile as she motioned Gregor to open the door. 'Then that is something we share, is it not, Mrs Grady?'

With a final wiggle of her fingers in Flynt's direction, Christy raised the hood of her gown and stepped into the rain. Gregor didn't trouble himself with any goodbyes, not even a final glower at Flynt. Mother Grady was not yet finished with them, for she stood in the doorway and screamed some words in her native Irish tongue, the meaning of which were unknown to Flynt but the sentiment they carried was not.

Jerome took her lightly by the arm and pulled her away, then closed the door. 'Leave it, Aunt, the night is too filthy for thy health and they don't pay you no never mind any road.'

She allowed him to lead her back into the foyer, where she fixed a flaring eye on Flynt. 'What is she to you?'

'She is nothing to me.'

'She seems to think differently.'

'I cannot help what she thinks.' He then addressed Jerome. 'You're fully recovered?'

Jerome gingerly fingered the bandage and gave Flynt a sheepish grin. 'A bump on head be all. I've had such before.'

Haven't we all, Flynt thought. 'Where is Mistress Belle?'

'She's in her chamber, Mr Flynt,' he replied.

'She doesn't wish to see you,' Mother Grady said, her words corroded by something liquid.

Flynt glanced up the stairs, contemplating testing that claim himself.

Mother Grady coughed slightly and swallowed. 'I've said this before, Jonas Flynt, but I say it here again and you might wish to write it down lest you forget it. You are trouble. I have no knowledge of your true connection with that wanton baggage and her hulking brute but I know this – it's no good you're up to. I knew you be thief and I knew you be adventurer but now I suspect there be more to you than that and, though I know not what it is, I don't like it. I don't like it being brought into my house and I don't like it touching my Belle.'

'Belle was not in any danger…'

'Perhaps not from that flighty Scottish piece, but I heard what she said and it was clear you will bring it to her soon enough, I wager. You are death, Jonas Flynt, and you will bring it to her, as sure as I'm standing here.'

She broke off with a paroxysm of coughing and Jerome reached out to help her, but she pushed his hands away and wiped her lips with a kerchief. 'Leave me be, for it is only a cough brought about by the dankness of the air.' Her voice was hoarse, however, and Flynt thought he saw a fleck of blood on her lips before she licked it away. The voice softened slightly when she addressed Flynt once more. 'Let the girl alone, man, for the love of God. She loves you and only the Almighty knows why, for she knows in her heart that you will break it.'

'That is not my...'

She raised her hand. 'You will not mean to, I know that, for though I have never fully warmed to you I know you are not a cruel man, though you have perhaps done many things that some might see as cruel. Yes, people talk and names are mentioned.'

'Not all of it is true.'

'But most of it is, eh? As for Belle, I believe you care for her in your way.'

'I do...'

'But that is not enough.' She coughed again, the kerchief again to her lips. She took a breath before she spoke again.

'Aunt, thee should be abed,' Jerome said.

'I will not be fussed over, Jerome.' The words were not sharp, but they were firm. 'I have things to say and by God, I will say them.' She returned her attention to Flynt. 'There are two types of men who come here, those who wish to sully us and those who wish to save us. I told you once before that women like Belle and I do not need men to be our saviours and to that I add this – but they can be our destroyers, and not just physically. I confess when I brought her here from the Indies she was just another girl to service my house but I think you know that I came to love her above all others, even as though she were my own child. I see much of me within her and by God she will need that in the years to come. I know she was forced into this life, and that perhaps preys a great deal upon my conscience these cold, dark nights, but she has become a strong, spirited lass. You didn't see her when she first came, for you did not make her acquaintance until she was fully grown, but she was a mousy little thing, all eyes and hair and fear. But I fancied I saw something else in her, burning through that fear, an independence of mind and spirit that might have been whipped out of her, or worse, had she stayed across the seas. She is intelligent, brave, and clear of thought. I like to think I had something to do with that, perhaps helped her discover a steel that might have been lost if she remained the property of some rich farmer, though I would like to think she is stronger than that and would endure. But when it comes to you, that steel seems to melt. You entered this house as a cull but you became something more and that in itself is unusual in our life. I counselled her against such feelings but emotions are like this damn wet weather, they seep into your soul, and they seeped into hers.'

She coughed again, the kerchief pressed against her mouth, then taken away and crumpled in her hand before he could check if there were any scarlet stains. She caught his quick gaze and gave her head a little shake, as if warning him against asking about it.

'You will break that girl,' she said. 'She loves you but you do not love her and when that finally seeps through like this weather, it will be the death of her soul.' Her eyes glistened as they took on a faraway look for a moment, as if she was remembering something. 'And that is a death I would wish on no woman.'

'What makes you believe I do not have affection for her?'

Her eyes sharpened again. 'Because you cannot even say the word, even to me.'

Only then did he realise what he had said. And what he had not.

24

'And who is this Andrew Wilson?'

They were travelling north to Moorfield in Colonel Charters' carriage, a rare honour for Flynt who had never before been invited inside. He was more used to what his countrymen called shank's nag, in other words walking, or being carried in sedan chairs that often bounced the passenger around like a dog shaking a rat. The closest he came to this mode of travel were hackneys but they were much less well appointed than this conveyance with its padded seats and headrests.

Flynt had told him about conversing with Madame de Fontaine and after assuaging Charters' initial anger over being disobeyed by explaining that she approached him, he revealed the identity of the Scotsman who had met with Lombre.

'He is a bailie in Edinburgh,' Flynt explained.

'And you have met him?'

Flynt inclined his head. 'I did, when I was in the city searching for Queen Anne's will back in '15.'

'What do you know of him?'

'I confess I thought him nothing but a functionary, you well know the sort, a middling office holder in city government. A nothing, a lickspittle, as he was described to me.'

Charters' smile was thin. 'A fine word. So exactly whose spittle did he lick?'

'At the time it was Lord James Moncrieff.'

Charters' eyebrows raised at that. 'Father or son?'

'Father. The son was not in Edinburgh while I was there.'

Charters took a moment to consider this intelligence. 'So what business does a petty official from Edinburgh have with Monsieur Lombre?'

'Christy didn't know.'

Despite his prevailing mood, Charters' familiar sparkle glistened. 'Christy, be it? Are you sure there is nothing more between you and that damned woman than rivalry?'

'I am certain, Colonel. And at this moment she is not a rival, for I would venture that it was you who helped her become acquainted with Sir Robert Walpole, on whose behalf she is currently employed.'

Charters was not thrown by the accusation. 'I always use the best person for the job and I knew of her connection with the Princess of Wales. They are two of a kind, those women, for the Princess Royal is also not averse to using her ample charms to bend men most subtly to her will. And it was Madame de Fontaine who began this Paladin nonsense, you say?'

'I think it was a prank more than anything.'

'A prank that could well have undermined the work you do for me, which I suggest was her initial intention. As for these personal missions of yours, Flynt, I do hope you have taken to heart my instruction to curtail them. I have overlooked your tendency to sentiment, even though it be something I find exceeding difficult to understand in a man such as you, but I can no longer.'

'I do what I think has to be done under given circumstances.'

'Perhaps, but whatever your motivations, you are no crusader for justice, Flynt, and I need you to concentrate on matters at hand and not some damn foolish displays of altruism.'

Flynt almost laughed. 'And what is this mission on which we are currently embarked if not one that has at its roots self-interest, Colonel? Had you not a personal stake in it, we would not have been following this.'

Charters had the good grace to be discomfited by this truth, but he still hit back. 'Yet had we not been following it then we would not have suspicions of Fellowship involvement, and I need not remind you that those gentlemen are very much our business.'

'We didn't know that when we began.'

'But we know it now and that is the end of it.' Charters glared at him. 'This Wilson fellow, do you think he might be Fellowship?'

'I would speculate yes. Christy did say he was most dangerous, despite his feigned exterior, something he does exceeding well, I have to say.'

Flynt recalled having the man under his gun in an Edinburgh apartment. He'd had no suspicion that the fright he displayed might have been affected.

Charters considered that. 'I spoke with Lord Moncrieff last evening, as you suggested. He denied all knowledge, of course, but when I intimated that it was a Scotsman who had been conversing with Lombre, I swear he knew who it was. He declined to speak further and I had the distinct notion that there was an oath involved. I would hazard that the Fellowship requires members to maintain silence regarding the membership and their activities.'

'That sounds exceeding familiar,' Flynt observed.

'The Company does not require an oath of loyalty,' Charters pointed out.

'No, the threat of Tyburn precludes the need for one.'

Charters seemed ready to argue the point when the carriage came to a halt, so instead he looked from the window and said, 'We're here.'

Flynt was not looking forward to this first visit to St Mary Bethlehem Hospital, shortened to Bethlem and then through common usage to Bedlam. Like Newgate and other prisons, visitations to this sanctuary for those of unsound minds had become a common pastime for Londoners, the poor tormented souls within had become fodder for the curiosity and delectation of those who revelled in the plight of the less fortunate. As they alighted from the carriage beside a long wall about eight foot high, Charters asked, 'Bethlehem means house of bread in Hebrew, did you know this, Serjeant?'

Flynt confessed he did not as he glanced the way they had come to see Charters' ubiquitous watchers idling on horseback a few yards away. The colonel himself lingered at the steps leading to a pair of tall wooden gates. The arrogance of a superior officer displayed within the carriage had gone and Flynt thought he detected an anxious quality he had never before seen in him.

'I have not stood here for near forty years. It has much changed. The new hospital had only recently been constructed, the old premises in Bishopsgate deemed not suitable for their purpose and this site near the old wall was selected. Beyond those gates stand an architectural triumph, Flynt, and I guarantee you will be most impressed.'

Flynt didn't know Charters' age but was confident he would not be even ten years of age when last he had gazed at those gates, so it was with some surprise that he said, 'You were here to view the inmates?'

'There is no need to adopt such a judgemental tone, Flynt. My father thought it advisable that I understand that there were people who were less fortunate than I. All society can be found beyond this wall and these gates, rich and poor, male and female. Nobles, paupers, artists, thieves, whores, for an unsound mind is no respecter of position or skills.'

'And was the visit instructive?'

'I failed to gain access. It was Whitsun, I recall, and as a holiday there was a multitude of visitors awaiting to enter. There followed a most disagreeable commotion nigh on this very spot. A young nobleman, no more than fifteen years of age, was deemed to have insulted a woman of the lower orders among the crowd awaiting to gain access and received a blow to the face for his trouble and was then thrown back down these steps. The young blood drew his sword and in his haste lashed out, stabbing a hospital porter. The mob turned upon him and would have torn both he and his mother to shreds had they not been whisked away into the safety of the grounds.'

'And what subsequently happened to this nobleman?'

'I have no idea,' dismissed Charters, 'for this was long before I took an interest in such things.'

Flynt could guess what happened to him. He would have pleaded self-defence and avoided any punishment thanks to his station in life. He let the matter lie, however, and instead made a study of the lion and unicorn crest on the gateway, the standard of Charles II, under whose reign the hospital was constructed. Then, as they climbed the steps, he raised his eyes to the massive stone carvings set above the tall gates, two men reclining, both hairless, both nearly naked.

Charters noticed Flynt's examination of the statues. 'Hewn from Portland stone by Caius Gabriel Cibber, father to Colley, the esteemed actor-manager of the Drury Lane theatre. They represent melancholy and mania, the two basic forms of madness. The fellow in chains be mania and I've heard tell that when it was hewn its likeness was drawn from a servant of none other than Oliver Cromwell, a seven-foot giant by name of Daniel, who was an inmate here for some years until his death. I believe his mania was of a religious nature, understandable given who his master was. I do wonder if he was as angry and dangerous as he has been presented here.'

The colonel's interest in the history of the city and its institutions had often been revealed to Flynt previously but this time it was different. This time Charters was displaying his knowledge not out of a desire to be pedagogue, but to camouflage the nervousness that fluttered behind his words. He was at once keen and in dread of what they might find behind these walls and both emotions were betrayed in his tone and in the now ever-present shadows under his eyes.

Charters pushed open one of the smaller wicket gates on either side of the taller ones and they stepped through into a most pleasing space of cultured gardens and well-tended walkways. Beyond them lay New Bedlam itself, which was in aspect very fine indeed and looked more like a palace than a hospital for the insane, hence another term used – the Palace Beautiful. At the centre of the long brick building was a pavilion of stone, taller than the roofs on either side, topped by a cupola and adorned by Corinthian columns. Similar, not quite so ornate, pavilions stood at either end of the structure. Each of the three floors was studded with windows, the tax obviously being of no concern for the board of governors. Attic rooms, signified by dormers, broke through the tiled roof.

'The architect, Mr Robert Hooke, took his inspiration from the French design,' Charters said. 'Have you seen the Tuileries in Paris?'

'I've never visited the city,' said Flynt as they threaded their way towards the main entrance through the formal gardens.

'If you had you might note some similarities. Of course, this is far finer than anything Louis could have had constructed.'

'I think perhaps you show your prejudices there, Colonel.'

Charters' smile was thin. 'Perhaps, but once an enemy always an enemy, I think I have already made that clear. You gaze upon an architectural triumph, Flynt, a symbol of the growth of this great city. Sir Christopher Wren it was who said that public buildings are the ornament of a country, and by God he was a man who knew whereof he spoke. When the people gaze upon his great cathedral, or even the hospital ahead, they come to know that their country is rising in stature and in influence, and it follows that they have a pride in being part of it.'

Again, Flynt was unsure of that being the case, but he had encountered fierce patriotism in the lowliest rogue. He himself acknowledged no pride in country, no obeisance to any higher power. He had followed the flag and drum into battle and witnessed carnage. He had fled when the slaughter became too much for him. He had seen friends and acquaintances die in order to gain dominion over a town or a village or even a few acres of dirt in some foreign field that nobody had heard of before armies clashed and nobody thought much of now. And all was done in the name of king or God or country and he would never do the same again.

Steps led to the main entrance set below an iron-balustraded balcony, and beyond it they were met by three figures, one of flesh and blood, the others artificial and dressed in the garb of the beggars. The breathing figure was a bulky, capable-looking man in a blue gown bearing a star motif and wielding a silver-headed staff, which he pointed in the direction of the figures, which Flynt now saw were actually vessels designed for the receipt of coin.

'Good day, gentlemen,' said the porter, his tone polite but dripping with official weight. 'Pray remember the poor lunatics within this place and with your own hands, insert your charity into these here alms boxes, if you please.'

'We are expected by Dr Richard Hale,' Charters said. 'I sent a messenger yesterday to inform him that we are come on official business, not as visitors.'

'Nonetheless, sir,' the porter said, almost achieving some level of respect in his voice, 'none shall enter here without putting up the alms. This here be a charity, sir, and to run a fine establishment such as this requires the coin. No coin, no entry, that be the simple fact of the situation, begging your pardon for my insistence.'

Flynt smiled, for neither the man's posture nor his tone revealed any real desire to beg pardon. He suspected that should they try to force entry, that sturdy staff would be wielded with considerable expertise. There was little likelihood that this porter would find himself run through by any recalcitrant visitor, be he noble or commoner.

Charters growled as he fished in his pocket and produced a coin. 'I understand that a penny or two is sufficient for admission but I have but a guinea on me, have you change?'

The porter shook his head, almost sorrowfully. 'I regret, sir, that I do not carry change. But a guinea is as welcome as a penny and for that you may both enter and with the thanks of the needy folks what find themselves here ensconced.'

Charters looked to Flynt in a wordless query and at first he was tempted to claim he had no money about his person but such a protestation wouldn't be believed. 'I have a crown here,' Flynt said. 'Would that be sufficient to grant my friend and I access?'

The porter looked somehow deflated but he grudgingly nodded and Flynt dropped the coin in the nearest box, hearing it clang against others within.

'Now,' said Charters, 'where can we find Dr Hale, for we have urgent business?'

'You will find him beyond these here penny gates, but I would introduce yourself first to the steward, who bides in his office to the right of the hallway yonder. He would not take kindly to you two gents simply making entrance to the consulting room without first being announced proper like.'

Charters said nothing as he turned away from the porter. Flynt smiled towards the man and nodded his thanks as he followed. Charters was a most complex man. He preferred his anonymity, especially when it came to the work he performed, but he did like his rank and social class to be recognised so to be treated as a mere patron by the porter had been an insult. He lingered in the wide hallway, leaving Flynt to address the steward who sat in his small office eating bread and cheese, washing them down with ale. He was another large individual, also dressed in blue and carrying the star badge, who stood as Flynt entered.

'You are the steward?' Flynt asked.

'That I is, sir, just having me some late breakfast, begging your pardon, and how can I help you?'

'My friend and I are here to see Dr Richard Hale. I believe he was expecting us.'

The steward craned round Flynt to eye the figure of Colonel Charters lingering in the hallway, then picked up a sheaf of papers from his little table. 'And what would be the name what the doctor was expecting, if I may make such inquiry, sir?'

'Colonel Nathaniel Charters.'

The steward ran a finger down a short list. 'Yes, sir, here it be, sir, your friend's name, and you would be Mr Jonas Flynt, with instructions here written to show you to the doctor immediate.' He dropped the papers back, then thrust the remainder of his late breakfast into a drawer, pausing only to drain his tankard and wipe his lips with the back of his hand. 'Begging your pardon, but it's been a busy morning and I has me a thirst that would choke a desert camel in that there African wasteland. Right this way, if you please.'

He led them across the passageway, where he knocked at a door and waited for a voice to bid him enter, which he did, closing the door behind him.

Charters said softly, 'Damn it, we could have entered that door without the preamble of calling upon the steward.'

'Every man has his function, Colonel,' Flynt said. 'We must respect that.'

Charters grunted, in no mood to respect the functions of petty officials.

The steward reappeared and motioned them into the room, where sat a full-figured man in a blue topcoat, his fleshy face stern but with a melancholy caste to his eyes, his head bare of wig, which was laid upon the desk near to his hand. He scribbled a few final words with the quill he held before rising from behind his desk and extending a hand.

'Welcome to St Mary's Bethlehem, Colonel Charters.'

'You received my note then? Concerning Nimrod Boone?'

'I did, and I must say I am most curious as to why you would be interested in this particular case. Most visitors come here to see the work we do *in totem*; those who wish to see individuals are generally related or friends. Do you have some connection to this poor unfortunate?'

Charters would have expected such a query and was ready with his response. There was no necessity to lie. 'I knew him in Flanders. He was under my command.'

'He was a soldier? I didn't know that.' Hale made a note on a piece of paper.

'Not a good one, however,' Charters said. 'He displayed his mania many years ago, when he slaughtered a family.'

Hale's eyebrows raised and he began making another note. 'And this occurred in Flanders?'

'It did, almost on the eve of battle at Malplaquet.'

Hale looked up from his writing. 'You were there?'

'We both were.'

Hale looked at Flynt as if noticing him for the first time and he glanced down at his notes. 'You will be Jonas Flynt?'

'I am.'

'Malplaquet was a most bloody affair, I understand.'

'The bloodiest,' Flynt said.

'But a magnificent victory for His Grace the Duke of Marlborough,' Charters added.

The French would say differently, Flynt almost said but decided this was neither the time nor the place to open that debate again.

The doctor asked, 'You say my patient committed murder, Colonel, and yet was not punished for the crime?'

'Regrettably he made his escape before justice reached its conclusion.'

Hale set his quill aside and settled back in his chair, his eyes fixed firmly on Charters. He raised his right hand and pressed two fingers against his lips. 'And you blame yourself for this failure.'

'He was under my command. I passed judgement. Naturally I feel some measure of responsibility.'

The doctor said nothing as he assessed Charters' words. The traces of sadness those eyes carried were perhaps the result of the tragedies he had seen in his patients, but they missed little. 'And what do you wish to achieve by this visit today? Do you still expect to mete out justice? To drag him from this place to the Sessions House at Newgate? I warn you, I would resist such a move, for this man is not able to plead, even if he is subjected to the rigours of the press yard. They could pile on every stone and still he would not yield.'

'I shall be frank with you, Dr Hale, I am here to see for myself that he is indeed beyond the realms of sanity.'

'I might argue that if he did indeed murder that family in Flanders, then that itself proves as such.'

'And I might argue that by escaping custody he understood the difference between right and wrong, and that distinction suggests some form of reason and makes him a danger to the public.'

'Then perhaps, but no more. You may rest assured that he is that most difficult of patients for a physician such as myself, the completely incurable. His mind is permanently unbalanced and no treatment we can offer here will restore that mental equilibrium. Nimrod Boone will never leave this place alive, I am sorry to say.'

Charters displayed no surprise. 'Had I been more attentive to my duty, as an officer and as a man, then I would have saved you the trouble of such care.'

'As a medical practitioner, my oath must take issue with such a sentiment, for I am bound to do no harm. But as a man, I understand that you feel guilt. You would wish to see him then?'

'Yes. I must gaze upon him myself if I am to regain any form of satisfaction.'

Richard Hale, his fingers once again pressed to his lips as he considered this, nodded after a few moments and rose, plucking the wig from the desk and settling it over his scalp. 'Very well. I would appreciate it if you would surrender any weapons to the steward. I allow none on the gallery floors and certainly not in the vicinity of Mr Boone...'

25

The noise came at them like a physical assault. Flynt was used to the hustle and bustle of the city – the cries of the hawkers, the rattle of cartwheel, the clip of hooves and the bellowing of cattle being led to market – but even though the gallery to which Hale led them was long and reasonably spacious, the din seemed to fill it, the walls and high ceiling not only containing it but also sending it back twice-fold. There was shouting and singing and the rattle of chains. There was weeping and wailing, moaning and groaning. A similar cacophony emanated from a further gallery above them, but those voices were female, for the genders were segregated. Most of the patients were within cells on either side of the gallery but some walked free, interacting with each other or the staff dressed in the blue garments Flynt now realised was a uniform. A few roamed alone, and one man marched towards them, his step not faltering and forcing them to part to allow him to pass. He did not thank them, did not acknowledge them in any way; he maintained his pace until he reached the locked grille when he spun smartly and trooped back in their direction once more, passing through them as if they weren't there to continue his perambulation.

Flynt glanced at Dr Hale but the physician offered no explanation, only led them onwards. Flynt saw two pairs of well-dressed men and women being guided by a member of staff pointing out cases of interest and peering into the cells that lined the gallery.

'I thought there was no visiting today,' he said.

'Sometimes exceptions are made,' Hale said.

Flynt couldn't keep distaste from his voice. 'If the price is met?'

The doctor's pace faltered just a little as he gave Flynt a severe glance. 'Do not judge these people or this institution so harshly, sir. Such charity assists us to meet our costs. This is a monumental endeavour and as such requires monumental funding. Those gentlemen are considering making a donation and so are entitled to view the work we do. I remind you, sir, that you are here for reasons that are not so charitable.'

Hale walked on and Charters glared at Flynt, whispering, 'Damn it, Flynt, keep your moralising to yourself.'

As they passed the group, Flynt made notice again of the symbol embroidered on the gown worn by the hospital guide. 'May I ask why the staff all bear the sign of a star?'

'It relates to the hospital name, St Mary Bethlehem,' explained Hale. 'The star represents that which not only guided the wise men to the birthplace of our Lord Jesus Christ, but also the first benefactor of the hospital, Simon FitzMary. As a crusader he found himself lost in the Holy Land and at the mercy of the forces of Saladin. He was guided to the safety of Bethlehem by such a star. On his return to England, he pursued a business and political career and finally pledged his Bishopsgate estate to the church for use as a hospital for the sick and the infirm. It was that first hospital, administered by monks, that became an institution to treat those suffering confusion of the mind and so it remains to this day. The star on the staff uniform pays tribute to that.'

Hale stopped at an iron-grilled gateway and signalled to the orderly beyond to unlock it. 'We house our more serious cases beyond this barrier.'

There were perhaps six cell doors in this section and as the orderly locked the grille behind them, Flynt saw that he was most powerful in build and armed with a stout truncheon.

'Boone's door, if you please,' said Hale.

The orderly nodded and selected a key from a heavy ring around his waist before unlocking the third door down.

'Gentlemen,' said Hale before the door was opened, 'I insist that you only view the patient from the vantage point of this corridor. On no account must you enter this room.'

They each nodded their assent and Hale motioned for the orderly to proceed. The heavy iron door was swung outward and Hale waved his hand to instruct Charters and Flynt to peer into the room. It was narrow, perhaps twelve feet long, with a crescent-shaped window allowing in daylight. A lunette, the style was called, and Flynt thought it most fitting that it be used in this place, for it and the word lunatic shared the same Latin root for moon, which was once believed to have influenced the humours of the brain.

Lying upon a narrow cot to the left was a man, heavily chained, the ends of which were attached to the wall by iron rings, the links wrapped around his body tightly, with only his legs free, for they thrashed on the thick blanket beneath him.

'He has been restrained thus since he was admitted, for on the very first day he attacked an orderly and bit the finger from him,' Hale explained, then indicated a bucket in the corner and a small stand with a washbasin. 'He can move from the bed to the bucket there for his necessaries but no further. He is most heavily sedated, a mix of opiates and wine is regularly administered, but even with that he remains extremely agitated at all times.' His sad eyes became fixed on the figure writhing and muttering on the bed. 'It is beyond my medical understanding as to what chaos has hold of this poor fellow's mind but it is most deep-rooted. We have attempted everything, bathing, keeping this room cold, as you can see there be no glass in the lunette window, but to no avail, for he remains ever thus.'

Charters' gaze was also centred on the man, his eyes slightly narrowed to focus on his face, which was deeply scarred and swollen. His shaved head was pockmarked with old and new scabs.

'Mustard plasters have been applied to the scalp,' Hale said, 'leeches also to draw out the ill humours of the blood, even the administering of hemp in order to calm his temperament, but none have worked. Robert Hooke, the architect who designed this building, was most convinced of the hemp's curative properties. Nimrod Boone is incurable, gentlemen, and none of my skills nor those of my colleagues can bring order to that disorder.'

Charters continued to make as close a study of the man as he could from the corridor. Flynt leaned closer to him. 'Is it he?'

Charters worried at his life with his teeth. 'I cannot be certain. He is of stockier build than I recall, but the years could have added meat to his bones. He carries the same look of mania in his eye but the disfigurement of his features is most substantial.'

'He was as you see him when he was admitted, I can assure you. Although restrained, and I admit there has been some force applied in order to achieve it and to pacify him, no lasting injuries were sustained while in our care.'

Flynt could see that the scarring to his face was not recent. 'And there is no opportunity for him to leave this place? He takes no exercise, does not mingle with visitors?'

Hale permitted himself a rare smile. 'He cannot leave this room, sir, and he receives no visitors. The only air he is permitted is that which penetrates yonder window. This door is kept locked and the grille there is also most secure. There is an orderly on duty in this corridor night and day. Boone is, as you can see, sturdily chained to the wall so unless he has the ability to transform himself into a puff of smoke and waft his way out, there is no opportunity for him to reach the outside world.' Hale paused. 'If I make so bold, Colonel Charters, given what you told me in my office about your connection to him, coupled with your companion's query, do you suspect him of the outrages perpetrated recently in Whitechapel and Lincolns Field?'

When Charters didn't reply, Flynt took it upon himself. 'We thought it possible.'

Hale's head shook as he looked back to his patient. 'It is not possible, I fear. This individual cannot leave here, will never leave here, for his reason is hopelessly and irredeemably lost, and I say that as a medical professional who once believed that no distemper of the mind was untreatable given time and study.' He sighed, as if he felt personally responsible for the failure. 'All that is left, I'm afraid, is a beast within the shell of what was once a human being.'

As if to prove that point the man leaped from the bed and lunged at them, his mouth twisted in a snarl, only to be brought up just short of the doorway by the heavy chains. His action had been so swift, so smooth, that Flynt, who by nature was permanently on his guard, was taken by surprise. He, the orderly and Dr Hale all stepped back involuntarily but Charters didn't flinch, his head cocked as he stared most impassively into the growling face just inches before him, flecks of foaming spittle flying from his lips, the eyes ablaze with hate. Charters leaned closer but Hale laid a hand on his arm.

'I beseech you, Colonel, go no nearer. What you see before you is the beast of which I spoke.'

Charters made no reply but he did take a half step backwards, although still making a study of the features in front of him. The man they had been told was Nimrod Boone snapped his teeth at him, straining the chain to its very limits, so after a flick of the hand from Dr

Hale, the orderly drew his truncheon and pushed him none-too-gently back from the doorway.

'Close the door,' Hale ordered, pulling Charters away. The orderly did as he was ordered while Hale gently propelled the colonel towards the grille, but Charters resisted, his eyes remaining fixed upon the now closed door.

'Does he whistle?' he asked.

Hale was confused. 'Whistle?'

'Does that man whistle?'

Hale glanced at the orderly. 'I have not heard him do so, have you?'

The orderly shook his head.

Charters breathed heavily. 'He does not whistle a specific melody? An old melody. "Greensleeves"?'

Something tightened in Flynt's gut. He had heard that tune the day before, after he and Wild had rescued Blueskin from the clutches of the angry mob.

'Colonel,' Hale said, showing concern and gripping Charters by the arm. 'I have said, we have not heard him whistle anything. Are you quite well?'

Charters looked to Flynt, his eyes lost.

'I cannot be certain if it is he,' Charters said, his voice strangely distant. 'But if he whistled…'

'He was admitted by his cousin,' Hale said. 'I would imagine he would know his kinsman.'

Flynt wished he could be as certain of that.

-

In the carriage, Charters stared at the city streets, the pedestrians, the chairmen, the coaches, the livestock, lost in his own thoughts. Flynt gave him the space and considered what he had just witnessed.

That the reason of the man in that little cell was unbalanced was clear, for if he was adopting the role of a lunatic then he would be better treading the boards at the Theatre Royal, because he had given them a most convincing performance. No, the central question was whether or not he was Nimrod Boone. Charters couldn't be certain, for the scars and lumps on his face had transformed his features. Dr Hale was happy to treat him as Boone simply because his cousin had stated it was so and had no doubt provided funds for his care. No further checks would have been made to his identity, the only question during the admission process would be whether he was deserving of a bed within Bedlam and that had been established beyond doubt. So, if he was not Boone, then who was he?

If Flynt accepted the premise that he was the man they had been seeking, then was it possible that he was responsible for the murders? Again, Dr Hale was adamant that he could not be, given his restraints and the security measures in place. But measures adopted by men could also be subverted by men. The possibility existed that Caleb Boone had his cousin placed within those walls as a means of screening his guilt, proof that he was nowhere near either Whitechapel or Lincoln's Fields at the time of the killings. The Latin word *alibi,* elsewhere, sprang to Flynt's mind. A porter, an orderly, is then bribed to free him from his shackles and help spirit him from the hospital and back again. It had been rumoured that there were staff within Bethlem who were open to siphoning off the money meant for the alms box and even accepting additional funds to make a further spectacle of the poor souls that the visitors came to view.

He realised that Charters had turned from his reverie beyond the window and was staring at him. Flynt had never seen him so distraught. He fancied he even saw tears forming. Despite the fact that the man had originally blackmailed him into doing his bidding, Flynt felt pity for him. He held himself responsible for the bloodletting of recent days and now his expression revealed that his normally astute and, it has to be said, convoluted mind had come to a halt.

'I couldn't be sure, Flynt,' he said, his voice scraped of his usual confidence. 'I couldn't be sure.'

'I understand, Colonel.'

Charters swallowed hard and rested his head back in his seat. 'What to do now? There is a killer roaming these streets and I feel powerless to stop him.'

'The first thing to do is to ascertain whether that creature back there is Nimrod Boone.'

'You think he is not?'

'As you say, we cannot be certain.' He considered telling him that he had heard 'Greensleeves' being whistled but decided not to mention it. The man was distraught enough.

Charters' head straightened. 'And how do we do make certain, for Caleb Boone will not tell us?'
'Leave it to me...'

26

Flynt sought Jack Sheppard at his place of employment but the carpenter said he had not seen the lad for days.

'His bed in the basement hasn't been slept in, Mr Flynt,' said Owen Wood, his tone apologetic. 'And he has neglected his duties. Right sorry I am, too, for that lad is the best locksmith I ever did see, he has a talent most natural for it. He can build and fit a lock in a door, and cut a key, faster than quicksilver. Those large hands of his have right nimble fingers, but then I reckons that is something you knows.'

This came as no surprise to Flynt but even so, sadness overtook him, not merely over the fact that Jack had abandoned his attempt at honest employment, but that in doing so he had disappointed not only him but also Owen Wood, who was a good and kind man.

'It can't be helped, Owen, but thank you for the obligement you did me in employing him in the first place.'

'He's a good lad, works hard and is bright as a button, but the vein of villainy runs deep within him. Honest work was never something that he would take to.'

That was something Flynt had suspected all along but he had hoped that learning the trade would divert him from that path. He thanked Owen and apologised for the inconvenience but the man dismissed it.

'It weren't no inconvenience, it were a pleasure being given the opportunity to assist you, Mr Flynt, for you has been right good to me and my girl, you has. What you did still outweighs what little service I could give you. There is always a boy whât wants to learn the trade and I will find a new one right smartish, you can be sure of that.'

By the time Flynt found Jack where he'd expected, in the Shakespear's Head tavern, his rage had risen. The tavern was unusually quiet and he spotted the boy immediately at a table sipping from a tankard of ale, Edgeworth Bess Lyons perched upon his lap, his free arm around her back and cupping her breast through a ragged dress unbuttoned as far as decency would allow. Obviously there had been some sort of rapprochement.

Flynt didn't wait to be invited to join them, he dropped his hat on the table and pulled up a chair. 'I would have a moment with Jack, Bess,' he said, his eyes fixed on the boy, who shifted slightly, knowing well that he had sparked Flynt's ire.

Bess, as was her habit, curled her lip. 'Who is you to order me around as if I were your...'

He didn't give her the chance to complete her comparison. He turned his cold gaze on her and repeated, this time with emphasis, 'A moment, Bess.' Then added, 'If you please.'

'Well, I don't please, so what do you say to that, eh?'

Flynt took a breath to contain his anger. 'Bess, there is something I must discuss with him, so...'

'I will hear what you has to say to him, because we is together now, him and me, and he no longer has to pay you heed. You filled his head with ideas above his future, you did, and involved him in your deeds, what is most dark and nefarious.'

Flynt looked back to the boy. 'Jack?'

Jack shrugged, took a mouthful of ale. 'You hears her, Mr Flynt. Sorry I is, but what she says is the true fact of it. We is together, her and me. I will be earning regular now and she's giving up the streets to be my girl. What you say to me can be said to her and that's the way of it, straight and simple.'

'You don't need to apologise to him no more, Jack darling, for he ain't your upright man,' Bess said, the pleasure she took in saying the words evident in her smile and the triumphant look in her eye as she regarded Flynt. 'You got your new upright man now and Mr Wild is more than this rum beggar.'

Flynt felt his heart sink with disappointment. 'You've aligned with Jonathan Wild, Jack?'

Jack avoided his gaze. 'I has worked for him before, you knows it, and he says he sees a future for me.'

'What sort of future, Jack? One that leads to Newgate and thence to the Tyburn trail? What did you say to me once, a short life but a merry one?'

Jack hunched in his chair, as though hiding behind Bess. 'You knows what work he has for me, Mr Flynt. He has thieving to be done and he says I am the best what there is. You've been good to me, you has, but I ain't a boy no more. I'm near sixteen now. I'm a man in the flash life and I has to make my way.'

'Mr Wood said you had a fine career in carpentry ahead of you...'

'The honest path ain't for me, you has to know that by now. I'm a thief and I'm a good one. Yes, I could've been a carpenter like me old dad but what good did it do him? Dead when I was but a baby. Mr Wood was good to me, though his wife could be harsh, but I won't be going back, Mr Flynt, no matter what you says, even if you threatens me, for if I did make my return and was locked in that basement room I would escape it. You knows I is capable of such.'

Flynt considered allowing his anger to show more openly to perhaps send the girl away in a fright, but he couldn't do it. He took a further breath to maintain control and let it out slowly. 'Very well, have it your way, lad. But you are making a mistake.'

Bess pitched in once more. 'Maybes he is, but it is his mistake to make.'

Jack agreed. 'That's the way I puts my peepers upon the matter, too, Mr Flynt. I thank you most solemn for what you has done for me but that is the way of it.'

Flynt looked from the boy to the young woman, sadness replacing his anger as he realised that there was nothing he could say that would change the course he had taken. Owen Wood had said that villainy ran deep within Jack Sheppard, and in his heart Flynt had always known this to be so. He had suspected that Jack would return to the streets one way or the other, but not under Wild's wing.

'Very well, you are master of your own fate and I must accept that, Jack...'

'And he won't be doing errands for you no more neither, Jonas Flynt,' Bess said with a sneer. 'You shall have to find yourself another boy to scamper over the city, doing God knows what for God knows what reason. I knows what you thinks. You thinks that he will end his days on Tyburn and perhaps that may be the case, for it could be the future for us all, even you. But working with you he might end up hushed anyway, so what's the difference?'

Flynt couldn't argue against that point. He had tried to keep the boy from harm when he performed those errands to which Bess referred, ensured as much as he could that he was out of harm's way, but there was always the chance that the lad would have asked the wrong question of the wrong person and had his throat cut because of it. He pushed the chair back and plucked his hat from the table.

'I wish you luck then, Jack, and would be obliged if you would do me one further service...'

'God's truth, is your listeners defective?' Bess said. 'He is done doing you any further service.'

'Let the man speak, Bess,' Jack said.

'Don't let him beguile you into—'

'Bess, for Gawd's sake will you let him speak his piece?' Jack's voice was harsher than Flynt had ever heard it. Perhaps he was growing up. 'If I don't wants to do it, I won't, but I owes Mr Flynt the courtesy of listening.'

'You owes him nothing, Jack,' she said, but folded her arms across her breasts and wriggled a little to make him remove his arm from around her.

Jack swung his arm free and gave Flynt a slight smile. He was used to Bess and her petulant ways and was unconcerned by this new display. 'What can I helps you with, Mr Flynt?'

'I seek a girl by name of Kate Miller, works out of the Rat's Castle.'

'She a moll, then?'

That brought a disdainful sound from Bess. 'If she works out of that place then she's a bunter pure and simple, for no moll with any respect of themselves would be seen dead working there.'

Jack nodded his agreement. 'Why does you seek her, Mr Flynt?'

'She was attacked by a cull a few months ago. He hacked off her ear.'

Recognition blossomed in Bess's eye. 'One Lug Kate, you means.'

'You know her?'

'Not intimate, like, as I said we work in different circles.'

'Can you tell me where I can find her?'

'You already knows she works out of the Castle, why not try there if you be on the lech to be in her mutton?'

'I've no desires for her services, I only want to talk with her.'

'Mr Flynt ain't got no need for girls like her, Bess, and you knows it,' said Jack.

Bess did indeed know that Flynt had no interest in tupping molls like Kate, or her for that matter. The antipathy she felt towards him stemmed from a time when she first propositioned him and then, in pique over his refusal, threatened to reveal his involvement in an incident in a Satan's Gullet basement. That and the bond he had with Jack was sufficient for her to dislike him intensely, though she had saved his life one time by putting a pistol ball into the head of a man who would almost certainly have killed him. She was a complex girl, was Edgeworth Bess.

'Where can I find her, Bess?'

She laughed. 'You think I is one to help you? Why should I?'

Flynt knew the only languages she fully understood. One was coercion, which he didn't want to do, the other was coin, which she could comprehend most fluently.

'This is why,' he said, holding up a crown between finger and forefinger. Her eyes fixed upon it and she reached out to grasp it but he snatched his hand away. 'Her location first, if you please.'

'Tell the man, Bess, for Gawd's sake,' said Jack.

Her greedy gaze still holding the coin in Flynt's grasp, she said, 'She has a crib above the sign of the Star and Sceptre, up a lane between Monmouth Street and St Giles Church. If she ain't working the Castle, then she lays her head there and occasional takes a cull back, though she's more a threepenny upright kind of girl.'

Flynt thanked her, then said to Jack, 'I wish you good fortune, Jack. You will need it. And Bess?'

Defiance blazed in her eyes as she waited for him to speak again, clearly expecting some kind of insult or even a warning. Flynt intended neither.

'Do your best to take care of him. At heart he is a decent lad, only he doesn't know it. I also believe there is some good in you, though you do your best to hide it. I wish you fair fortune too.'

And then he turned and left the tavern.

-

Another corridor, another stairway...

The inn at the sign of the Star and Sceptre was one he had never before visited until he inquired within for Kate Miller and was referred by a landlord, who barely paid him heed, to a narrow lane at the corner of his establishment. The door lay open and led to a flight of stairs ending into darkness. Not that it was much lighter outside because the day waned fast and the rain had begun to fall once more. Flynt was wearied by the weather. Cold he could take, for it could be kept at bay by thick clothing and movement, a blazing fire if he was stationary, but, as Mother Grady had observed, the rain and dampness of the air penetrated all attempts to keep it out. Water could eat away at solid rock over time and the rain that had fallen most steadily since the end of the previous year was most certainly washing away at him.

Another doorway...

He paused to listen at the flimsy wood, as was his practice, and detected the moan of a woman within. Kate had a cull with her and though he regretted disturbing her while she was earning, he knew he had little time, but as he raised a gloved fist to knock, he heard a new voice, one he recognised, that of one of the men he had encountered outside Patience Boone's crib. Neither he nor his fellow were fair featured so it was possible looking as he did he would be forced to making the pursuit of pleasures a commercial exchange, but it was equally as likely that he was about nefarious business. Flynt pressed his ear closer to the door and this time heard another voice, one he also knew from the alleyway in the Sanctuary. A threesome, perhaps, but instinct told him that if that were so it was not a pleasurable one.

It was time to make his presence known.

He couldn't risk gunfire alerting the rest of the building. A short walk away nestled the Rookery where such exchanges would not pass unnoticed but would go unreported, but this lane was not in St Giles proper, so he loosened the blade from its sheath, stepped back, took a deep breath and kicked at the door with his right foot, immediately stepping over the threshold, taking in the image of Scarface and Toothless standing over a cot on which lay the body of a woman Flynt took to be Kate Miller, her legs twisting. The men leaped apart, the knife in Scarface's hand dripping blood, Toothless reaching for a pistol in his belt. Flynt leaped across the small room, his sword piercing Toothless's hand, pinning it to his belly. His eyes bulged and he spluttered in pain but Flynt had already plucked his blade free to leap back as Scarface lunged, swinging its hilt hard against his temple. The man dropped to his hands and knees then went down completely when Flynt slammed the solid handle with considerable force into his crown.

Toothless shrank against the wall, his fingers clutching his wounded gut, his breathing a series of gasps. Flynt pulled the man's pistol free from his belt and threw it into a far corner.

The woman thrashed on the bed, her stomach dark and glistening in the light of the single candle on the mantle. He glared with considerable venom at Toothless.

'I didn't touch her,' the man sputtered, a trail of saliva oozing from the corner of the lips. He nodded to the groaning Scarface on the floor. 'It were Thomas did the cutting.'

Flynt didn't waste any words. He raised his foot and smashed the sole of his boot into Toothless's face, who jerked away, blood spurting from his mouth, his hand automatically stretching for the knife Scarface had dropped, then thinking better of it, he tried to push it away, but Flynt had already stamped his heel down hard, hearing bones snapping. Toothless howled. Flynt smiled.

A scrape on the floor behind him made him turn as Scarface attempted to regain his feet. A kick to the side of his head stilled him.

Satisfied that neither man was about to move again, Flynt attended to Kate Miller. The slices and gouges in her flesh were deep, though she clung yet to life. He reached down with his free hand to grasp hers, trying somehow to give her comfort but knowing there was little he could do. Even if he managed to find medical help, her wounds were of such severity that she would soon be dead. A paroxysm of pain gripped her and she gasped, her fingers tightening on his hand. He held her until the agony lessened and she relaxed, but only slightly.

'I'm sorry, Kate,' he said, feeling something burn behind his eyes. He hated being so powerless.

She seemed to understand and moved her head slightly to gaze towards the mantle. There was something there she wanted, so Flynt eased his hand free then stepped over the prostrate Scarface to the fireplace, where he found a locket draped around the candlestick. It was a cheap piece of jewellery, the chain thin and tarnished.

'You wish this?' he asked the woman, and received a weak nod in return.

'You has broke my hand,' Toothless wailed.

'It would be best if you said nothing for now,' Flynt said, his voice tight with rage as he placed the locket in Kate's trembling hand. Her fingers closed around it and she breathed something that may have been gratitude as she clasped it to her bloody breast.

Toothless was not for remaining silent. Something high-pitched leaked from his throat. 'My hand... my guts... they hurts most terrible bad.'

'Good.'

'Show some mercy, mister. Send for a physic, or a apothecary...'

Flynt didn't even look at him. 'I'll show you the same mercy you showed the lady.'

A lump of blood was ejected from Toothless's mouth. 'We was to put her to the question only, maybe cut her a little, but it was Thomas what ripped her guts open, like he was competing with...'

He brought himself up short as he realised he had been about to say too much.

Flynt turned his face slowly towards him. 'Competing with who?'

The man forced his gaze away. 'Nobody, not nobody. I is agonised here, and doesn't know what I is saying.'

'Nimrod Boone perhaps?'

Toothless's head drooped to his chest. 'I ain't sayin' nothin'. It's more'n my life is worth to say.'

'Your life at this moment is a commodity that isn't worth spit.' Flynt sneered as he hefted his sword. 'I hold it in my hands.'

Toothless tried a brave smile. 'You would hush me in cold blood? I don't believes you is the sort.'

The woman's breathing was slashed and ragged like her body. Her eyes were closed and her lips moved in silent prayer. Flynt watched her for a moment, feeling so damnably helpless, so when his returned his gaze towards Toothless, he knew what the coldness of his eyes and tightness of his lips would reveal. 'The world is filled with misplaced belief.'

Toothless recoiled, his head swivelling. 'I can't tells you, I can't...'

'Then I'll tell you,' Flynt said, jerking a thumb towards Kate. 'It wasn't Nimrod Boone who disfigured this woman, was it?'

He shook his head. 'It ain't for me to say...'

'No,' said a weak voice, 'it's for me to say.'

The woman struggled to talk, and when she licked her lips the blood coating her tongue smeared across her teeth.

'You should rest, madam,' Flynt said.

Kate Miller's smile was so fragile it was hardly present. 'I shall rest soon enough, I think, for these here bastards have done for me right proper.' She summoned the strength to spit bloody phlegm towards Scarface on the floor then swallowed hard. A moan built from the depth of her pain, her face contorted and her free hand reached out. Flynt took it and her fingers once again tightened on his. Kate's expression relaxed a little but her grip remained firm.

'It weren't no Nimrod Boone what cut me,' she said, her teeth clamped together as she forced out the words. 'I was told to... say that name, but it weren't him...'

'Who did it?'

'A cove by name... Lawrence Bullock. Desperate lunatic... frothing... moaning... speaking in gibberish.' She paused again as a further spasm rolled through her and she rolled a little to her side, her body doubling up. 'Oh God, this be hell, mister, this be hell...'

Flynt gently brushed the hair from her forehead, revealing the stump of her ear, and ran the backs of his fingers down her face, trying to soothe her. 'Who told you to say the name Nimrod Boone?'

A subdued scream bled through her gritted teeth. 'Caleb...' she managed to say.

Flynt glared at Toothless. 'And you were sent to silence her?'

The man flinched and groaned. 'Oh dear Jesus, I will be hushed now and there ain't no denying it...'

'Shut up,' Flynt said.

'He is not a man to be crossed...'

Flynt's anger broke and he whirled on him, the tip of the sword pointed straight at him. 'I said be quiet, or by God I will quiet you for good.'

Toothless shrank away, still cradling his injured hand, but made no further sound.

The woman bit back another scream as pain erupted. When it subsided she fixed him with a surprisingly clear eye. 'You must finish me.'

'I cannot...'

'You must... I begs you.' Further pain surged through her and she jerked free from his grip to clutch her stomach, the locket in her other hand still pinned tightly to her chest. 'You... must...'

He hesitated, the sword he held suddenly heavy. Kate squirmed, her face rigid with the pain, sobbing now. He closed his eyes against the sight, not wishing to do it, but knowing that he must. She would succumb to her wounds. He was certain she would not survive what atrocities those vermin had perpetrated upon her body, but until death took her, the agony would be intense and unremitting. And yet, he could not bring himself to raise the sword.

'In the name of God,' Kate panted, 'you must help...'

He placed the tip of his sword over her breast, rested both hands on the hilt. Closed his eyes.

He could not do this.

He must do this.

Opening his eyes, he found find Kate staring at him. She nodded, mouthed thank you.

He leaned into his blade, felt it pierce her flesh as easily as if it were cheese. She sucked in a single sharp breath, then fell still, her eyes wide and staring at something only she could see, the air escaping in a low hiss between her lips, her limp hand sliding free to hang from the side of the cot, the precious locket dangling from her lifeless fingers. Flynt retrieved it and clicked it open to reveal a wisp of golden hair, which he probed delicately with one finger. It was golden and soft, like a baby's. He knew nothing of this woman, didn't know if it was Kate's own hair from childhood or that of a loved one, perhaps a child who had not lived, but it had obviously been precious to her. Familiar guilt stabbed at him. If he had been a few minutes earlier in arriving, if he had walked faster, if he had spent less time with Jack, if he had climbed those stairs more swiftly, she might yet be alive and breathing. But she was not. As usual he had done what needed to be done and, as usual, he felt a little piece of himself die.

He dropped the locket and chain into his pocket, rested her hands upon her breast then most tenderly eased the lids of her open eyes together.

'You murdered her,' Toothless accused, his voice hoarse. 'You did her in cold blood.'

Flynt knew what he had done. It had been cold. But his blood was heated now. He turned to face the man propped against the wall. Toothless understood what was coming and tried to kick himself away but his feet could gain no purchase on the floor. Finally realising he had nowhere to go, he fell still.

'It weren't me,' he wailed. 'It were Thomas…'

'I will attend to him presently,' Flynt said, stepping closer.

27

He didn't notice the rain as he stalked the streets. He didn't notice the cold. It couldn't penetrate now, for he was colder within than without. He had become one with it. He suspected Boone would be waiting for him, but he didn't care, in fact he welcomed it. He knew the Rookery's upright man would have Harry and John at his back, but he was prepared for that too. He believed that he understood Harry and John, and indeed, the plan taking shape relied upon that judgement being sound. If it wasn't, he would find himself in some jeopardy, but that was the chance he had to take. As he had said to Belle, life was a game between destiny, ambition and death and he was about to throw the dice.

As he moved, he pieced together what he knew and even though there existed gaps in his understanding, which he hoped Caleb Boone would fill, it all fitted.

Under the pretext of shaking the rain from his hat as he entered the tavern, he surveyed the room, filled as ever with men, women and children, perhaps believing that there was more safety here that their meagre homes in the hovels of the Rookery could allow. Through the eternal fog he found one face he recognised. Jury Leg sat by himself as usual, nursing a bottle, seemingly impervious to his surroundings, but Flynt knew better. That was Jury Leg's gift, the ability to be present and not be seen, for he who is not seen can hear and he who can hear can turn idle gossip into coin. He stopped by his side, his eye fixed on the door beside the stairway to the tupping parlour above.

'Caleb Boone.'

Jury Leg didn't even look up. 'Ain't seen him, Mr Flynt.'

'Don't lie, Jury, I'm not in the mood.'

The man now raised his head and realised this was not the time for their usual byplay. 'He's in the back room.'

'Anybody else in there?'

'He ain't never on his lonely, Mr Flynt.'

'How many?'

'Three.'

John, Harry and Ratty, Flynt surmised. If that was all, then it was manageable. At least, he hoped that was the case. He handed a crown to Jury. 'I wouldn't linger here.'

Gnarled fingers wrapped instantly around the coin. 'Old Jury thought as much. Thank you kindly, Mr Flynt, you was always a gent.' He pulled himself upright and touched the brim of his hat. 'Whatever occurs, I hopes you leaves this place in good health so you can continue to be as generous.'

As he hobbled away quickly, displaying his dexterity with his wooden leg, the landlord eyed Flynt with suspicion. He and the two men at either end of the bar watching the customers and ever alert for trouble looked capable and Flynt had little desire to breach the rules of the house, but if events turned bloody he would have them to deal with. Hopefully that was an issue that could be resolved somehow.

At the doorway, he adjusted his coat to afford easier access to Tact and Diplomacy, then twisted the lock of his cane. Taking but a moment to even his breath, not too long for to tarry for any length of time would only deepen the landlord's wariness, he turned the handle and stepped inside.

Boone was unsurprised to see him. Believing he was well insulated from attack by the sturdy figures of Harry and John on either side of him, he sat back in his chair and crossed his legs.

'Jonas Flynt, how can I help you this day?' Boone's tone was relaxed. Flynt intended to do his best to make him less comfortable.

'I had occasion to interact with two of your men, Boone, fresh from murdering an innocent woman.'

'Is there such a thing, I wonders?' Ratty giggled but was silenced by Boone's raised hand.

'Where are my men now?'

'Once again, they will not be attending us,' Flynt said, noting that he didn't ask who the woman was. 'Ever again.'

Boone's eye creased with amusement. The woman's death, even those of his men, meant nothing to him. 'You have come here to finish the work you began with them then?'

Flynt took a moment to reply, aware that though Harry and John had not moved from Boone's side. 'I've come here for the truth.'

'The truth, is it? Now there's a thing, eh? Is it not the case that one man's truth is another man's fantasy? Don't our monarchs and politicians and priests depend on that for their livelihoods?'

'The facts then, for they are irrefutable. I will have them from you, one way or another.'

Boone laughed. 'You are bold, I'll give you that, Jonas Flynt. You come here, into my domain, alone mark you, and yet you still feel at leisure to make threats. I understand that you like to gamble but there is such a thing as a losing bet and if you look around, you must surely see that you are, at this moment, making such a wager.'

'Perhaps, but when I say my piece it is possible that those odds will not seem quite so daunting.'

Boone was so confident in his superiority that he didn't notice Flynt giving Harry and John a meaningful glance, nor less see them frown as they sensed his last comment was directed to them. Yes, Flynt was correct about these men. They were smart. The question now was, how would they react when the time came?

'Then say your piece, cast your bones,' Boone said, rising and taking the few paces to the wine on the small table, 'and let's see where they land.' He poured himself a glass then held it up towards Flynt in an unspoken query.

Flynt declined with a shake of the head. 'Let's start with your cousin. He's not dead and buried across the sea, he's not in Bedlam, he is at liberty. The man who you claimed was Nimrod was in actual fact Lawrence Bullock, who was the one who attacked Kate Miller and you seized the chance for a bit of deflection.'

Boone returned to his chair, his smile suggesting he was enjoying this encounter. If all went well, he would not enjoy it for long. 'Why would I do that, I wonder?'

'In case the work on which Nimrod was engaged generated inquiry and somehow led first to him and then you. If he was in Bedlam at the time of the murders of the families in Whitechapel and Lincoln's Fields, then he couldn't possibly be responsible, could he?'

'You have no evidence that Nimrod was responsible.'

'Only that he is predisposed to such acts. And the fact that you covered for him. Kate Miller told me herself that it was Bullock who cut her and not Nimrod Boone. But your cousin is guilty of much worse.'

He risked another look towards Harry and John but neither reacted. Had he misjudged them? Did they not only know what their upright man had done but had also accepted it?

He pressed on to make the gravity of those acts clear. 'Children, Boone, Nimrod murdered children. Four of them, slaughtered in a most obscene way because that's how Nimrod takes his pleasure, is it not? He enjoys inflicting pain. He's been like that since he was a boy, hasn't he?'

'Patience has been spinning her lies again.'

'Not lies. Truth. He did it in Flanders, he's perhaps even done it elsewhere during the intervening years, and now he has done it here.' He flicked another look at the two men behind Boone and emphasised the victims for their benefit. 'Children. We have few rules in this world of ours but one is that we do not harm children.'

Boone dismissed this with a jerk of the head. 'Children are harmed every hour of every day. They are beaten, starved, worked to death, sold for pleasure. Life is hard from birth to earth and we must accept that.'

Flynt almost smiled, for a sharp look from Harry towards Boone suggested he had made an error. 'True, but there are those in our profession who take a dim view of the men who prey on children for their own pleasure. It's what separates the professional from the beast. There is cruelty enough in our life without that.' He hammered home his message. 'Children, Boone. Murdered in their beds, their parents already dead. Ordinary families, loving families, straight arrows.'

'Our profession, Flynt, takes a dim view of nothing but survival, because that's what life is for our kind. Survival. We steal, we cheat, we lie, we prostitute ourselves, we kill, all to survive, all to maintain our position or to make progress in this dungheap we call a world.'

'I agree, in the main, the flash world is filled with those who baulk at nothing but a few, not many perhaps, but a few do follow some rules, spare though they are.'

'Honour among thieves and killers, is that what you say?'

'Something like that.'

'And you are one of those few with such honour.'

'I am. But I'm not alone.'

At least, he hoped he wasn't alone in this room. Apart from that single look from Harry, neither he nor John had reacted further. Boone drained his glass then held it out. Ratty, who had melted away from them, scuttled to his side to relieve him of it.

'Does you wish another, Mr Boone?' he asked eagerly.

'Do I wish another, *do* I, not does. But no, not at the moment, thank you.'

Ratty replaced the glass on the small table before edging backwards into the shadows again. Boone crossed his arms. 'Let us assume, then, that my cousin is responsible for this, what blame lies with me?'

'You covered for him.'

'He is my cousin, my blood. I love him. I was perhaps misguided but if you wish to accuse me of loving family overmuch then so be it. There is honour in that, surely.'

Flynt's smile was more of a grimace. 'What you did wasn't for family.'

'Then what was it for?'

Flynt paused, then said, again for the benefit of Harry and John, 'Because you ordered him to do these things.'

Finally, another look was exchanged between the two men. This time he thought – hoped – he detected a measure of unease. He was making progress. Boone was correct when he said he was gambling. He had no idea how much these two men knew of what had occurred and it was always possible they cared little. But he had thrown the dice and they appeared to have landed in his favour. At least so far.

Boone laughed. He was relaxed, so confident in his position. 'Now, there's an accusation, a most serious one. Why would I do such a thing?'

'You said it yourself, we steal and we kill to progress ourselves. And you are extremely keen to progress, aren't you? You told me you wished to better your position. You have all but cast off your Sanctuary roots in both speech and manner.'

'And how does killing these families progress me?'

Flynt gave it a beat. 'You hate the Admiral. He had you run off the waterfront.'

'What of it?'

'The father of the Berthon family in Whitechapel had a professional and personal connection to the Admiral.'

'So?'

'Killing them hurt him.'

'That doesn't improve my position.'

'No, but involving Jonathan Wild might. He reached the scene of the murders very quickly, far more quickly than if he had merely heard the word on the street. Someone let him know almost as soon as the atrocity was committed.'

'Or he was responsible,' Boone countered. 'If this Berthon fellow was connected to the Admiral then Wild has the most to gain, for there is no love lost between them and they struggle for control of the waterways.'

'Yes, that thought did occur to me. But then the second family was murdered and they had a personal and business connection to Wild.'

'The Admiral, striking back.'

Flynt shook his head. 'No.'

'You are so sure of that?'

'Yes.'

'How can you be?'

'Because he assured me he did not.'

Boone laughed. 'You take the word of a masked wharf rat?'

'I do, because he is a professional like me. And others.' Another glance to Harry and John. 'He would not countenance the murder of innocents, nor would Wild for that matter. He has few scruples but I believe that is one.'

'But I would.'

'You would, Caleb. You did. By doing so, and by planting the seeds of suspicion in each camp that the other was responsible, you designed to set off a direct confrontation. Such a thing would leave them open and vulnerable, for they would either slaughter each other or the survivor would be left so weakened that you could move in.'

'In the name of God, I am most calculating...'

'You are sly, Caleb, but I submit you didn't think of this yourself. You had assistance. Someone far more cunning dropped the notion into your mind.' He faced John and Harry again. 'Tell me, gentlemen, shortly before the last time I was here, did Boone meet with someone here? A meeting, perhaps, at which you were not required.'

Boone had by now realised that Flynt knew more than he should. 'I've heard enough of this yarn spinning. Harry, John, take him out back and deal with him.'

Neither man moved and Boone swivelled his head to glare at them. 'Did you hear me?'

'I think we shall hears the rest of what he has to say,' said Harry.

'That we will,' said John.

Boone shot to his feet and whirled to face them. 'You defy me?'

Harry considered that. 'I think we do.'

'It's most interesting,' said John.

'I likes a good yarn.'

'And this truly be a good 'un.'

Unlike Flynt, Boone had misjudged these men. His fists opened and clenched as he tried to hold on to his temper. He had been a formidable fighter but he would know that these men would kill him in an instant so he made no move to attack. He swore and turned to where Ratty had been standing but was no longer. He had been astute, far more than Boone, and he had fled the room while nobody was paying him any attention.

'It appears the rat is deserting your rotten house before it falls,' Flynt observed.

Boone swore softly, then snarled at Harry. 'I will have you hushed for this, by God I will. I dislike treachery.'

Harry seemed unconcerned by the threat. He even smiled a little, as if the very thought was nonsensical. 'We has done many a job for you, Mr Boone. We has damaged people and we has threatened them.'

'That is what we does,' said John.

'It is. But Flynt here be correct, there is rules…'

'A code.'

'It ain't hard and fast and there be many what don't adhere to it, but we does.'

Boone sneered. 'You're weak and you're stupid and you're hypocrites. You're killers by profession and killers by inclination. One death is no worse than another.'

'That's where you're wrong, Mr Boone,' said Harry. 'We may kill to live…'

'And there may be a bit in us what lends us to it natural,' said John.

'For there is a bit of the devil in us all, ain't that right, Mr Flynt?'

Flynt nodded his assent.

Harry continued, 'But see this here snuffing of children?'

'It ain't right,' John said.

'It ain't fitting. And we don't hold with it.'

'We don't hold with it at all. And we don't want no part of it.'

'And here's my thinking on it,' said Harry. 'You knowed this from the off, which is why you kept us apart from meetings in secret with coves we didn't know.'

'But we knows about it now, thanks to Flynt here.'

'Yes, we do, and you will pay a price for it.'

'We kill to live, Boone,' repeated John.

'But unlike that cousin of yours,' Harry said, 'we doesn't live to kill.'

Boone remained silent now, his body rigid, his jaw clenching and unclenching. 'You have caused my men to mutiny with your lies.'

'No lies. Facts, as I said.'

Boone said nothing but his expression spoke volumes. He stared at Flynt as if calculating new odds, whether he would reach him before Harry, John or Flynt himself took him down. He obviously didn't like the end result so he took his seat again and in a bid to be nonchalant crossed his legs and clasped his fingers over his knee.

'You has the upper hand, Flynt, so you may as well continue with your yarn spinning.'

'Thank you,' said Flynt. 'And I *have* the upper hand, not has. Your diction is reverting to type, Caleb.'

Boone's only riposte was to spit something onto the floor.

'I will say only a name, Caleb. Lombre.'

A flicker of the lips, a twitch of the eyebrow.

'You know that name, don't you, Caleb? Don't deny it – it was he who first put forward this scheme, was it not?'

Flynt was guessing and by the little smile that crept across Boone's lips he realised he had been wide of the mark. 'Ah, it was your idea, then? You suggested this killing spree.'

'Who is this cove Lombre? He a froggie?' John asked.

'Nobody really knows for sure, John,' Flynt replied. 'He works for the French, or for the Jacobites, or anyone who pays him, but in this case I think his employers are somewhat closer to home, though they remain enemies of ordinary people. I apologise, Caleb, I gave Lombre credit for the inhumanity of this scheme but it appears you are indeed exceeding calculating.'

'So who is these employers?' John asked.

'It's a group of men who style themselves a fellowship. Their aim is to progress themselves financially, no matter the cost to others. They would sacrifice you, me, anyone in order to profit. They control politicians and kings and manipulate them to protect their businesses or to feed off public funds. They promulgate wars to benefit from the sale of arms and, afterwards, the rebuilding of countries. I've even heard that they began the great fire in order to reap the rewards of the reconstruction, and though I hold little credence to that I wouldn't be surprised. I rather fancy that Caleb here has ambitions to join them. I know that Lombre is in London and he has met with a Scotsman by name of Andrew Wilson, who I believe to be a member of the Fellowship. I saw Lombre leaving the Castle the other day and suspect he met with Caleb in this very room. Although you gentlemen were not present, you will have seen him. A tall man, wanting of an eye?'

The look Harry and John exchanged confirmed Flynt's conjecture.

'He is an enemy of the country and Caleb here is in league with him.'

Their faces hardened as they glared at the erstwhile employer, an example of the depth of patriotism that could lie in the hearts of even the lowliest of rogues. And Harry and John were far from lowly.

'Greed is man's curse,' Flynt said, 'and the Fellowship attracts greedy men. They have already taken control of legal enterprises and even government but that's not enough, is it? So what's their aim, Caleb? To set the Admiral and Wild at each other's throats and then profit from their illicit organisations, with you at the helm?'

Caleb didn't reply. All he did was spit on the floor again.

Flynt took that as a yes. 'Where's Nimrod?'

Caleb managed a bitter smile but remained silent, so Flynt gave the man's erstwhile bodyguards a querying glance.

'We never had the pleasure of meeting him,' Harry said.

'We heard his name, though,' said John.

Caleb emitted a short laugh. 'You'll never find him. He is most expert at vanishing.'

'I'll find him,' Flynt said. 'And when I do, I will kill him.'

The smile became mocking. 'Then you best be quick, for his work is near done.'

Flynt stepped forward. 'What do you mean?'

Boone looked at Harry, then John, and sighed. 'This very night it all ends. By cock crow, your precious Admiral and, if there be any justice, that puffed up bag of pus Jonathan Wild will be dead, and Nimrod will be in the wind.'

'Where is he, Boone?'

A sly gleam shone in his eye. 'Such knowledge comes with a price.'

Flynt knew what that price was. 'Very well, if you tell me I will show you mercy.'

'I has your oath upon that? The oath of an *honourable* thief and husher of men?'

'You do.'

Boone accepted that. 'Then I will tell you this and no more: the Admiral, may the devil roast him, will this very eve be drawn to a place where he feels safe and the wheels are already rolling.'

'On the waterfront?'

'No, somewhere beyond his turf. And word has been given to Wild, evidence also.'

'What evidence?'

'A bloody scarf belonging to the woman in Lincoln's Field, carried to him by one of the Admiral's own men, who was known to Wild. Coin can go a long way to shift loyalties.'

'Who is this man?'

A divisive shrug from Boone. 'It matters not, he is already dead at Nimrod's hand, for if he would betray one he would betray another and such disloyalty should be used, not rewarded. As we blather here, I suspect Wild is already gathering his troops. Nimrod will be waiting for them, for he likes to linger to witness the effects of his work.'

'Where?'

'That's for you to work out.' Boone's smile broadened. 'Exciting, isn't it?'

Flynt's mind raced. Somewhere the Admiral felt safe but not on the waterfront, so not the inn at Wapping. Of course, Boone could be lying, but he thought not. He sheathed his sword, replaced his pistol under his coat and turned to the door.

Behind him he heard Harry say, 'Up you stand, Mr Boone.'

'Flynt!' Boone shouted. 'You gave me your word.'

Flynt looked back from the doorway to see Harry and John hauling him to his feet. 'I gave you *my* word that I would show you mercy. I didn't give your theirs…'

28

Flynt had last seen young Jack in the Shakespear's Head but when he looked now there was no sign of him or Bess. An inquiry with the landlord revealed that Sheppard had been fetched by Blueskin Blake, so Flynt at least knew he was on the right track. Wild wouldn't do anything without Blake at his side.

He tried three other taverns before he found Bess in the White Lion, just off Wych Street and not far from where Jack should, at that moment, have been lodging in the basement of Owen Wood's carpentry shop. She was at the bar, rubbing herself against a cull, a merchant by his mode of dress. So much for her not working the streets. Flynt weaved through the tables towards her, his customary survey of the room revealing Daniel Defoe in a corner, scribbling in his notebook. They acknowledged each other with a nod. Bess affected a smile as he approached but her eyes flashed a clear warning.

'I'm with this here gentleman, dearie,' she said, her tone light but underneath he detected a tightness in her throat. She was being pleasant for the sake of the cull. 'You shall have to wait your turn.'

Flynt had no time for any niceties. 'Where's Jack, Bess?'

Irritation crumpled her brow. 'He's gone, ain't he, off to work.'

Off to work. He could be out thieving but Flynt feared that wasn't the case. Wild had called him to arms. A boy, a nimble-fingered boy. He was no fighter, no killer, and yet he may have been conscripted to do both.

Bess gave her cull a reassuring smile and tugged a little at his arm, pulling him away. 'Now then, my love, why doesn't we buy ourselves a bottle and go to a place I knows where we can take our leisure most comfortable.'

Flynt stepped in their path. 'Where has he gone, Bess?'

The man's masculinity decided to take umbrage. 'Perhaps you didn't hear the girl, sir, she's with me for the moment. Once she and I am done with our business you can take your turn…'

His words drawled as though they were thick wine poured from a bottle. Flynt made an attempt at being reasonable. 'I will have her attention for but a moment, sir.'

The cull pulled himself up to his full height, towering over Flynt. 'Perhaps you misunderstand, sir, you will await your turn and my pleasure…'

Flynt sighed. He didn't have time for this. He stared into the man's eyes and spoke softly. 'I've had a long day and I face a long night so I would advise you not to test me, friend. My fuse is short and it would take little to ignite it.'

The man was sufficiently sober to see that Flynt was not one to be trifled with and took a step back. Then another and another.

'Good decision,' Flynt said, then turned to Bess. 'Where did Jack and Blueskin go, Bess?'

Her smile was gone now and her customary glare had taken its place. 'Why should I tell you? He ain't yours to use no more.'

He thrust his face closer to hers, his whisper hoarse. 'Because he could be hurt, Bess. Wild is going to war with the Admiral over lies and Jack will be nothing but cannon fodder.'

'I don't believe you…'

'Damn it! There's been enough killing already. Families, children, One Lug Kate…'

That shocked her. 'Kate's dead?'

'Yes, murdered by men sent by Caleb Boone.'

No, Jonas, a voice said, *you killed her. They began it but you finished it.*

Bess remained suspicious. 'How does I know you is speaking true?'

He rummaged in his coat pocket to produce the locket and chain. 'You recognise this?'

'That's her locket. I seen her wear it often.'

'Would she part with it willingly?'

'You could have stole it from her… hushed her yourself…'

He blocked the image of his sword piercing Kate's breast, his hands clasped on the hilt.

My God, this young woman was stubborn. He attempted to ungrit his teeth but found it impossible. 'Why in God's name would I steal such a trinket? It's worth nothing to me and if you knew her at all then you would know this was everything to her. In addition to which, you know me, and you know the killing of women is not what I do.'

But it is, Jonas, you have...

He couldn't let those thoughts slow him down. He forced his guilt away. He was accomplished at doing that. 'Now, where did he go? I know he would tell you, Bess, so if you have any affection for him I beg you, don't delay me any further.'

Her lips pressed together as her feelings for Jack's wellbeing battled with her desire to oppose Flynt.

'Bess...' Flynt began, desperation heavy in that single word.

'Whitechapel.' The location escaped from her lips as though it was drowning and seeking air. She took a deep breath, then said quietly, 'Blueskin Blake comes here to fetch him and I hears them say Whitechapel.'

Boone had said the Admiral was to be lured to a place he felt safe and there was only one location in Whitechapel where Flynt knew he was even remotely comfortable.

'When did Jack and Blake leave?'

The thought of replying no further obviously crossed her mind but she relented. 'Not ten minutes since.'

There was yet time then. Wild would be gathering his forces, which might take a little time, and they would come together at a rallying point before moving east.

'Thank you,' he said and was about to turn away when he remembered the locket in his hand. 'Do you know of Kate's people? Parents? Relatives?'

'I doesn't... didn't know her that well. I heard tell there was a cove what she was sweet on once but when he found out about her means of income he turned his back.'

He reached out to take her hand. She flinched but he gripped her wrist and dropped the locket and chain into her upturned palm. 'Speak to her friends, Bess. This meant something to Kate and it may mean something to someone else. It should be returned to them.'

He turned away before his voice, his face, his eyes betrayed something of himself. He was confident she would do as he asked. Bess was hard and she was grasping and her lifestyle of culls and gin would age her before her time, but he had seen how tenderly she could treat other women of her profession. If that locket and the strands of hair within were precious to someone, she would find them.

Defoe waited for him in Wych Street as he left. 'You have the appearance of a man on a mission, Jonas,' he said. 'Do you require assistance?'

Another hand – another weapon – might prove useful. Before he left the Rookery he had contemplated asking Harry and John if they would be willing to accompany him but he doubted if they would. Their sense of honour might have been dented by Boone having children slaughtered, but they would not involve themselves in a struggle between two warring upright men. That held no profit for them. He couldn't bring himself to place the writer at risk, though there was something he could do for him. 'Do you know where Colonel Charters lives, Dan?'

'Of course, I have dined there often.'

This man truly was a friend to the colonel. Flynt had never been invited to Charters' home. 'I need you to make all haste and deliver a message. Tell him that I believe the end of our little quest lies at this moment in Whitechapel, at the mount.'

'Good God, that place be a hive of evil at this hour.'

'More than you can ever know, Dan.'

Flynt turned towards the Strand and Defoe frowned. 'You will attend this hellish location alone?'

Flynt gave him a smile he did not feel. 'Don't worry, Dan, Tact and Diplomacy will see me through…'

-

I is ready. Everything be in place. Tonight will be a most beauteous thing to see, to be sure. Them pricks Wild and the Admiral will have at it against each other and I shall watch from this here hill.

It be most pleasant here, despite the rain, but I've always liked the rain. It washes all clean, lands, streets, people. Not that I needs washing clean, even though there be those what believe I is monster. I ain't no monster. I is just true to my nature, is all, and a man must be as such if he is a man.

Caleb has big plans but I care not a fart for them. He wants to be the most upright of upright men but that means nothing to me. I live for my work and my work is ripping, and it is possible that this night I will get to do some, for Wild will come here team-handed. The Admiral will be more or less on his lonely, perhaps that fellow Pickett what I has seen him with, but it be possible that I can pick off a Wild man or two in the dark. The dark is my friend and I am one with it.

And then, when this work is done to my satisfaction, I shall turn my mind to Jonas Flynt.

–

Flynt would have preferred heading back to Charing Cross and the stables where he lodged Horse, his mare, but it would take too long, so instead he set off eastwards at a brisk pace, his eyes scanning the rain-swept streets for a hackney. It took him some time to find one idling on Fleet Street and convince the driver to take him beyond the city wall.

'It be late, sir,' said the driver, 'and the Whitechapel Road ain't a place to be going after dark. There is cutthroats what roams there.'

More than you know, friend, Flynt thought as he promised to pay the man three times his fare.

The driver considered this. 'I will take you as far as St Mary's, no further. I ain't going nowhere near the mount. Not under nightfall.'

It would have to do. He told the man to make haste and settled himself in the cabin as best he could while the driver proved as good as his word, rattling through the streets as though the devil himself was pursuing. But the devil wasn't behind them, he was somewhere ahead. In the dark. Waiting.

They crossed the old city wall twice, once at Ludgate then following the route he and Daniel Pickett had taken on his last venture to Whitechapel to pass through at Aldgate, going beyond the Castle tavern where Flynt had met Charters only days before. My God, much had occurred since that day, he mused. So much blood had been spilled and there was more yet to come. He checked and double-checked Tact and Diplomacy, making certain their loads remained intact. He sheathed and unsheathed his blade ensuring its ease of movement. He knew the weapons were as they should be, but he had to keep his hands busy. Caleb Boone and his damned cousin had been one step ahead of them all along, aided by Lombre and Andrew Wilson. He wondered where Lombre was now, whether he would also be present to see the final hand dealt in this game of chance.

It seemed to take an age before the hackney came to a swift halt, almost pitching Flynt from of the seat. The driver thumped the roof and shouted, 'This be as far as I risk.'

Flynt disembarked, glanced at the stone steeple of St Mary Matfelon, which was topped by a square battlement-style platform. If Flynt had the time he would dearly loved to have utilised it as a vantage point in order to spy out the land ahead, but he knew he had to press forward. He paid the driver his agreed fee and stepped aside as the man instantly wheeled round and whipped his horse into motion back towards the city, the hackney's wheels splashing dirty water from the rutted road.

Flynt broke into a run towards where Whitechapel Street became the road to Mile End. Looming through the rain and darkness was the darker shape of the mount, and twin pinpricks of light moving at the base. Torches, but not enough for it to be Wild's small army. He picked up the pace and closed in.

As he drew closer he began to make out the dark shape of a familiar coach, its lamps lit and standing beyond it the Admiral, Pickett and another individual, the latter two bearing the torches. Pickett heard his footfalls and whirled, a pistol already level.

Flynt stepped into the dim circle of light, his arms held wide. 'It is I.'

'You're late, Jonas,' said the Admiral. 'I was about to leave...'

Flynt understood immediately. Boone had used a message supposedly from him to draw them to this place. 'I didn't ask to see you.'

The Admiral nodded, as if he had already suspected such. 'Then who did?'

'You've been lured here, Admiral. Jonathan Wild and his men are on their way for a reckoning.'

'Wild did this?'

'No, Caleb Boone and his cousin, Nimrod.'

'To what purpose?'

'To engineer a confrontation leaving one of you, but preferably both, dead. Boone will then step into the void created by your absence and profit from the organisations you had created.'

'And if only one of us is dead?'

Flynt scanned the hulking mass of earth rising above them. 'Then Nimrod Boone is here to finish you off.'

The Admiral looked around him. He was calm, Flynt noted. This was a man not easily unnerved. 'You know this for fact?'

'I have nothing tangible to produce but I know it to be true.'

The Admiral thought upon this for a moment. 'And Caleb Boone is here also?'

'No.'

The Admiral caught the finality in Flynt's voice and nodded. 'I assume Mr Boone will trouble us no further.'

'Admiral, it would be best if you left,' Flynt said. 'Let's not play their game.'

Pickett as usual watched and listened impassively, and the Admiral first stared at him then cocked his head a little before saying, 'I think not, Jonas, for you are too late.'

Flynt was surprised and confused as the Admiral gave Pickett a nod before reaching with both hands into the deep pockets of his thick coat to produce two pistols. Flynt heard it then, wheels clattering and splashing on the uneven road from the city. He turned, saw their lamps bouncing in the murk, heard the snort of the horses and the creak of the coach bodies. He counted four of them. Wild had come fully prepared for an all-out assault.

'This may well be a ruse,' the Admiral said, 'but this night has been coming for some time. It might as well be now.'

The coaches came to a halt and Wild, Blake and Jack emerged from one. Doors opened and closed as a further dozen men alighted. Some carried lamps, others stopped to ignite flambeaux. All were armed. Knives, cudgels, swords, pistols, one or two muskets were brandished as faces tightened in resolve, the mix of orange and red light causing lines in flesh to deepen and dance a little.

Wild came to a halt a few feet away. 'Jonas Flynt, be that you?' He squinted in an exaggerated fashion. 'By God's beard, it is! Shown your true allegiance at last, I see.'

Flynt chose not to deny it, for he knew the truth was that he held more loyalty to the Admiral than he did to Wild. He stared across the void between them at Jack's slim features, forcing him to cast his eyes at the muddy ground.

'Walk away, Jack.'

'Leave the lad be, Flynt,' Blake said, his arm resting around Jack's shoulders in a show of both camaraderie and possession. 'He's here to make his mark.'

'He's no fighter, Blake.'

'Time he learned then, ain't it?'

Jack resolutely refused to meet Flynt's eye but even in the light of the lamps and torches it was obvious he trembled, and not just from the cold and damp. The boy knew he should not be here but he had either been coerced or had recognised this as a test of loyalty by Wild and Blake. Either way he had taken a side.

'It is you who be best advised to walk away, Jonas,' Wild said. 'You have backed the wrong nag.'

With a final imploring look at Jack, Flynt said, 'I'm here to stop the bloodshed, Wild. You have been gulled, both you and the Admiral.'

'I think not,' Wild said. 'I have proofs that your friend here is guilty of infanticide.'

'The Admiral didn't have that family killed, no more than you did the Berthons.'

'I have a bloody shawl taken from the Newell house and found in the Admiral's possession...'

'That's a lie,' said the Admiral.

'The man who brought it to me has sworn it be true, that he took it from your crib in Wapping. I know this man and he has no reason to lie, for he holds no love for me, but he is, like any right-minded person be they rogue or no, most horrified by the murders. I recognised the garment, it was one worn by the wife of Walter Newell many times. How came he to have it if he not speak the truth?'

Flynt almost laughed, for the answer to that was obvious. 'Because the true murderer gave it to him and he was paid to carry it to you. Don't you see this, Wild?'

Wild shrugged, and in that moment Flynt understood that he didn't want to address the obvious answer. He wanted this fight.

The Admiral moved closer, his eyes roaming the faces of Wild's men. 'Who is this accuser? Bring him to me.'

'He is not here, but he will willingly take his oath upon his statement.'

Flynt knew that to be a lie, for Boone said the man was already dead. Nevertheless, he pressed the point. 'Then let's take this to the courts,' he said. 'Let's put him to the test.'

Wild shook his head. 'No courts, not for us.'

Flynt couldn't contain his exasperation. 'Dear God, what madness has taken hold of you both? You would sacrifice each other, yourselves, your men because you have been manipulated by one man who was mad with ambition and another who is just plain mad?'

Wild frowned. 'Who are these men?'

'Caleb Boone intended to have you both removed and place himself at the head of your respective enterprises. He had his cousin Nimrod do the killing. The man who came to you was paid to betray the Admiral, the shawl having been taken from the Newells' house the night of the slaughter.' Flynt half turned towards the Admiral. 'The Boone cousins have played us all and Nimrod is here now, watching us. If you fall for this ploy then you will merely be dancing to his tune. I implore you, don't give him the satisfaction.'

Wild pursed his lips. 'Let us suppose what you say be true...'

'It is...'

'That does not change the fact that this here between us is merely the culmination of years of antagonism, be that not so, Admiral?'

The Admiral inclined his head in agreement. 'If not now, when?'

Flynt whirled on the man he thought friend. 'Then you are as mad as Boone, Admiral. Look at this.' He waved a hand towards Wild's men strung out before them like skirmishers. 'Look at these odds. He has you outnumbered, can't you see that? There are but three of you, you cannot possibly hope to emerge victorious if hostilities erupt. See sense, man.'

Silence fell, with only the sound of the rain drilling the ground and the guttering of the torches. The Admiral's gaze moved along the line of faces before him, then rested on Pickett, who understood the unspoken command and emitted a loud whistle. In the murk beyond the range of the illumination, shadows moved and a host of men stepped forward. They were all burly and all armed with cutlasses, pistols, clubs, knives.

'I suspected you would never ask to meet me here after dark, Jonas,' the Admiral explained. 'So I took precautions. I'm not mad, my friend, but I am cautious.'

Flynt, standing between the two factions, looked from the Admiral to Wild and back again. 'Have you all lost your reason? Are you so swept up in your narcissism that you will lead men...' he aimed a finger at Jack, '...boys to the slaughter? And for what? Power? Position? Profit? And where is the profit when you are dead or crippled? You hate him and he hates you and so you will condone needless bloodshed just to prove it? What in the name of Christ is the point of this?'

'The point, my friend Jonas, is that as long as he lives,' the Admiral pointed a pistol at Wild, 'he is a threat to me and my interests. And as long as I live, I am a threat to his.'

Flynt swore and paced up and down. The evidence presented was flimsy and they both knew it, but they were intent on this confrontation. He gazed at each man's face as he passed, recognising none of the Admiral's forces but picking out Godfrey and Hal from Lincoln's Inn Fields. 'Do you wish to die, Godfrey? Do you, Hal?'

Even by the light of the torches, he saw how pale Hal was. Godfrey was of sterner stuff but he at least dropped his gaze. Flynt whirled around, waving his arms at the men clustered around him. 'Do any of you wish to die? Because some of you, perhaps most, will, and simply because these two men desire it in the name of profit and power.' He raised a finger in turn towards Wild and the Admiral. 'They hate one another with such fervour that they have willingly allowed themselves to be manipulated by a madman. And who will gain? Certainly not you men. Not you Godfrey, not you, Hal.' He looked over his shoulder at Jack, who was edging back, only to be tugged into line by Blueskin Blake. 'Not you, Jack. Not you Wild, or you Admiral, for Nimrod Boone lurks out there and will ensure neither of you leave this place alive. Is it worth your blood? Is it worth your lives?'

Doubt flickered as men looked to their neighbours and nervously shifted their feet. But nobody made a move to leave the field. No man wanted to be the first to leave.

Flynt sighed, deciding on another tack. 'Very well, as you are so set on shedding blood this night, why not limit the damage? If you two are such mortal enemies, then spare your followers death or impairment and face each other, man-to-man.'

He couldn't see under the mask, but Flynt was certain the Admiral was smiling when he said, 'You suggest a gladiatorial struggle?'

'Yes, you and him, on this neutral ground between you. And to the victor goes the spoils.'

Wild shifted his stance a little, his eyes revealing little appetite for the suggestion. 'And if we both lie dead?'

Flynt affected a shrug. 'What do you care? You'll be gone, he'll be gone, this enmity between you will sink into this earth with your blood.'

Neither upright man spoke.

'Come, gentlemen, let's see what you're made of.' Flynt was warming to his idea. 'Trial by combat. Here. Now. Your men can go home to their families or sweethearts if they have them. The young...' another glance to Jack, '...will be spared for another year or two. And Nimrod Boone, up there on the hill somewhere, will have fulfilled his mission.'

Flynt again studied the faces around him. Some of the men on either side nodded, others seemed reluctant to make their feelings known. Blueskin glared at him while Jack continued to stare at the ground. Pickett remained inscrutable.

The Admiral spoke again. 'First blood or to the death?'

Damn it, this was no time for half-measures. 'First blood solves nothing permanently. Sooner or later you two would be at each other's throats again. To the death is the only permanent solution. Agreed?'

The Admiral inclined his head. 'Agreed.'

Flynt faced the Thieftaker General. 'Mr Wild?'

Wild looked at Blueskin, then across the divide to the Admiral, then to Flynt, his hand squeezing the hilt of his sword. There was something in his eyes, not quite fear, not quite calculation, but a mix of both. He had shown some courage when facing the mob in Lincoln's Inn Fields, but in that situation he used his position, self-administered though it was, as a shield. Here no man cared that he had adopted the title of Thieftaker General. The Admiral could be quaking behind that mask but nobody would know, so Wild had to hide behind a mask of his own and he found it a struggle. If he refused he would lose what respect his men bore him and they would be less likely to fight for his cause. If he agreed he could find himself dead. His struggle between asserting his superiority and his sense of mortality was plain. Flynt banked on him choosing self-interest and, hopefully, walking away. It would not end the rivalry with the Admiral, but it would, at least, delay bloodletting and deny Nimrod Boone any satisfaction.

'Come, Wild,' Flynt cajoled, 'you have allowed these cards to be dealt, now you must play them.'

Wild swallowed and opened his mouth to speak, but Blueskin must have sensed the confusion of his thoughts so jumped in ahead of him.

'Champions.'

All eyes turned to him as he stepped forward.

'It be unseemly for a cove in Mr Wild's position to grub around in the dirt on his lonely with this here masked creature. It ain't right, it ain't dignified.'

Wild would have been happy to see his men do the grubbing, Flynt thought, and had little doubt that he would have ensured he be well away from the hostilities. For some reason Flynt was proud of Blueskin. He was a rogue and he was brutal but he was devoted to Jonathan Wild, misplaced though that loyalty was, for Flynt had occasion previously to point out that he would be sacrificed if it was ever to the thieftaker's benefit. Of course, there was always the possibility that he recognised that Wild was no match for the Admiral and wished to protect his own position. Without him, Blueskin was just another thief.

'So what I proposes is this. We set champions to fight. And I will be the one what takes up the cause for Mr Wild here. What does you say to that, Mr Masked Admiral? You wishes to nominate someone to battle in your place?'

The Admiral stared at Blueskin for what seemed a considerable time, before a raspy chuckle escaped him. He glanced first towards Pickett, who Flynt expected to be nominated, but then his mask turned in his direction.

'I choose Jonas,' he said.

Damn it, Flynt thought, I should have seen that coming…

29

Blueskin perhaps had predicted the choice, for a satisfied grin spread across his face.

'Guns or knives, Flynt,' he said. 'You has the choice.'

Flynt gave the Admiral a glare, saw the amusement in his eyes. The man was enjoying this and knew that Flynt could not refuse the challenge, for if he did then it would risk the commencement of open warfare between the two forces, and Jack had to be protected somehow.

'Guns or knives, Flynt,' Blueskin repeated.

'Neither,' said Flynt.

Blueskin was puzzled. 'What shall we be doing then? Firing insults at each other?'

Flynt took off his hat and his coat then handed them both to Pickett. 'Fists,' he said.

That surprised Pickett as well as Blake. 'Fists? You wants us to brawl here in the rain and the mud?'

Flynt didn't want to use weapons. He didn't like the man but held no particular antagonism towards him, while he still felt he owed him something for pulling him from the freezing Thames in the winter of 1716. With a fist fight, there was less chance of either of them losing their lives, although he was certain Blueskin Blake would do his best to beat him to death. He, in return, would do his damnedest to avoid that.

As the opposing factions ranged themselves in a circle, instinctively forming a ring, the Admiral sidled closer to him and whispered, 'Those were harsh words, Jonas.'

'Did I hurt your feelings?'

A slight chuckle rumbled under the mask. 'I'll get over it. Are you sure this be the best course to take? Why not simply shoot the fellow and be done with it?'

'Nobody dies tonight, if I can help it,' Flynt said, raising his eyes to the mount. 'Apart from one.'

The Admiral craned round to follow his gaze. 'You are truly convinced this Nimrod Boone fellow watches us?'

'He's there.'

'How can you be so certain?'

'Because I can feel it.'

Blueskin had taken off his coat and hat and Flynt's disappointment in seeing that he had handed them to Jack must have reflected in his face, for he grinned again. He is ours now, that grin said.

'Be on your guard, Jonas,' the Admiral said, 'I know this fellow Blake. He is extremely mean-spirited and quick to anger.'

That's what I rely upon, Flynt thought.

'Good luck, Mr Flynt,' Pickett breathed. 'You'll need it.'

Flynt nodded his thanks and edged towards Blueskin, who paced the perimeter of the ring, his fists half raised, his lips still sporting a smile that Flynt hoped was prematurely triumphant. Forcing his shoulders to relax, and focusing on his breathing, Flynt moved in the opposite direction, the torrent streaming between them, turning the already soft ground ever more treacherous. Many of the torches had already burned themselves out or been extinguished and those that remained guttered, the flames flicking back and forward in the breeze. The covered lamps continued to burn and there was sufficient light to enable Flynt to watch Blueskin's face intently, knowing he would see the first attack in his eye before the movement began. He saw it almost immediately.

Had Blueskin not given out a little roar as he surged forward, head down, he might have hurtled into him and brought him down. Flynt neatly sidestepped the charge and delivered a sharp punch just behind Blueskin's ear. The blow wasn't of sufficient strength to drop him but it did make him pause and shake his head a little. His eyes narrowed and Flynt knew he wouldn't make that mistake again.

They circled each other once more, Blueskin more wary, Flynt more alert. Men on both sides shouted encouragement, some showing impatience and demanding that they engage. Flynt had no intention of engaging until he saw an opening. Blueskin was all muscle and hatred and if he even once managed to sneak a blow that floored him, then it might all be over. Flynt had to bide his time and remain watchful. Blueskin would make an error, he was that type.

Then he made his own mistake.

As they ranged around each other, Flynt's eye wandered towards Jack, who clutched Blueskin's coat to his chest, his face awash with concern. Beside him, Wild smirked, his confidence in the superiority of his man apparent. The splash of a heavy foot in the water lying water between them alerted him to Blueskin's next attack, his big right hand swinging. Flynt managed to block it with his left and swung a blow of his own but Blueskin ducked under it, darted nimbly behind him to wrap his arms around him, one locked on his throat, the other tightening on his chest, both intent on squeezing the life from him. Flynt pushed back, his feet slipping and digging into the mud, hoping to force Blake off balance, but he steadfastly remained upright. Flynt struggled against the grip, hauling at his opponent's hand and wrist, seeking a weakening of the grip, an opening, anything that might give him the opportunity to free himself, but it had to be soon because one damned arm was about to crush his throat while the other his ribs.

He thrust the heel of his boot into Blueskin's leg, scraped it down his shin, then jammed it with as much force as he could muster into his foot. It wasn't much but the sharp agony was enough to cause Blueskin's hold to loosen, just for a split second, but it allowed Flynt to jerk his head backwards and crash into the man's nose. A grunt and the arm eased a little further, so Flynt ignored the pain jagging through his skull to deliver another butt. Blueskin staggered, his grip easing considerably, giving Flynt the chance to jerk his own arm free in order to jab his elbow sharply just below his ribs, followed by a third powerful head blow. Blueskin croaked and Flynt managed to stumble free, losing his footing to land on one knee in the mud, pain slicing through his brain, but pulling himself erect quickly to whirl and face Blueskin who was coming at him again. Flynt dodged out of his way, his head a little foggy thanks to the powerful blows he had delivered. They circled one another again, Blueskin's mouth curled in a snarl, the rain streaming red around his mouth and down his chin. He wiped the blood away from his upper lip with the back of his hand before, his temper aflame, lunging again but Flynt danced out of reach. Blueskin tried once more, his arms outstretched, a low growl rumbling, but again Flynt avoided him.

Flynt waited, his eyes firmly fixed on his opponent. He couldn't be distracted again. He mustn't be distracted again. He couldn't let this man get him on the ground, for that would be the end.

Blueskin straightened, his chest heaving as he fought for breath, his bloody nostrils flaring, his eyes burning through the lancing rain. Flynt slowed his own breathing and though he was resolved not to take his eyes from the man now slowly edging to the left, he was aware of a movement beyond the line of men surrounding them. Somebody stood against the dark bulk of the mount, but kept himself at the edge of the circle cast by the lamps and the remaining torches. A spectator, keeping himself hidden, barely caught by the flickering light.

Nimrod Boone had come down for a closer look.

Blueskin closed in again, his fist flying, but Flynt swayed back to let it skim past, while at the same time lashing out with his foot, aiming for Blake's groin but misjudging and catching him on the knee, which wasn't ideal but it landed with force enough to make Blueskin grunt. It was now or never. Flynt banged both fists onto his ears with as much force as he could muster. A strangled moan rasped from Blueskin's throat and he stumbled, both hands automatically shooting to clutch his injured ears. Flynt whipped his foot up again, slamming the sole of his boot with full force on the knee again. The leg gave way and Blueskin slumped. Flynt stepped in, jabbing the heel of his hand into his nose, once, twice, three times. Blood sprayed and Blake's head rolled backwards but he remained upright, knee buried in the mud, other leg bent, foot flat and holding him erect. Flynt stepped back, knotted the fingers of both hands together and swung his arms like a club against his jaw. Blake spun and pitched sideways into the mud. Flynt bent over him, his hands on his knees, sucking in deep lungfuls of air. Blueskin moaned, rolled onto his back, his hands splayed into the sodden ground, his feet seeking purchase as he tried to rise. Flynt sighed. He had to keep him down, so he stamped hard on his groin. A squeal, a contortion of his back, but Blueskin still tried to haul himself up. Flynt kicked him again, this time on the chest, forcing the air from his lungs, then pressed his boot hard onto his ribs, forcing him down. When he was satisfied he wouldn't try to rise again, he backed away, though he continued to monitor Blueskin's movements, slight though they were.

He became aware of the Admiral at his side, holding out his pistol. 'Finish it.'

Flynt pushed the weapon away but the Admiral thrust it back towards him. 'To the death, remember? Finish it.'

Wild watched them intently and when he caught Flynt's eye, nodded. 'An agreement was reached.'

The figure watching them had vanished again, but Flynt could still feel his eyes on them. He took the pistol, weighed it in his hand for a moment, then moved back to Blueskin, who still gasped for breath, his legs curled slightly against the pain in his groin, his nose squashed even more than before, rivulets of blood streaking his cheeks. He opened his eyes, saw Flynt towering over him, the pistol hanging loosely in his grip.

Blake managed a small laugh, revealing blood-caked teeth. He coughed a little, turned his head and spat out a blob of scarlet phlegm, then looked up at Flynt again. 'Do it, damn you. I wouldn't hesitate if it was me standing over you.'

Flynt raised the pistol. Blueskin was still smiling but it was strained. His eyes, though, remained defiant. 'I can't believe you bested me.'

'You let your anger guide your instincts. A fight is an exercise in thought as well as brawn.'

'I don't need no learning from you, Flynt, so just smoke that barker and give me peace.'

Flynt pulled back the hammer with his left hand, adjusted his aim slightly, and pulled the trigger. The shot was remarkably loud, louder than he thought he had ever heard before, but perhaps it merely seemed that way. Some of the men exclaimed, even Jack cried out. Wild's face was blank.

Blueskin stared at the hole left by the ball in the mud just an inch from his head.

'Now we're even,' Flynt told him, then turned away to return the spent pistol to the Admiral.

The gathering broke up soon after. Wild said nothing as he headed back to his carriage, leaving Godfrey and Hal to help Blueskin to his feet. Jack, still carrying Blueskin's coat and hat, lingered for a moment, and Flynt could feel the boy's eyes upon him as Pickett wrapped his own coat around his shoulders.

'Go, Jack,' Flynt said over his shoulder. 'You've made your choice, now you must live with it.'

'Mr Flynt, I...'

Flynt raised a hand to silence him. 'I don't wish to hear it. You're with them now.' He turned away again. 'Leave my sight.'

Even though he didn't see it, he knew Jack hesitated for a time before he trudged through the rain and mud after his new friends. The Admiral watched him leave, compassion evident in his eyes.

'That was also harsh,' he said.

'It's a harsh world,' Flynt said.

'You love that lad like a son.'

Only then did Flynt look back in Jack's direction in time to see him climb into Wild's carriage. 'Sons often disappoint their fathers.'

The Admiral pressed no further and Flynt shrugged himself fully into his coat. His waistcoat, shirt and breeches were soaked through, his hair matted to his head. The excitement that had sustained his body during the fight had evaporated to be replaced by aching bones and muscles. His knuckles tingled, his head throbbed, his bones chilled to the very marrow. He wanted to leave this place, find a warm fire, perhaps a warm bed if Belle was willing but his own lodgings if not, and he wanted – no, needed – to sleep for hours.

He knew he could not leave, though. The work was not yet done. He stared into the darkness, searching for another glimpse of the figure he'd seen, but saw nothing. The Admiral knew for whom it was he searched.

'You believe him still to be there?'

Flynt didn't believe a reply was called for. He breathed in deeply. 'I need you to take your men away.'

'You'll face this man alone?'

Flynt's attention diverted to Wild's convoy of coaches pulling away. 'I work better alone.'

30

It didn't take long for the Admiral to gather his forces and order them to go. The men merged with the darkness as easily as they had appeared.

'You will need our help with this creature,' the Admiral insisted but Flynt shook his head as he peered into the night.

'Boone will simply vanish if he sees anyone other than me linger.'

'I have a personal stake in this, Jonas.'

'I know, but it's me he wants.'

'How can you know?'

Flynt declined to answer, unsure how to put into words how he knew, knowing only that he did know. Finally, recognising that Flynt knew his business, the Admiral wished him luck, Pickett patted him on the arm and then they too left, the rhythmic clip of his horses and rumble of carriage wheels receding until they could be heard no more.

Standing in what had been the fight area, the ground churned by so many feet, Flynt breathed in the damp air, appreciating the sense of peace, short-lived though it may be, the silence now broken only by the rain rattling on his hat brim and pattering on the watery land. A discarded flambeau lay on the ground, its flames dying. Flynt stamped on it to finish the job, then stooped to pick up a single lamp left behind, opened the gate and blew out the wick. He needed the darkness in order to see.

Drawing both Tact and Diplomacy, he found a rough path leading up the hillside, stopped to listen, straining for a footfall somewhere in the dark but all that met his ears were the rain and the breeze disturbing scraggy bushes that had erupted from the hillside over the years. The mount might be a dust heap, the result of generations of refuse, but life always finds a way.

So does death.

He took the uphill grade slowly, weapons held before him, twisting his body from side to side. The path levelled a little and he came to a halt, every nerve alive. Boone was near, he could feel it in the air, like the charge after a lightning strike.

And then he heard the whistling. 'Greensleeves', and most tunefully too. Boone lay somewhere ahead but moving away, drawing Flynt further up the hill. He followed. He had no other choice if he was to end this. He swivelled both pistols before and around him. Together they climbed further, the whistling from the unseen Boone acting as a guide. The path levelled at the summit. To Flynt's right he could see lights bobbing upon the river, shifting and blurring in the rain. He grew weary and decided to bring the game to a halt.

'Caleb's dead,' he shouted.

The whistling stopped.

In the dark, Flynt grinned. That had hit home.

The whistling began again, but the tempo was slower, the notes slightly off key. Now for the final push and for that he needed to bend the truth a little.

'I killed him, Boone.'

Again the whistling halted, as if the sound had been cut with a knife. In its place the rain wept. The wind moaned.

'I killed him,' Flynt repeated, 'and I left him in the muck of the Rookery. He lies there yet, I'll wager, his flesh a feast for the pigs. I do hope he doesn't upset their stomachs.'

Flynt tensed. If the Boone cousins truly were like brothers then he calculated that image should cause some kind of reaction.

'I knows you, Jonas Flynt.'

The familiar voice came from the darkness, very close, and Flynt turned to face the direction from which it came, both weapons now aimed. Slowly a figure emerged from the night, not tall and slimly built, carrying a sabre. The face remained shadowed but recognisable.

'Ratty,' said Flynt.

'I told you previous, Flynt, that ain't my name.'

Flynt should have seen that coming, too. He had entertained the notion that Lombre was Nimrod Boone but it was a mental plaything only. Ratty, he saw now, was the obvious choice. His features were unremarkable, as Charters had pointed out, and he was forever by Caleb's side. There was no familial resemblance, for Caleb had the face of a brawler but Nimrod's features, if one were being charitable, had the appearance of one who leaned more towards books. Looks, though, could deceive.

'It be fine that we get to face each other like this, Flynt. You and me, we is alike,' Boone continued.

Flynt bristled. 'Now, there's an unpleasant thought.'

A faint laugh. 'Like knows like,' said Boone, 'and you and I, we is both hunters. I knowed it as soon as I set my peepers upon you in Whitechapel and proved it to myself when I sees you deal with them two at your lodging.'

'You sent them?'

'That I did, for I wished to see you in action. I thought you'd hush them but you didn't, perhaps halted by that fellow what was with you. But I knows you and I sees it that night for certain. We both live for the kill.'

The words of Harry and John echoed in Flynt's mind. We kill to live, not live to kill. That was what he believed too, but he thought it would be a waste of breath to deny Boone's assertion. Boone didn't seem to expect any response.

'You feels it, don't you? The thrill of the claret as it surges through you, the prospect of the kill, the anticipation, then the final release as the blade falls and you sees the light fade in their eyes and hear them takes their final breath. I've stared at them for an age, wondering where they goes after they leave this world behind. Them pious coves will tell us that it is to a better place and maybes that be true, 'cos anywhere is better than this world of piss, ain't that so? So, it seems to me that I be doing them all a favour, sending them to that place. A service, you might calls it.'

'Is that how you justify the horrors you have wrought?'

'I doesn't justify it at all, for it is what it is and I is what I is. As is you, Jonas Flynt. Oh yes, I knows you well, for we is brothers under the skin. Caleb was my cousin but he weren't no brother. I loved him like one and I mourns him but we takes our chances in this life of ours, do we not? You hushed him, you says, and maybes that be the truth of it, but I saw the way of things in the Rat's Castle...'

'Before you fled...'

Boone laughed. 'I had business elsewhere, as you know, and I was a-seeing what you was about with Harry and John, even if Caleb didn't. Always had a inflated opinion of hisself, did Caleb, believed people was loyal or afeared or both. I will miss old Caleb, but him and me, we wasn't truly alike. He didn't do no blood work himself, apart from brawling, he had others do it for him, others like me. He had ambitions, did Caleb, and they got the best of him, I reckons. Overreached, is that the way of it? But me? I doesn't have no ambitions but to keep doing my work, 'cos I do loves it so. You understands that, I reckons. You understands that all too well, for like knows like.'

He paused, perhaps expecting a reply, but Flynt held his tongue, loath to even consider that he and Boone might share some kind of kinship.

But the image of his sword penetrating Kate Miller's flesh flashed in his mind. His rage as he killed Scarface and Toothless. All necessary. Further acts of the past, some he could attempt to justify, others that were more problematic. He knew he was capable of killing but he took no pleasure from it. No, that wasn't true. There were times when he had experienced… satisfaction. Men who deserved to die, men who had hurt others, who would continue to hurt others if they were not put down. He recalled his pleasure as he crushed Toothless's fingers under his boot heel…

Like knows like…

He had known in the riverside tavern that Lombre was the man he sought before he had even seen his face. He had seen something within Harry and John and used it to his advantage…

Like knows likes…

He had known Nimrod Boone was up here on this hill, watching, waiting…

Like knows like…

No, he thought, I am NOT like him…

Another laugh, then a few notes of 'Greensleeves' before Boone spoke again. 'You is denying it to yourself, ain't you? See, I knows you, maybes even better than you knows yourself, because you won't admit to your true nature, like I has. I knowed what I was since I was a boy and I embraced it. Him what spawned me, he was a bastard, he did more than just beat me. He showed me that this here life ain't nothing but hell and we is all nothing but the devil's minions, so I act according. Her what give me birth let him do his evil, didn't raise no finger. I hushed him good and proper when I was old enough, and should've done her too but she is my mother, after all, and despite all her shortcomings I loves her, so I stayed my hand.'

'You love her, yet you left her to fend for herself in the Sanctuary.'

'I let her live, didn't I? And I prevails upon Caleb to ensure she is cared for. A boy should love his mother, eh? For they is what brings us this life. Fathers just provide the seed but it's the mothers what grow us and cultivate us.'

'You killed mothers. You killed children.'

Nimrod Boone grinned. 'That I did. As Caleb once said, I is just a whole mess of contradictions.'

He fell silent again. No more words, no more whistling. The rain was carried by the breeze to slip under the brim of Flynt's hat but he couldn't risk diverting his aim to wipe it away. He was tired and he was wet and he was cold and his body ached. He studied Boone's features. He had been the sweetest child, Patience Boone had said, but he had changed. This was the man who had once wept over the death of a kitten, who proclaimed love for a mother he had abandoned, and yet he had slaughtered entire families and talked of it as sport. A mess of contradictions was putting it mildly.

Boone stretched out his arms to the side. 'Here I is. You could easy take me down with your barkers. I don't use them, much prefer this here blade. I'm sure old Charters told you to do for me, but you doesn't and I wonders why.'

Just shoot the man, Flynt told himself, but something held him back, perhaps the fact that he was only armed with that sabre, or perhaps because he found himself held rapt by the man's monologue.

'I knows why you don't pull them triggers,' Boone said. 'It's because though you be at the denying of it, you knows, deep down, that what I says be true. Like knows like and you and me, we is connected. You knows you has to kill me but you delay, because you ain't comfortable yet with that side of your nature. You looks at me and you sees a man who is at ease with his skills and takes his pleasures from them.' Boone lowered his arms. 'You're scared. I can feel it. Ain't nothing wrong with being scared. Being scared means we is alive. It means that the claret still pumps.' He leaned forward as if imparting a great secret. 'I freely admits that I'm scared, too. Always am scared. The only thing that stops me being scared is the hushing. I ain't scared then, not no way, 'cos then I controls it, see? Then I is GOD.'

That final word was practically screamed, startling Flynt, but Boone had stepped back into the darkness. Flynt triggered Tact, the muzzle flash momentarily revealing Boone darting to his left. He strained to see anything further in the dark, still slowly revolving with Diplomacy at the ready. He shouldn't have hesitated, he should have put him down as soon as he revealed himself. But instead he had held his fire, let the man talk, his need to understand why Boone was what he was overcoming his caution.

Or the fear that whatever lived within that man also occupied part of him.

The attack came from behind, a powerful shove, hands thrusting at his back, pitching him forward onto the soft earth, Diplomacy escaping his grasp. He hadn't heard Boone rush him nor did he see him now. The man had once again merged with the night. Only his whistle could be heard. Flynt was coming to detest that damned tune.

The whistling stopped with a laugh. 'I could've had you there, couldn't I? It would have been so easy to stick you with this here blade but I didn't.'

Flynt pulled himself to his feet, eyes dropping quickly to search for the lost pistol, but it lay in a small pool of water, the muzzle slightly buried in mud, the pan already waterlogged. Tact he had already discharged and now Diplomacy was useless, except as a club. He slid his cane free from his belt.

'Why didn't you?'

'Don't be so hasty, your time will come, you can be sure of it.'

Flynt whirled in the direction of the voice. 'You're certain of that?'

A chuckle. 'As certain as death.'

He unsheathed his sword. 'You'll forgive me if I don't fall easily to your wishes.'

'Of course, but fall you will, on that you should be having no doubts.'

Flynt had faced men who wished to take his life many times. None had succeeded, although one had come close on the frozen Thames. On that occasion, and once on a hill in Scotland while a battle raged below, he had grown weary of life and had given himself up to death's embrace, only to be saved by circumstance. There was something about this man that filled him with dread but he would never allow him to take him. They might both die but Boone had to be removed from this world, on that he was resolved. He'd had matters too much his own way thus far. It was time to end this.

'Then let us have at it,' Flynt said.

'You is most eager for your end.'

The words came as a near whisper to Flynt's left but when he jerked in that direction he saw nothing but the falling rain.

'Jumpy, isn't you?'

Cursing himself for showing his nerves, Flynt forced a laugh. 'Impatient. I am eager for my supper.'

'With that African strumpet, I'll have no doubts.'

Flynt felt his skin prickle at the thought of Boone knowing of Belle.

'You must put her from your mind,' Boone said, his voice moving in a circle again, Flynt following. 'You will never be at the tup with that piece again, nor less eat yourself a supper. And she is destined for a hushing, too, so perhaps you will be reunited with her...'

'You'll never live to touch her.' Flynt's words came out with more passion than he intended, even though it was sincere. He didn't wish to let Boone know he was in any way unnerved.

Boone laughed. 'Oh, it ain't me what will have the doing of it. I don't have no ill will towards the bobtail, though it would be pleasure to acquaint myself with her. But the honours is being handled by that one-peepered foreign cove what Caleb was transacting with, punishment, says he, for your meddling in his affairs.'

Lombre... going after Belle...

'It may even be done yet, for alls I knows, though I suspects he might have his pleasures of her first...'

Flynt focused on the voice, tensed, crouching low, eyes and ears straining even keener than before.

Boone loomed to his left, a sabre raised, a grin that seemed to be fixed to his lips, Flynt turned, raised his sword, blocked the downward stroke towards his head, the power of it vibrating along his arm, the man's mania feeding his power rather than muscle, failing to see the man lash out with his foot, the blow catching him in the stomach, the air ejecting from his body as he was propelled backwards, his footing unsteady in the slick mud, the sabre arcing downwards, this time in both hands, it was a heavy blade, a sharp blade, and sturdy though his own sword was it would not parry this strike, especially as he began to tumble backwards, his feet finally losing their purchase.

Belle, he thought…

Forgive me, he thought…

Belle, he thought…

'Private Boone!'

The voice was strong, commanding and carried force sufficient to halt Boone's movement entirely. He craned into the darkness, his eyes narrowed. 'I knows that voice.'

Colonel Charters stepped into view, a pistol held steady, and Boone let his sword arm drop as he grinned. 'Ah.' The single syllable was replete with satisfaction. 'I was a-wondering when you would show.'

'I might not have, had you not felt the need to provide a commentary to guide me in the dark. I don't recall you being so loquacious.'

'A man changes with the years.'

'Not you, Boone, you're still the vicious, gutless little shitrag I remember.'

Boone feigned hurt. 'Hard words, Colonel, for an old man wanting a wing.' He raised his sabre once more. 'Come closer and let me even that up for you.'

'I think not.'

The curled lip was scornful. 'You is scared of me?'

'Of course I am, man. Any reasoning person fears the likes of you. Distemper of the mind such as yours is most disturbing.'

Flynt had scrambled to his feet and moved out of range of the sabre, his own sword at the ready, but Boone barely gave him a glance. 'Well then, we has us a situation, do we not? How is it to be resolved?'

Charters said, 'Come with us, Boone, face the king's justice.'

Boone made a pretence at considering this option. 'Nah, I think that is not my way forward, thanking you all the same.'

'You will not leave here alive otherwise, on that you have my oath.'

Boone gave Flynt a sideways glance, then tilted his head towards Charters. 'I believe I shall take my chances. It is my calculations that I can take one of you before I goes. The question is, which one?'

Charters gritted his teeth. 'You have killed your last living creature, Boone, that is my calculation.'

Another half glance at Flynt. 'We shall see, we shall see…'

He moved suddenly, not at Flynt but towards Charters, the sabre raised, a scream of fury rending the air, followed by the report of Charters' pistol. The ball caught Boone square in the chest and stopped him dead. He stared at the bubbling well of red and slid to his knees, his sabre still gripped in his hand. Charters was calm as he slid his pistol into his pocket and stepped closer to Flynt, his hand outstretched.

'Your blade, Serjeant, if you would be so kind.'

Flynt handed his sword over and the colonel turned to Boone, who tried to raise his sabre but the pistol ball had sapped him of all strength save that which held him upright, albeit on his knees. Boone retched, blood oozing between his lips. 'You think you can kill me this time?' He straightened. 'I am not...'

Charters tutted. 'Oh, do be silent.'

Charters thrust the sword. Boone gurgled as the steel entered his throat and the tip pierced the back of his neck. He hung there for a second until the blade was pulled free, then pitched to the side. Charters stared at him for a moment, his face impassive, before returning Flynt's sword. 'Thank you kindly, Serjeant.'

Flynt asked, 'You have a coach?'

'Of course, do you think I walked to Whitechapel?'

Flynt was already rushing back down the hill, having snatched Diplomacy from the mud. 'Then we must get to Mother Grady's with all haste...'

Ignoring the protests from his body, he prayed to a god in which he didn't believe that he wasn't too late.

31

As soon as Jerome swung the door open, Flynt rushed in. 'Has a man with one eye called upon the house? A foreigner?'

Jerome sensed from his demeanour that something was amiss. 'Aye, there be a man short of an eye upstairs but he is no foreigner, he's as English as me.'

Flynt doubted that but was already running to the staircase. 'Is he with Miss Belle?'

'Nay,' Jerome shouted after him. 'He's with Miss Sadie, said he had a taste for flaxen hair...'

'Where is Belle?'

'In her chamber...'

He took the stairs two at a time while Jerome welcomed Charters and his two guards, who had waited by the carriage at the mount.

The gunshot sounded as Flynt rounded the head of the stairs.

Belle...

He swore, drawing Tact as he pounded along the corridor, alarmed cries leaping from behind the various closed doors and, behind him, hurried footsteps ascending the stairs. He couldn't be certain where the report came from. Sadie's room was at the far end, overlooking the rear of the house, but he doubted Lombre would be with her, so he made straight for Belle's door. He didn't waste time listening at the wood, he threw it open and stepped in, his pistol at the ready.

He had expected Lombre to rush at him but he didn't. He was slumped on a chair, his left hand clasped to the bullet hole in his opposite shoulder, his stiletto on the floor at his feet, his single eye blazing towards Belle, who stood on the other side of her bed, smoke still rising from the muzzle of her little pistol.

'You certainly took your time getting here, Jonas,' she said, her voice steady as she took in his bedraggled appearance. 'I see you have been in the wars again.'

Flynt kept his pistol on Lombre. 'I regret my appearance, Belle. It was unavoidable.' He risked an appraising look in her direction. 'Are you hurt?'

'No, I didn't afford him the opportunity.'

The relief that she was unharmed made him smile. 'Monsieur Lombre, I would be obliged if you would kick that blade in my direction.' He raised a warning finger with his free hand. 'Gently now, I have had a most taxing evening and my self-control is not what it should be.'

Lombre winced as he moved his foot gingerly to push the stiletto towards Flynt. 'I assume Boone breathes no more?'

'Your assumption is correct.' Flynt pulled the blade further away from his reach with his boot but left it lying on the floor sheet.

'You did this?'

'It was I who despatched Nimrod Boone,' said Charters from the doorway.

Lombre was unsurprised. 'Charters.'

'Monsieur Lombre, I wish I could say it is a pleasure to make your acquaintance.'

Lombre's smile was thin with pain but he didn't respond.

'Jerome,' Flynt said without removing his eyes from the agent, 'you had best see to Sadie.'

Jerome left and Flynt retrieved the stiletto. Belle made an intense study of Charters.

Charters had also noted her scrutiny and gestured to his men. 'Gentlemen, please provide Monsieur Lombre some assistance in rising and we shall take him to a place of safety.'

Lombre was hauled none-too-gently to his feet, the men ignoring the agonised protests as they dragged him from the room.

'Madame,' Charters said, with a slight bow, 'I regret we have not the leisure to make your acquaintance, for we must take this gentleman to lodgings that will be considerably less comfortable than these.'

Jerome returned. 'Miss Sadie lives but she is unconscious. I've sent for a physic...'

Belle's eyes flared towards Lombre, who was being propelled from the room, as she reached for Flynt's pistol. 'Give me that, Jonas, and let me take his other eye out.'

Flynt laughed and stepped out of reach. 'Calm yourself, Belle. There's been killing enough this night.'

She gave Lombre a withering look and then said, 'I shall sit with Sadie until the doctor arrives. And you and I, Jonas, will have something to discuss when I return, so do not disappear.'

Charters motioned Flynt to follow him into the hallway, where Jerome ushered curious and startled women and their culls back to their rooms, assuring them all was well and that the disturbance was well in hand. Charters nodded towards Belle who was at that moment entering Sadie's room then, ensuring they were well out of earshot of all, said, 'You will handle this situation?'

'I'll try,' Flynt said.

'How will you explain?'

'I have no idea.'

Charters smiled. 'In my experience, a version of the truth is best, for the moment at least.' He gave Belle an admiring glance. He knew about her, of course, and of Flynt's association with her, but this was the first time their orbits had intersected. 'She is a fine woman who can acquit herself most admirable and she deserves to be treated well, Flynt. When events are more settled I would appreciate an evening's conviviality.' He raised his hand when Flynt flinched. 'Not in any priapic sense, of course, but the three of us. A meal, some wine, conversation. And perhaps,' he looked at Belle again, 'that conversation would concern the lady's future.'

His meaning was clear. He was considering folding Belle into the Company. A courtesan of her quality, with a fine house, would yield rewards and his advice to give her a version of the truth regarding the night's events would act as precursor to that recruitment. Flynt was unsure how he felt about the prospect, but he knew better than to interfere on Belle's behalf. She was more than capable of deciding for herself.

A thought occurred to him. 'On that note, Colonel, there is something perhaps you could do for me…'

–

Flynt had eased off his coat, waistcoat and muddy boots and was washing his face and hands with hot water he'd asked Jerome to send up when Belle returned.

'Sadie is well?' he asked.

'The doctor is with her now and says her head will ache for a time but there should be no other after effects.' She stopped to examine him. 'Should I ask him to tend to you?'

'I have no wounds, just bruises, and I am used to them.'

She snorted. 'That you are.' She lifted his coat from where he had dropped it on the floor, tutted in distaste at the mud caked upon it, and hung it on a nail behind the door. 'It is well that Mother Grady is not to home this evening. I think it possible that she would take what has occurred somewhat ill and hold it against you.'

That provoked a wry smile. 'I think perhaps you're correct. Although I would have enjoyed seeing her deal with Monsieur Lombre. Somehow I believe he would find it preferable to have your ball in his shoulder than whatever she would dish out.'

'My aim was off, I was aiming for his heart.'

Flynt was grateful for that, for he would not wish her to experience the ordeal of having taken a life. 'When I heard he was coming for you, I feared the worst. He is a most expert killer, Belle, how did you gain the upper hand?'

'You have your friend Madame de Fontaine to thank for that. Had she not mentioned his single eye and the scarred face, then I might have thought him just another cull. But I saw him enter and even when he repaired upstairs with Sadie I suspected him. I made a show of entering my room ahead of them and waited for him with my pistol primed. If I was wrong there was no harm to it. If I was right then I was ready. The rest you know.'

Flynt grinned, then winced as he touched a tender spot on his face.

'Who was the one-armed gentleman?' she asked.

'An old...' He paused, unsure how to describe Charters correctly. Friend? Comrade? 'He was my commander in Flanders.'

'The one you pulled from the field?'

'Yes.'

Her face remained impassive. 'And yet, he is more than that, I feel.'

Belle, like many of her profession, had the uncanny ability to read men.

'He is,' he admitted.

'He is someone who uses your... eh... skills most regular, I would hazard.'

Flynt turned to face her, unsure what version of the truth he was going to give her. 'He does.'

'He is thief?'

'No.'

'Then what is he?'

A version of the truth…

No, she deserved better.

So he told her the whole truth.

32

One week later

Mr Handel was at the harpsichord, the gentlemen of White's gathered around him, some appreciative of his skill, others wishing he would stop and leave them to their pleasures. Charters was seated in his favourite chair, awaiting the maestro's impromptu recital to end, when Lord James Moncrieff stopped by his side. After the pleasantries, the Scottish noble asked, 'I trust the matter we discussed recently has been resolved?'

'It is, my lord, most satisfactorily, too.'

'The perpetrator of the horrors has been taken into custody?'

Charters permitted himself a little smile. 'Let us say that he will alarm decent people no further.'

Moncrieff seemed troubled still, and Charters realised that his query did not solely concern Nimrod Boone. However, he left the man to stew a little, unwilling to meet him even halfway.

'And the man Lombre?' Moncrieff asked, in a conversational manner. 'You have him?'

'Yes.'

'And he will go to trial?'

'Ah, unfortunately he suffered a tragic accident while in custody.'

'What manner of tragic accident?'

'A deadly one.'

There was never any question of the man ever seeing the inside of an English court, let alone address a crowd at Tyburn. He was found dead in a private cell within Newgate, the cause being widely believed – because Charters had circulated such – to be a sudden and unexpected stoppage of the heart, the prisoner having complained of tingling of the fingers and shooting pains in his chest and arms. Of course, Lombre's heart had stopped, though it was not caused by any weakness of his body but by the garrotte wielded with considerable expertise by a jailor in

Charters' employ. Thus those agents of the Crown who Lombre had himself despatched were avenged.

Moncrieff seemed to be appreciating Mr Handel's playing when he asked, again casually, 'And I assume then you have the name of his employer?'

Charters was enjoying this exchange. 'And what care is it of yours, my lord?'

Moncrieff maintained his outward laissez-faire. 'He is a countryman of mine and there is shame attached to him being attached in any way to such heinous acts.'

Charters thought there was some measure of truth in that. 'I understand totally. It was a fellow by the name of Andrew Wilson, would you know him?'

Moncrieff was unsurprised. 'It is a common enough name among my countrymen.'

'To be sure, but I will find him, on that you can depend.'

'Then you know not where he is?'

'I would assume Edinburgh, for he is a dignitary of that city.'

Moncrieff affected shock. 'Do you mean Bailie Wilson?'

'I do.'

'My God, I cannot believe that!'

His disbelief was almost convincing. Almost, but not quite.

'And you will send people after him?'

'In the fullness of time.'

'Jonas Flynt?'

'Perhaps.'

Mr Handel had risen from the harpsichord and was accepting the praise of the patrons while White's employees began to manhandle the instrument out of the room to return it to where it was usually kept. Charters rose, too. 'I regret I have to wish you good evening, my lord, for I must have converse with Mr Handel.'

Moncrieff gave him a bow. 'But of course, Colonel, I wish you well in your dealings with Andrew Wilson. I feel sure he will answer for his crimes.'

As he extended his hand in the composer's direction, Charters knew for certain that he would.

Edinburgh, two weeks later

Andrew Wilson had contemplated visiting the Widow Gilchrist that night but had decided against it. He knew that since the death of his wife she had expected to become the new mistress of his household but he had resisted such a move, for Annie Gilchrist was good only for the tupping not the marrying. She was a most accommodating lass in the bed chamber but she was not the one to be forever by his side and to act mother to his girls and his only son. So, even though he'd spent an arduous day on town business and would have appreciated some enthusiastic physical relief, he made for his home off the High Street. His children were with an aunt in Falkland, across the Forth in Fife, so he would have peace to be with his own thoughts, along with a brandy and a full pipe.

It was his turn to be surprised when he entered his parlour to find Lord James Moncrieff awaiting him, a glass of his best sherry already poured and half consumed.

He'd had to affect the guise of the slightly dithering bailie at the council meetings all day. Such subterfuge wearied him and he often longed to cast it off to show his true nature, so his anger rose easily. 'What right do you have, lad, to enter my home in such an easy manner?'

Moncrieff was unperturbed by the vehemence in the Grand Master's voice. 'Sit down, Andrew.'

'You dare give me orders in my own parlour? Are you somehow dighted? Have you taken leave of your senses, man?'

Moncrieff sharpened his tone. 'I said, sit down, Andrew, and be quiet.'

'I am the Grand Master and you...'

'You are Grand Master no longer. You have overreached, Andrew, and you have left our Fellowship exposed.'

Wilson sneered. 'In what way?'

'Your recent adventure with Monsieur Lombre and denizens of London's Rookery. You used the agent as go-between between you and a certain Caleb Boone, but the endeavour has collapsed, as it always would. Lombre is dead, the men he employed also dead, and Nathaniel Charters knows far more than he should.'

Wilson obviously knew. 'No matter, there is no direct link to the Fellowship.'

'There is a link to you, Andrew, and that could lead to the Fellowship.'

Wilson shook his head. 'No, Lombre didn't ken my real name, I used an alias.'

'Charters knows of your involvement, Andrew.'

Wilson was shocked into silence for a moment, his initial anger now overcome by his concern. 'How could he know...?'

'That would be my doing, Andrew.'

Christy de Fontaine emerged from the bed chamber, her Russian bear as ever at her back. Andrew Wilson, despite his show of fogginess to the outside world, was sharp and he put everything together quickly. He narrowed his eyes towards Moncrieff. 'You had this creature inform Charters of my name?'

'After your surprise visit to my home I made inquiry. I knew that Madame de Fontaine was in London so I made an arrangement to meet her. She already knew of Monsieur Lombre's presence, of course.'

'It's a small place, this shadow world of ours,' said Madame de Fontaine.

'She used her considerable skills to tease from him the intelligence that he was embarked on a mission for a Scotsman. He even provided a description.'

'Teased from him?' Wilson shot her an accusatory look. 'You slept with him?'

Christy tilted her head. 'A woman has to do what is necessary. And he had a certain amount of trust in me.'

Wilson sneered. 'Trust in you, madame, is most misplaced, for you are a treacherous jade.'

Christy gave him a smile, not insulted in the least.

Moncrieff asked, 'What I wish to know is what you hoped to gain from this adventure, Andrew?'

'Profit, boy, profit, what else is there? It is that for which the Fellowship exists. There is silver to be had from illicit enterprises, perhaps even more than from honest trade if organised properly.'

'And you could organise it properly?'

'It's halfway there, thanks to Wild and the one who terms himself the Admiral. The city streets and the waterfront are the key to London's prosperity and if the Fellowship controls it, then the silver would flood into our pockets. We already have the politicians and the merchants in our hand, why not the criminals too?'

Moncrieff's voice lowered to a gruff whisper. 'So you had children murdered?'

Wilson had decency still to look ashamed. 'That was a miscalculation. They were meant only to kill the bookkeepers that were close to Wild and the Admiral, and then lay a false trail to lead them to each other. Their own enmity would do the rest.'

'A miscalculation,' Moncrieff repeated. 'Is that what you call it?'

'Aye, the man Boone sent the wrong man to do the job. It is regrettable but not my doing.'

'Regrettable, yes indeed,' Moncrieff intoned. 'This whole enterprise was regrettable, Andrew.'

Wilson sneered. 'I wouldn't be taking too superior a tone, boy, for your adventure in the north of England in order to bring down your half-brother was far from perfect.'

Moncrieff saw Christy de Fontaine raise an eyebrow. He would rather she not know anything of his personal life but it was out there now. All he could do was press on with the matter at hand. 'Your own misjudged adventure has captured the attention once again of Colonel Charters and his Company of Rogues. It's only a matter of time before you are visited by Jonas Flynt and it will not end as pleasantly as your last meeting.'

'You need have no fear of Flynt, boy. I have made arrangements, I told you...'

'I have no fear of him, but nevertheless, this misadventure brings an end to your tenure as Grand Master.'

'That is not your decision to make. I am Grand Master in perpetuity, Fellowship rules dictate it so, and no member can remove me.'

'That is true, you do indeed hold the office in perpetuity.' He paused. 'Only death can end your tenure.'

In that moment, Andrew Wilson knew what was to become of him. He stared open-mouthed at Moncrieff, who returned his gaze with impassive mien. He then looked at Christy de Fontaine, who gave him that damnable smile of hers as she stepped aside to allow the big Russian to move forward, his metal hand clawed and already reaching for him.

Epilogue

Belle looked glorious. That was the only way Flynt could describe her. Her skin was flawless, her hair magnificent, her slim body sheathed in a gown of such quality silk he regretted it having to as much as brush the ground as they crossed the Piazza. He had prevailed upon Joseph Hynes at the Black Lion to grant the use of his private room, the very one in which he and Colonel Charters regularly met, and had ordered a most sumptuous meal, which the landlord had provided most proficiently. They had visited the Theatre Royal in Drury Lane for a production of Kit Marlowe's *Tamburlaine* and he noticed admiring glances from both men and women in the foyer and the playhouse itself. He couldn't help but feel pride to be seen with such a beauty. There were other, not so admiring looks, but he managed to ignore them, even though that deep, primal part of him wished to slap their prurient faces. Belle was enjoying her evening, her eyes shone with such delight, and he would not spoil it. She had accepted a great deal about him, not the least his admission of working for Colonel Charters and lying to her all these years about it.

On their return to Mother Grady's, Jerome gave him a surreptitious nod so Flynt suggested a final drink before they retired.

'Truly, Jonas, I don't think I could swallow one more drop,' she said. 'The meal was superb, the wine also, but if I ingest anything further I would, I think, burst.'

He couldn't accept no for an answer. He took her hand and gently manoeuvred her towards the parlour door. 'Just one more, Belle. A brandy, perhaps, to aid the digestion.'

She laughed. 'Jonas Flynt, you have been most solicitous this night and I am beginning to think that you have been replaced by some faerie glamour.'

He laughed. 'No faeries, Belle, just a need to make up for lost time and missed opportunities.'

'Do I detect guilt, Jonas?'

He saw his friend Rab fall from his horse, struck down by a bullet. He saw another friend dead at the hands of a mob. He saw Belle's young friend Sam bleeding to death in a Newgate cell. He saw Kate Miller die once again. Had she ever had someone in her life who cared enough to take her to the theatre, or enjoy a meal together? Or was her life as mean and brutal as her manner of death?

'Regret perhaps,' he said.

The smile in Belle's eyes died when she detected the shadow in his. 'You have no need of guilt or regret, Jonas. I now understand how complex your life has been, and remains so. And we have dined out before.'

He pushed the images that had briefly flooded his mind away. 'Yes, but there is one thing we haven't done, and that will be remedied this instant.'

He opened the parlour door and immediately a sprightly air was struck by a quartet of musicians led by Mr Handel. Belle's hand flew to her mouth as she stared at the room, set aglow by a myriad of candles and the beaming faces of the girls in her employ and their special patrons. Even Mary Grady, standing by Colonel Charters, smiled.

'Madame,' Flynt said, affecting a bow, 'would you honour me with a dance.'

Her eyes filled as she gazed at him. 'Jonas, you don't dance...'

'Regrettably, that will be most evident in the next few minutes, but I believe a man must face his fears. I'd appreciate it if you would face them with me.'

Belle looked at Jerome behind them. 'You knew of this?'

Jerome grinned. 'That I did, Miss Belle, and I carried that there harpsichord from t'street.'

Belle took Flynt's proffered hand and together they stepped into the room, the furniture having been pushed back to create an area for dancing. Immediately, at the order of Mr Handel at the harpsichord, the music changed to a minuet. Flynt took a deep breath and tried to remember the steps that Colonel Charters had taught him over the previous few days. His movements were clumsy, in complete contrast to Belle, who was grace itself. He was further discomfited with the eyes of the assembly upon him but he did his best to combat it. This was something he had to do. This was something he wanted to do, for Belle, for them both.

The spey-wife had been correct, someone had tried to come between them. He had thought perhaps it was Christy, but then Lombre had intruded. Belle had dealt with both in her usual capable way.

As the music changed, slowing now to Mr Handel's own sarabande, he realised he wasn't dealing with the steps in any capable way. As long as there was a sprightliness to it, he could equip himself reasonably well, but the slowness of this dance revealed his lack of prowess and he feared he would trip over his own feet somehow. He wondered at his ability to be fleet of foot when wielding a sword and yet here he was reduced to a lumbering oaf. Belle didn't notice, however. Or at least engineered not to notice.

Eventually, some of the others released him from his ordeal by also dancing, Charters taking Mrs Grady by the hand and leading her out. Jerome, standing by the door, looked over his shoulder and then left the room.

Belle was laughing now. She was happy and he was glad to see it, glad that he could in some way bring her joy. She leaned closer and whispered, 'I never want to lose you.'

He held her gaze. 'You won't, Belle, not if I can help it.'

She understood that his life did not lend itself to making promises of longevity, but he was sincere in his resolution to live as long and as content a life as he could, given the pressures of the work he did for Colonel Charters. He knew now that he wanted to live that life with Belle. When he thought Lombre was about to kill her he had felt a stabbing in his heart that he hadn't experienced for a long time. Guilt he was used to, stirring of conscience also, but the prospect of losing her was something he couldn't bear.

'I love you, Jonas Flynt,' she said.

Now's the time, Jonas, say it. Three words. Say it.

'Belle, I…'

Jerome tapped him on the shoulder. 'Begging thy pardon, Mr Flynt.'

Flynt almost groaned with exasperation at the interruption but Belle laughed. 'Salvation, Jonas,' she said.

'What is it, Jerome?' Flynt asked, his tone sharper than he meant it to be.

'There's some people at the door asking after thee. I tried to explain that thee was otherwise engaged but they wouldn't brook no refusal. I put them in small room across hall.'

Belle laughed again. 'Go see who it is, Jonas.'

Sighing and giving her an apologetic look, and shrugging in reply to Charters' unspoken query as he danced with Mother Grady, Flynt followed Jerome from the room and across the hall to the small reception room. Jerome opened the door and stepped aside to let him enter.

His heart began to hammer and his brain froze slightly as the woman turned to face him, a young man at her side. He had grown in the more than two years since he'd last seen him and his features had formed even further. It was like gazing into a looking glass at himself at the boy's age.

'Jonas,' said Cassie, as ever wasting no time, 'I need your help...'

Historical Notes

The inspiration behind this story came from the Ratcliffe Highway murders of 1811. Two families were murdered in two separate attacks, but the main suspect, John Williams, took his own life before he could stand trial. I have taken only the notion of two home invasions and grafted my own storyline on them.

Most of the inns and taverns I mention existed, including the Rat's Castle in the Rookery. My description of it is based on a later description of the premises, although I have applied my usual licence.

The entertainment to which Eliza Berthon referred regarding the animals did actually take place in the public house I mention. The advertisement for this barbaric event did mention African tigers, but as there have never to my knowledge been tigers on that continent we can only surmise what creatures were used. Cheetahs, perhaps, or merely lions.

The violent incident on the Bedlam steps described by Charters also took place. In 1677, the 15-year-old noble Digby, Lord Gerard, was involved in an altercation with the woman and her husband, resulting in constables wading in to rescue him and his mother. During the confusion, the porter was wounded in the stomach by the young man. As far as I'm aware no punishment was meted out and, if one source is correct, he died seven years later following a drinking contest in a Covent Garden tavern.

Obviously, Daniel Defoe and George Frideric Handel were real people and I have remained as close as I feel I needed to historical fact in creating their characters. And yes, Defoe did act as an agent for the Crown around the period of the Act of Union.

The royal split between King George and his son did take place, and it was claimed that the prince challenged Lord Newcastle to a duel, although he later denied it. Walpole used the division between father and son, via the Princess of Wales, in order to curry favour with the future king. Christy's – and by extension Charters' – involvement is my invention.

Acknowledgements

A book is very much like a child. It has to be raised, nurtured, eased gently and kindly onto the right track. They say it takes a village to raise a child and the same is required for a book, for though the author alone gives birth, others assist in helping it grow from a nebulous idea, born while walking the dog, to something that lives and breathes on a printed page.

My village includes my agent Jo Bell, who always has my back, my editor at Canelo, Kit Nevile, line editor Miranda Ward, the sales and marketing teams, the booksellers who give the titles space on their shelves – hopefully, face out (hint) and on tables (another hint), the readers who buy them and tell their friends and the reviewers who review them.

Special thanks go to Sarah Frame who read this one for me when I was at the point that I didn't know if it made any sense. Yes, she's my partner, but she didn't pull her punches and made some telling points.

Thanks also go to fellow authors Caro Ramsay, Denzil Meyrick, Michael J. Malone, Gordon Brown and Jane Hamilton who are always available to advise, guide and cajole me.

I must make special mention of Isla Coole, of Criminally Good Books in York, who successfully bid in the 2023 Children in Read appeal to have her mother's name appear in a Jonas Flynt. It all happened too late for this one but Madeleine Richards, née McRobert, watch out for *Ship of Thieves*!